Elena thought about that tension she had been feeling for so very many years. Was that—magic?

The old lady nodded with satisfaction. "So. You have felt it. All over the Five Hundred Kingdoms, there have been countless girls like you for whom the circumstances were not right. And magic keeps gathering around them, trying to make it all work— and by the way, we call that *The Tradition.*

"It never goes away. Sometimes, it just builds to the point where a magician notices it, and it gets—" she waved her hand vaguely "—siphoned off. Sometimes neatly, with the person's consent, though the effect is that it leaves them quite ordinary. Nothing magical will ever happen again to her—or him—but at least their life will go on."

Perhaps it wouldn't be so bad to be ordinary—

But even though not so long ago, Elena would have welcomed the prospect, she knew that this was not the right answer anymore.

"And sometimes," the old lady went on, "if the person has attracted someone who is a magical guardian, something else happens."

She smiled, a warm smile that felt like a comforting arm around Elena's shoulders, and Elena smiled back without knowing quite why. "I am that *something else.*"

MERCEDES LACKEY
The Fairy Godmother

LUNA™
www.LUNA-Books.com

LUNA™

Recycling programs
for this product may
not exist in your area.

First edition January 2004

THE FAIRY GODMOTHER

ISBN-13: 978-0-373-80333-0

Copyright © 2004 by Mercedes Lackey

www.LUNA-Books.com

Printed in U.S.A.

More Tales of the Five Hundred Kingdoms from

MERCEDES LACKEY

and HQN Books

The Snow Queen
Fortune's Fool
One Good Knight
The Fairy Godmother

Be sure to catch Mercedes's next
Tale of the Five Hundred Kingdoms

The Sleeping Beauty

Available July 2010!

And don't miss *Harvest Moon,* available October 2010
Featuring "A Tangled Web"
An all-new Tale of the Five Hundred Kingdoms novella!

Dedicated to the members of the FDNY, lost 9/11/01

Battalion 1
Paul Mitchell
Matthew Ryan

Battalion 2
Richard Prunty
William McGovern

Battalion 6
John Williamson

Battalion 7
Orio Palmer
Stephen Harrell
Philip Petti

Battalion 8
Thomas DeAngelis
Thomas McCann

Battalion 9
Edward Geraghty
Dennis Devlin
Carl Asaro
Alan Feinberg

Battalion 11
John Paolillo

Battalion 12
Fred Scheffold

Battalion 22
Charles Margiotta

Battalion 47
Anthony Jovic

Battalion 48
Joseph Grzelak
Michael Bocchino

Battalion 49
John Moran

Battalion 50
Lawrence Stack

Battalion 57
Joseph Marchbanks, Jr.
Dennis Cross

SOC Battalion
Charles Kasper

Safety Battalion 1
Robert Crawford

Tactical Support 2
Joseph Mascali

Special Operations
Timothy Higgins
Michael Russo
Raymond Downey
Patrick Waters

Division 1
Thomas Moody
Joseph Farrelly

Division 11
Timothy Stackpole

Division 15
Martin Egan, Jr.
Thomas Haskell, Jr.
William O'Keefe

This is not the way to spend a beautiful spring morning! Elena Klovis thought, as she peered around the pile of bandboxes in her arms. They were full of hats, so they weren't particularly heavy—unlike most of her stepmother's luggage—but they were very awkward to carry. There was a lark serenading the morning somewhere overhead, and Elena wished with all her heart she was him and not herself.

Still, if nothing went wrong, in a few hours she just *might* be free! If not as free as a bird, at least better off than she was now.

She took a few more steps, feeling her way carefully with her bare toes, and caught sight of the neighbors peering over the rose-covered wall as she passed by their perch. They must have been standing on boxes or a bench to do so, and even at that, all that could be seen of them was the tops of their caps, a few little greying curls escaping from beneath the lace, and two sets of eyes, blue and bright with curiosity.

Their curiosity would have to wait. She didn't have time to satisfy it right now.

Elena felt her way on towards the carriage, the bandboxes swaying dangerously with each step. Madame Blanche and Madame Fleur knew better than to call out to her when she was in the middle of a task, and even if they hadn't been, she wouldn't have answered. Not now. Elena was not in the mood to take either her stepmother's sharp tongue nor the blows of her cane, and if the carriage wasn't packed soon, Madame Klovis would be delivering up both.

She made a few more careful steps. It would have been easier if she'd been properly shod instead of barefoot, but the only shoes she had were the wooden clogs she'd carved herself for winter, and the wooden pattens for rain. The last time she'd asked for shoes, her stepmother had flown into a rage and beaten her so hard that her back ached now at the memory.

Sometimes she thought about what would happen if she snatched that cane away and struck back—and wondered if it would be worth what would follow.

It wouldn't, of course. The girls would run to get help, and Elena couldn't possibly get away before she was caught. First would come the constables, who would charge her before the magistrate for assault, and the law was on her stepmother's side. An unmarried girl was the ward and property of her parents, who could do whatever they wished with her. Of course, most parents were good and kind, and would never hurt their children, not even when they were the children of another marriage—but when they were not, well there was no recourse for the child, none at all....

Well, the magistrate would certainly have *his* say. Then would come ten strokes of the lash at the hands of the town gaoler, followed by a session in the stocks in the town square. Then things would go right back to the way they were, except that Stepmother's hand would be even heavier.

Even if she was twenty-one, an unmarried maiden was still a child in the eyes of the law, and nothing could free her from her parents but marriage.

When she was much younger, Elena had dreamed about running away; now she knew better. A boy could run away, perhaps, and become a soldier, or a wandering man-of-all-work, or perhaps a tinker, or join the gypsies. It was different for a girl. It was a dangerous world out there for a girl. Oh, it was dangerous for everyone, true—there were bandit bands, rogues, thieves and tricksters, not to mention storms and wild beasts—but there were worse fates for a girl if her luck ran out. Stepmother was bad; being kept as the captive of bandits for their pleasure would be infinitely worse. *Probably*.

She got to the carriage, and handed the bandboxes up to Jacques, the single servant that the Klovis household still possessed, after Madame and her daughters had finished running through the family fortune, or what had passed for their fortune when Elena's father died. The dour, sour man, thin as a spider, balding, with a nasty long fringe around his pate, and evil-tempered as a toad, took them from her and began strapping them to the top of the carriage, adding them to the luggage already there. Elena turned back towards the house for more.

She heard whispers from the other side of the sandstone wall as she hurried up the mossy cobbles of the path that led from the front gate, through the formal garden, to the front door. She didn't have to go far; there was more luggage piled up just outside the stained, oak door. She loaded herself up with as much as she could carry, and repeated her trip.

She had been loading the luggage since dawn, first dragging the biggest trunks and boxes to the hired cart, which had left before the sun cleared the pointed rooftops, then piling the rest onto the old family carriage. The carriage was huge; it had been built to carry a family of eight with reasonable luggage for all of them, and by the time she and Jacques were finished, Madame, Delphinium, and Daphne would hardly have room to fit.

"It looks as if they're taking everything they own!" came a slightly louder whisper, as she handed Jacques more boxes and calico bags. A bit of breeze teased the ragged edges of her skirt and tickled her bare legs.

Yes they are, she thought sourly. *And quite a bit that they don't own.* All of her mother's property, which should have come to Elena, for instance. And never mind that the dresses were decades out-of-date; the fabrics of fine silks and satins, velvets and lace, were still good. Elena had no doubt at all that they would soon grace the backs of Madame and her daughters. Here, anyone who saw those dresses would know where the fabric had come from—but in another town, no one would know, or whisper. Let Elena go in rags with but two skirts and two blouses to her name—*they* would, if they could not find the money to pay the silk-merchant's bills, *still* have new dresses.

And as for Theresa Klovis's jewels—or what was left of *them*—once Madame and her daughters were safely in a place that didn't recognize those either, the necklets and bracelets would go to a pawnbroker or to ornament the Horrids.

That was what Elena called them: the Horrid Stepsisters. Would that they had been ugly as well, their outsides matching their insides! If there were any justice in the world, they would both have the faces of greedy monkeys.

But no, they were not particularly unattractive; Delphinium, the eldest, was a little too thin, her nose a little too long for beauty, and her perpetual look of hauteur was going to set extremely disagreeable lines in her face one day, but right now, she was not so bad to look at. Her sister Daphne was just like her, except for tending to plumpness rather than bones. Both had beautiful raven hair, like their mother, and if their eyes were rather close-set, they were still a fashionable deep blue. Never venturing outdoors without a hat or a parasol kept their skin as pale as any lady could wish, and their hands, which never lifted more than a needle or a spoon, were white and soft.

They were no great beauties, but they were pretty enough. And if they lacked for suitors here, well, that was partly due to the fact that they wouldn't consider anyone without a title or a fortune, and preferably both.

The rest of it, of course, was because—

"Elena!" came the inevitable screech from above. *"E-le-na!"*

"Coming, Madame!" she called, and handed Jacques the last of the bags in a rush. If he dropped them, she didn't care; let him take the blame for once.

They were such shrews, such harridans, that any sensible man in this town would have cut off his right hand rather than wed either of them. Only a sizable dowry would have enticed anyone *here* to court either of them—dowries which neither of them possessed.

She pushed past the pile of boxes and bags still awaiting her inside the door, and ran up the dark, oak staircase. *"Elena!"* came another screech, this time in Daphne's unmusical voice. "Where are you, you lazy slut?"

No, there wasn't a man in the town who didn't wince at the idea of hearing *that* voice coming from within his house.

She didn't trouble to answer, just pushed open the heavy door into Madame's room.

It was the largest room in the house, of course, a pleasant chamber, with whitewashed walls and dark beams supporting the ceiling, furnished with a peculiar mix of the fashionable and the ancient. The canopied bed, for instance, was generations old, and was too heavy to move. Two of the chairs and the little dressing-table where Madame sat were spindly-legged, delicate items in the latest mode, painted white, and gilded. The wardrobe was the same age as the bed, plain and dark, with little carving, but the bedside table was the sibling to the dressing-table, ornamented with carved curlicues and flowers. The remains of the breakfast Elena had brought up earlier were still littering the bed-side tables, the window-seat, the massive oak mantelpiece, and the floor.

Madame had been tugging at the laces of Daphne's corset, but let go as soon as Elena entered. Daphne hung to the post of the disturbingly bare canopy bed. The bed had been stripped of its linens and embroidered hangings as soon as Madame rose this morning; those were some of the first things on the coach. Yes, Madame was taking every-thing that was remotely portable, and the only reason she wasn't taking the modish furniture was that she had al-ready sent on as much of that as she could manage.

Madame didn't have to say anything; Elena took her place behind her daughter and wrapped the long corset-laces around each hand. Not as long as they *should* be; Daphne was putting on weight again; the wider gap between the edges of the corset proved that much. If she didn't leave off the cream cakes and bonbons, soon no amount of corset-ting would make her fit her dresses. Elena put her knee in the small of Daphne's back and pulled with all her might.

Daphne squealed a protest as her waist gradually be-came several inches smaller with each pull of the laces. Madame, however, was having none of it. "Pull harder, girl," she ordered, looking down her nose. "If she *will* eat two cream teas in an afternoon, then she'll have to suffer the consequences."

"I was—being sensible!" Daphne objected. "It would—only have—been thrown—away!"

Elena gritted her teeth at that. The food *wouldn't* have been thrown away; Elena herself would have gotten it. It would have been nice to have a cake or two instead of stale, dry toast and the watery remains of the tea. Greedy pig. She'd stuff herself sick rather than see Elena have a single treat.

Elena obeyed by pulling on the laces until she wondered if they were about to snap—this was one of the few tasks she enjoyed doing—and the corset narrowed again. When the edges finally met, she tied the laces off, leaving Daphne red-faced and panting in tiny breaths, while she picked up the froth of three pink silk petticoats with their trimming of ecru lace from the floor. They rustled and slid softly over her work-roughened hands.

"You really are getting as fat as a pig, Daphne," said Delphinium from the window-seat, still dressed in nothing more than her corset, shoes, stockings and drawers. She looked out the window as she spoke. "You'll have to marry a peasant farmer before you're through if you keep eating like you have been, because no well-born man will be seen with a hog in satin—"

"Mother!" whined Daphne, as Elena dropped the three petticoats over her head and tied them in place. And when Madame feigned to ignore them both, went on, viciously, "Well, no one would look at *you* twice—you're getting lines around your mouth and nose from all the scowling. And starving yourself like you do gives you bad breath and no breasts—you're as flat as a boy, a boy with the face of an old hag!"

"Huh. Better thin than looking like a pregnant sow," Delphinium replied, but as Elena took Daphne's dress from the chair on which it had been left, she saw Delphinium surreptitiously pick up her hand-mirror and examine the area around her mouth with a certain alarm.

"Enough, girls, both of you." That order, in Madame's coldest voice, shut them both up. Elena dropped Daphne's pink-and-green silk dress over her head and tugged it in place over the petticoats, then laced up the back while Daphne stood still.

Once Daphne was gowned, Madame rose from her dressing table and gestured imperiously; obedient for a change, Daphne took Madame's place, while Madame attended to her hair. All three women wore their hair piled high on their heads in elaborate designs of pompadours and ringlets, and as a consequence, never actually took their hair down and combed it out more often than once a month. They slept with their hair protected at night by huge, stiff paper cylinders, so that in the morning, Madame didn't have to do a great deal to set it to rights. Ever since she'd learned this, Elena had thought they were mad to fuss so much, and she still did. No one else in the town wore their hair that way unless they were going to attend a ball or some other important event. It couldn't be comfortable, sleeping like that, and she shuddered to think what could move in and set up housekeeping in those untouched hair-towers. It was stupid to go about dressed and coiffed like that every day.

Why, not even the Queen went to such pains over her appearance! You could see that for yourself, if you went to the Palace about the time she took her afternoon stroll in the garden with her son, the eleven-year-old Prince Florian. That was one of the chief entertainments in their town of Charbourg, in fact—going to the Palace in the afternoon to watch the Royal Family walk about in their gardens, then take a stroll yourself when the Royals had gone into the Palace and the gardens were open to the public for an hour. Not that Elena ever had the time for such a diversion, not since Madame had come to be her stepmother—but she remembered back when her mother was alive, when the baby Prince was just big enough to toddle about the grass. The people of Charbourg loved their King and Queen, and in fact, everyone in the Kingdom loved the King and Queen; Otraria was a good Kingdom to live in. The land was fertile and the climate gentle, the tax collectors never took more than was reasonable, and sometimes gave what they took back, if someone had fallen on hard times. In spring, there was never a frost to blight the blossoms; in summer there was always enough rain, and never too much. The King listened to the needs of his people, and met them, and the King and his Queen were good, kind, caring stewards of the land. Not like some of the Five Hundred Kingdoms....

Or at least, life was good here for anyone who didn't have Madame for a stepmother.

With Daphne dressed, it was Delphinium's turn to be gowned and coiffed, and the elder sister slid off the window-seat with a scowl, and turned her back to Elena. Delphinium's bony shoulder blades protruded over the back of the corset like a pair of skin-covered winglets; Elena wondered why she bothered with a corset at all. Perhaps only because it was fashionable to wear one; perhaps because the corset gave her a place to stuff balls of lambswool, to give her the illusion of breasts. The corset didn't exactly need tightening, just tying, and Delphinium's petticoats of yellow, and her dress of blue and yellow, were soon slipped over her head and laced on.

All the while that Elena had been dressing the girls, she had heard Jacques going back and forth to the carriage, carrying off the baggage that had yet to be stowed. There was a single basket on the floor, and a single case on the bare mattress; when Madame finished with Delphinium's hair, she turned to Elena.

"Put the toilette articles into the case," Madame said imperiously, "and pick up all the china and put it in the basket, then bring both down to the carriage. Come, girls."

The three of them sailed out the door, and as Elena hurried to attend to this final task, she heard the sound of their elegant high-heeled shoes clacking on the staircase as they made their way down.

She would have liked to just throw everything in the case and basket, but knew better. Madame would check. So she fitted the brush and mirror, the comb and pick, the powder-box and powder-puff, the cologne bottles, the rouge and lip-paint and the patch-box all in their proper places, then stacked dainty floral-figured saucers, cups, teapot and silver in the basket with the soiled napkins around them to keep them from jouncing. At least this was one set of dishes *she* wouldn't be washing. With the case in one hand and the basket in the other, Elena hurried down the stairs and out the door.

They were already waiting in the carriage, with Jacques up on the driver's box, the hired horses stamping restively. She handed up case and basket to Daphne, who took them and stowed them away somewhere at her feet.

Madame thrust her head out the window.

"Keep the house tidy," Madame ordered.

"Yes, Madame," Elena replied, throttling down her joy. They still might change their minds—something might happen. Madame might get cold feet at the last minute.

"Don't let any strangers in."

"Yes, Madame."

"We will write to inform you of our address. Send any invitations from the Palace on *immediately*."

"Yes, Madame."

Stepmother looked down at her, frowning, as if trying to think of something else, some order she had not yet given. Elena held her breath. There was *one*—she prayed that Madame would not think of it.

And she did not. She moved away from the window, sat back in her seat, and rapped on the roof of the coach with her cane. Jacques cracked his whip and snapped the reins over the horses' backs. With a clatter of clumsy hooves— they *were* nothing more than carthorses, after all—the carriage lurched into motion. It wallowed down the cobbled street, over the arched granite bridge, then around the corner and out of sight.

Elena waited, listening for the sound of returning horses. There were too many things that could go wrong. They could discover that they had forgotten something. They still could change their minds....

Madame could remember that she had not ordered Elena not to leave the house and grounds.

The rose-scented morning breeze pressed her shabby brown skirt against her bare legs. Her bare feet began to ache from standing on the hard cobbles. The larks overhead continued to sing, and a pair of robins appeared and perched on the sandstone wall beside her. The sun climbed a little higher. And still she waited.

But the clock in the church tower struck the hour, and though she watched with her heart in her mouth, there was no sign of them. No rattle of wheels on the cobbles, no clatter of hooves on the stone. Only the song of larks overhead, the honking of geese on the river that flowed under the stone bridge, the whisper of the neighbors on the other side of the wall—

"You can come out now, Madame Blanche, Madame Fleur," Elena called. "I think they're really gone."

Two thumps, and the patter of footsteps, and the two old women burst out of their own gate and hurried over to Elena. They were as alike as two peas, these neighbors; sisters, round and pink and sturdy, dressed in handsome linen gowns with a modest trimming of ribbon, no lace, and white linen mob-caps over their grey-streaked dark curls. Blanche wore grey, Fleur wore blue; Fleur's gown was sprigged with tiny flowers in darker blue, Blanche's was faintly striped grey-on-grey. Elena was very fond of them; they had done their best to help her whenever they could, though they had to be careful. Madame Klovis would punish Elena for taking anything from them, if she discovered it. And Madame *hated* both of the sisters. "Common," she called them with distaste, though they were no more common than Elena's father had been, and not being given to speculation, had kept the money they had intact.

"What has been going on?" asked Blanche, at the same time as Fleur burst out with "Where are they going?"

"To LeTours for now, and if necessary, right out of the Kingdom entirely," Elena told them. "And," she continued sourly, "as soon as the creditors find out, I expect them to come for the furniture."

Both little rosebud mouths formed identical, shocked "o"s.

"I didn't know it was that bad," Fleur said, after a moment. "She kept it all very quiet! What are you going to do?"

"They can't claim the house, of course, since it was willed in equal shares to all of us, and I haven't run up any debts," Elena continued. "So at least I will have a place to stay for the moment."

"But what will you do? How will you manage?" Blanche asked at last. And "Why did they leave?" asked a more bewildered Fleur. "All they would have had to do to discharge the debts would have been to sell some jewels, live more frugally—"

Then Fleur stopped as both Elena and Blanche favored her with sardonic looks. "Oh," the old woman said, and grimaced. "I forgot. This is Madame and her daughters we are speaking of."

Blanche shrugged. "She still could have lived frugally," the elder sister said. "She could have decided to lose those airs of hers, and act her station, instead of miles above it."

Elena just shook her head. "There are a great many things she could have done. None of them suited her."

The old women tittered, and Blanche took Elena's elbow. "Come, dear," she said, in a kindly tone of voice. "I would guess that Madame didn't leave you so much as a crumb in that house, and Daphne ate everything that had been saved out of the cart before they left. Come over to our house, and we'll give you breakfast. I always enjoy cooking for you."

Just at that moment, a clatter of wooden wheels and a rattle of hooves made all three of them look up—

But it wasn't the carriage returning. It was Monsieur Rabellet. His wife was the town's most fashionable dressmaker, and there was still a mighty outstanding bill from Madame and her daughters at that establishment.

He was driving a commodious cart, and he had a very determined and angry expression on his face.

"Word spreads quickly," Elena sighed. "Thank you, Madame Blanche; I *am* hungry, and I gratefully accept your invitation. I would rather not be there as the corpse is stripped."

They heard more carts arriving as they worked together in the kitchen, and soon voices were raised in angry argument on the other side of the fence. Presumably those who had arrived were just now finding out how little had been left behind that was of any value at all. The heavy, old-fashioned furniture that had been in Elena's family for generations was not only hard to move, it wasn't worth a great deal. Most of the fashionable items that had been left would need repair— Madame and her daughters were not easy on their possessions. There tended to be a lot of fighting between the sisters; teacups were hurled, tables upset, and the delicate legs of the new-fashioned furniture didn't hold up well to such mistreatment.

Elena tried to ignore the shouting. There was one thing

that she was certain of; there was *nothing* in her little garret room that was worth taking. If they even bothered to go up there.

When her father had remarried and brought home his bride and her two daughters, the first thing that Delphinium had done was to claim Elena's room. Daphne had taken the next-best chamber, and Madame had made over the remaining rooms into sitting rooms for the three of them, except for the one that went to her very superior lady's maid. Elena had taken a little garret room at the top of the stairs; at least, with the chimney running through the middle of it, it was warm in the winter. When her father had died, they had actually tried to force her out of her garret, claiming that it was needed for Madame's new assistant lady's maid, and for a hideously uncomfortable several years, she'd been forced to sleep on the kitchen hearth, giving her a permanently smudged appearance and the nickname in the town of "Ella Cinders."

But the maid had eventually decided that a garret room did not suit her lofty standards, and Daphne had to give up her sitting room. Elena got her garret back, and as the family fortune was burned away in a funeral pyre of gowns and fripperies, the servants began to leave.

"What would you like in your omelette, my dear?" asked Blanche, breaking into Elena's reverie. Elena flushed, realizing that she had been standing there, lost in memory, staring at the blank garden wall across from the kitchen door.

"Oh, please, Madame, let me—"

"Nonsense," Blanche said firmly. "You have been on your

feet since before dawn. Now just sit down and let us feed you, and then perhaps we can help you make some plans."

"Mushrooms, then, please?" she replied, "If you have them."

Fleur laughed. "Elena, please! Fancy *us*, without mushrooms!" And the two women set about making a handsome breakfast for all three of them. There were only three servants in their household—a man-of-all-work, a housekeeper, and a little maid to help the housekeeper. No cook—Blanche liked to cook—no lady's maid, no coachman, no great state at all. Certainly nothing like the small army that Madame had thought needful, an army that Elena had eventually come to replace all by herself. Then again, their little house was half the size of Elena's.

Madame Blanche was an excellent cook; her husband had been a very plump and happy man with her as his wife. It was, by far, the best meal that Elena had tasted since the last time that Fleur and Blanche had smuggled her over to eat with them.

An ugly shouting match began on the other side of the wall as they were finishing their tea. "Oh, my," Fleur said, cocking her head to one side. "I believe Monsieur Beavrais has discovered that he has come too late. I hope this doesn't put my chickens off laying."

"And speaking of chickens," Blanche said, firmly taking the reins of conversation into her hands. "If you're going to be left with nothing, as good neighbors, I cannot even think of allowing you to starve. I think we could spare you three hens and a rooster, which would give you three eggs a day. I doubt that the creditors will bother to tear up your kitchen garden, so once that begins to produce, you will have eggs and vegetables."

"You can probably trade the vegetables for bread," Fleur added helpfully. "And perhaps you could take in washing? With no one there but you, there won't be nearly as much work. Everyone knows what a hard worker you are, and that you were the one that has done everything in that house that Jacques wouldn't do."

"Perhaps," Elena agreed, although she already had ideas of her own on that score. But she let them rattle on, reveling in the fact that here it was midmorning, and she was actually sitting down in a cozy kitchen, with a cup of tea in her hand, and nothing whatsoever in front of her to do!

And when the last rattle and bang from next door had died away, the last set of boots clumped off, the last dust settled, she took her leave of her kind friends, and went to see what the vultures had left her.

Elena paused at the gate to take a good long look at the house she had lived in all of her life, *seeing* it, really seeing it, for the first time in a very long time. She tried to look at it as if she was a stranger. It was a handsome place, which Jacques had miraculously kept in good repair—but then, since it was made of the same beautiful golden-grey stone as the wall around it, and had a stout slate roof, perhaps that hadn't been all that difficult a proposition. Once in a great while, a slate would slip and need to be replaced, or a windowpane crack, but that was all.

The lack of cloth fluttering at them told Elena that the creditors had taken all of the curtains.

And the urns with their little rosemary bushes that had

stood on either side of the front door. *And* the statue of
Venus that had held pride-of-place in the center of the
flower-bed in this, the front garden. The bills must have
been very large indeed, for creditors to take the garden
statuary.

At least they hadn't taken the glass out of the windows.
But perhaps they couldn't—the glass was part of the house,
and as yet, they could make no claim on the house itself.
They would have to go before a magistrate, and Elena could
plead her cause there, and possibly even win. And even if
she didn't, she could take her cause to the King at his weekly
audience, and probably win. They said that the King had a
notoriously soft spot for orphans, having been left one himself, but that might just be a bit of idle gossip.

She lingered for a moment, steeling herself for the inevitable, then walked up the path. The door had been imperfectly
closed, and opened with a touch. It creaked on its iron
hinges, and for a moment, Elena winced, expecting Madame
to shriek a complaint.

But no. Madame was no longer here to complain. She relaxed again.

Madame had taken as much as she could, but most of the
downstairs rooms still had been furnished before the creditors had arrived. Even Madame Klovis could not manage to
carry off an entire household of furnishings in a carriage
and a hired cart. Most of what Madame had added in the
way of decoration to the public rooms of the house had
been in soft goods—rugs, tapestries, cushions. Those she
had taken with her, leaving the heavy pieces behind. Now
the morning light shining through the open windows

showed nothing but bare walls with paler patches showing where the tapestries had been, and bare wood floors, marred with deep scratches where the heavy furniture had been dragged out. Elena began wandering through the rooms, taking inventory of what was lost.

The sitting room; here there had been a fine, heavy settle beneath the window, a handsome cabinet made for displaying the family silver (Madame had taken the silver), a table and chairs at the fireplace, a second settle against the wall opposite the window. All of the furniture had been made of dark walnut, lovingly rubbed and waxed until it glowed. The only thing left now was the inglenook seat built into the fireplace itself.

The dining room, where the furniture had been made of the same oak as the beds upstairs; table, twelve chairs, sideboard. All gone.

Her father's office; desk, chair, cabinet where he had kept his records. Now a mere memory. The tiny room seemed much bigger now.

The library—she opened the door and stepped into the room, and stifled a hurt gasp at the sight of all the empty shelves. It had not been a large room, no bigger than the dining room, but it had been her favorite in all the house. This was, perhaps, the greatest loss for Elena, for not only were the stout chairs and desk gone, and the huge, framed map of the Five Hundred Kingdoms that had hung over the door, but so were all the books and ornaments that had stood between them. The ornaments had never interested her a great deal, but the books—those books had been the consolation of lonely hours, the things that took her away when she was unhappy. Madame had not taken any of the books; she had no use for such things, and had not seen their value.

But to Elena, who had hoped that the creditors would not see the value either, the loss of each book was as if she had lost a friend. She had known each of them, read them all countless times, knew every foxed page, every scar on every binding. Tears sprang into her eyes, her throat closed, and she jammed the side of her hand into her mouth to keep from sobbing aloud. Blinded by her tears, she turned away, quickly.

The pantry had already been empty, every bit of food loaded into the carriage, and she did not pause to examine it. Nor would she trouble to go down to the cellar; there was nothing there, either, and for the same reason. Madame never stinted herself on fine wines, and what she didn't drink, without a doubt, Jacques would. The kitchen, however, had still been furnished—Madame did not intend to have to cook for herself, and had no need of kitchenware. Only the fine china had been packed away and taken. But now it, too, was bare, stripped as completely as any other room, every knife, every pot and pan, excepting only the dishrags she had washed and left to dry, two heavy, brown-glazed dishes and three mugs made of the commonest clay, all of them chipped and worn, and two pots made of the same substance. So, she *could* cook. But otherwise, even the spit, the crane, and the pothook in the fireplace had been taken.

No need to look in the stillroom. What Madame didn't take, they'll have now.

She went upstairs, and did not bother to check the bedrooms on the second floor. If the creditors had been so thorough down below, she doubted that they would have left anything other than dust. Instead, she climbed the stairs to the attic, and her garret room, to see if anything at all had been left there.

She opened the door to her own room and for a moment, she felt frozen with shock. Her few belongings had been tossed about the room as if a mad dog had been playing with them. Her poor, flat little pillow was gone. Her ragged blankets were thrown into the corner. Her other change of clothing wadded up and tossed into the opposite corner. The box that held her few little treasures had been upended, and the comb with teeth missing, the bit of broken mirror, the feathers, bits of pretty stone, and dried flowers kicked everywhere, the string of beads broken and scattered. Her pallet of straw-stuffed canvas had been torn open, the straw scattered about the room. The place was a shambles.

For a second time she fought back tears, but she truly wanted to fall to her knees and weep at the thoughtless cruelty of it. *Why?* Why tear *her* poor things to bits? Could they possibly imagine that there had been anything of value hidden up here? How could they even *think* that she would have been allowed to keep anything? Hadn't the entire town been aware of her shabby state? Why, the town beggars went better clothed than she!

Perhaps another girl would have been paralyzed with the grief that shook her—but Elena had learned to work even while her heart was breaking and her eyes overflowing a long time ago. And if her hands shook as she carefully picked up and shook out her spare skirt, bodice, and blouse, her worn-out shawl and kerchief, and folded them up to set them in the window-seat, what was left of her bits and souvenirs in a mound atop them, well, there was no one to see. And if she sprinkled the straw she regathered from the floor with her tears, there was no one to mock her grief. But it was hard, hard, to have the little she had saved of her past life ground into dust as those poor flowers had been. At least she was wearing the locket with her mother's portrait in it around her neck on a ribbon—Daphne had stolen the chain long ago.

She sobbed quietly as she collected every bit of straw; she would need something to sleep on tonight. It had to be done, and no one would do it for her.

She stuffed it all back into the empty canvas sack that had been her bed. And at least there was one small blessing; she always kept her needlecase in the pocket of her apron, and had they found that, they probably would have taken it as well. So she was able to stitch the mattress back up again, sitting cross-legged on the bare floor. They had torn the seams open, rather than ripping up the canvas, and although she had to remake it a little smaller, when she finished it was not in much worse shape than it had been before it had been torn apart. It was a hard thing, though—to find that men whom *she* had never harmed, who should realize that she had been just as ill-treated as they, should take out their anger on her.

And when she thought about how the flowers from her mother's grave had been crushed, the few things she could call her own left in ruins, her eyes burned and new sobs choked her—

"Ahem."

She squeaked and jumped, and cast startled eyes on the open doorway.

There was a man standing there. He stepped into the light, and she saw that it was Monsieur Rabellet. He carried a bundle under one arm, and his face was suffused with guilt.

"I am sorry, Ella," he said, flushing with shame when he caught sight of her tear-streaked face. "They were looking for valuables, and they started in on your room before I could stop them. It was the latecomers, you see, the ones who got nothing because—"

She sniffed, and wiped her cheeks with the back of her hand, but said nothing; she just stared at him, and let the tears come, weeping silently. She was *not* going to make this easy on him. If he'd cared to, he could have stopped them. He was a big man, only the blacksmith was bigger.

"At least I kept them from tearing up your clothes!" he protested, and flushed again. "At least—no more than they already were...." He coughed, and swallowed audibly as she fixed him with a look that she *hoped* would stab him to the heart and double his guilt. "The wife gave me a piece of her mind when she found out."

Well, *Madame* Rabellet had always been kind to Elena, who had given her the respect due to a fine craftswoman, and always been ready to lend a hand at the fittings, proving herself so useful that Madame Rabellet had never needed to bring her Apprentice girl with her.

"Anyway, when she found out, she sent me back here with this—" The man took two steps forward into the room and thrust the bundle at Elena, who automatically put out her hands to take it from him. "She said it wasn't fair—said

God gives blessings to the charitable—said—" He was backing up as he babbled, as if the accusations in her eyes were arrows, wounding him, and when he reached the door, he whirled, and fled, leaving her alone as his hasty footsteps on the floor and the staircase echoed through the empty rooms. She sat there, unmoving, until the slamming of the front door woke her from her shock.

She looked at the bundle in her hands. It was fabric—it was woolen, dyed a golden-brown. Not new, but sound, in good condition, and so far as she could tell, not stained, either. She unfolded it, to find that it was a large, plain shawl, and it was only the covering for a bundle of clothing.

A skirt, a blouse, and a bodice; like the shawl, the fabric was not new and the skirt and bodice had been re-dyed. The skirt was a heavy twilled linen, and there was a kerchief that matched, dyed a dark brown, the bodice was black, and the blouse a pale color that was not quite white. They all looked to have been made from much larger garments, cut down when the seams were too worn to hold, but the fabric itself was still good.

They were *not* patched, *not* torn, *not* darned. In fact, they were stoutly-sewn and well re-dyed. These were the sorts of things that a dressmaker assigned to a new Apprentice to make, simple garments to teach her to sew a "fine seam."

They were the best pieces of clothing that Elena had owned since her father had died. They were also *exactly* what she needed to carry out her plan.

When the rest of the town discovered—as it must, given that Madame Blanche and Madame Fleur were two of the most inveterate gossips in the Kingdom—that Elena had been left behind to live as best she could in the empty house, a few of the more guilt-stricken arrived to leave small offerings at her doorstep. Most she never saw; she heard footsteps on the path, and by the time she got to the front door, the gate was swinging shut and there was a basket or a bundle on the doorstep. In fact, except for Monsieur Rabellet, she didn't get much more than a glimpse of a skirt or a pair of legs.

But the offerings were welcome—indeed, desperately needed. A warm woolen shawl, a kitchen knife and a very old and very small frying pan, a loaf of bread, a ball of cheese, a blanket, a pat of butter, a pannikin of salt and a twist of tea. So she wouldn't go hungry tonight, nor cold. Madame Blanche completed the offerings in person, delivering a half dozen eggs and some bacon just as the sun began to set.

She found Elena on her knees at the hearth in the kitchen, getting the fire going again, and ready to toast some bread and cheese for her supper.

"Well!" she said, looking with approval at the food. "I was hoping *someone* would have a guilty conscience! Good." Her mouth firmed with satisfaction. "So, now the robbers have taken care of what you need for now, but have you thought about what you're going to *do?*"

Elena sat back on her heels and looked up at her kindly old neighbor. "I have, actually—I thought it up the day Madame told me that she and the girls were going. I just—" She shook her head. "I wanted to tell you, but Madame swore me to secrecy. She told me that she was going to leave me here to look after the house, and that was when I made up my mind what I was going to do when she was truly gone."

"You did? Well, good for you!" Madame Blanche went out into the kitchen garden and came back with some bits of herbage pinched off the new growth in the herb bed. "Here you are, dear. Those will go nicely in coddled eggs. So, what are you going to do?"

She took a deep breath. "I'm going to leave. I'm going to leave here and never come back."

Madame Blanche blinked, as if she could not quite believe what she had just heard. "I don't suppose you would care to explain that?"

"Tomorrow is the Mop Fair," Elena elaborated. "Anyone who is looking for a servant is going to be there. And you said yourself that everyone in the town knows that I've done every bit of cleaning, mending and tending in this house for—years, anyway. I'm only a plain cook, but anything else, I can do."

"But—but you're *not* a servant!" Madame Blanche said, looking blank. "You're from a good family, Elena! Your poor mother—if she knew, she'd be weeping at the thought. It's one thing for me to do my own cooking, but—"

"I may not have been born a servant, but that's what I am now," Elena said firmly. "I'm too old to become an Apprentice in any decent trade even if I had the fee, so that is what I am good for now." She bit her lip, and continued, bitterly, "You know that's the truth, that it's *all* I'm good for, now. Madame Klovis saw to that; I have no dowry, no prospects, nothing to offer a young man but myself, and what young man would marry an old maid of twenty-one who brings him nothing but her two hands and a few house-keeping skills? Unless I dispute it, within days, the magistrates will turn this very house over to the creditors. Even if I do dispute it and win, what am I to do? It won't be long before Madame Klovis returns—for you surely don't think that she'll have any better luck elsewhere in her fortune hunting any more than I do—and I will be back to being her unpaid slave."

"Well," Madame Blanche said, blankly, "I suppose that all of that is true...."

"So there you are," Elena said, trying to sound deter-mined, and not bleak. "This is my only chance to get away from her. And if I am going to have to spend the rest of my life, mending and tending and cleaning, then I am—by Heaven!—going to be *paid* for it!"

And at least I'll have three meals a day and two suits of cloth-ing a year as well, she reminded herself. Every servant, no matter how lowly, was entitled to that and her bed and board and pay. It would be more than she had ever gotten out of Madame Klovis.

Madame Blanche took a deep breath, as if she was about to dispute Elena's view of the situation, then let it all out in a tremendous sigh. "I am afraid, my dear," she said sadly, "that you are correct. And you are a very brave girl."

Elena shook her head. "I am not brave at all," she replied, and a little of her despair crept into her voice, despite her attempts to keep it out. "I am terrified, Madame Blanche. If I were brave, I would go to the King and find some way to get everything back again. If I were brave, I would reclaim this house at least, and sell it, and use the money to set my-self up in a little cottage somewhere, with a cow, and some chickens and geese, and a little garden of my own. But I am not brave. I am afraid to face all of the creditors and the magistrate, I am too terrified to even think seriously of going to the King. I am running away, Madame Blanche, and I was not even brave enough to face my stepmother and tell her what I am going to do. When she returns, she will find the house has been sold and I am gone, and if I am working for some family here in town, I will hide until she goes again."

Madame Blanche regarded her gravely for a long moment, the light from the fireplace casting strange shadows on her face. "You may be right, Elena, in saying that this is the only thing you can do. But I think you are wrong in saying that you are not brave." She paused. "May I tell Fleur what you have told me?"

"Of course!" Elena replied. "I would be happy to have—" now it was her turn to pause, to choose the right phrase "—her kindly thoughts."

"And I am sure you will have them, my dear," Madame Blanche said warmly. "Well, I will leave you to make your supper in peace."

And she bowed a little, before she turned and left.

Elena sighed, and put a pat of butter in the skillet to melt. After everything had been taken, there were two things left; there had been wood in the woodshed, and a bucket on the pump. She made and ate her dinner—eggs and bread and a little tea. She cleaned the dishes in the light from the fire.

Then she banked the fire until morning, washed her face and hands, and, for lack of anything else to do, went up to bed.

There were no candles, of course, for even if her stepmother had left any, the creditors would have taken them, so Elena climbed the stairs to her room in the dark, and made up her bed (with the new shawl bundled around her old clothing for a pillow, and the new blanket over the old, tattered ones) by the light of the moon coming in her window. She carefully took off her outer clothing and slid into the bed in her shift, and if the pallet was a little lumpier than it had been, it was also warmer beneath the new blanket.

And this was the earliest she had been able to go to sleep in as long as she could recall. Usually she was awake until after midnight with all of the tasks she had to finish—later than that, if the Horrids had been to a ball or a party, and she had to stay up to help them undress. She usually didn't get to go to sleep on a full stomach, either.

It had been a very long day, nevertheless, and an emotional one. She was tired, as tired as she ever had been.

And no one is going to wake me with a scream for something, she realized, as she felt her muscles relaxing in the unaccustomed warmth. The empty house felt—odd. There was a hollowness to it. There were no little sounds below her, of people moving about or making noises in their sleep.

Through her open window, which overlooked the kitchen-garden, she heard voices coming from the house next door. Not loud enough to make out what was being said, but loud enough to know that it was Blanche and Fleur, and a third, unfamiliar voice.

She smiled a little. It was probably a client of Fleur's;

someone like Fleur usually saw a lot of clients after dark. Few people wanted to be seen patronizing a Witch, even if that Witch was someone who had a heart full of only good, true as a priest, and honest as a magistrate.

Everyone knew that Fleur was a Witch of course, and had been since she was very small indeed, though no one every actually said the word aloud. This was why they called her "Madame," although, unlike her sister, she had never had a husband. You just called a Witch "Madame"— it was respectful, and it didn't do to treat a Witch with disrespect. That was why Elena had chosen her words so carefully when she'd asked for Fleur's "good wishes," and why Blanche had asked so carefully if she could "tell Fleur." Words took on extra weight, and extra potency, when there was a Witch involved. You were careful about words around Witches.

Not that Fleur had a great deal of magic of the sort that tales were made of. No, Fleur's power lay in healing and herbs; she was a very small Witch, as Witches went. Ask her to cure your child or get your dry cow to give milk again, and there was no problem. Ask her to cast a love spell or break a curse, and she would look at you helplessly, and shrug.

As she had the day that Elena, weeping after having had yet another possession appropriated by one of the Horrids, had come running into the neighbor's garden and begged Fleur to make Madame go away.

Fleur had only looked at her, sadly. "I cannot, dear," she said, slowly. "I am bound to tell you the truth, my pet. Somewhere, Madame obtained a very powerful love spell, and your father is entrapped in it. I cannot break it, though I wish with all my heart that I could. I could not even begin to guess how to break it, in fact."

Elena stared at the moon framed in her window as she remembered that dreadful moment. It had been an epiphany of sorts. Until that moment, she had believed that all endings were happy ones, that all good adults could help children, if only the children asked, and that good things happened to good people, if only they were brave enough. In that moment, she had learned that sometimes good people were helpless, that terrible things happened to good people, that there were sad endings as well as happy ones.

Worst of all, she had learned that no matter how brave and good you were, bad people often won, and that her father was lost to her forever.

From that moment, she mourned him as if he was dead—and indeed, for all intents and purposes, he might just as well have died. He came less and less to protect her from her stepmother and stepsisters, until at last he did nothing at all. He scarcely seemed to realize that she existed. He totally forgot that he had ever been married to anyone else, and spent his every waking moment trying to find some new means of pleasing "his Madeleine."

It almost came as an anticlimax when he sickened and died within that year of wedding Madame. She thought, looking back on it, that she had known, deep in her heart, that this was what would happen. Love spells did not last forever, not even powerful ones, and Madame was not the sort to allow her power to ebb away.

But this was the peculiar thing; Elena had spent her time

since her father's death wrapped in a growing sense of tension and frustration, as if *something* was out there, some force that would make all of this better, if only she knew how to invoke it. That there was a way to turn this into a happy ending, and that her life was a coiled spring being wound ever tighter until it would all be released in a burst of wonder and magic that would give her back everything that had been taken, and more. The longer things went on, the more she felt that climax rushing towards her, or she towards it—

But it never happened. Not on her sixteenth birthday— the primary moment of magical happenings according to every tale that *she* had ever read or heard—nor on her eighteenth, which was the other possibility. No, things stayed exactly as they had been. No Fairy Godmother appeared, not even Madame Fleur, somehow empowered to take Elena out of her miserable existence. No handsome prince, no prince of any kind, appeared on the doorstep to save her. There was not even a marriage proposal from the blacksmith's son or the cowherd, both traditional disguises for wandering princes. Nothing. Only more and more back-breaking work, and the certainty that nothing was going to change, that Madame had things arranged precisely as she wanted them, and that Elena would be "Ella Cinders," the household slave, until she died. And her despair grew until it matched the tension inside, until it overwhelmed the tension inside, and the only escape from either she ever had were a few stolen moments inside the covers of a book.

For years while she still had hope, she had eased her sadness by telling herself stories like those she read in the books and heard old women tell their grandchildren. "Once upon a time," they always began, "there was a poor orphan girl who was forced to slave for her Wicked Stepmother." And they ended with, "And the orphan girl married the prince—" or the duke, or the earl, or the handsome magician "—and lived happily ever after."

Then, gradually, the stories had changed, and the rescuer had not been a prince. By the time she was sixteen and a day, she had abandoned all thoughts of royalty, and instead, prayed and hoped with a clawing despair for romance. Just a little. Just an ordinary love of her own.

No, the dreams she had told no one were no longer about the unattainable, but about the barely possible—if there were, somewhere in the town, a man willing to brave Madame's wrath to steal her away.

Day in, day out, in the market, by the river, or from her garret window, she had watched other girls with envious eyes as they were courted and wooed by young men. They seemed so happy, and as her sixteenth, and then eighteenth birthdays passed, her envy for their lot grew. As did the stirrings in her heart—and elsewhere—as she spied on them from behind her curtains, or while pretending to select produce in the marketplace, when their sweethearts stole kisses and caresses.

And if only—if only—

She dreamed of the handsome young men, the jaunty Apprentices, the clever journeymen, the stout and rugged young farmers—then watched them court and marry someone else, time after time, never giving her as much as a glance.

Then she dreamed of not-so-handsome, not-so-young men, the widower with two children, the storekeeper with an aged mother, the work-weary bachelor farmer—who did exactly the same.

And when she found herself contemplating with wordless longing the balding, paunchy Town Clerk, who at least had kind eyes, only to weep in her pillow with despair when he married the cross-eyed daughter of the miller, she knew that she had reached the end of dreams.

At least, those sorts of dreams.

All that had been left her was a single, simple longing. *Let me get away. Dearest Father in Heaven, let me get away!*

And finally, at long last, this one little prayer had been answered. Well, now that she had a chance to get away, she was going to seize it with both hands. She would dream of getting a decent place, then working her way up with hard work and cleverness, becoming a cook, or a housekeeper. That was real; that was attainable. Not some *feeling* that her life was a tightly-coiled spring that would shoot her into a life of ease and a path strewn with stars. Feelings were nothing; the only thing that counted was what was in front of your eyes, what you could hold in your hands.

Tomorrow was the Mop Fair; that was what it was called here, in Otraria. Other places called them Hiring Fairs, she had heard, but here the occasion was named for the mops that women wishing to be hired as servants carried with them into the town square. In fact, it wasn't just women who presented themselves to be hired, it was men, too; the women would line up on one side of the square, the men on the other. Each of them would have some token of his or her skills about them. A maid-of-all-work would have a mop or a dust rag, a cook would bring a pan, a shepherd would have his crook, of course, a farmhand a twist of wheat in his hat, a drover a whip in his hand or a twist of whipcord in *his* hat. Each of them would have his or her belongings bundled up at his feet, and those who needed servants would come and examine them, make an offer, and be accepted or refused. That wasn't the only thing that would happen tomorrow, of course—it was a *Fair*, after all, and all of the booths and games, the displays and amusements typical of a Fair would be going on in the center of the square as well. It was a very *large* town square, with more than enough room for a lively Fair with space left to spare.

But the hiring was the chief thing, and tomorrow she would be ready for it. She would wear her new clothing, with the frying pan in her hand and a dust rag tucked into the band of her skirt, showing that she was an all-around servant. And she would take the first offer that came from anyone who looked kind. That was all she wanted; kindness, and a good master or mistress.

But she still had hopes, even if they were much reduced, and when the moon had left her window, she fell asleep, thinking of them. *A kind old priest, whose housekeeper has gone to live on the generous pension he granted her. A busy scholar, absentminded, who needs looking after. A large family, with a dozen children, happy and easy-natured. A great lord, whose housekeeper is looking for maids who can be trusted....*

And so at last, her hopes became dreams, and her treacherous dreams sent her down paths she had given up, or thought she had—into stories—

—and the handsome son of the great lord fell ill, and no one would tend him but the brave little scullery maid, who nursed him back to health at the risk of her life. And when he came to himself, and looked into her pale, grave face, and knew what she had done, he fell in love—

She awoke at dawn, with Fleur's roosters telling the whole world that it was more than time to be up and about. And if there were tears soaking her makeshift pillow, there was, at least, no one to see.

Fleur's roosters had the habit of crowing before the sun was actually up—but Elena was used to getting up that early anyway. Madame Klovis had been a demanding mistress, and her daughters took after her. She had managed to keep a full staff busy; when all that was left was Elena and Jacques, there had always been too much to do, and not enough time to do it in.

So this morning she woke, as she always did, immediately and alert, and although she could have gone back to sleep again, for the first time in years, to sleep late, she knew that this of all days was no time to be lazy. If she wanted a choice spot at the Mop Fair, she needed to get there soon after sunup, and she wasn't going to do that by lying in bed.

In her belongings had been the tag-end of the bar of coarse, harsh laundry soap. Somehow it had escaped being mashed into the floor, squashed into her clothing, or otherwise destroyed. Appearances were terribly important at the Mop Fair, and she was determined *not* to be "Ella Cinders," not when she was trying to make a good impression.

So once she had finished breakfast, she brought everything she owned down into the kitchen and filled the sinks and all the pots with water from the pump. She packed up everything but her new clothing, a dust rag and the pan in a bundle, then stood naked in the middle of the kitchen and scrubbed and rinsed herself until she was pink, and her hair and skin squeaked with cleanliness. Only then did she put on the new clothing. She bound up her hair, braiding it tightly and confining it under the kerchief. Then she shouldered her burden, and marched straight out the front door. She took a deep breath on the threshold, and closed the door behind her, walking away without looking back, because she knew that if she did, she would never have the courage to go on with this.

She paused for a moment in the thin, grey light of morning, looking at the silent—well, silent except for the roosters—house next door. She had hoped that Fleur or Blanche would be about—but there was no sign of either of them as she passed their front gate. She closed her eyes, made a last, silent prayer, and strode resolutely towards the square, and (she hoped) her new future.

The town square had some movement in it, a few people walking about among the stalls and along the shops. The sun was just below the level of the buildings now. The rooftops and ridges were gilded with sunlight, though the square was still in shadow. The men lined up on the cattle-pen side, the women, along the front of the Town Hall. The most desirable spaces were at either end, for those nearest to the ends would be seen first, and Elena took one next to the first-comers, in a place that would be in shade during most of the afternoon. She was one of the first to take her place, right behind a plump woman with a suspicious eye, a pair of young girls with dust rags who looked like sisters, and an old lady with a nursemaid's cap and a motherly look to her. The stalls and booths for the Fair had been set up last night, but only a single hot pie stand was manned this early. Her mouth watered at the smell of the fresh pies—but pies weren't for the likes of her, without even a sou to her name. She had the bread and cheese made up into sandwiches in her bundle. That, and water, would have to see her through the day.

More and more women and girls straggled up to join the line as the Fair came to life. More stalls opened, and the air began to fill with the shouts of barkers hawking their wares or entertainments, the scent of fried food, sausages, meat pies, sweet-stuffs. Eventually, by the time most folk had finished breakfast and the shops were opening, the Fair was in full voice, and the first prospective masters and mistresses were walking the line, examining what was on offer there.

The two girls went first, to a woman in a farmer's smock, who was looking for a pair of maids-of-all-work. They seemed perfectly pleased to be chosen, and Elena took that as a good omen.

Every time someone paused in front of her, Elena looked them straight in the eyes, recited her abilities, and prayed. *Someone kind. Someone kind.* But most merely looked at her and moved on. For some, the reason was obvious; women with husbands with hungry eyes, or sons old enough to begin thinking about girls. No one wanted to hire a girl who could, all too readily, become the plaything of someone in the family. It was hard enough to keep a girl away from the trouble that came from fellow servants and farmworkers; at least there she could presumably be relied on to have enough common sense not to fall into a haymow and into pregnancy unless there was a wedding in the offing. But a pretty girl had no defenses against a predatory master. As a sheltered girl of a wealthy family, Elena had known nothing of such things; as one of the lowly servants, she had learned a great deal. Madame's servants gossiped constantly, and it hadn't been long before they were ignoring her as so unimportant that it was safe to gossip in front of her.

For the rest of those possible employers, though, she could not even begin to guess why they passed her by. It wasn't that she was expecting too much; in fact, she could have asked far more than the wages of a maid-of-all-work. The lowest wages, all that she asked for, were set by law; she was a plain cook and general housemaid, and she should get a shilling a week, two suits of clothing (or household uniform), bed and board and twice a year, a three-day holiday. So why were so many people looking at her, taking a second look, then passing on to choose someone else? It became harder to understand as the noontime came, and the strongest, brightest-looking, and most competent of the other girls were chosen, leaving her clearly the best of the lot available.

At noon, a boy with a bucket came along the line with water. Elena took out her sandwiches and the least chipped of the mugs, and got a drink. The bread was dry on the outside, but she had used all of the butter on the inside, and it was no worse a meal than many she'd had under Madame.

By now, the sun was very warm, and she loosened the neck of her blouse a little, fanning herself with her dust rag; she would be glad when the shadows of the shop-buildings to the west would fall on her and the others still waiting.

Now those who were examining the women and girls moved down the line more slowly, examining the candidates with great care, for the choices were fewer. And now, something peculiar was happening.

These people looked her in the eyes, and looked away. One or two stopped, and asked her name after she had recited her qualifications. "Elena Klovis," she said, and after a moment of blankness, they would say, as if to themselves, "Ah—Ella Cinders." Then they would shake their heads and move on.

Finally, the explanation came, after a harried-looking woman seized on the sight of the old nursemaid with relief and a cry of "Oh, Nanny Parkin! I did not know *you* would be here!" The old woman quickly made an advantageous bargain for herself, but then turned to Elena just before leaving the line.

"I didn't want to blight your hopes, dearie," Nanny

Parkin said, in the kindliest of tones, "but no one will hire you."

"But—" Elena stammered.

"They know who you are, you see," the old woman continued. "Everyone knows Ella Cinders now. Those that didn't know your tale surely do now, after what happened yesterday. No one wants to face Madame Klovis when she returns. They know she'll return, and there won't be anything left here of value when the creditors are finished but you. You see? She'll want you, she'll have some rights to you, and if someone else has you, there will be the devil to pay."

And she picked up her own bundle, and followed her new employer. Elena stared after her in shock and dismay. And when she glanced over at some of the others in the line, she saw nods—or else, averted gazes.

She almost gave up. But—

No, she decided. *No, I will not give up. There are still farmers here, and merchants, and maybe they need someone. They won't be able to make a choice until their goods are sold and their purchases made. I will stay.* People from outside of town wouldn't be afraid of Madame. They would know that Madame would never stir out into the countryside to find the flyaway stepdaughter. There was still a chance, a good chance....

But as the shadows stretched across the square, as time passed and stalls and booths closed, as the line of women thinned, and finally the two lines of those who wished to be hired were combined into one, men to the right, women to the left, her hopes thinned also.

Still, she stayed. Stayed as the last of the food-stalls closed and there was no one left but a dubious-looking sausage-seller hawking equally dubious sausages, as even the disagreeable-looking cook was trundled away by a cross old man. She stayed, until the sun was setting and there was no one left except her, the dispirited sausage-seller, and one other. This was a gangly boy with no tokens of experience, all elbows and knees, wearing clothing that was three sizes too big for him apparently made of tent-canvas. There *was* another person as well, but he was not hoping for hire— this was the father that was keeping the boy company.

"Y'ant t' go naow?" the man said to the boy, who shook his head stubbornly, though his face bore an expression that was as desperate as Elena felt.

The moment the last of the sun went below the horizon, she would *have* to go. The Fair would be over, and there would be no chance of finding a place until next year. Oh, officially it wasn't over until midnight, but no one would be *here*, looking for someone to hire, after the sun set.

Laundry, she thought, despondently. *I can take in laundry. At least, as long as I can keep the creditors from taking the house. I can keep those hens that Blanche offered me. The kitchen garden will feed them and me both. At least, as long as I can keep the creditors from taking the house—*

Then, just as the sun sank behind the buildings to touch the horizon, came an unexpected noise—

It came from the street leading into the square, the sound of hooves and wheels rattling on the cobbles. Which was odd—the stall-holders would not come to take down their booths and stalls until tomorrow, and anyone coming to stay at the inn was already there. Could it be—was there the slightest chance—?

She looked up, peering down towards the street.

The vehicle rattled into the square; an odd little dog-cart, driven by a little old lady dressed in a quite eccentric outfit of clothing. It could have been gypsy clothing, if gypsies were neat as a pin, impeccably groomed, and wore beautifully sewn and ornamented garments that looked far newer than Elena's. It was certainly bright enough to be gypsy clothing; scarlet boots with black stitching, blue skirt embroidered with red and yellow flowers and green leaves, black bodice, yellow blouse, scarlet vest, and wildly embroidered black shawl. The old woman wore her hair in a fat knot at the back of her head, from which little curling wisps were escaping.

The cart was as odd as the driver, also scarlet, painted all over in multicolored flowers. And the horse—or perhaps, pony—was the oddest of all. It was grey with huge eyes, had floppy ears, a hunched back, and was no bigger than a mastiff, but it was wildly strong, for it pulled that cart with no perceptible effort at all, and looked altogether jaunty and proud of itself. And it wore a straw hat, both floppy ears pulled through holes and falling over the brim.

"Ah!" the old lady said, pulling up in front of Elena. "Good. You haven't gone home; that speaks well for your spirit! I'm very glad to see it. Would you like a position?"

"Ah—" Elena said, looking startled, into a pair of the bluest, kindest eyes she had ever seen. *Someone kind*— She did not even have to think. It didn't matter what was wanted. "Ah—yes! Yes, please!"

"In with you then, my dear!" the old lady said, and Elena wasted not a second; she tossed her bundle into the back of the cart and scrambled up beside the old woman. She didn't even stop to ask what the position was—

As they drove out of the square, she heard the man ask his son again, "Y'ant t' go naow?" and heard the boy say, stubbornly, "No. Tain't tomorrow, yet. I'm stayin' till midnight." She looked back at them, until the cart turned a corner and they were lost behind buildings, wondering what would happen to the poor lad.

The little horse picked up speed, trotting with all his might and main, still showing no signs that the cart was too heavy for him, acting as if, in fact, it was lighter than thistledown. As they passed under the wall that encircled the town, and through the town gates, dusk descended.

The little horse picked up his pace, until he was galloping, his tiny hooves flying—

There was a *bump*, and Elena clutched the side of the cart. The old woman was making no attempt to rein her horse in, and he was going awfully fast. In fact, they were right out of sight of the town walls now, the cart bumping and rattling along at a rate that put her heart right in her throat!

The cart gave a lurch, a bump, a wiggle, and a huge jolt that sent it flying into the air—

—and—it—didn't—come—down—

She gasped, and clutched at both the side of the cart and the old lady's arm, as they rose right up into the twilight sky, heading for the stars.

She tried to cry out in fear—instead, she squeaked. The

old lady laughed, and tied off the reins. Elena looked down at the ground, and immediately regretted it.

"Don't look again, my dear," the old woman said, cheerfully. "At least, not until you get used to it."

Elena tried to say something, but nothing would come out of her throat. Panic was the mildest description of what she felt right now—

A Witch! She must be a Witch! That was the only *possible* explanation for this. A powerful Witch—a *very* powerful Witch, one that made Fleur look like—like—Elena! *No wonder she wasn't afraid of Madame, the way everyone else was. If she can make a cart and horse fly, she could turn Madame into a toad with a snap of her fingers!*

But what did she want with Elena? Well, Witches ate, and presumably needed their houses cleaned. Maybe it was easier to hire a servant than to do it all by magic.

The old lady rummaged under the seat, nonchalantly taking out a basket. She flicked a finger, and a little round ball of light appeared over their heads, illuminating both of them. "I'm sure you're hungry, Elena," she said, with a cheerful smile. "Would you help me with this?"

She began handing Elena napkins, a plate of sandwiches, another of little iced cakes, and cups of tea that somehow emerged steaming from the hamper. The cart was as steady as a house, and the seat between them became their table, spread with plates of food, a teapot, a small milk-jug, a bowl of sugar. It was absurd, impossible, ridiculous—and the very ordinariness of the cloth set for two, in the midst of all this impossibility, gave her a kind of anchor, something to grasp at. At this point, Elena's store of shock was beginning to run out—she accepted a sandwich and cup in a numb daze.

"Well," said the old lady, in a nonchalant, matter-of-fact tone. "I expect you would like to know what this is all about."

Elena took a bite of her sandwich, automatically, because—well, because that was what you did with a sandwich. It was ham and watercress. Very good ham. In fact, she hadn't had ham quite this good since she was a small child. "Yes, please," she said in a small voice. Overhead the sky was a deep black strewn with the brightest stars she had ever seen. Beneath the cart was nothing but darkness.

Which was altogether better than looking down on houses no larger than toys.

"Well, where to begin?" The old lady sipped her tea. "I suppose I should begin with this. Elena, I am your Fairy Godmother."

Elena blinked, and a thousand thoughts raced through her head. Uppermost was, *then where have you been all this time when my stepmother was starving and beating me?* The thought did not have the heat of anger in it—yet. But in a few moments, it would.

"Actually, to clarify, I am the Fairy Godmother to this entire Kingdom," she continued, and Elena was suddenly glad that she had not blurted out what had been in her head. A Fairy Godmother to *her* was one thing; a Fairy Godmother to all of Otraria was quite another. Being angry now would be like being angry at a thunderstorm because it happened to rain on *you*. "You *do* know about the King of Otraria, I presume? And his Queen—who used to be the Princess Who Could Not Laugh?"

Elena nodded.

"Well, that was my doing—the goose, and all those people stuck to the goose and each other." She smiled, and patted her hair with every sign of pride. "One of my best efforts, I think. So, in that case, you already *know* how tales come true—for *some* people."

Something about the way she said that made Elena repeat it. "*Some* people?"

The old lady nodded. "Indeed. You see, whenever there is a person whose life begins to resemble a tale—the brave little orphan lad, the lovely girl with the wicked stepmother, the princess with the overly protective father—something begins to happen, and that something is *magic*." She paused, and ate a dainty quarter of sandwich. "Magic begins to gather around them, you see, and in fact, there are even certain people to whom that begins to happen from the moment they are born. That magic begins to try to force their lives down the path that their circumstances most closely resemble, and the longer it takes for that to happen, the more magic begins to gather around them."

Elena sat stock-still, her cup clutched in both hands, thinking about that *tension* she had been feeling for so very many years. Was that—the magic?

The old lady peered at her, and nodded with satisfaction. "So. You *have* felt it. Good, then you understand. That magic has been trying very hard to propel you down the path of a tale to a *happily ever after*, and you've been well overdue for *that* ever since you were sixteen."

"But—" Elena began.

"Among the many other things they do, the Fairy Godmothers are supposed to help that sort of thing along, like midwives," the old lady continued, right over the top of Elena's "but." "Which is why we always turn up when something goes horribly wrong, to counter the Bad Fairy's curse or the invasion of an Evil Sorcerer. But quite often, I'm afraid, in fact more often than not, circumstances around that special person are just not going to allow the happy ending that the magic is pushing for. Take your case, for instance. You do realize what was *supposed* to happen in your life, don't you?"

Well, of course she did! How could she not? She'd day-dreamed it often enough. "On the Prince's birthday, there would be a great ball," she said, automatically. "I would get a gown, somehow—my mother's spirit would weave it of flowers, perhaps, or—"

She looked penetratingly at the old woman.

"—or your Fairy Godmother would conjure it out of the rags left from your mother's old gowns, yes, or Brownies would sew it and leave it for you in the garden. Exactly. And then?"

"Well, I would go to the ball, and no one would recognize me, the Prince would fall in love with me and I with him and he would take me away and I would live—"

They finished in chorus, "Happily ever after."

"Exactly so. Unfortunately, my dear, in your case, though your stepmother and stepsisters are fully *wicked* enough to justify that sort of happy ending, Prince Florian is a mere boy of eleven." She paused just long enough for Elena to begin to feel horribly *cheated* somehow, then continued. "Nor are you the only girl to whom this has happened *with this par-*

ticular tale. All over the Five Hundred Kingdoms, down through time, there have been countless girls like you for whom the circumstances were not right. Their destined princes were greybeards, infants, married or terrible rakes, or not even Princes at all, but Princesses! And the magic keeps gathering around them, trying to make it all work— oh, and by the way, we call that, *The Tradition.* The way that magic tries to set things on a particular course, you see. And there are dozens and dozens of other tales that The Tradition is trying to recreate, all the time, and perhaps one in a hundred actually becomes a tale."

Elena nodded, pushing off that feeling of being cheated with all her determination. "All right, I do see, but—"

"So all of that magic is building up around the person— you, in fact—like a snowball rolling down a hill. It just gets attracted, the same way that white cat hair is attracted to a black velvet bodice, you know." Now the old woman was watching her, closely. For what?

"I see, but—"

"It never goes away. Sometimes, it just builds up to the point where a magician notices it, and it gets—" she waved her hand vaguely "—siphoned off. Sometimes neatly, with the person's consent, and to the benefit of the person, though the effect of that is that it leaves them quite ordinary. Nothing magical will ever happen again to her—or him— but at least their life will go on rather as everyone else's life goes on. And if the person's circumstances are truly dire, usually the magician who benefits by the magic gives them a helping hand to a set of better circumstances, which, of course, breaks The Tradition so that the magic stops building up around them. And sometimes—it is siphoned not so nicely." Her expression darkened. "If that happens, Elena, they are generally left dead, and if they aren't—well, believe me when I tell you that they are worse off than if they *were* dead."

Elena went cold all over. Was *that* why the old woman had offered her a position? Did she only want the magic?

Perhaps it wouldn't be so bad to be ordinary—

But at that moment, even though, not so long ago, she would have welcomed the prospect, she knew that this was not the right answer anymore. Not now.

"And sometimes," the old lady went on, "if the person has attracted someone who is not only a magician, but a magical guardian, something else happens."

She smiled, a warm smile that felt like a comforting arm around Elena's shoulders, and Elena smiled back without knowing quite why. "I am that *something else*, at least in your case."

"What sort of—something else?" Elena asked, cautiously. Her mouth felt very dry and automatically took a sip of tea. It was stone-cold, but before she could do more than make a face, the old lady wiggled her finger at it, and the cup was suddenly steaming again. Elena felt dizzy.

"Someone has to become the Fairy Godmothers. And the White Wizards, and the Good Witches. It has to be someone who already has enough magic gathered around her—or him—so that she can properly learn how to use that magic and how to get more before what she has accumulated is used up. As I said, I am the Fairy Godmother for all of Otraria, and I am getting old and tired. I need an Apprentice. That would be *you*."

Elena had expected to hear any number of things. This was not one of them. "Me?" Elena squeaked.

"That is where all of those Good Magicians come from, dear," the old lady said. "All of those people like you, whose happily-ever-afters just aren't going to come, but who still have too much that is special about them to ever be content with being ordinary. You're ready. You are more than ready. You're brave, sensible, clever, and extremely magical. You have a kind heart, and a good mind. You are certainly proper Godmother material."

Elena thought about that for a moment, and thought about how she had felt, just before the old woman turned up. Angry, and full of fear and desperation. "Excuse me, but—what happens if one of those same people goes bad? Turns ugly and nasty over what they're having to go through?"

"Where do you think evil sorcerers and wicked Witches come from?" the old lady asked darkly, and paused. "Not Bad Fairies though, nor Good Fairies. Those are Fair Folk, and something else entirely; they're born that way. But the Wicked Witches—the Bad Wizards—the Dread Sorceresses? Oh my, yes."

Elena took a deep breath, and closed her eyes for a moment. She didn't precisely *think*, she simply let all that she had been told sink in. Fairy Godmothers, Bad Witches— The Tradition—the magic. It all fell into a pattern in a way that life never had before. She opened her eyes.

"Oh. I think I see. And the position you offered me—"

"As my Apprentice, yes, is for life. And one day, you will choose someone like you, and make her the same offer." The old lady nodded. "Now, you can refuse it if you like, and if you like, I can take all that magic from you and make you like everyone else. You'll still have a position; I'll see to that. I know several kind folk who could use a plain cook or a housekeeper. And actually, that is something else that a Godmother does. There are far more people who want to be rid of the magic than want to become our Apprentices. It can be hard work — and it can be dangerous. After all, *we* stand in the way of what *they* want." She cocked her head to the side, and waited for Elena's response. She did not have to say who *they* were.

Where do you think the evil Sorcerers and bad Witches come from?

And some of those were very, very evil indeed.

But Elena really did not have to think about her answer for very long. Given a choice between an ordinary life, and a magical one—well, it was no choice at all.

"I would love to be your Apprentice, Madame," she said, solemnly, as if she was making a pledge. "And I do accept."

"Grand!" the old lady crowed. "Now, you may call me Madame Bella, my dear, and I believe we shall get along capitally. Oh, look!"

She pointed, just in time for Elena to see a shooting star streak across the heavens in front of them.

"A good omen! Quickly, make a wish!"

"I—don't have to," she said, slowly, feeling the deep truth of her words even as she spoke them. "I already have it."

Madame Bella smiled. "Then I believe that we shall make all speed for home. *Your* home now, and for as long as you care have it so."

Home. What a wonderful word that was. And words were powerful for Witches. For a Fairy Godmother, it should be very powerful indeed. More than powerful enough to make it all real.

Quite as matter-of-factly as if they were sitting on a bench in a starlit pleasure-garden instead of on a flying cart, Madame Bella packed up the hamper with Elena's help, and stowed it once more under the seat. Madame made the little ball of light vanish when she was through, leaving them sitting side by side in the darkness.

Now, in spite of the fact that they were *flying* through the air, rather high above the ground, the only real indication of this was that there was nothing but darkness below them. Madame Bella was as calm and composed as if she did this every day, and the motion of the cart—well, there just wasn't any perceptible motion, only a bit of breeze from their passing. It was surreal, to tell the truth, giving Elena a sense of peculiar dizziness and disorientation.

She blinked, and for the first time, wondered if she really *was* flying through the night sky above the countryside. The whole situation was very dreamlike, after all.

Dreamlike; *was* it a dream?

The more she thought about it, the more certain it seemed. Why, at any moment now she would awaken and discover herself on her pallet in the deserted, barren house, with the depressing prospect of no position and very few options in front of her.

Oh, surely this was a dream. When had anything this wonderful, this fantastic, ever happened to her? Never, of course. She stared out at the darkness. This was like something out of a tale; entirely like one of those dreams she used to have, stories she used to tell herself.

After all, how could a horse and cart be flying in the air like this? When had she ever heard of a flying cart?

But a little voice inside her, stubborn—or perhaps desperate—insisted that this was no stranger than things she already knew were true. *Well, how can Witches fly about on broomsticks? Even Madame Fleur can do that; I saw her, once.* Only once, and in the company of (she presumed) another Witch, but still—

"Madame Bella, what's keeping us in the air?" she asked, hesitantly.

The Godmother gestured at the little horse, who tossed his head. "I prevailed upon my little friend Sergei," she said, cheerfully. "He's part of his own set of tales, but when he's not needed there, he often helps out the Godmothers and Wizards. His mother is the Mare of the East Wind, you know."

"Oh," Elena said, at a bit of a loss, for in fact, she *didn't* know. She hadn't even known there was such a thing as the Mare of the East Wind.

"Oh, silly of me, of course you don't know." Madame Bella chuckled. "And there you see why I need an Apprentice; I'm getting so muddle-headed, it is *more* than time that I stepped down, before I try to put a magical lamp into Cap'O'Rush's hands! Sergei and his mother are from another line of The Tradition, another set of Kingdoms and tales. Take it as read that Sergei is a sort of magical creature rather like one of the Faerie Folk and with equal powers."

"A magic horse. Like a—" She strained her memory, but could not think of another such. At least, not one with power enough to make himself and the cart he drew fly. "Like a Wizard?" she hazarded.

"No, more like a dragon," Bella told her. "Or a Unicorn. His mother is truly powerful, much more so than he is; but then, she is more than half a spirit creature. She was mated to a mortal stallion once, for some reason that escapes me. He has two brothers who are really remarkable to behold; quite the most handsome horses I have ever seen. But sad to say, they have not a smidgen of magic in them; he got the lot. Didn't you, Sergei?"

The little horse tossed his head and whickered. It sounded rather like a snicker.

"Yes, I know, you got all the brains in the family, too," Bella laughed. "Which is probably why you are your mother's favorite child. It's quite true though," Bella continued, turning back to Elena. "Sergei is rather brilliant and terribly crafty, which makes him invaluable to us. For instance, had your stepmother unexpectedly returned, I am fairly certain that *he* would have found a way to get you away from her long before I did."

The horse whickered again, and Bella clapped both hands to her mouth in feigned shock. "Sergei, you *would not* have!"

From the bray that came out of the little horse's throat, whatever it was, Elena was entirely certain that, yes, Sergei *would* have.

She wished Bella would tell her, but the Godmother just shook her head. "Just as well that nothing happened, then. Your town would never have gotten over it, and The Tradition would have been kinked for years. That sort of thing can have serious consequences, dear, and a grave flaw in The Tradition gives an evil one room to move in. I'm not saying that would have happened this time," she hurriedly added, "but just that you have to be very aware when you cross Tradition lines or break Tradition that you do it in a way that impacts the fewest people."

"I thought that The Tradition was only important for— for the special people," Elena said hesitantly.

"Oh, no—The Tradition rules *everything* in the Five Hundred Kingdoms." At least Bella didn't sound at all impatient with Elena for asking so many questions. "Why, for instance, do you think that everyone in Otraria loves King Colin and Queen Sophia? That no one would ever whisper a word of treason about them, even though the only army he has never does much except march in parades and the only guards he has are old men inclined to nod off at their posts?"

Elena shook her head. "The Tradition?" she hazarded.

"Exactly. Goose-boy Colin brought a smile to the face of

the Princess Who Could Not Laugh, and *that* brought joy back to Otraria, as well as won him her hand and Kingdom. Now, precisely because of this, The Tradition makes certain that *everything* in the Kingdom runs sweetly and smoothly, from the happiness of the King and Queen down to the weather."

"Oh, surely not!" Elena objected. "Surely the *weather* isn't affected!"

"You think not?" Bella laughed, but there was a sad sound to it. "Then early in your training I should take you to a Kingdom that is laboring under an evil ruler, a despotic one. You'd see then that The Tradition guides everything down to the least and seemingly insignificant detail. Otraria is happy, Colin is a good King who rules well and wisely, and so—the land is fertile, the people are content, the weather is perfect in every season, because The Tradition creates a Kingdom to match the King and Queen. It would be very, very hard for an evil Witch or a dark Wizard to move into Otraria now; in fact, the only way that one *could* would be either by an invasion, which would take a *very* great force of arms, or by a combination of magic and treachery. Believe me, when it comes to the latter, *that* will not happen while I am Godmother here, nor as long as any Apprentice I train is overseeing things."

There was a steely tone to Bella's words that made Elena sit up a little straighter and give the old woman a sideways glance. Not that she could see very much in the dark but—she had the feeling that if she *could* see Bella's face, she would discover that the slightly dotty old woman that had offered her a position had transformed for a moment into something very like the iron-spined general who commanded Otraria's tiny army. Both of them might be old—but they knew their duties, and they would drive themselves and everything and anyone under their authority to see to it that those duties were performed.

"But there—that's one of the things we do, you see," Bella continued in a more normal tone. "We see to it that the conditions are fulfilled to make things as pleasant as possible for everyone. The main problem is that there is quite a bit of work, and not very many of us; there are Kingdoms that don't have a Godmother or resident Wizard, Kingdoms where the assigned Godmother is overworked, or falls ill, or dies without an Apprentice in training. So things can, and do, go wrong. That is when The Tradition works against us, and for the evil folk of the world— The Tradition doesn't *care*, you see, whether the outcome of a story is a joy or a tragedy; if the circumstances are there, it just makes things follow down set paths. And since we can't fix them directly, we have to help the heroes who can."

"But why can't you fix them directly?" Elena asked, now truly puzzled and confused. "If you have all this power—"

"Ah. The answer to *that* is why you will be serving as my Apprentice for some time," Madame Bella replied, wisely. "But the quick answer is that it would take all the magic of a hundred Godmothers working together to correct a single one of those problems if we had to go counter to The Tradition. *We* do not figure as heroes, you see. Whoever heard of a dotty old lady in shining armor?"

Elena giggled at that; why not? She was going to wake up, after all, and things would not be nearly so pleasant when she did, so she might as well enjoy this dream. And it was such a *good* dream—she would very much like to be a Godmother's Apprentice. And it was somehow comforting to have an explanation for why her life had gone from bad to worse, no matter what she had done to try to change things.

"And you have to remember that the evil ones are always on the prowl, looking for their opportunities to make The Tradition work to *their* advantage, and they have one thing on their side that we do not," Madame Bella continued. "Once one of them finds a place to work, *they* can concentrate on that one Kingdom, while *we* are spread out over many."

"How many?" Elena asked, sobering. This might be a dream, but it certainly sounded as if this Godmothering business was quite hard work.

Not that *she* was afraid of hard work, for heaven's sake! But she had to wonder just how many Kingdoms Bella was responsible for, if there were so few of the Godmothers.

"At the moment, I am Godmother directly to two dozen of the Five Hundred Kingdoms, and I can be called upon to help with another twelve or fourteen," Madame Bella said, and sighed. "And I am not getting any younger, alas. I have been looking for a good Apprentice for some time now."

Obscurely, Elena felt a surge of disappointment, even though this was a dream. So she had not been the only person that Madame Bella had considered!

But in the next moment, Bella's words made the disappointment vanish. "In fact, I have really been looking, in one way or another, from the day that I became the God-mother for these Kingdoms. I have seen too much tragedy come into the world because a Godmother left looking for her Apprentice until it was too late. I must say, though, in all that time, I never had a bit of hope until I found you. And I was not going to even hope that you could be what I was looking for until after you passed your eighteenth birth-day."

"Why then?" Elena wanted to know.

"Because if ever you had a satisfactory end to your per-sonal tale—if, for instance, you had found a sweetheart who had successfully taken you out of that house—it *had* to be by then." Bella sounded melancholy. "Far too many of the young women I have watched over the years did, in-deed, make that sort of end. Why it should be before the eighteenth birthday, I do not know. Perhaps it has something to do with being willing to—to *settle* for less, to stop dream-ing—to give up on hope. And then, perhaps the magic around you arrows in on whatever you can get, rather than what you hope for. I don't know for certain, because I have never asked those young women about what was going on in their minds."

Elena licked her lips thoughtfully, tasting the last, faint hint of sweetness from an iced cake upon them. Yes, she *had* re-cently stopped dreaming—or at least *day*dreaming—but it had not been until after that critical eighteenth birthday. Even then, could she really say that she had given up on dreams? Not when she had continued to look out her win-dow at handsome young men and make up lesser stories, smaller dreams about them.

And in all that time, had she ever really tried to *do* anything about those dreams? Oh, she could argue all she wanted that her stepmother would never have given her the time to go meet a young man, but in her heart of hearts, she had to admit that if she had tried, she probably could have stolen the time, somehow, to go and meet one of those young men, to flirt a little, as she had seen so many other girls do.

Why had she never tried? It wasn't that she was shy. It wasn't that she had some withered sprig of pride left, that insisted that Elena Klovis was above the common young men she saw in the streets. Perhaps, if she had seen a man that her heart had really longed for, perhaps she would have defied her stepmother and grasped for love with both hands. She sat back in her seat and thought, hard, about all the men, young and old, she had watched, and she had to admit that no, it had never been the *man* she had longed for—only the escape that marriage, marriage to anyone, represented.

Well. That was certainly interesting. And perhaps a little disturbing—*why* was that true? Was it the men? Or was it her? Was she just as cold in her way as the Horrids, who cared nothing for the men who courted them, only the wealth or status that they represented?

It was a nasty thought, and one that gave her pause as she considered just what all the implications of it were.

"Perhaps," Bella sighed, "Perhaps for the rest of those others, it was just as well. Every one of them discovered someone she truly loved, and in the end, they were happy. The Tradition works in small stories as well as large, you know."

But if I had tried, would I have found a true love? she thought, somberly. It was hindsight, of course.

"I certainly had plenty of opportunity to go that route myself," the old woman continued, as if musing aloud. "It wasn't as if I had a terror of a stepmother dogging my footsteps every waking moment of the day. I merely had two spoiled older sisters, and it wasn't that I was their slave, it was just that they were too bone-lazy to take the task of housekeeper, so I did. I had plenty of time for myself, and I was the only one who decided what I would do and when I did it. My sisters had plenty of beaus haunting our house; I suppose I could have had, too, if I'd been in the least interested, but there wasn't one of them that I cared to exchange more than a few words with."

"What about—" Elena hesitated "—after?"

"*After* I became a Godmother?" Bella laughed. "Heavens, child, when would I have found the time to look out for a young man? I had so much work on my hands I hardly found the time to sleep! Ah—look! Down there! We're almost home."

The old woman pointed down and ahead of them; Elena couldn't see much; just a faint light, that seemed to be hidden among trees. But as soon as she spotted it, she realized that the light was getting closer, and the treetops nearer, *very* quickly indeed! She could *see* what was below them now, instead of it being a vague darkness, and all her fear came back. She clutched at the side and the seat of the cart convulsively, as they skimmed over the top branches, tiny twigs hitting the underside and the wheels, and then, while her stomach lurched with fear, they were above a clearing, in the center of which was a cottage with lights in every window and what was surely a garden surrounding it.

Then as her breath came short and her heart pounded, they were no longer above it, they were dropping down quickly.

Too quickly!

She wanted to scream, but nothing came out of her paralyzed throat, and a moment later, the little horse's hooves touched the ground in front of the cottage. Then the wheels set down with a *bump*, the horse halted, the cart rolled to a gentle stop, and there they were.

Elena felt limp with relief; Madame Bella patted her hand. "There you are, my dear. Safe on the ground." She laughed. "I know you don't think it now, but one day you will let Sergei pull you across the sky without even thinking about it."

Oh, no I won't! Elena thought, as her heart slowly calmed.

Madame Bella climbed down off the seat, and it was obvious as she moved that although she *sounded* as lively as a much younger woman, she certainly moved like an old one whose joints pained her. Not excessively, just enough to slow her down a bit, and make life—difficult for her.

She opened the garden gate, and the little horse drew the cart inside and up the garden path without being asked. But when he stopped at the front door of the cottage, Elena also jumped down from her perch on the seat. Dream or no dream, she wasn't about to sit about while poor Madame Bella struggled with harnesses and straps.

"Where is the stable, Madame?" she asked, coming to the little horse's head.

"Around to the side—will you lift your bundle down for me?" the old woman asked.

"I'll bring it myself," Elena said firmly. "And I will unharness the little horse." Dream or no dream, she wasn't about to show so little respect for a good old woman like Madame Bella as to make *her* do work that Elena was better suited to.

Madame Bella smiled. "Bless you child; I am pleased to see you wishing to take up your duties already. Sergei won't stay the night, but the cart should be put away. Sergei?"

The horse whickered and trotted off, going around the side of the cottage and taking the cart skillfully with him. When Elena followed she discovered a neat little stable, into which Sergei had already backed the cart. She had him unharnessed in a few moments; though he insisted on keeping the hat. She looked for and found a currycomb, but the horse shook his head at her merrily, and with a leap, vanished—upward.

Yes, this was surely a dream. Bemusedly, and wondering when it would end, she picked her bundle out of the back of the cart, and for good measure, the basket of dishes and leftovers from under the front seat, and carried both of them around the corner and in at the front door.

And there she got yet another surprise, for although the cottage looked small on the outside—cozy for one, but perhaps a little confining for two—on the inside, well, although it was no palace, it was *certainly* far larger than it appeared.

Ah. This could be nothing but a dream. What she was looking at was simply not possible.

Before her was a modest antechamber, with a pair of benches flanking the door. Beyond that, was apparently a fine sitting-room, with furniture the equal of anything that the Klovis household had boasted. It was all of that older, heavier style, and had been so well-polished that it glowed in the candlelight. There were two doors beyond that within Elena's vision, and a bit of a staircase. From all appearances, this place was about the size of the Klovis house.

On the inside. On the outside, it looked to be a two-room cottage.

I had no idea that I had such a good imagination.

Madame Bella was talking to two peculiar little creatures. They were about the height of children—coming to just about Elena's waist—but their hair was silver, and they looked like a pair of gnarled and wizened old men, dressed in leather trousers, immaculate linen shirts, and red vests. Both of them wore soft, pointed brown caps, and both were barefoot.

"Ah, Elena! This is Hob, and this is Robin," she said as Elena paused on the threshold. "Hob is in charge of anything to do with mending in my household, and Robin is in charge of anything to do with making." The little old fellows turned grave, dark eyes on her and bowed solemnly. She curtsied in return, and her mind belatedly caught up with what she was seeing. These must be Brownies, or House-Elves; one of the lesser branches of the Faerie Folk.

And they were, evidently, serving Madame Bella. *Mending and making? An odd way to divide the duties.* Still, if it suited the Brownies, who was she to criticize? "Is working in the garden mending or making?" she asked both of them. "What I saw of it is lovely."

"Ah. That'd be *tending*, and that'd be Lily, Mistress," said Hob, with a finger laid aside his nose and a nod. "She be gone to bed anow. 'Tis Robin's Lily as does the tending, and my lass Rosie who does the cleaning."

"And when Robin lets me, I have been known to do the cooking," Madame said with a silvery chuckle. "They'll be staying on to help you when you are Godmother here."

Elena noticed immediately that Madame did not say, *serving*. So, the Brownies were not servants; given what little she knew from nursery tales, to call them servants or treat them as such would be a deadly insult.

Robin evidently anticipated the question she was afraid to ask. "'Tis our honor and our duty to help the Godmothers and White Wizards and Witches, Mistress," he said solemnly. "For when the Black-Hearted Ones move in, it is our kind that are the first to suffer."

"You'll learn all about that later, dear," Bella said, as Robin took her bag from her, and Hob the basket. "Come along now, and I'll show you your room."

Through the sitting room they went, and the candles in the antechamber went out by themselves as they exited.

Well, it is a dream, after all.

Hob went through one doorway, and Madame Bella led the way through the other, to that staircase that Elena had glimpsed. With Madame in the lead, and Robin following behind, Elena climbed up to the next floor—and the candles in the sitting room also went out by themselves.

At the top of the stairs, it was quite obvious that Madame

liked an old-fashioned sort of house, with no hallways, just one room leading into another. This one was meant for display, apparently, but Elena could not quite understand what the theme was, or even if there was one. Shelves lined the walls, floor to ceiling, and there were objects carefully arranged on them. But what *odd* objects! A cap made of woven rushes. A fur slipper, but quite the smallest that Elena had seen, clearly made for an adult woman, but the size of one meant for a child. A knitted tunic that was made of some coarse, dark plant fiber. A golden ball. A white feather. There were hundreds of these odd objects, and Elena would very much like to have looked at them further, but Madame Bella gestured to her left, and Robin was already carrying her bundle through the left-hand door.

"Your rooms—the vacant ones—are that way, dear," Madame Bella said, and covered a yawn, which triggered a similar yawn from Elena. "The two suites are identical, mirror-images, so I know you'll be comfortable. Good night."

And with that, she passed through the right-hand doorway, leaving Elena to follow Robin on her own. So she did, and once again, as soon as she left the chamber, the candles in the sconces on the wall behind her went out of their own accord.

I really do have the most remarkable imagination.

The first room was a sitting-room, and Elena very nearly stopped right there, for it was fitted on two sides, floor to ceiling, with bookshelves. And they were all full. She stopped dead, and stared hungrily, only vaguely aware that there were other furnishings here.

"Mistress?" came Robin's plaintive call from the next room.

I'm dreaming, she reminded herself. *These books aren't real.* And for a moment, she felt her eyes burn and her throat close, and the dream didn't seem quite so amusing anymore....

"Mistress?" Robin called again, and she sniffed and hastily wiped her eyes with a corner of her apron, and hurried on to the next room.

If Madame Klovis could have seen this room, she would have turned a rainbow of colors with envy.

To begin with, it was carpeted with quite the most beautiful rug that Elena had ever seen, the sort of thing that many people would put on a wall, not a floor. It looked like a meadow of the deepest green, dotted with flowers, and was softer underfoot than kitten-fur. The furnishings were of that same old-fashioned style of the rest of the house, but not even Madame Klovis would have discarded these in favor of the newer styles, for they were carved so beautifully that every piece was a masterwork of art. The twin wardrobes were made to look like castles covered with vines so realistic that Elena half imagined that they had grown there instead of being carved. The dressing-table resembled the stump of a giant tree, supported by carved, sinuous, bare roots. The chair beside it was made in the form of a little throne of vines cradling a moss-green velvet cushion, and the divan beneath the window matched it. There were tapestries on the walls portraying a magical forest full of fantastic animals and birds, flowers such as she had never seen. The bed, curtained in heavy green velvet embroidered with thousands of flowers, with a counterpane to match, could have slept four comfortably. So perfectly was it appointed that the headboard had a candle sconce built into it at the right height for reading in bed, and there was a bookshelf already full of books beneath it. Robin stood anxiously in the middle of the room, her bundle at his feet. "Would you like *me* to unpack for you, Mistress?" he asked, as if he wasn't entirely certain just how one did unpack.

"Oh, heavens no, Robin, thank you," she told him quickly. "I'm quite used to waiting on myself."

"Very well, Mistress," he replied, sounding relieved. "There's a nightdress beneath your pillow. Good night, Mistress."

And before she could reply, he had whisked himself out, so quickly, he might have actually vanished.

A nightdress beneath my pillow! This dream really was extraordinarily detailed! She set her bundle aside, and turned down the covers, revealing three magnificent goosedown pillows, encased in snowy white linen. And beneath the center one, there was, indeed, a nightdress, such as she had not worn since she was a child.

Madame Klovis would have died of envy on the spot.

It was made of pale green silk, tied at the neck and wrists with silken ribbons in a slightly deeper hue, and bordered at all hems with lace three inches deep, made of silk thread as fine as cobwebs. When Elena pulled off her coarse, workaday clothing and slipped it on over her head, it caressed her skin like a soft sigh, and felt so light and ethereal it was as if she was wearing nothing at all.

She folded up her clothing and set it on the chair—even

if this *was* a dream, she was not going to start being untidy!—then climbed into the enormous bed. She sank into the feather mattress with a sigh, as the candles in the rest of the room, saving only the one in the sconce in the headboard, went out of their own accord.

She reached at random for a book, and got something called *The Naturall Historie of the Lives of Curious Beastes,* which sounded impossibly dull. But—

This is my dream. If I decide the book is going to be interesting, it will be!

And so it was. The first "Beaste" in the book was the Unicorn, which evidently led a much more complicated life than she had ever imagined. For a start, it was only male Unicorns who were attracted to virgin maidens; females were only drawn to virgin, chaste men, which, the author observed, were more difficult to come by. "So it is of no usse, to even attempt the capture of the femalee of the species," he concluded.

He then went on to the courtship rituals of these shy creatures, and it was at that point that Elena found she was having a great deal of difficulty in keeping her eyes open.

She had never fallen asleep in her own dream before—nevertheless, although she had no real idea of what would happen, she was not going to fall asleep now. She was going to enjoy every moment of this until she was forced out of the experience by waking up. So she fought the impulse, then the need to put down the book, to close her eyes, fought it even though the words on the page stopped making sense, though her lids drooped until she could not even see the page, and until the book dropped from her numbing fingers and her last conscious thought was that the candle in the sconce above her head had just gone out of its own accord.

"**G**ood morning, Mistress!"

The cheerful voice startled her awake, and even if it had not, the ruthless pulling aside of the curtains at the windows to let in a flood of sunshine surely would have.

Elena sat straight up in bed. A real bed. The same real, luxurious bed she had dreamed that she had climbed into last night. And she was in the same, gorgeous, glorious room that she had imagined in her dream.

Except that she was awake, very much awake, and she was still here. Those were her clothes folded up on the chair, which a little brown woman who probably stood no higher than her waist—whose ears, she could see, were rather pointed—was picking up, unfolding, and *tsk*ing over. She was dressed in a miniature, muted version of Madame Bella's eccentric costume.

She must be a Brownie, like the two old men last night. Which meant that they, too, were real.

"Oh, Mistress, these'll never do, these *garments* of yours," the Faerie woman said firmly, and with, perhaps, just a touch of disdain. "Maybe for working in the garden after rain, but not for every day. Not for an Apprentice."

She had not been in her position a day, and already she was making mistakes, it seemed. This wasn't a very auspicious start. And last night, Madame Bella hadn't said a word about clothing.

"But I'm afraid they're the best I have—" Elena said, weakly. "I'm terribly sorry, but my stepmother—I'll wear whatever you like—"

The Faerie woman interrupted her, with a wave of her hand. She didn't seem annoyed; relieved, perhaps, that Elena had volunteered to wear what *she* chose. "Oh, not to worry, not to worry. You won't need the whole turn-out for weeks and weeks yet, and Robin will have it all tailored up for you by then." The little woman bustled about the room, unpacking Elena's few things and folding them away in a chest. "Till then, I expect some of Madame's things will do. You're much of a size." She opened one of the two wardrobes and began pulling clothing out.

Remembering Madame's rather—flamboyant—style of yesterday, Elena wondered if she ought to say something. Not that Madame Bella's clothing wasn't good but—

But fortunately, it seemed, the little woman's taste was a good bit quieter than Madame's. Out came a fine white linen shift and petticoat, a white blouse liberally trimmed at the cuffs with lace, a black twill skirt piped in green, and a black vest embroidered in green and purple, and a sash to match. Still far more colorful than anything Elena had worn in years, but by no means as eye-popping an ensemble as Madame's.

No corset, so there wasn't any need for help with dressing; and just as well, as Elena would really rather do without a corset if she could. Before the old woman could make a move to serve as a body-servant, Elena quickly climbed out of bed and put the clothing on, feeling an unaccustomed urge to giggle with nervousness. It wasn't that she was shy about disrobing in front of a stranger—years living among the rest of the servants had cured her of any such illusions of modesty. No, it was the giddy and dizzying rush of realizing that this was real.

It wasn't a dream—it wasn't a dream. She was the Apprentice to a Fairy Godmother. She was living in a house that was bigger on the inside than the outside, waited on by Faerie Folk.

I am going to learn magic. Magic! How incredible could this be? Here she was, with Faerie Folk all around her, and she was going to learn magic herself!

The old woman—much less wrinkled, and much more apple-cheeked than the old men, Elena noted—surveyed her with hands on her hips when Elena had finished dressing. "You'll do," she said brusquely. "Those colors suit you. Foot."

"Excuse me?" Elena replied, now utterly bewildered.

"Your *foot*, girl, show me your *foot!*" the old woman repeated, and with absolute confusion, Elena lifted her skirt and held up one of her feet.

The old woman seized it in a hand as hard as horn, and looked it over, muttering to herself. Then she let go, to Elena's relief, and bustled over to another chest.

From there she took a pair of soft slippers of the sort that tightened with ribbons to fit, and handed them to Elena. "Barefoot only in the garden, Mistress," she said, in a tone that warned that there would be no arguing with her. "Shod elsewise. People *come* here, Mistress. You must be a credit to the Godmother as her Apprentice. People have to respect you, as they respect her."

Meekly, Elena took the shoes, and the stockings that the Brownie woman handed to her, and put them on. The shoes were of a leather that was as soft as velvet, and she was terribly afraid that she would have them ruined within an hour.

Still, if this was what was proper—

The Brownies were known for strict adherence to the truth. Rose—for surely this must be Rose, who did the "cleaning"—would not tell her to do something that was not correct. Very well. If these were the shoes that were right, then she would wear them.

It's all true.

"Right then, Mistress. Come along." The little woman opened the door and stood there, beckoning. "Time to break your fast and start on your work. You've a lot to learn, and you're a bit late coming to it."

"Are you Rose?" Elena asked, as the little woman made

impatient shooing motions with both hands, as if Elena was a giant chicken.

"That would be me. Come along, then. Madame doesn't stand on ceremony at breakfast and luncheon, unless there's guests; we all eat in the kitchen, and I'm to show you the way." An odd little sniff showed Elena that Rose did not precisely approve of Madame Bella's informality with the staff. *Poor Hob! She must lead him a merry dance! I wonder if all Brownie women are like this?* Rose had all the hauteur of Madame Klovis's oh-so-superior lady's maid, packed into a package half the size of the human.

Out they went, with Elena glancing at all the books waiting for her in her sitting room with longing, down the stairs, and out towards the back of the cottage, at least so far as Elena could tell. First they passed a little dining-room, then a pantry, then a milk-room with pans of milk already set out for the cream to rise, and at last came to the kitchen. This was a fine, well-appointed room, complete even to a sink with a hand-pump, bake-ovens built to either side of the fireplace, and plenty of pothooks for kettles and a spit with a clockwork turner. *And* there was a very modern stove, as well, which set into a much larger hearth, one that could have once roasted an ox whole. Its presence surprised Elena. The cook in the Klovis household had often lamented that they had no such thing, and had described one in detail, though Elena had never actually seen one.

The kitchen had an immaculately scrubbed flagstone floor and whitewashed brick walls, two big, sunny windows with real glass in them, and it smelled deliciously of baking bread. There were two tables there as well, a large worktable in the middle, which would have been low for a human, but was waist-high to the Brownie, and under one of the two windows, a table with benches beside it. Madame Bella was already there, dressed much as she had been yesterday, except that the predominating hue in her wardrobe was red today. Robin was at the stove, and besides baking bread, Elena smelled porridge, eggs, and frying ham. He turned at her entrance, nodded at Rose, and asked, "Did you sleep well, Mistress? What would you care to eat?"

"Very well, thank you, Robin," she replied, carefully. "And I'm not particular, anything at all will suit me."

"Come sit here, Elena," Madame Bella said, waving at a stool beside her. "I trust your rooms suit you? Ah, I see by your face that they do."

Before Elena could even get properly seated, Robin had bustled over with porridge for her. There was already cream and sugar on the table and Elena helped herself to both, with a sense of giddy freedom, for other than when she had eaten porridge with her neighbors, all she'd had for years was the scrapings from the kettle, seasoned with a little salt. She had not even finished pouring the cream over her breakfast, when Robin returned with a plate of eggs and fried ham. This was a feast!

"Now, today, my dear, I will need to prepare you for your position," Madame was saying as she dug into her breakfast. "In fact, we'll begin now. A wineglass, please, Robin, and something to take the taste away afterwards."

Robin brought two glasses, one empty, the other half full of something that sparkled darkly in the sunlight. "Ah, blackberry cordial, just the thing," Madame Bella said with approval. She reached for a tiny decanter that was already on the table and poured a few drops into the empty glass. "Now, you toss that right down, and never mind the taste, just get it all down and follow it with the cordial."

Elena looked askance at the glass, but did as she was told. It wasn't as if there was anything to fear, after all. Firstly, Madame Bella was a *good* magician, and secondly, why in heaven's name would she bring Elena here just to poison her? But the liquid in it was black and oily-looking, and seemed to warn that it was not going to be nice.

She picked up the glass, took a deep breath, and tossed it all back.

And nearly choked.

It was worse that she could ever have imagined. Horribly bitter and fiery at the same time, it was so powerful and so awful that her eyes filled with tears and she had to struggle not to spit it all out. She groped with one hand, and Madame put the other glass into it, which she took and quickly downed the contents of.

The cordial managed to wash away the awful taste, and she shook her head as she put the glass down and wiped her eyes with a napkin. "What *was* that?" she choked.

"Dragon's blood, undiluted," Madame said, apologetically. "Fresh, or relatively so; I got it yesterday before I went to fetch you. Now you'll be able to understand the languages of the birds and beasts."

Dragon's blood? Real *dragon's blood?* There seemed no reason to doubt it, and Elena nearly choked all over again. She reminded herself how often she had eaten things like blood sausage, and tried not to feel too sick.

Perhaps some porridge— She took a mouthful before she asked her next question.

"Why would I want to do that?" she asked, hoarsely, feeling as if she must be missing something that should have been terribly obvious.

"Because the birds and the beasts are everywhere, and often have a great deal to tell you," Madame replied. "You'll see. At any rate, this was best taken care of first, as the rest of the spells are a bit more complex. But first, Elena, do finish your breakfast. It's going to be a busy day, and it has just begun."

The morning began with a tour of Madame Bella's "cottage," which was quite as large inside as Elena's old home had been. The difference was that very few of these rooms were devoted to show, especially on the ground floor. There was no formal dining room, and what Elena had taken for a drawing room was, in fact, a second library, the first already being crammed so full of books that they had spilled over into this room, where they were in a fair way to take over. Elena felt her eyes going round with astonishment at the sheer number of books. The only spots on the walls that were not covered with floor-to-ceiling bookshelves crammed with books were where the windows and doors were let into them, and where the fireplace, mantel, and chimney were let into the wall. There were hessian curtains on these windows, old, faded rugs on the floor, and the only furniture in either room were more low bookcases surrounding a desk and a chair.

"Genealogies, histories, and tales. Also some spell-books,

but most of what a Godmother does is about what is appropriate to the moment, is impelled and powered by The Tradition and the magic that The Tradition has accreted around the hero or heroine, and doesn't require the same preparation as a Witch's or Wizard's spells." Bella looked around the walls with what seemed to Elena like weary satisfaction, and Elena noticed that there was a book lying open on the desk, with pen and ink beside it. "What you *do* need to know is who is related to whom—absolutely necessary to trace missing heirs and potential usurpers. You need to know your enemies; you'll find them in those books, like as not, and potential enemies for the future as well. And you should be familiar with every tale that any Godmother has ever been involved with. In your turn, you are expected to write up every Tradition Line that you steer—you *can* read and write, I hope?" Suddenly Bella looked very anxious, and Elena was pleased to be able to reassure her. "Ah, good. Well, that will be one of the spells that you *will* have to perform; once you finish writing a tale, there will be an identical book in the library of every other Godmother and Warding Wizard, and those White Witches and Wizards who are powerful enough to have libraries like ours will also have a copy." She shook her head. "And this, of course, is why I no longer have a drawing room. I thought about performing the spell to add a room, but I never got around to it. That will be your duty, I expect. I can't see how many more books can be added without spilling into some other room—and Lily would be most vexed if that happened."

"How is it that this is nothing more than a cottage from

outside, and all this on the inside?" Elena asked, pleased for the opening at last to ask what she had been dying to know.

"Ah. That is rather difficult to explain. In fact, I'm not entirely certain that I can, except to say that it is magic, and it is necessary." Madame Bella shrugged. "There is nothing to show on the outside that this is not the abode of an ordinary White Witch, or even some peasant who has chosen to live apart in the forest. I told you that we have enemies, and it has happened in the past that in order to facilitate their schemes, they began by eliminating the region's Godmother. Not often, but it has happened."

"Oh," Elena said, sobered. So, this Godmothering business was dangerous. She felt a little touch of fear at that moment. She wasn't used to *danger*. Life with her stepmother had been hard, lonely, unhappy and unpleasant, but not precisely dangerous. Danger was something that happened to other people—why, hadn't she considered and discarded the idea of simply running away and taking her chances because of the danger?

Difficult, complicated, and now dangerous. But on the other hand, I will never be bored, and no one will be making a slave out of me. There was a great deal to be said for that, and as for the danger—

I will be helping to make other peoples' dreams come true.

"You will make dreams come true, Elena," Madame Bella said, softly, in an uncanny echo of Elena's own thoughts. "And dreams are dangerous things in and of themselves." She cast another look around the library. "Look at them! Dreams and nightmares, hopes and fears. Compared to some of the trials that our heroes and heroines must face in order to earn their happy endings, what we Godmothers encounter is really trivial so long as we are careful to keep our true nature hidden. You'll see, when you come to read them, for not every tale has that happy ending. Not every hero is brave enough, resourceful enough, or lucky enough, even with our help, to triumph in the end." There was a shadow on Madame Bella's face, and she seemed to be recalling something that was very sad indeed. Then she shook her head. "Read the books, Elena, and you will see."

The rest of the ground floor was given over to working rooms. There was a dairy-room, a stillroom, the kitchen, of course, a little office, a sewing-room; in short, everything this establishment needed to be self-sufficient. "We take care of a great deal of our own needs here," Madame said with pride. "There are two villages within walking distance, and we have arrangements with people in both of them for things like flour and so forth. The villagers all believe that I am a White Witch, and often come to me for spells and cures, and pay me in things that we need." She smiled. "Which, of course, is another reason why my home appears to be a simple cottage on the outside. You will soon see that we do not squander magic on the things we can supply by the same means as anyone else. We help our local people, earning our way the same as any other craftsman, and our local people, since they do not know that I am a Godmother, assist in creating the illusion that I am just the local White Witch. They will see nothing amiss in my having taken an Apprentice; in fact, I suspect that they will be somewhat relieved."

"That sounds like an excellent arrangement to me," Elena

replied, feeling relieved, for she could not envisage herself as a farmer, and the House Elves did not seem young nor strong enough to be farm-workers. Of course, according to the tales she had heard, there was no telling with Elves; they might look frail, yet be strong as an ox.

"In the same way, we aid the local Faerie Folk in return for their help, both in terms of the service that Hob and Robin and their wives give us, and in magic. They, however, know that I am a Godmother, and by now, they have heard about you." Madame Bella smiled broadly. "The Faerie Folk always seem to know about something within the hour of it happening."

Outside the house—which *still* looked, and from all angles, like a simple two- or three-room cottage—were the gardens. In the front were the flowers and ornamental plants; two on either side were herb-beds. The culinary herbs were to the right of the cottage, the healing herbs to the left. Of course, there were some herbs that served both purposes, but as Madame pointed out, having them in both gardens meant only that she could be sure that there would always be enough.

In the rear was the kitchen-garden, with handsome red hens industriously scratching among the planted rows, looking for insects or weed-sprouts; this was where they found the Brownie Lily, working diligently among the young cabbages.

And as she listened to their quiet clucking, she got a shock. She certainly heard clucking—but she also heard something else.

"Greedy, greedy, greedy," muttered one hen, jealously eye-

ing a choice patch of ground that a bigger hen was scratching. *"Not enough bugs,"* grumbled another, and the rest simply evidenced contentment.

She could, indeed, understand the speech of animals.

It took her a moment to catch her breath when she realized the truth, it seemed as if, for now, her life was going to
be one disconcerting moment after another.

Finally she caught her breath, so to speak, and turned her
attention back to what Madame was saying about her garden.

If ever there was a model vegetable garden, this was
surely it—the rows were as straight as could be, the young
plants healthy and flourishing. And if Elena was any judge,
the gardener had started her plants in stages, so that there
would be vegetables at the perfect state to harvest all summer long. It was difficult to manage, and took a great deal
of skill, as well as careful management of cold-frames. Elena
had never managed it properly, and only knew two farmers at home who had done it—and *their* produce almost always went straight to the Palace.

"Ah, Madame Bella!" said the Brownie, rising to her feet
and brushing soil from her canvas apron. "I've some lovely
sparrow-grass coming; not for dinner today, but definitely
for tomorrow. This would be Mistress Elena, then."

"Yes," Elena answered for herself. "And you are Lily;
these are wonderful gardens!"

"Oh, I do my best," Lily replied, with a shrug. "It's good
to be where people appreciate that."

The last of the tour took them to the byre at the bottom
of the garden, with the stable beside it. There was a donkey

in the stable—presumably unmagical, since it gazed on both of them with supreme disinterest and went back to the hay in its manger. It was an old beast, by the grey of its muzzle.

In the byre were two red-brown milch-cows with mild eyes, who were equally disinterested in the two humans. Well, that explained where the fresh milk and cream were coming from. Fortunately, they didn't say anything. Elena wasn't at all sure she could cope with talking cows as well as talking chickens at the moment.

Altogether, this would have been exactly the sort of situation where Elena would have been happy as a servant. She certainly had never envisioned herself as the mistress of such a place. It was a little daunting.

And when you added in the talking animals—

How am I ever going to be able to eat meat again? she wondered with sudden dismay. But then, she remembered just how incredibly *stupid* the chickens had sounded. She had always known that chickens weren't bright, and the fact that she could understand what they were saying to each other hadn't changed that. All that was different, really, was that instead of merely intuiting the meaning of their calls, she actually *knew* it.

It occurred to her, as Madame Bella opened the garden gate and beckoned her to follow out into the woods surrounding the cottage, that there was another aspect to all of this. In the tales that she knew, there were often animals that were, well, *more* than mere animals. Whether they were magic beasts, or from the Faerie Realms, they were always the equal and sometimes superior in intelligence to humans—

—like that little humpbacked horse that had drawn Madame's cart last night, for instance.

And now she would be able to speak to them, as Madame could, which was probably Madame's entire reason for giving her the dragon's blood to drink.

Madame followed a path winding among the enormous trees of this forest, and Elena followed her, though once they got under the deep shadows cast by the heavy growth, she looked back at the sunlit gardens longingly. Elena was town-bred, and in fact, since Madame Klovis had taken over the household, she had never been any farther from her house than the market-garden. The trees she knew were all tame things, neatly trimmed and confined to gardens, surrounded by seats or planted in jardenierres. These were wild trees, huge, taller than the clock tower, so big that three girls could have stood around them, stretched out their arms and barely have been able to touch their fingertips together. The thick bark was green with moss, and beneath their branches the woods lay in a murmurous twilight. Anywhere that there was a gap in the canopy, the undergrowth ran wild—where there was no place for the sun to penetrate, mushrooms made little colonies, moss carpeted the ground and the fallen tree limbs, and the occasional odd, pale flower bloomed.

Every time a twig snapped or a bird called, Elena jumped. And it didn't help that she could understand what those birds were saying, either, because it was mostly, *"Hey! Hey, hey, hey!"*

So what were they shouting about? What was lurking out there, hidden in the tangles of vines, behind the fallen trees, in the shadows. Bears? Wolves?

Worse?

"Madame Bella?" she whispered, not wanting to make any noise louder than that. "Where are we going?"

The Godmother glanced back at her. "I need to show you to the Faerie Folk—their official representatives, that is; my Brownies don't count. Most of them can't abide salt and cold iron, so they cannot come to us, we must come to them."

Elena shivered. The Brownies were one thing; they were small and earthy, and impossible to be afraid of. But there were all manner of Faerie Folk that she wasn't at all sure she wanted to be "shown" to. Dangerous creatures dwelled in the Faerie Realms, and even when they were marginally friendly to mortals, they were chancy to deal with; unpredictable and easily offended. What if she offended one of them?

Perhaps worse, what of one of them took a fancy to her? No mortal could resist Faerie glamour; she could be lured away, only to discover, when her Faerie lover tired of her, that when she tried to return home, she would turn into a withered old crone, or even die, once she set foot outside those charmed precincts. For while weeks or months had passed for *her*, hundreds of years would have passed in the mortal world.

But it was too late for misgivings now, for there was a glow ahead of them that was not sunlight breaking through the heavy canopy, and there were bright and dark figures moving in that glow.

As they neared the spot, Elena saw that it was a clearing in the woods, ringed with palid mushrooms, carpeted with deep green moss studded with tiny golden flowers. In the center, two stumps and a tightly entwined series of ancient vines formed a pair of thrones, cushioned with leaves so dark a green they looked at first glance to be black, and ornamented with huge, trumpet-bell flowers in of pale pink, pale blue, and cream. Two tall, thin, impossibly beautiful creatures sat in those thrones, creatures with leaf-pointed ears, cascades of silver-gilt hair, and garments of that damasked silk that only the Elves could weave. Their skin was so pale and translucent they could have been carved from moonstone, but their enormous, curiously slanted blue eyes were alive enough as they watched Madame and Elena approach.

Surrounding the thrones was a crowd of other creatures, most of which Elena could not put names upon. There were Unicorns, silken-soft and cloven-hoofed, and tiny, perfectly formed, perfectly naked winged women no more than a foot tall. There were tall, shrouded creatures that seemed to bring a deeper shadow with them, and Elena instinctively knew that she did not want to look under their cowls. There were green-skinned women clothed in leaves and flowers, and men with goat-legs, tiny horns half-hidden in their curly brown hair, and sly, knowing eyes. And those were just the ones that Elena could see.

Madame led her to within twenty paces of the sylvan thrones, and stopped, making a deep, but not servile, bow. "Majesties, this is my Apprentice, Elena."

The two on the thrones, who evidently must have been the King and Queen of the Elves in this Kingdom, if not all of the Faerie Folk, turned their impassive gaze on her. And, after a long moment of scrutiny, nodded.

"A good choice, Madame Bella," said the woman, whose musical voice was as lovely and indescribable as her face. She stood up, and beckoned to Elena, who reluctantly came nearer. "So, Apprentice, have you been warned? Do you know the dangers as well as the duties?"

"I left that to you, Majesty," Madame Bella said, serenely. "As is the custom."

The Elven Queen smiled, coolly. "So you do remember. It is well. Mortal woman, stand before me, and see. These are the foes you will contend with, mortal and immortal."

The Queen extended the slender willow-wand in her hand until it touched Elena's forehead.

And in a single moment, it seemed, a torrent of images poured into her mind. None were pleasant, and many were terrifying.

It was one thing to be warned about the evil magicians, and to remember all of the things she had read and heard. It was quite another to *see* them at work, in rapid succession. And some—were horrors.

Some of the horrors were blatant—entire countries laid waste, the inhabitants made into hopeless slaves, afraid to do anything but obey because of the cost of disobedience. Some of the evil ones were precisely as she might have expected, gloating despots squatting on thrones they had no right to, torture and exploitation the hallmarks of their reigns.

But some were subtle, and once Elena realized what she was seeing, the implications were chilling. Often the evil one was not on the throne itself, but was the power behind it, whispering into the monarch's ear. The effect was insidious; rather than creating despair for all, the dark one created factions, pitting the privileged, wealthy, and titled against those beneath them, placing the effort of exploitation one layer below the monarch. This kept despair from being total, for there was always the hope—"But when the *King* learns of this...."—even though the hope was destined never to be fulfilled. These spiders spun a cunning web, beginning as they always did by eroding conditions gradually, with rights converted to *privilege*, then the privilege revoked on one pretense or another, always for an excellent reason, always on a "temporary" basis, until the next "privilege" was taken and the previous grievance forgotten. Then as one hand took away, the other, the King's, would give—something trivial, but pleasurable. Games perhaps, or entertainments. Nothing controversial, of course. A competition that would elevate the winner into the ranks of the wealthy and prominent—so that the illusion was maintained that this was possible for everyone. It was as if wholesome bread was being taken, and a tastier bread made with sawdust used to replace it.

Or, perhaps the one behind the throne would start a war on some trumped-up cause—a little war, of course, against a weak but convenient enemy, one that would be difficult to lose, that would stir up patriotic fervor, one that would, of course, entail "sacrifices for the good of all and the security of the realm" under cover of which more "privileges" could be "temporarily" taken.

Clever and insidious, and damnably difficult to counter.

And all the while, the spider spun his web, battening on the misery and depression, growing fat and ever more powerful, and in the darkness behind the throne, indulging himself in secret cruelties against the "enemies of the state."

These, more than the others, were the ones that were the most dangerous to the Godmothers, the White Wizards, the Good Wizards. The first class were brutal, but seldom thought past the moment. The second planned ahead, months, years, decades—anticipated opposition, and moved to counter it well in advance. These were the ones who swiftly cleansed their countries of resident magicians, either directly murdering them or instigating the local peasantry against them, and then ensured that no one else would move in by creating intense hostility against "foreigners" and "outsiders," cleverly engineering their rhetoric so that the blame for *anything* that was bad would be laid to the door of "outsiders." Since that effectively made isolationism a certainty, it protected the evil ones further, for anything outside the borders became suspect, even hated, and there would be no chance for anyone to learn that things might be better, elsewhere.

Elena saw, in detail, what was happening to the "outsiders" in several of the infected Kingdoms...imprisonment was the least of it. In rapid succession, she saw Faerie Folk being driven into grim encampments hedged around with cold iron and salt and spells, there to wither and die, or suffer torture at the hands of sadistic guards. She saw a Godmother dragged to the center of a town and burned alive, a White Wizard buried in the rubble of his own tower, a coven of Good Witches torn to pieces by a pack of savage hounds.

It all played out with dreadful immediacy in front of her eyes, and sent her heart into her throat.

But more than that, it made her *angry*. This was what her stepmother had done to *her*, writ large on the face of the world. She had been powerless to stop it then, but she would not be powerless now, and she would not stand idly by when there was something she could do.

So that when, after it all was shown to her and the Faerie Queen took the wand from her forehead, she emerged from the nightmare fueled with rage and determination.

It must have shown on her face, for the Faerie Queen gave her a penetrating look, then a nod of satisfaction.

"Good," she said. "You are made of stern materials. You are an iron bar, lady. We will give you the tools to be transformed to a sword."

She beckoned, and an ethereal creature, outwardly sexless, winged like a dragonfly and garbed mostly in its own flowing hair, drifted forward, handing her what appeared to be a rose petal. "Eat it," the Faerie Queen commanded, and wary of what had happened the *last* time she had followed a similar command, but obedient to Bella's nod, she did so.

It tasted like nothing—but a moment later, she was seeing things—ribbons and auras of intense blue, surrounding and drifting between the Faerie Folk for the most part, but also around Bella, more faintly running everywhere she looked. And also, *very* strongly, around herself.

A second creature, another Brownie, came forward with what appeared to be a small stone. Again she ate it, and now, added to the ribbons of blue were ribbons of gold. A shining bird dropped what appeared to be a hot coal in her hand, which gave her ribbons of fiery red, and last of all, a girl clothed in water-weeds with a water-lily in her hair dripped a single drop of clear water into her hand, which granted her emerald-green ribbons and auras.

"Now you see the magic around you, of air and earth, fire and water," the Faerie Queen told her. "What you see, you can use. Use this gift wisely."

That seemed to be a dismissal, for the assemblage of Faerie creatures formed up around their monarchs, and the King and Queen descended from their thrones. An arch of vines at the far side of the clearing that Elena had taken for an accidental arrangement of wild plants over a natural pathway began to glow, faintly, with soft moonlike light, and fill with mist. The mist glowed, too, and there were hints of figures moving in it. The unearthly Court formed up in a rough line and began to file through it.

The King and Queen were the last to depart; the Queen passed through the arch without a moment of hesitation, but the King stopped for a moment, and looked deeply into Elena's eyes. She could not have looked away if she had wanted to—but she did not really want to. Although his narrow, high-cheekboned face, with its winglike eyebrows, strange, slightly slanted, enormous eyes, beardless as a boy's, with long midnight-black hair any woman would be proud to boast of, was not what *she* would have named as attractive before this moment, she understood exactly what was meant by "Elven glamorie." She felt powerfully drawn to him, and knew that if he had cared to, he could have had her by snapping his fingers.

But he did nothing of the sort; he merely looked deeply into her eyes, as if weighing and measuring her as his consort had done. And then, without a word, he touched her brow with a delicate forefinger.

Something passed between them, though she could not have said just what it was. A great shudder shook her, a moment of dizziness, and for a moment she heard a sound as of the rushing of great wings all about her. The hair stood up on the back of her neck, yet at the same time, she was filled with such intoxication she might have been drunk.

Then the moment passed; the Elven King smiled faintly, turned, and passed through the gate behind his consort. The light within the gate faded; the glow of the framing vines faded.

And Elena and her mentor were standing in a perfectly ordinary clearing, in the dim light filtering down through the myriad branches of the trees above them as a bird called somewhere in the middle distance.

Bella was regarding her Apprentice with a look of great thoughtfulness. "Well," she said at last, "he certainly never did that with *me!* What happened between you?"

"I don't know," Elena said honestly. "I haven't the faintest idea." She blinked as she said that; the pale glows and colors were everywhere now, and she was having to get used to the *sight* of magic all about her.

"Interesting." Bella tapped her cheek with one finger, thoughtfully. "Well, whatever it was, it's something that King Huon thinks you'll need, and we'll have to let it go at that. He's too subtle for the likes of mere mortals." She beckoned, and smiled. "Come along, Apprentice. We have to choose your wand."

But as they left the clearing, Elena could not resist looking back for a moment, wondering.

"Curious, Apprentice?" Madame called over her shoulder. Elena hurried to catch up.

She wanted to ask why the Elven King had been interested in her, but she heard herself asking a different question entirely.

"Why are the Fair Folk—" she groped for a word "—involved?"

"Ah. Well, very long ago, *all* of the Godmothers were Fair Folk; that is the reason some folk call us Fairy Godmothers still. Some still are, and there is an equivalent to Wizard that you hear of very, very seldom, and that is the Elven Knight. But most Godmothers are human now," Bella told her, as they walked back towards the cottage.

"Why?" Elena asked.

"I suspect because there are so few of the Fair Folk and so many mortals," Bella said wryly. "They soon discovered that if The Tradition is to be served and directed properly, they needed help. Since their very existence depends upon The Tradition, they did not have a great deal of choice, it would seem."

She could not imagine at the moment why the existence of the Elves would depend on The Tradition, but she supposed that her reading or lessons would eventually tell her. "So that is why the Queen has to accept an Apprentice?" she hazarded.

"Exactly." Bella seemed pleased that she had made the connection. "Having been the originals, they are best at judging who will be appropriate. And of course, their understanding is much deeper than ours; they can do with a touch things that require great effort from a human."

That last only made her wonder the more, as they continued down the path. They can do with a touch....

So what had the Elven King done to her?

Choosing a wand turned out to be nowhere near as complicated as Elena had thought it would be—given the complexity of nearly everything else that had happened to her from the moment Madame Bella entered her life.

It was, oddly enough, the House-Elf Lily who helped her with the task. Robin she had expected, but not Lily. After all, Lily did the tending, didn't she? So what would she have to do with the business of finding a wand?

Lily was waiting for them on the path, and smiled with satisfaction when she saw them. "Ah, good, you have the King's Favor as well as the Queen's!" she said and looked to Madame Bella, as Elena wondered *how* she had known of the Elven King's odd behavior. Then, just as she wondered that, she *saw* it; more of the swirling color she now knew was magic, a haze, a dusting of pale silver (which must have been the Queen's mark) and pale gold (surely the King's) that drifted around her exactly like dust motes drifted in warm air. Bella didn't have that cloud about her, nor did Lily. *How peculiar. I wonder if it will wear off?* This business of seeing magic was going to take some getting used to.

"Is she ready for her wand?"

"No reason to put it off," Bella replied. "I have some things to attend to; this will take until luncheon?"

"Oh, at least; after Robin makes the wand, he wants to take her measurements for her costumes, and after this, you're going to keep her too busy to take the time for proper measuring," Lily replied, and turned to Elena. "Come along, Apprentice, and don't look so wary; this won't be anything like that nasty business over breakfast."

I certainly hope not! she thought, following Lily with an apprehension that she hoped she veiled adequately.

They ended up in a little workshop where Robin already was at work, laying out lengths of perfectly straight wood on a workbench, placing longer, similar pieces of wood leaning against a wall. "The wand," Robin said, with immense dignity, as if he was lecturing, "is not a thing of magic in and of itself, as most outsiders believe. It is merely the extension of the magician, a tool to help focus magic. Actually, practically any old stick will do in a pinch so long as it is made from a wood that the magician feels comfortable with."

"Ah, but now, that's the trick," Lily said, taking up the lecture as smoothly as if she and Robin had rehearsed it. "And that is where I come in. All of these bits of wood have been harvested over the years from trees I grew from cuttings or seeds, trees I nurtured and tended, and they *gave* me these lengths freely, as a gift. Not one piece was cut. There was no pain in the culling of these branches, and as a consequence, there is nothing here for the darker magics to work on. No Black Witch or Sorcerer can make a wand made from *this* wood turn against its Godmother."

There it was again, that warning of danger. But she had accepted the risk, and though she shivered, she set her chin. She would no go back on her given word.

"So would I need a little wand like that one—"

With the colors and currents of magic drifting all around her, Elena found that easier to accept than she might have before the Elven Queen bestowed the gift of Magic Sight to her. In fact, as she pointed at one of the wands, she saw and felt the potential of magic building up, as if the were act of *pointing* at something energized the magic to flow in a particular direction.

"That will depend on your costume; you will have your everyday clothing, of course, and probably a small wand like this—" Robin held up a slender, polished stick no bigger around than her little finger, and no longer than a foot. "When you are in your most impressive garb, the sort of thing you will wear to attend Royal Christenings, for instance, you will bear a full-sized staff like this." He hefted a length of wood about a foot shorter than she was.

"Have you ever seen a man concentrate the sun with a lens to make something catch fire?" Lily asked. Elena nodded; when she was younger, one of her playfellows used to purloin his granny's glasses to amuse his friends with just that trick. "Well, there you are. The wand acts for magic as a lens does for the sun; it concentrates and focuses it. It won't matter a pin if one of your wands is broken—we'll keep several made up for you in each size. And you can certainly cast your spells without one—but it will be easier for you to use magic if you have one."

"Now, please, Mistress, go along the ranks of these small lengths, and tell me when you have found a wand that feels right in your hand," Robin said, stepping aside so that Elena could approach the bench. She did so, and picked up the first of the rough-finished wands. And it felt like—nothing. A stick of wood. She tried the next, and the next, with similar results. Finally, about halfway through the ranks of samples, she found it.

And that mere act surprised her, because she had begun to think that she wasn't *feeling* whatever it was she was supposed to sense, and would have to just make an arbitrary selection. Then the next wand she picked up came alive in her hand.

There was no other way to describe it; the rest had been as inert as an old broomstick; suddenly *this* one felt like a living thing in her hand.

"Ah!" Lily said, taking it from her—and she found that she was incredibly, inexplicably reluctant to let go of it. "That would be the birch in the water-meadow. A good choice." And as she set the wand in a vice, Robin cleared away all the other lengths of wood but seven.

"I'll have this finished for you in a trice," Robin said matter-of-factly. "The others will take longer, but this will give you something to work with."

In less than an hour, Robin fashioned a wand for her of the polished and waxed birch, tapered, with a simple spiral carving to it so that it looked like the horn of a Unicorn. It was lovely, and although she had watched him make it, she could not imagine how he had finished it in so short a period of time.

"You'll find a long, narrow pocket in your skirt," said Lily, and when she hunted for it, she found that indeed, she did. The wand fit in there as perfectly as it had in her hand.

"The other wands can wait," Robin said, and gave her an unreadable look. "Next, we need to fit you for proper clothing."

So she spent an uncomfortable two hours with every inch of her being measured by the little Brownie. This would be for her "Fairy Godmother" costumes, which Bella assured her, when the Godmother looked in on the fittings, were as vital a tool as her wand, if not more so.

"What people think of you is important," Bella insisted. "If you don't look the part, they won't believe in you, and if they don't believe in you, you might not be able to get your job done right."

Quite frankly, Elena was feeling very intimidated, and it got worse as Robin held up one length of fabric after another against her face. She was afraid to touch the delicate fabrics with her work-roughened hands, and thought that she would probably look a fool in the kinds of dressmaker's confections that her stepsisters had worn.

She was even more intimidated when Hob brought in the trays of jewels, the bolts of trimmings that were to adorn these putative costumes. It was bad enough when they held up lace as fine as cobwebs, or gorgeous, heavy stuff shining as only bobbin lace made with silk thread could shine; it was far worse when they brought in the trimmings made with real gold and silver threads, and began selecting pearls and other gems to be added to the ornamentation.

"I can't wear these things!" she finally burst out. "I'm not—"

"You *are*, Mistress," Hob said sternly. "You are every bit as important in rank as an Empress, and when the time comes, you *must* wear these gowns, and wear them without a second thought. Appearances are important, Mistress, and the time will come when you will speak with Royalty and they will know you for their superior, the gracious bestower of gifts that *they* have humbly asked of you."

She shook her head, unable to even picture that in her own mind.

"But don't worry so much," Lily told her, with a wave of her hand. "Most of the time you'll be dressed like Madame does around here—because most of the time you need to look like one of the common folk."

"Oh, not exactly like Madame," Robin demurred. "Madame's choice of colors is—well, in a fine lady of her age, it is delightfully eccentric. In a young woman—" He visibly groped for words.

Lily did not. "You'll look like a motely fool, or a color-blind Gypsy," she said bluntly. "Don't worry; you'll not be mistaken for a mountebank in what we give you."

Finally the measuring and selection—none of which she got any chance to make for herself—was over, and the Brownies let her go. She sought refuge in the kitchen, where

Madame was making a cold Ploughman's luncheon with her own hands, slicing meat, onions, bread, and cheese.

Of course, this was a better luncheon than Elena had seen in months, perhaps even years.

"Ah, they've released the prisoner. Come have something to eat," Bella said cheerfully, and Elena hurried to help her with the platters which they placed on the table. "Eat well; you'll be working very hard this afternoon."

When luncheon was over, with her wand in her pocket, Elena followed her mentor to a secluded room at the back of the house. Her heart was literally in her mouth, but she kept her chin high and told herself that if she was not fearless, she could, at least, *look* fearless.

Bella closed the door; the room was utterly empty except for a few shelves that held a book or two and some oddments. But Elena did notice something odd.

The swirls of magic around her did not drift through the walls as they did elsewhere in the house. In fact, they never got closer to the walls than a foot, and the same held true of the floor and the ceiling.

"Elena, do you *see* magic, now that the Queen has given you her power?" Madame asked. And the way she emphasized the word "see" made Elena very careful with her answer.

"I think it's magic," she said carefully. "It's like swarms of dust motes that glow the way dust motes glow in the sunlight, only in different colors. It's rather thick around me," she added, hoping that was helpful.

"Ah good." Bella's expression cleared. "That makes things easier."

"Some people don't?" Elena hazarded.

"It does vary. *Most* people see it, but I know of Godmothers and Wizards who hear magic as music, some who taste or smell it." Now Bella pulled her own slender wand, a bit of walnut carved with a delicate hint of vines and leaves, out of the pocket of her skirt. "Right, well, since you can see it, now you'll learn how to move it about."

Elena spent what was possibly the most curious afternoon of her life, the flying cart notwithstanding, as she herded flocks of colored dust motes about, first with, then without her wand. It *was* easier with the wand. As she did the herding, she began to notice that some of the motes would always escape, drift towards her, then—vanish. "Why am I losing magic?" she finally asked.

"Because you're using it. The only power in this room is yours and mine, and I've pent mine away from you." Bella half smiled, and raised an eyebrow. "You are moving your own power about, the power that has built up around you, trying to bring your life into The Traditional path. You will probably use most of it up, *learning* how to use it."

"Oh." Then what am I supposed to—

"And part of that learning will be how to acquire more power," Bella went on, before she could voice the question. "Though if you absolutely *must*, there is no other choice, and you can convince them that it is in their best interest, the Elves will probably share power. But you do recall how I told you that others like you often wish to lead ordinary lives? That is one source of power that we often avail ourselves of, and there are others that I will teach you."

Ah.

"And now, my dear, we must get back to work."

On the face of things, these lessons would have sounded to an outsider as if they were easy, and so, in a way, they were, just as walking is easy. But suppose that someone was possessed of two good, healthy, strong legs, yet had never used them, and had not, in fact, ever known that they *could* be used? This was the position that Elena found herself in now.

It was, to put it fine, *hard* work. It took real physical effort, and more concentration than she had ever put into anything in her life. Finally Madame called a halt to the lessons, which by that point had graduated up to containing the power.

She might not have been sweating, but she certainly felt limp with exhaustion when Madame sniffed the air, declared that she could smell supper, and allowed her to stop her current exercise. "Go tidy yourself up, child," Madame told her, with no sign whatsoever that she was exhausted. "We'll hold the meal until you join us."

The sun was just starting to set, and deep golden light poured in through the western windows, a light as thick and rich as honey. The walk up the stairs was as hard as it would have been after an entire day of running about tending to the household chores and multiple errands for her stepmother and stepsisters.

But there was water in the ewer beside the basin in her room, waiting for her, a luxury she hadn't enjoyed for so long.... With her face and hands washed, she felt much more like herself, and trundled back downstairs. It couldn't

be said that she did so in a *more* cheerful frame of mind, because, despite the hard work, she was enjoying herself. This
was challenging, she was doing things she had never even
dreamed of, and it was all real—

But now she was able to feel something besides exhausted, and ready to do full justice to whatever was on the
stove for dinner.

For some reason, Rose seemed a trifle more friendly over
supper. Lily chatted away, sounding very much like Madame
Fleur, and Robin and Hob, though mostly silent, made it
clear even in their silence that they approved of Elena. So
evidently the entire household was happy with her now; she
didn't *know* why, but she could guess.

The Elven King's approval had impressed Lily, and probably that was why the atmosphere had warmed all the way
around. The Fair Folk all bowed to the Elven King and
Queen, no matter what race they were; the Royal Pair were
the supreme authorities in their sphere. Apparently, having
the Queen's blessing was one thing, but earning the King's
was quite another level of achievement.

"I'd say she's made good progress today," Madame Bella
was saying, as Elena brought her wandering attention back
to the conversation and the meal. "I must say, there is a great
deal to be said for bringing in an older Apprentice; there's
nothing flighty about you, my dear."

Elena was saved from having to say anything by having
a mouth full of excellent rabbit pie.

"Some of the stories I've heard," said Rose, with a disap-
proving *tsk*. "Girls whining and complaining about being
buried in the country—as if they were going to have time

for *anything* but learning the job of Godmothering! Girls half afraid of everything around them. Girls carrying on with young men—"

It suddenly struck Elena—Bella had intimated that she had been a maiden lady all her life. Did this mean that Godmothers were not supposed to have anything to do with men? She felt a moment of mingled shock and dismay.

Not that any man ever showed any interest in me—but is it worth giving up the possibility?

"There is nothing wrong with a young woman being interested in young men," Bella retorted.

"A young *woman*, certainly. But a young Godmother?" Rose snorted. "Madame, think of the risk! The Tradition has no room in it for wedded Godmothers! And any young man falling in with a Godmother is going to be *forced* by The Tradition into *some* familiar path! So what does that leave?" Rose gave none of the others a chance to answer that question. She counted off the options on her fingers. "The Rogue, who will leave her broken-hearted, and perhaps in difficulties. The Betrayer, who will lead her enemies to her. Or the Enemy himself—whether he *is* the Enemy or later *becomes* the Enemy...."

"Or something new," Madame said firmly. "The Tradition can be redirected. Witches have married Wizards and made good matches of it, and Sorceresses joined to Sorcerers, and there used to be no place in The Tradition for that."

Rose snorted again. "Only *if* the Godmother is strong of will, and if it isn't *only* the Godmother who has the will to steer it into a new path. And from what I've heard, there wasn't a one of those girls that had the will to turn a goose from grass, much less The Tradition from its chosen path."

Madame laughed, and shook her head. "Only rumors, dear Rose. And really, if a girl is that unsuitable, she's generally run away from all the hard work before the Queen gives her blessing. I would not have taken Elena to the Queen if I had not thought that she was suitable, and the Queen has her own means of weighing candidates."

Rose nodded grudgingly. "Well, you were careful, Madame, and there have been those that just took the first girl to cross their path with a wreathing of magic about them." Finally she turned to Elena. "I have to say, even though I thought Madame was rushing you, I must admit that Madame was right about you. I've never heard of the Queen giving a blessing to anyone on their first day of being an Apprentice."

The talk turned then away from Elena, and to, of all things, the small doings in the nearby village. Elena did what she had learned to do among Madame Klovis's servants when she wanted to learn things.

She stayed quiet, and listened.

This was how she learned that Madame Bella not only *was* thought of as one of the local White Witches, but that people made the long trek out through the forest to the "cottage" on a regular basis. Furthermore, there was a less-powerful Witch who served as Bella's agent in the sale of potions, healing draughts, and herbal remedies, with a stall on market day in the square of the largest village.

Finally Rose seemed to realize that Elena was there. "I

don't suppose you know much of concocting," she said, dubiously.

"Common things, yes," Elena replied, and pulled a face. "My stepmother never spent a penny on anything other than herself and her daughters, so I had charge of the still-room—"

"Ah, good!" Bella exclaimed. "Then tomorrow we'll work there, and I'll see how well you follow a recipe. If I am content, I will leave you to work alone, and once you have produced the actual potions, I will show you how to infuse a little magic into them. Not a great deal, but enough to make them work efficiently and effectively."

Elena's look of surprise must have been very obvious, for Bella laughed, and so did Rose. "Godmothers aren't always going about lobbing magic swords in the paths of rightful heirs, or giving younger sons the right answers to riddles!" Rose exclaimed. "They do as much good with the little magics as they do with the great ones, I'll be bound. It's more working *with* The Tradition; the happier and healthier a Kingdom is, the harder it is for the Evil Ones to insinuate themselves into it."

"Meanwhile, your day isn't done yet, my dear," Bella said, as Hob cleared away the dishes and Elena moved to stand up. "I want you to come along with me."

Now what? she thought, with dismay. It had been a very, very long day—

But Madame led her straight to the library, and after studying the shelves for a moment, selected three books and handed them to her. "Here you are, your work for tonight," she said. "Read them, and ask me for more when you've finished."

"What are they?" she asked, turning the books over and seeing no title worked into the leather covers.

"The earliest histories of the Five Hundred Kingdoms," Bella replied. "Priceless books, in their way; I don't think there is more than a handful of copies in existence that are *not* in a Godmother's library. I want you to read them, see how The Tradition has grown and changed over the years."

Elena nodded, but felt a thrill of greedy glee. As if being told to *read* was some sort of work! She took the books and went upstairs, where the lamps were already lit.

She settled in with the books, and paused to look about herself, and marvel at how her life had changed. It was, literally, unbelievable.

I had better get used to believing in the unbelievable, then, she told herself, and turned her attention to the first of the books.

After the first few pages she realized that above all else, Madame was right; she had a lot to learn. But it would not be the first time, and she had everything to lose—

—and everything to win.

Every waking moment of every day from that moment on was filled and overfilled with *something* having to do with being a Godmother's Apprentice. From the lessons about magic to the work in the stillroom, from the forays into the forest to collect the wild herbs that would not grow in a garden (though those were few, with a Brownie being the one doing the tending) to her long nights studying the history of the Godmothers and their work in the Five Hundred Kingdoms, she had no time to spare and little opportunity to think of herself.

Not that Madame was unkind! But she was an implacable taskmistress, expecting no less than total dedication, for that was what she herself gave to the job.

For virtually every waking moment of Madame Bella's day was given over to Godmothering, and Elena could easily see why Madame wanted to pass her position on to someone younger. Within the first three days, Madame was gone for nearly an entire afternoon and evening, and only returned well after moonrise. Elena heard her weary footsteps on the path to the door, and flew to open it for her.

Elena had been in the stillroom this afternoon and had not seen Madame leave; she loved being and working in the stillroom, for it was the one place where she was on firm ground. She had made up dozens of items in the Klovis household when the housekeeper had quit. Madame Klovis was "above" dirtying her hands in the stillroom, there was no one else who cared to take on the task in addition to their own, and Madame would not spare the money to purchase needed infusions, tinctures, and ointments in the market. Perfumes, face and land lotions, goodness yes, but common burn ointment was a "frippery." So, as usual, it had been Elena who had found herself with the task on her hands.

She had enjoyed it, though; stillroom work was anything but boring, and it wasn't hard labor. Here in the Godmother's stillroom, it was even more enjoyable, for she had the finest of ingredients to work with, in generous measure, and a recipe book that featured such delights as rosewater, jessamine lotion, and tincture of lavender. Bella had spent no more than a quarter of an hour supervising her initial labors; after that time she had laughed, stated that there was nothing she could teach her Apprentice *here* but the final infusion of magic, and left Elena with a list of what needed to be made up.

It made Elena very happy to know that here, at least, she was actually contributing to the household. When she had a bit of free time, she was making up scented candles and as a special surprise, a pair of scented gloves for Madame.

She busied herself until darkness fell, then after a dinner with the House Elves, went to her books. Madame did not return until an hour after that.

Elena heard her at the door and ran down the stairs to open it for her. When she opened the door, she saw to her astonishment that Madame was garbed in what Rose called "the full rig-out," from the top of her powdered wig to the silver buckles on her satin-covered high-heeled shoes. No ball-gown could have been more resplendent; the rose-pink, lace-festooned confection fitted her like the proverbial glove. The lace alone probably cost enough to buy the nearest village; the satin overskirt had been embroidered with an all-over pattern of rosebuds, and the underskirt was festooned with cascading tiers of more lace, sparkling with tiny faceted beads of rose crystal. She carried a staff rather than a wand; made in the manner of one of the highly fashionable, tall walking-canes, it was surmounted with a globe of rose-quartz caught in a winding of silver vines. Madame leaned on it heavily; she looked exhausted.

Rose took charge of her the second that Elena opened the door; she somehow whisked Madame away before Elena had time to realize that Bella *needed* help. And roughly half an hour later, Rose summoned Elena from her own rooms to cross into Madame Bella's.

It was the first time that Elena had been there, and she was not at all surprised to discover that the rooms were furnished in an older style than her own. Madame favored the medieval; the walls were hung with tapestries, the furniture looked too heavy to move, and the overall effect was frankly sumptuous. Madame herself had been stripped of her festive gown and elaborate wig and was sitting before the fire, wrapped in a dressing-gown, sipping a cup of tea.

"Ah, Elena!" she said, and Elena was glad to see that some of the weariness was gone from her face. "I'm sorry I did not tell you that I was leaving, but you were busy— and you will discover for yourself that although we may know for some time in advance that we will find ourselves with a particular task to perform, we don't know exactly *when* that task will take place. Today I was needed, along with six of the Fair Folk, to guide a prince to where his captive maiden was waiting for him, and to make sure he knew the secret that would defeat the one who held her captive." She smiled ruefully. "Then, of course, I had to remain long enough to see whether or not he was victorious."

"But—" she protested. "Why wouldn't he be?"

"Because, my dear, no outcome is *certain*, not even with The Tradition pushing it along. I brought you here, however, to show you how I know when I am going to be needed, and where. It is time for you to meet Randolf." She gestured at something on the wall opposite her fireplace—something like a painting, or perhaps a mirror, but one with heavy velvet curtains hung in front of it. "Go over there, and draw the curtains."

With curiosity eating her alive, she did so. It *was* a mirror, and there was a face staring at her from out of its inky depths.

It wasn't *her* face.

She gave a startled little squeak and jumped back; the face in the mirror looked surprised to see her—then stuck thumbs in each ear and waggled its hands at her while making a facc. This, of course, with nothing except the face and hands being visible.

"Randolf!" Bella snapped. "Stop that this instant!"

The face flushed, and the hands vanished. "I apologize, Madame, Apprentice. The temptation was overwhelming."

"Randolf, this is my new Apprentice, Elena," Madame said next, without moving from her chair. "Elena, this is Randolf, the Slave of the Mirror. I got him from a Dark Sorceress after she was destroyed."

"And *what* she'd been using me for—!" the face said, rolling its eyes. "What a *bore*! Never allowed to look at things for myself! Every day, it was always the same thing, 'Mirror, mirror, on the wall, who's—'"

"Well, you get to exercise your powers to the fullest now that you live with me, Randolf," Madame chuckled. "Show her my afternoon—a precis, if you please."

"Charmed," said the face, and vanished. It was replaced by a series of scenes that played out in the depths of the mirror as if it was no mirror at all, but a window on a place far from here.

For not even in rumor had Elena heard that there was a sleeping princess nearby, immured in a castle surrounded by a thorn hedge a good twenty feet high, twice that in thickness. She recognized the tale, of course. The Tradition seemed to favor the tale of the Sleeping Princess.

Bella appeared to the Prince as he was despairing of ever getting past the wilderness and into the castle. He looked pathetically glad to see her and the six Ladies of the Fair Folk that accompanied her; he was even happier to see the magical boat drawn by swans that brought them through the marsh. His face fell when he saw the thorn-hedge, however at that point, his sword and buckler probably seemed woefully inadequate. But it rose again, when the Fairies gave him a sword and shield of glass; it didn't take a lecture to tell him that these items were magical and could help him cut his way into the castle. And once inside, not even the Sorceress in the shape of a Wyrm could stop him.

"This was the first Sleeper *ever* in that Kingdom, so it was important that someone with experience be in charge. No one wanted this one to go wrong, and I had a certain personal interest in the outcome as well."

"Now, now, Madame," Randolf chided from the mirror. "The whole truth, now."

Bella grimaced. "The Sorceress and I have history together. She has tried to kill me on several occasions. I wanted to see her eliminated, once and for all."

"Ah," Elena said, with understanding.

"Now, here's the rub—over the course of this Tale, there have been several Princes who had come close to the site, but none passed the ordeals to come to the point where they were entitled to Faerie aid, so there was no telling the exact moment when I would have to make my appearance. I had to invoke the 'All Forests Are One,' spell in order to get there in time," Bella said, as the story played out, the Prince slaying the Wyrm with his glass sword, and awakening the Princess by ringing the bells of the Palace chapel. "Most exhausting."

Elena already knew about the "All Forests Are One" spell—it was a very important one, that enabled a Godmother *or* the person she was supposed to guide to cross their paths, no matter how far apart they really were.

"And a good job she made of it, too," said Randolf cheerfully, invisible behind the moving picture of the Prince being greeted by the awakened Princess and her entire Court. "Is that enough, Madame?"

"Quite enough, thank you, Randolf; I'm sure she has the idea by now."

"Randolf shows the future?" Elena hazarded.

The face appeared in the mirror again, and gave an exaggerated sigh. "Alas, no, fair maiden. I show only the present and past. But I show the present as it happens, with enough warning and fully in time for the Godmother to arrive."

Well, that put an interesting complexion on things! Elena had wondered just how Madame had managed to keep track of her all these years, and now she knew.

"Amazing," she managed. The face in the mirror beamed. "Oh, Madame!" it said. "Don't forget the Christening tomorrow. You asked me to remind you."

"Yes, thank you, Randolf. Elena, you may give him his curtains back."

It seemed cruel to imprison the poor spirit behind heavy velvet drapes, but it didn't seem to mind. "Doesn't he get bored in there?" she asked.

Bella laughed. "Ah, my dear, unlike his former mistress, I have freed him to use his powers to look anywhere he cares to. He doesn't need to eat or sleep; what he enjoys is watching over my charges, the Kingdoms for which I am responsible, with some little time to view players, minstrels, and musicians! I give him the freedom and the magic power to enjoy himself when he is not watching on my behalf, and he keeps me apprised of what I need."

Kindness, Elena thought, with satisfaction. A little kindness to Randolf had won Madame a powerful servant. Here, at last, she was in a place where kindness was rewarded. "So you are attending a christening tomorrow?" Elena asked, disappointed, as she thought she was making some real progress in her magic lessons and frankly didn't want them interrupted.

"Oh, yes, a Royal Christening," Madame said, and gave Elena an opaque look. "I'll be there.

"And so will you."

A carriage had appeared from nowhere, at least, so far as Elena was concerned. It had simply turned up at the door when Madame Bella and Elena had both been gowned and coiffed to Rose's satisfaction. There certainly wasn't a carriage, nor a carriage-horse in the tiny stable, and this wasn't the sort of equippage you would find in any of the nearby villages. While not large, it was excessively opulent, a little mauve-and-gold jewel-box of a carriage drawn by a single, handsome grey horse, and driven by a curiously silent foot-man in mauve livery with a great deal of gold braid on it.

Elena, recalling all of the tales, had to wonder if this carriage was really their little farm cart, and the horse that old donkey. As for the footman, well, he could be anything; a frog, a mouse, a rabbit—even old Hob or Robin, transformed.

Their coach took them into the edge of the forest, where Madame paused to invoke the "All Forests Are One Forest" spell. This was the first time that Elena had seen this Great Magic at work, and it was—remarkable.

Madame got out of the carriage, walked to the road just in front of the horse, and raised her staff, and it was as if she was the center of a whirlwind of the green dust motes of magic—but it was a very slowly moving whirlwind, and a soundless one. Denser and denser they became, and brighter and brighter, until Elena had to squint in order to see, and just as the light became painful, Madame thumped the end of the staff three times on the ground.

The light, the magic-motes, all vanished, and Elena got the strangest sensation, as if someone had dropped the carriage out from beneath her, at the same time thumping her in the middle of her chest.

Madame came back to the carriage and the footman handed her in, quite as if nothing whatsoever had happened. They entered the deep green depths, and no more than a mile later, emerged again. But this time, they were nowhere near the little village that *should* have been on that road. According to a signpost, they were in the Royal Forest of Leskamidia, very near the Palace. A mile after that, and they came out of the trees and into farm fields, the Palace clearly visible in the middle distance. Within a half hour, the footman was handing them out at the foot of the stairs, lined with guards in handsome uniforms, to join the throng of bewigged, bedecked and bejeweled guests moving into the Great Hall and the Throne Room beyond.

And difficult as it might be to believe, the Godmother was outstanding even in this group. Once again, Madame Bella was resplendent in her full Fairy Godmother glory, with no sign of the eccentric old lady about her. This time, the color of the outfit was a pale mauve, matching the carriage and the footman's livery, which was probably why the Major-Domo who announced them kept referring to her as "Her Grace, the Lilac Fairy." Her jewels were a chain of amethysts and pearls, amethyst rings, and amethyst and pearl buckles on her mauve satin shoes. The lace of her gown was beaded with tiny faceted amethysts, and seed-pearls ornamented the bodice. She was even wearing a tiara of little flowers made of amethysts, with emerald leaves and pearls for centers on her powdered wig. Elena was grateful that, as the mere Apprentice, she didn't have to look nearly as splendid. No tiara, no powdered wig, not even powder on her natural hair; in fact, all that Rose had done with her hair was to make it curl—though apparently even Brownie magic was not sufficient to make it form into neat ringlets. Her gown was a more subdued version of Madame's, with a great deal less of lace and no gemstone-beading at all; her jewels were a simple rope of pearls and her shoe-buckles of plain silver. For the first time in her life, she was wearing satin slippers, and truth to tell, she felt quite elegant enough. She had a wand instead of a staff, though it was a much longer wand than she was used to using now, and for some reason, Robin had elected to put a gilded star on the end of it. "Otherwise, it's just a stick," he had insisted. "People will *ex-*

pect it. How will anyone know you're Madame's Apprentice without a wand with a star on top?"

"The gown just might give the game away," she had pointed out dryly. "It might as well be livery, seeing as we match. And that wand looks, well, silly. Like something out of a book of tales."

He'd waved his hands in frantic triumph. "That's the *point!*"

She knew when she was beaten. But she still thought it looked silly.

Apparently no one else did, however. People did give her a wide and wary berth, and as she moved through the gathering in Madame's wake, they actually bowed slightly to her, with deeper bows reserved for Madame, who graciously nodded her head in return. That was gratifying, since there wasn't a single one of these people who would have looked at Ella Cinders with anything other than pity and disdain, and fretted lest she somehow dirty the hems of their garments from five feet away.

The Throne Room dazzled with color and light; name a hue, and someone was wearing an elegant, jewel-embroidered suit or gown in that color. Flowers garlanded the creamy marble walls and were twined about veined marble columns; a thousand scented candles twinkled in sconces and chandeliers. The room was full of delicate scent and light.

It was, to the last detail, the sort of celebration that Elena had only read about—the sort to which not even Madame Klovis could ever have dared aspire. Not one guest here was of common blood; Elena suspected that even the servants considered themselves to be a sort of nobility. And among the dukes and counts and barons, were a sprinkling of another sort of nobility altogether—

Fair Folk. Well, some of them, anyway. The Major-Domo called them *all* Fairies, and identified them by the colors of their gowns, but that was probably because he didn't know any better, or perhaps, hadn't been told their true identities. Possibly the latter; better to call them all Fairies, for there were some folk who were unreasonably prejudiced against Witches and Sorcerers. Three of the guests were genuine Fair Folk indeed, Elves of the sort that Elena had already seen, gowned in rose, silver, and gold; four were quite powerful Witches, if the haze of power surrounding them was anything to judge by. One was a Sorceress.

Now, Elena only guessed at that last, but there were signs, for someone who had been reading as much of the history of the Five Hundred Kingdoms and The Tradition as she'd been. Fairies were immediately identifiable, of course, by their eyes and ears—and two of them had mischievously elected to cause tiny butterfly-wings to sprout from their shoulders, perhaps in mockery of some of the sillier stories Elena had read about them as a child. The Witches were all in earthy colors—russet, green, wheat-straw, and grey—and their staffs and the ornaments they wore, though fashioned of silver and gems, were modeled on vines, leaves and flowers, or beasts and birds. The one that Elena reckoned to be a Sorceress wore a very dramatic gown of brilliant blue and white, and her ornaments, made of silver, diamonds, and sapphires, were *not* representations of natural things. She looked a bit spiky, truth to tell, very splendid and aloof—

but as Madame crossed her path, she winked at both of them in a conspiratorial manner, and there was a definite twinkle in her eye.

Madame was met by a page as she glided serenely across the ballroom floor, and conducted to the King, Queen, and the new little Princess, with the crowd parting before her as if someone invisible was shoving them aside. The nearer they drew to the thrones, the more tiaras and coronets there were—

Good heavens! Elena thought, catching sight of a haughty little head with a confection of gold, velvet, and ermine atop its ornate, powdered wig. *Is that a* crown? *It is, and there's another! There are foreign Princesses here!*

Princes, too, it seemed, as Elena caught sight of another crown, this time on a male head. Elena concentrated on Madame's back, and remembered that she was a Godmother's Apprentice, and that a Godmother's Apprentice didn't gape at the guests at someone else's party.

And then they entered the empty space around the dais, all eyes upon them, and Elena had to remind herself that she *belonged* here, and that someday it would be *she* who was the Godmother. It took a lot of reminding; her initial reaction was to want to stammer an apology and run off to the kitchen.

"Madame Bella!" said the King, rising from his throne and descending the two steps to take Madame Bella's free hand in both of his. "I cannot tell you how grateful we are—" He lowered his voice. "But are you *sure* nothing will go wrong? She *did* say she would be here, and we've done everything you said, but I just know that she'll find something to be offended by—"

Elena was utterly mystified by some of the King's words, but she had a good idea of the sort of things that Traditionally went wrong at Royal Christenings. There was usually an evil Witch or Sorceress who hadn't gotten an invitation—or if she had, she would find some great affront when she arrived. She would wait until she thought every magician there had delivered up his or her magical gift to the baby, and then descend with her own curse.

The young Queen—both the King and Queen were very young, Elena noticed; certainly no older than she herself was—leaned forward on her throne, one hand protectively on the edge of a canopied cradle spilling over with pink silk and lace coverlets. If anything, she looked more anxious than the King; perhaps he was better at hiding his feelings than she was.

"I've taken care of everything, don't worry," said Madame, soothingly. "But if you want to be sure it will work, Bertram, you and Linette *have* to look carefree, as if you are expecting no trouble whatsoever."

"We'll try," the King replied, and forced a smile onto his face, kissed Madame's hand, and let her go.

Madame bowed, and retreated with Elena still following like a faithful shadow. She moved off a little ways to the side of the throne, and took up what seemed to be a *position*, or at least, it felt that way to Elena. "I expect you're wondering what all that was about," she said in an aside to her Apprentice, as she nodded and smiled to other guests who wandered by, bowed to her, and passed on.

"Well, I *know* all the things that can go wrong at a Christening," Elena replied, dubiously.

"And so do Bertram and Linette; in fact, Linette is one of my Princesses, so she's doubly aware," Madame acknowledged. "Which is why, when their firstborn turned out to be a girl, they sent word begging me to take care of all of the—special arrangements—at the Christening. Not only did I make sure that all of the desirable magicians of the Kingdom got their invitations, I had Randolf spend a considerably store of his free time covering every square inch of this Kingdom, looking for the Evil Sorceress I knew had to be here. Then I made absolutely certain that *her* invitation was put right into her hands."

"But that's no guarantee——" Elena began, when suddenly——

She felt an inexplicable plummeting of her heart. A chill wind moved across the room, making the candles in the chandeliers flicker, and the guests shiver. Frightened silence spread from a point near the entrance, moving across the crowd like a ripple in a pond.

A shadow passed over the room. People edged away from something that was moving towards the thrones. And in the center of that moving point of silence Elena saw her first Evil Sorceress.

No great surprise, she was gowned all in black. From the shoes to her own tiara, she wore not a single hint of color. Her gown was a black velvet overdress, a black satin underdress, with faceted black crystals winking among the folds. More black crystals made up the tiara in her elaborately-styled ebony hair. Her staff was black, with a black serpent carved twining around it, and it was surmounted by a globe of black obsidian. As she drew nearer, Elena realized with a touch of reluctant admiration that even the black lace adorning her gown was very different from the swags and garlands on everyone else's garb—it had been made in the pattern of spiderwebs.

She glared about her, hostility and anger radiating from her, and it was then that Elena realized that she was, in fact, no older than the King and Queen, or even Elena herself. She exchanged a glance with Madame; hers startled, Madame's knowing. Madame nodded.

Sometimes, the ones who were "supposed" to have the happy endings go to the bad.... There was so much anger in the young woman's eyes, so much resentment, and so much pent-up pain, that Elena could not imagine how Madame was going to stop this creature from just exploding then and there, like a fermenting bottle—

Then, from out of the shadows where he had somehow been concealed behind the blue-and-white Sorceress, another figure stepped.

It was a young man; he wasn't handsome, and he clearly wasn't all that wealthy, but he had the most interesting and intense face that Elena had ever seen. He, too, wore black; a little threadbare, but *not* ill-kempt. Clearly, though he might be poor by the standards of the rest of the guests here, he was proud, but with the right sort of pride that will not be beaten by so small a thing as poverty, and insists on what Madame Fleur used to call "certain standards." Elena sensed that even if he had to mend and clean his clothing himself, he *would* be clean and mended. If he had to go without a meal, he would give no hint of it.

He moved into the Sorceress's path as if she was a lodestone, and he a needle. And when she paused in surprise, he seized his moment, and her hand, and bent nearly double to kiss it.

"Madame Arachnia, I presume?" he said, and his voice was so melodious that it made Elena yearn to actually hear him sing rather than speak. "Madame, I would never have accepted the invitation to come here this day, if it had not been that I knew that *you* had also been invited."

The Sorceress was taken so completely by surprise that she could only stare at him in shock. "You—you did?" she stammered, completely taken aback. "But—"

"I had to meet you," he replied, staring into her eyes with hungry intensity. "And please—could we come away from these—ordinary people?" Now his voice dripped disdain for those around him. "I sense that we must talk."

Still in shock, the Sorceress let him lead her, all unresisting, out of one of the double doors that led to the garden.

The shadows and the chill passed from the room with them.

Elena managed to drag her eyes away from them long enough to look at her mentor.

Madame Bella was watching with every evidence of satisfaction, and when the pair had gone out the door into the garden, she smiled. "That went well," she said, and winked at Elena. "I knew I could count on Miranda."

The celebration went on—presumably, without either Madame Arachnia—that had to be an assumed name!—or the young man. There was entertainment; dancers, musicians, mountebanks. Then, at last, came the moment to present Christening Gifts. And to Elena's horror, Madame Bella was the first of the magicians to grant hers—

"I grant her the gift of a caring heart," said Madame, and bowed over the cradle. A swirl of lilac mist rose about her, and settled over the baby; Madame smiled and retired, to make way for the Sorceress in blue and white.

"What are you doing?" Elena hissed frantically, as Madame resumed her place beside her Apprentice. "That *creature* is still outside! Why didn't you go hide or something, so that when she comes in and curses the baby—"

"You will be the one to turn the curse, because Arachnia has probably forgotten about you completely," Madame replied, looking completely unruffled, as the Sorceress bestowed "lips like cherries and teeth like pearls."

"Me?" squeaked Elena, "But—"

"Hush. And watch, and listen, and learn."

As Elena fidgeted and fretted, the other magicians gave their gifts, all, to her mind, singularly useless. What good was "hair as gold as sunlight," and "the voice of a lark," to someone who was probably going to *die* on her sixteenth birthday, unless an untrained Apprentice could figure out a way *and* muster the power to turn the curse of a very powerful Sorceress?

Finally the last of the Fair Folk gave her gift—"the grace of a swan on the water"—and, with utter predictability, Madame Arachnia appeared, the crowd drawing back from her, that shadow hanging over her, a cold wind coming with her.

Except that—she wasn't alone. That young man was still with her. And the shadow that surrounded her seemed thinner, the cold wind not so much icy as merely cool—and the expression on her face was one of—

Bewilderment?

The King and Queen clutched each other's hands, trying to put on a show of bravery, and failing utterly. Arachnia stood before the cradle, uncertainty in her very pose. She looked down at the baby, looked into the eyes of the King and Queen, and then—

—then looked back at the young man, who gazed at her with trust, worship and tenderness.

"On the morning of her sixteenth birthday—" Arachnia began, her voice rolling across the crowd in sepulchral tones. But then— she stopped.

"Her sixteenth birthday—" she began again, but now her voice was not so threatening. In fact, it sounded hesitant. She looked back at the young man.

He smiled. She tried to turn towards him, but something was holding her there. The struggle between Arachnia and this invisible force was palpable, visible, and it was making her angry.

She turned back towards the cradle and gathered herself together. She drew herself up. She pointed at the infant in the cradle—but when she spoke, instead of threat, the voice was full of—irritation.

The tone said, *I know I have to do this; I feel The Tradition forcing me into it. I don't have a choice, but pardon me if I just go through the motions.*

"On the morning of her sixteenth birthday, the Princess will awaken with her hair so knotted it will look as if birds had been nesting in it!"

There was a halfhearted little rumble of thunder. The shadow passed for a moment. Arachnia turned back to the young man with a look of triumph. He held out both hands to her; now it was she who was drawn as steel to a lode-stone, and they walked away from the King and Queen and Princess and right out the door together, as if no one else existed.

But then the shadow gathered again, the cold fell heavily on the room, as The Tradition gathered all of *its* strength to warp that ineffectual curse into something horrible. Elena felt the *potential* of the curse still hanging over everything, and she knew The Tradition and what it could do—if the curse wasn't quickly countered, it would descend in some ghastly form that no one could anticipate, no matter how weak the actual curse might seem to be. She grasped her wand in a sweating hand, and stepped forward, the youngest of them all, and her mind was working frantically. How to turn the curse into a blessing? How to take all that power of The Tradition and turn it against itself? She had to be clever; had to give The Tradition what it wanted. That was not only a curse, but a reward for someone worthy. The poor little Princess would have to endure *something*, and at the same time, the end of the tale had to provide something for another person that *she* had to "name"—

What could you do with hair that was horribly knotted and keep it from tangling around someone's throat to choke off her breath? It had to be *something* that would cost some pain, for The Tradition demanded pain for a curse—who could untangle something hopelessly snarled?

It came to her, and as she stepped forward towards the infant's cradle, she was carefully phrasing her counter, hoping no one noticed how her hands were shaking. She gathered all of the power she could see swirling around her in a rainbow skein of magic; prayed it was enough, and waved her wand three times over the baby's cradle. Shining motes of power followed the circling of the star on the tip of her wand, and spiraled down into the sleeping infant.

"The Princess will awaken with her hair binding her to her bed, so knotted that she cannot move."

There. That was surely enough of a curse to satisfy The Tradition.

"Scissors will be blunted, knives useless, and not any of her handmaidens will be able to loosen so much as a single knot. All will seem lost."

There was the despair that was needed.

"Nor will magic avail the day. No man's hand will free her."

That left things open for a girl, a female, anyway. The Tradition liked these little, sly loopholes.

"But a rescuer will come; noble by nature, not by birth, gifted with patience and common sense, drawn by pity and not hope of reward. With her own two hands, the rescuer will free the Princess from the prison of her own hair, and win her freedom and her friendship."

Just like the popping of a soap-bubble, the dreadful *potential* vanished. Elena almost wept with relief.

Now everyone sighed, some with relief that matched Elena's, some not understanding what had happened, laughing nervously at the apparently absurd "curse." Only the magicians among them moved forward to congratulate the new Apprentice on a clever counter, for only they realized that The Tradition had been poised to make the Princess strangle in her own hair, or be smothered by it, or take some other dreadful form. Now it, and all of its potential, had been bound into a harmless, yet logical form. The Princess would live, and there would be a "happily ever after" for the nameless rescuer, some humble girl somewhere who would have the patience to untangle the Gordian-hair-knot when everyone else had given up.

The celebration went on, but *their* work was done, and Elena felt as drained as if she had been running for a mile. The King called for the musicians to play, and Madame Bella quietly went to him to explain what was going to happen in sixteen years.

Elena found a convenient pillar and put her back against it, feeling limp and drained. Eventually Madame Bella returned and took her gently by the elbow, and steered her into one of the little side-rooms that had been set up for the convenience of a few guests who wished to converse together. Somehow she was not at all surprised to find the other magicians there, being served with refreshments and chattering amiably among themselves.

"Miranda, my dear, you exceeded my wildest dreams!" Bella said, as they entered, and the Sorceress beamed. A seat was immediately provided for Elena, and the Witch in russet pressed a glass of wine into her hand. Elena drank it down at a gulp.

The Sorceress nodded graciously. "It was a stroke of luck finding him. Do you know he's a Prince as well as a poet?"

There was a gasp and a laugh from the Witch in green. "No! Oh, my word, that *does* make a great deal of sense! No wonder Arachnia gravitated straight for him!"

What? Oh—oh, of course, if she's like me, she was sup-posed to have a Prince and somehow didn't get one. Only she turned bitter and hard and wants to make everything around her hurt as much as she does. But The Traditional attraction is still there.

"What sort of Prince?" Bella asked, plying Elena with a slice of cake. It was far too sugary—or at least, would have been if she hadn't been so famished.

"A *Frog* Prince, the poor thing, and he'd been that way so long that his Kingdom had passed right into the hands of a collateral line. Decades at least; maybe more, I couldn't be sure. Kissed by a Princess, all right, but she was only six years old, and in the habit of kissing every bird and beast that crossed her path!" Sorceress Miranda shook her head with pity for the poor man's situation. Elena winced. Bad enough to have the first part of your "destiny" thwarted, worse to no longer have a home to return to, but then to have insult piled on top of injury like that—

"Oh, the poor lad!" exclaimed the Witch in grey, with sympathy warming her voice. "No Princess, no Kingdom—no prospects—"

"But a talent for brooding poetry. Well, I would be broody, if I'd gone through all of that," Miranda replied. "He's good enough to keep from starving, which for a poet, is a pure mir-acle, frankly. I found him just as you suggested, Bella, by looking for slim volumes of recently published verses full of suffering and anguish and longing for death—and a morbid fascination with the trappings of darkness, but not the sub-stance."

"And you tracked the poet down—" Bella prompted,

handing a plate of little sandwiches to Elena, who felt as if she was so starved there was a hole in the bottom of her stomach.

"Just as you said—I knew I had the right sort of fellow after watching him a while. He might speak longingly in excellent rhyme of wanting to be united with the powers of darkness and descend into the blackness of never-ending night, but in his little garret he was feeding sparrows with bread he could hardly afford to part with." Miranda smiled merrily. "I took on the semblance of a Royal Messenger, delivered the invitation, and made sure he knew that the notorious Madame Arachnia would also be there. And when he arrived, I just made sure to position him properly, and you saw the rest."

"But Bella," the Witch in green protested. "How did you *know* this would fall out in this way? How did you know that Arachnia wouldn't still put a really powerful curse on the babe?"

"She didn't, not exactly," said an aged voice from the door. They all turned, and two of the Witches leaped to their feet to aid the bent and withered old woman who stood there into the room and into a chair.

"She didn't," the old woman repeated, with a cherubic smile, and a voice creaking with age. "I was to be her emergency counter, in case the curse was too dreadful for her clever little Apprentice to work out. Not," she added, "that I think it would have been. Once a truly dreadful curse has been laid, The Tradition usually makes the counter fairly easy to think of and set."

"'Not death, but sleep,'" quoted Miranda. "And no one

would ever have looked for you here, Madame Veronica. I thought you never traveled anymore."

"I do not," the elderly Godmother replied. "This is my Kingdom, and I told Bella to be ready when I knew the Queen was expecting. I am one of the Royal Nursery-maids—and that was a good touch, couching the counter so that the savior is a low-born girl, young Elena," she added. "I shall have to be sure there is someone worthy of reward and gathering Potential in that position when the time comes."

"But still, Bella, how did you know you would find a young man that would find Arachnia irresistible?" the Witch in green persisted. "I can see where you could turn her, if you could only find someone who would see her and love her, but how did you know such a fellow existed?"

Bella tilted her head to the side, and a wry smile touched her lips. "You find them in any Kingdom," she said, "if you look hard enough. Young men, and young women, too, who believe that they are in love with evil, death, and dark-ness, but in fact, are in love with *mystery*. Mind, it wouldn't have worked if Arachnia herself wasn't so young, and still able to be turned, if only one could find the key to her lone-liness. I expect she'll be your charge now, Miranda."

"And happy to take her on," the Sorceress replied. "I'd go through fire and ice to turn someone with her power. And believe me, I have bound that young man with so many spells I'm surprised he can move."

"You didn't put a love spell on him!" said the Witch in grey, aghast.

"Great heavens no! I'm not that stupid!" Miranda exclaimed. "Arachnia would have spotted *that* in an instant, and she'd have been so angry she probably would have cursed the whole Kingdom! No, all I did was hedge him around so that he can't become the Rogue, the Betrayer, the Cad, or the Seducer, and I let his own romantic feelings do the rest."

"We can count on that," Madame Bella said, with a decided nod of her head. "I think that he may be in love with an abstract now, but it won't be long before he's in love with Arachnia herself, and she won't be able to resist *him*. I know; thanks to Randolf, I've had a look at her Library. A good half of it is slim little volumes of darkly romantic poetry, and I wouldn't be at all surprised to discover that some of them are his. In no time—well, probably by tonight!—they'll be haunting the battlements of her castle together as bats flutter overhead beneath a gibbous moon."

Two of the Witches heaved sighs of relief, and Madame Veronica nodded.

"Well, that seems to have it all settled and sorted, then, and I must say, a more clever way of turning The Tradition I have never seen," the Witch in russet said with contentment, and turned to her fellows. "When shall we four meet again?"

"Thursday next would be good," said the one in grey. "But this time, I am supplying the cards! Your deck likes you altogether too much, Penelope!"

In the carriage on the way back to the cottage, as shafts of light penetrated the forest canopy, creating slashes of golden light across the green shadows, Elena turned to her mentor. "Did you really arrange all of that?" she asked in wonder. "However did you even think of it?"

"It only worked because Arachnia—that's not her real name, by the way; she changed her name when she turned to the darkness—is young, and although she is a seething mess of anger and resentment, she is also enduring a truly crushing weight of loneliness," Madame replied, as the carriage wheels rolled over a dry stick, breaking it with a sound that made Elena jump. "She spent all of her young life, much like you, despised and exploited. She was sent into the wilderness by her stepmother, who told her to gather berries before any such thing was ripe, and taken up by an Evil Sorceress and made into a slave."

"Then what?" Elena wanted to know.

"Well, the Sorceress had many such 'servants,' all of whom hated her, but none of whom dared to defy her. Arachnia bore it as long as she could, but the moment came when she was both strong enough and had the opportunity, and she managed to kill her mistress. That was when she decided that she must be an Evil Sorceress, and The Tradition obliged by supplying her with some sort of tutors, as well as the workroom and library of her former mistress and all the other Evil Magicians who had lived there originally."

"So—she studied magic and The Tradition on her own?" Elena hazarded. Bella nodded.

"That's what usually happens, actually. The dark magicians don't have a great deal of tolerance for one another." Madame Bella glanced over at Elena, perhaps to see if she needed to elaborate on this point, but it was pretty obvious to the Apprentice. Dark magicians didn't have much tolerance for any sort of rival.

"Well, when Randolf found her for me, I began using him to watch her, but to tell the truth, it was easy to see that her heart wasn't in the business of evil for its own sake. She had the proper trappings, but it was mostly show. Her garden has as many roses as nightshade and henbane plants. She keeps only nonvenomous spiders and snakes. The bats live in their very own tower, and every raven and owl that has decided to roost at her castle is so well-fed that several of them are too fat to fly."

"But if that's true," Elena said, her brow wrinkling, "Why didn't you do something to help her *before* she killed her stepmother?"

There was a very long moment of silence.

"Because," Madame said at last, with such deep sorrow that Elena almost regretted asking the question, "I did not know *any* of this until I had Randolf go looking for the Evil Sorceress that I knew must be there. And I was lucky in Arachnia."

"She could have been—" Elena was not sure how to phrase it.

"She could have been truly evil. This isn't the first time that I've hoped to turn The Tradition this way, been disappointed, and had to rectify matters in the usual way. But that is why I sent Randolf looking, as I always have, hoping that I would be lucky." Madame looked steadily into Elena's eyes. "I knew that if just once I could find the combination I was looking for, I could turn The Tradition, not just this one time, but open a new possibility for the future. *You* felt it—

all that potential, how it just slipped aside when your counter was cast."

Elena nodded, warily. She *thought* she'd felt that, at any rate.

"The potential magic you used was just a fraction of what was available, and the rest of it went into cutting a new Traditional Path," Madame said, with just a touch of gloating. "Now, just you wait and see, the tale of Arachnia and her impoverished Poet Prince will become its own part of The Tradition, and perhaps that knowledge will help another Godmother turn some other Dark One in the future."

"Or maybe it will keep one from going to the Dark at all?" Elena hazarded.

"We can only hope, my dear," Bella replied, as the carriage came within sight of the cottage, its thatched roof gleaming like gold in the evening sunlight. "But it is a goal worth pursuing at almost any cost."

Elena had no difficulty whatsoever in agreeing with that.

Day by day, week by week, Elena mastered the arts and skills of magic, and "fine art" of being a Godmother. Midsummer's Day came and went, and summer drowsed towards haying time in the villages near Bella's cottage. Haying time brought a spate of women to the cottage, the wives and sweethearts of farmworkers, seeking charms against cutting and ointment for wounds; haying was dangerous work, and the men who swung the huge, razor-sharp scythes could be cut and bleed to death if the worst happened. Bella taught the making of these to Elena, and after the first few, it was she who supplied all such things to their visitors.

Some few of the farmers themselves came looking for help as well, but what they wanted was not a charm, but a prediction; hay needed five hot days to dry properly after it was cut, five days of no rain and no dew. Bella herself saw to that.

"It's easy enough," she said with a chuckle. "Weather moves from west to east. I simply have Randolf look west from here, and find me at least a five-day span of clear weather, then give me a notion of when it will start. At this time of year, when we have far more sun than rain, that's not so hard."

That struck Elena as supremely clever. It didn't require trying to see into the future (which she had learned was very difficult and became more so the further ahead you tried to look). It also didn't require *changing* the weather, which she had been warned was something that could cause more problems than it solved. Sometimes, it seemed, the business of a Witch or a Godmother was not so much *using* magic as knowing when *not* to use it.

Sometimes she felt as if she was learning so much so fast that her head was stuffed full of it all, and if she had to master one more thing, her skull was going to burst.

While Witches and Hedge-Wizards tended to control and direct magic by using *things*, (creating complicated potions and talismans), the Sorcerers and Sorceresses controlled magic with words using a special language of words of binding and loosing, that minutely described the effects a magician wanted. But a full Wizard or a Godmother worked strictly by will and intention. Oh, that sounded so very easy! But you had to learn how to focus yourself completely, so that nothing distracted you; you had to learn how to chart an exact course and commit yourself completely to the course you had decided on. And you had to learn to think on your feet, so that you could frame something that would steer The Tradition in the way you wanted it to go the moment that an opportunity presented itself.

This was why Arachnia, despite her best effort, had not thwarted The Tradition with her pseudo-curse. This was why Elena, shaking with fear and effort, had been able to counter the curse in a way that satisfied The Tradition. Faced with her first crisis, she had been so focused on it that by the time her will had been imposed there was no room for The Tradition to move except in the direction she wanted it to. Thanks to all her reading, she had known enough of The Tradition by then to be able to give it the path of least resistance in the direction she wanted it to go.

But the more practiced she became, the more experience she had, the more important the ability to focus would become. She would not have that fear to narrow her concentration down to the sharpest point. With familiarity came, if not contempt, certainly a loss of urgency; she had to learn how to make up for that with internal focus.

Wizards and Fairy Godmothers did more than merely counter curses; they also tested and guided Questers and dispensed punishments to seekers who failed the tests.

The little old lady in the woods, who after being treated kindly, dispensed the clues that a Quester needed to find his goal—those were Godmothers. The ferryman who had the answers to questions—also Godmothers, or Wizards. The hag at the bridge, the watcher at the door—

And when there was more than one Quester, when, for instance, it was a Quest by several young men, only one of whom would be worthy, it was the job of the Godmothers and Wizards to test these seekers to find the one who was worthy to pass on. And, if they did not measure up, to allot a punishment or send them in another direction that would, hopefully, teach them and correct their behavior. Many a Prince who had failed the test of kindness on the way to the captive Princess later became the hero of his own story— or, at the least, became the wise and virtuous King of his own land at the death of his father.

That was Godmother and Wizardly magic.

Wizards were fewer than Godmothers, and usually elected to be solitary, apart from the dwellings of men, living in caves or wild forests as hermits. But because Godmothers often acted as the local White Witches, they also had to learn Witchery in order to help their communities and maintain their fictive disguises; thus, Elena had not one, but *two* sets of lessons to master.

Of the two, the Witchery was the easiest; in fact, so far as she was concerned, it was something of a doddle. All you had to do was to follow the recipe to create the potion, whose purpose was determined by the ingredients. Then you infused the potion with a touch of power. Witches and Hedge-Wizards worked in subtle ways, attempting to make their influence felt, not at the crisis, but before there was any hint of a crisis. They operated at the lowest level of magic, where small changes might bring larger results. As a result, even the most powerful of Witches generally used the smallest amount of magic needed in order to bring about the desired result. More often than not, they did not use magic, as such, at all.

For instance—being kind to the abused and exploited stepdaughter of a neighbor...giving her encouragement and the odd meal, helping her to cope with a cup of tea and a word of advice. Yes, Elena's neighbors had been Witches—*both* of them. And, among many other things, they had kept a careful eye on Elena, guiding her, keeping her spirit from being crushed. Had she ever truly wanted, with all her heart, to become ordinary, they would have called on Madame Bella to come and take the weight of all of that Traditional Potential away from her, and she probably *would* have managed to find either a kind husband, or a position as a maid-of-all-work, when Madame Klovis departed on her search for another wealthy victim to wed. Probably the latter, though there was no telling for certain.

As it was, when they knew that Elena was determined to escape, no matter what it took, they had called Madame Bella to examine this potential Apprentice for herself. *Those* were the voices that Elena had heard that night, murmuring over the wall next door.

For their part, Sorcerers and Sorceresses intervened when things had gone so wrong that only enormous magical effort could save the day. They accompanied heroes and heroines on the quests, and when they did, the odds were usually stacked against them. They often watched over the children who *would* become heroes as they were raised in hiding. They fought at the side of heroes when the armies of good and evil clashed. They could go their entire lives without ever fulfilling that particular destiny, however, so they also served another set of functions. They often assisted Godmothers; they frequently devised the trials and tests that lesser questers had to pass. And, perhaps because of their affinity for language and deep, long thought, they were frequently mystics, being sought for their wisdom as well as their magic. A Sorcerer's life was often spent in long years of patient study and waiting, and it sometimes ended in a frenetic and peril-filled span of mere months. When there was combative magic darkening the skies, it was most often the Sorcerers and Sorceresses who were in the thick of it.

Yet, such times were few, and it was just as well that this was so, or the landscape would have been shattered by the scope of such conflicts. Most Sorcerers and Sorceresses never once raised a wand in anger. They lived and died in their distant, lofty towers, seldom venturing out, studying the heavens and the earth in splendid isolation unless someone happened to call upon them for some trifle or other.

Elena decided rather quickly that she would not much enjoy being a Sorceress.

She might have enjoyed being a Witch, but—

But could she have ever acted as her neighbors did, remaining apart from the people she served, staying out of their day-to-day quarrels, living *in* her town, yet apart from it? Witches and Hedge-Wizards could not take sides, could not become involved, dared to make no judgments, allowing events to judge themselves.

She didn't think so; she could *not* just stand apart from things and let them run their course without trying to set them right. She would never, for instance, have been able to stand being next door to her younger self, seeing how that self was mistreated by Madame Klovis. In fact, she probably would have marched right in one fine day after a beating and turned Madame and her two daughters into toads.

It was the passion to set things right that defined the Godmother and the Wizard; and this was also why they did *not* live among the people. To be a Godmother meant that you *did* become involved, and you used your strong emotions to help you focus. But Godmothers and Wizards did not remain so utterly apart from people as the Sorcerers and Sorceresses did—they needed to have *some* contact with people, to remain anchored in humanity and keep their own emotions alive. It was a difficult balance to maintain—but it wasn't boring.

In all of the magical work she was doing, Elena was constantly concerned that at some point, that store of magical power that The Tradition had surrounded her with would run dry, and finally one day during the haying, when she had made half a dozen charms against cutting (a little talisman made of tiny leaden scythe with no edge at all, a sprig of High John, and a bit of cloth with the person's blood on it) she voiced that concern to Madame.

Bella was out in the garden, deciding, with Lily's help, just which herbs would be cut that night in the light of the full moon. When Elena stammered out her worry, Madame gave her a long and considering look.

"It is true that with nearly anyone else, I would have taught you how to harvest power by now," she said at last. "The reason I haven't is that you arrived with so much you haven't yet expended half of it. But something could happen to me—" she paused at the sight of Elena's stricken look, and laughed "—no, no, I'm not anticipating anything!

No premonitions, no predictions, I assure you, just the common sense that things *can* happen that no one foresees. So, since those talismans and a few other things have to go to the village anyway, you might as well come along with me, and I'll show you how it's done."

"I'll harness Dobbin," said Lily instantly.

"You go change your apron and get your hat," Bella told Elena. "I'll have Rose make up the basket."

So by the time Elena had changed her apron for a clean one, tied a kerchief over her hair to keep the dust out and placed her wide-brimmed, flat-crowned straw hat over that and was down the stair again, the donkey and cart were at the front gate, and Madame was already on the driver's bench.

Although he wasn't nearly as fast as the Little Humpback Horse, the donkey could keep a surprisingly quick pace for one so old and small. A pleasant hour brought them to the village of Louvain, and Madame was hardly over the little stone bridge before the women who had commissioned those charms came running to meet them.

"You're just in time," said the first of them, a cheery, round-faced woman who had three happily grubby little children trailing along behind her. "Haying begins tomorrow! I don't know what we'd have done if you hadn't come today."

"Tell those dolts to be extra careful, that's what we'd have done," said another, thin and careworn, with a grimace. "Still, they're men! You never *can* depend on them not to play the fool when there's a lot of them together!"

The last of the women, a sweet-faced girl with a furrowed brow, took her talisman but whispered to Madame when the others were just out of earshot, "Madame Bella, it's—can you—"

"That's why I came today," Madame whispered back. "Just let me leave my simples with Brother Tyne, and I'll see you before I leave."

Elena had expected from the name that Brother Tyne was a priest—but in fact, he was an apothecary with a little shop on the village square, the sign of his trade—a large, round-bottomed bottle—hanging above his door. When they drew up to his shop, he came out and took the basket from Madame, handing her down afterwards as if he was a footman. "Come along, Apprentice," Madame called over her shoulder. "You'll be doing this eventually, so you might as well see our arrangement."

They didn't stay long in the tiny shop; Brother Tyne counted what they'd brought and apparently there was a set price already for Madame's goods, for there was no haggling. They emerged with a little purse of copper and silver and an empty basket, and a paper with the prices that the Apothecary would pay for each potion on a little slip of paper in Elena's pocket. And on the way out of town, Madame pulled the donkey up beside the gate of a tiny, rose-covered cottage with the prettiest yard Elena had ever seen. The entire place was as cheerful as you could ask, and Elena was struck by the notion that not that long ago, *she* would have been happy living in such a place. "Rosalie!" Madame called. "Have you got that butter I wanted?"

The same young woman who had whispered so urgently to Madame appeared at the door of the cottage. "I have, and please come and choose the pats for yourself," she replied. Madame hopped down off the cart, and Elena tied up the donkey to the hedge at the front of the yard and followed her.

Once inside the cottage, it was clear that butter had been nothing more than an excuse to come inside, away from the prying eyes of the neighbors. "I feel that hemmed in, it's like I can't breathe sometimes," the young woman was saying, as Elena joined them in the tiny kitchen. "I can't imagine why it's got so bad, so quickly this time."

It was then that Elena noticed what she had not before; that the young woman was just beginning to show her pregnancy. Ah, this must be something to do with that, Elena thought—but then wondered. She *knew* this village had a midwife, and a good one. Why ask Madame Bella for help?

"Well, this should be the last time it's this hard, my dear," Madame soothed. "Now just you remember, if you get a craving for *anything* out-of-season, you send straight to me, that minute, and I'll make a special trip here or send my Apprentice. I don't think you will, once I've done with you today, but it's still possible. Now, Elena, *watch* and listen."

When Madame said "watch" in *that* tone of voice, it meant magic.

Elena blinked, and saw the whirls of magical power swirling tightly around the young woman, so thick that her features were blurred, as if she wore a veil.

"Rosalie, do you surrender your power to me, freely and of your own will?" Madame asked, slowly, carefully, and clearly. She held her wand just over the crown of the young woman's head. "Do you renounce this power, not only for yourself, but for the sake of your unborn child?"

"I do," Rosalie replied, bowing her head slightly. "I renounce it for the life I have chosen, for the sake of my unborn child, and for the love that I bear my husband."

With each word that the young woman spoke, the power slowed, and somehow *relaxed*, until it no longer bound her like coils of wire, but lay about her like loose hay.

"Then I assume it, for the pledge I have made, for the sake of those who will need it, and my duty to those who call upon me," Madame said, circling young Rosalie's head three times with the tip of her wand—and the power followed it, flowing around and upwards, vanishing *into* the wand, as if it was somehow sucking it up. That was the only analogy that Elena could make—

The *spell* was a simple enough one, but she saw by the frown of concentration on Madame's face that the effort to make it work was intense. And before all of the power had been absorbed, she stopped.

Rosalie's head shot up. "You aren't done!" she cried, accusingly. "I can feel it—"

Madame held up her hand. "Hush, dear. We'll take the burden from you, no fear—but I want my Apprentice to take a hand and finish the job."

Rosalie looked at Elena doubtfully, but did not voice those doubts, perhaps because she was too polite to do so. Elena took Madame's place, her wand outstretched. "Rosalie," she said, carefully, "do you surrender your power to me, freely, and of your own will? Do you renounce this power, not only for yourself, but for the sake of your unborn child?"

The power had begun to wrap Rosalie in its coils again when Madame had released it; now, as Rosalie repeated what she had said to Madame, it relaxed again.

"Then I assume it," Elena said, "for the pledge I have made, for the sake of those who will need it, and my duty to those who will call upon me." And as she circled Rosalie's head with the tip of her own wand, she concentrated, fiercely, on doing the *opposite* of what she had learned to do so far—not to dispense power, but to take it in.

It was a great deal more difficult than she would have guessed. Not only was she fighting against the training she'd had so far, but she could feel the whole weight of The Tradition bearing down on her in a kind of sullen resistance. The Tradition *wanted* this young woman for something. It bent its power towards making her into that something. It was like an enormous, blind, insensate beast, *pushing* her towards that end, and it did not want to let her go down some other path.

But Rosalie did not want to go there. She was happy with her little cottage, her gentle, simple husband, happy to be ordinary and fit in with the rest of the village as a pea fits among its neighbors in a pod. The more The Tradition pushed her, the more she pushed back, and that was what made it painless for her to give up the power that was collecting around her.

Given the amount of it, Elena had a good idea of why she had seemed so distressed. *She* knew that sort of distant-storm tenseness that the coiled-up power around you made you feel; the sense that there was something, somewhere, you urgently had to do. It was not unlike feeling that a dreadful headache was poised, waiting to strike you the moment you dropped your guard. It wore on you, until all you could think about was this *weight* on you, the feeling of nerves stretched thin. Slowly, reluctantly, the power let go of Rosalie and passed to Elena—

Where, exactly, it went, she couldn't really tell. But she could feel a sort of weight to it, and felt it join her power, as if she was a vessel, and it was water flowing in from some outside source.

Finally the last of the power was gone. There was no more magic sparkling and glowing around Rosalie than there was around any of her perfectly ordinary neighbors.

Rosalie might not have been able to see the difference, but she certainly sensed it. Her shoulders straightened, as did her back; she opened her eyes and smiled, and her brow was no longer furrowed.

"Well, Apprentice!" she said, her voice bright with pleasure. "I expect you'll not be an Apprentice much longer!"

Elena flushed. "I still have a lot to learn," she murmured, embarrassed, as Madame chuckled.

"We'll be off, then," was all Madame said. "Now that you're sorted. But remember, *any* craving, and you send to me! That may not sound like much, but believe me, it's important!"

"I will," Rosalie promised.

"All right," Elena said, once they were well out of the village, "what was all *that* about?"

"Rosalie is a rare one," Madame replied. "In fact, you

won't find a girl like her in a hundred years. She's a dou-
bler—when she was younger, before she married her
sweetheart, The Tradition was trying to make her into a Fair
Rosalinda."

"Oh good heavens—" Elena said, her hand going to her
lips in consternation.

The Tradition was not *all* happy endings. "Fair Rosalinda"
was one of the uglier directions that The Tradition could go
into—the beautiful peasant orphan girl who is seduced by
a King, set up in her own secluded bower, and murdered by
his Queen when she discovers his philandering.

"Oh, yes," Madame said grimly. "A fine romantic tragedy,
if it were to happen to someone else, long ago and far
away...not such a fine thing if it was supposed to happen to
you."

Elena had read of several "Fair Rosalindas" already; magic
entered the picture only after the poor thing was dead—
poisoned or strangled and the body buried somewhere hidden—

But usually, the Fair Rosalinda was drowned. Then a mu-
sician would enter the tale. Sometimes he would make a pipe
or some other instrument of the reeds or the tree growing
from her hidden grave—in the most macabre and disturbing versions, he would make a harp from her bones and
string it with her golden hair. And then he would go before
the King, who was grieving for his lost love, and when he
played, the instrument would have but one song—

"The Queen hath murdered me," Elena murmured.

"I will *not* have one of those in *my* Kingdoms," Madame
said fiercely. "I found her before the King did, before her

breasts began to bud—she, in her turn, had already begun to feel the coils of the power around her and when I had explained something of what was going to happen, begged me to take it from her. Which I've been doing, and I had hoped that when she wedded, The Tradition would give over and let her go. But it hasn't; I had some suspicions as to why, and I think they've just been confirmed now that I know she's with child. Failing to make her a Rosalinda, The Tradition now wants to make her child a Ladderlocks."

"Oh, *please!*" Elena said, as much in disgust as anything else. "What has the poor thing done to be so put-upon?"

The Ladderlocks story was more fantastical and less— but only a trifle less—unpleasant than that of Rosalinda. The mother of a Ladderlocks child would be overcome with a craving for some out-of-season food to the point where she could eat that and only that. Naturally, the only place her distracted husband can find this food would be in the garden of some Black Witch or Evil Sorceress. He would steal it, be caught, and pledge to give the woman his child to save his own life. On the birth of Ladderlocks—always a girl— the Witch would take her away, lock her in a tower, and among other things, forbid her to cut her hair...and the rest of that tale was familiar to any child in any Kingdom that Elena had any knowledge of. It might end well, but there was often a great deal of horror before the end came—

"I can't even bear to think about being locked up in a tower for sixteen years," Elena replied. "I don't know why the girls don't go mad."

"Some of them do," Madame confirmed. "I know of one who hung herself with her own hair."

Elena shuddered, and looked away for a moment.

"And then there's the dozens of poor young fellows who die at the hands of the Dark One before one of them manages to get to the tower," Madame continued, frowning fiercely. "A Ladderlocks is nothing more than bait for a deathtrap, and I *won't* have one of those in my Kingdoms, either!"

Elena nodded, knowing that even when a young man managed to get to the tower, climb the hair, and win the maiden, he still might not escape the Witch unscathed. They were almost always caught, and sometimes the poor young man who fell in love with Ladderlocks found himself blinded by the thorns around her tower, or sometimes worse than that. A Ladderlocks tale often had more tragedy than triumph about it.

It was a tale best prevented.

"I wish I knew why The Tradition was so set on having *her*," Bella replied. "But as long as I keep draining her, at least until her first-born is actually *born*, the magic won't attract the other half of the equation."

"The Evil Witch." Elena nodded. "She knows, of course?"

"I've drummed it into her head often enough," Bella said grimly. "And it will have to be *her* that prevents it; her husband is kind, sweet, gentle, handsome as the dawn, and as dense as a bag of stones. She loves him, but she knows very well that he is prime material for the loving but stupid husband who climbs the wall around the Witch's garden to steal her rampion. And it would not matter how many times she warns him about it, he won't remember. The Tradition can shove him about like a coin in a game of Shove Ha'penny."

At that moment, Elena felt a surge of anger at The Tradition, that faceless, formless *thing* that pushed and pulled people about with no regard for what they might want or need. She met Madame's eyes, and saw that same anger there.

"Yes," Bella said, softly, only just audible over the sound of hooves and wheels on the hard-packed road. "I hoped you would feel that. I hoped when I took you as my Apprentice, that you were cut from the same cloth as me. Some Godmothers are only willing to assist in the making of the happy endings. *I* am of a different mind."

"There will be no Fair Rosalindas in *my* Kingdoms," Elena said, just as softly, but just as firmly.

Madame gave a quick nod, as if she and Elena had just made a pledged pact. And perhaps, they had.

"Good," was all she said, then she turned her attention back to the road.

Madame changed the topic to something innocuous. Nothing more was said on that subject.

But then again, nothing more needed to be.

As harvest turned towards autumn, the days became noticeably shorter, and the air grew chill at night, Madame took to leaving Elena in charge of the cottage for several days at a time. "Keep Randolf company," was all she usually said, before she went off on whatever mysterious errands were taking her away. "He gets lonely sometimes. He'll chatter at you about plays he's been watching; just nod and make appreciative noises, even if you can't understand half of what he's nattering on about."

Elena was growing very fond of the Slave of the Mirror by this point; Randolf was perhaps the most artless person she had ever known. Despite everything he saw, and everything he had lived through, he maintained a kind of innocence. He had no pretenses, nothing about him was a sham.

Furthermore, he had beautiful manners, and was perfectly pleased to give her the one set of lessons she found it difficult to accept from anyone else in the household—the lessons in what he called *deportment* and *she* called "fitting in."

Madame just simply seemed to change everything about herself without thinking, depending on what costume she wore, from dotty old peasant woman to gracious Lady of exalted breeding and impeccable pedigree. Lily had just laughed when Elena had broached the subject, and advised her to "just be yourself, and be damned to them as doesn't like it."

And the haughty Rose, Elena thought, would be so critical that the lesson would get lost in the criticism.

Ah, but Randolf had not only been *watching* Kings and Queens for two hundred years or more, until recently he had been the prized possession of several queens of the evil sort. So, when Madame Bella was away, Elena would spend several evening hours in her sitting room, not merely keeping Randolf company, but learning from him.

"Just what *does* Madame do, off on her own of late?" she asked him one night, after a long and complicated session on Precedence. Randolf was not showing her anything but his own face at the moment; she had gotten so used to conversing with a disembodied head that it no longer seemed at all odd.

"Oh, you could ask her yourself, it's no secret," Randolf said airily. "But I can tell you easily enough. She pays visits around to other magicians in her Kingdoms; she's likely to start taking you about once you've mastered enough that you can meet them as an equal rather than an Apprentice. And she likes to keep an eye especially on the ones she's turned."

"Well, I can see why," Elena replied, struck that the answer hadn't already occurred to her. "Good heavens, the *last* thing she wants is for one of them to turn back!"

"Hmm, that *would* be a nasty surprise," Randolf replied. "I do suggest to her that she could do so just as well through me, but she seems to think that the *personal* touch is more effective."

"Using both would be a better idea, it seems to me," Elena said judiciously. "After all, even though you might get a better notion of something odd going on by being there yourself, people are on their best behavior when visitors arrive. It's when they're alone, or think they are, that they let things slip."

Randolf *tsked*. "Truer words were never spoken," he agreed brightly. "Like that little pair of turtledoves from the Christening you went to! Bless their hearts, they're so like every other pair of new lovers I've ever watched—they *so* want people to believe that everything is always perfect in their little world! If there was anything wrong between them, you wouldn't see it unless you had *me* look in on them."

"Is there anything wrong?" Elena asked, suddenly anxious. She felt rather—proprietary about those two. She *didn't* want there to be anything going wrong between them—

Randolf laughed. "Bless you, sweetheart, not a bit of it! In fact—well, look for yourself!"

The mirror went to black, and for a long moment, Elena thought that Randolf was having her on, for there didn't seem to be anything at all in the mirror. But then, her eyes gradually adjusted, and she realized she was looking at two deeper shadows silhouetted against the night sky.

Then the moon rose, a huge and golden Harvest Moon, flooding the top of a tower upon which the two were standing, close together.

Arachnia had changed.

It was a subtle change, but to a Godmother's Apprentice, quite noticeable. Her hair was down, cascading over her shoulders and down her back; she still wore black (at least insofar as it was possible to tell in the moonlight) but the lines of her gown were softer. In fact, everything about her was softer. Elena got the vivid impression of a fortress whose walls have not been breached, but eroded, and covered with vines and flowers.

As for her Poet, there were changes in him, too. He stood straighter, and yet there was an easiness about him that had not been there before. In his case, Elena had an image of a man who has put aside a mask he no longer feels compelled to wear.

As Elena watched, Arachnia leaned her head on the Poet's shoulder, and he snugged his arm around her waist as they watched the moon rise. A moment later, she turned her head a little, and he turned his face to meet hers; their lips met, and—

—and at that point Elena couldn't tell if it was the Sorceress who flung herself passionately into the embrace, or the Poet who crushed the Sorceress to him. Probably both. All that she knew for certain was that the two silhouettes became one, and from the way the one was moving, it might not stay upright for very much longer—

And she felt heat rushing to her cheeks, a tightness in her chest, and a slow tingling excitement all over, but particularly centered at the cleft of her legs that—

"Thank you, Randolf, I believe I understand you," she somehow managed. She wasn't sure how. Her throat felt very thick, and her face very warm.

Randolf's guileless face emerged from the blackness. "Nothing wrong *there!*" he laughed. "Unless you're fussy enough to insist on a wedding before the—"

Her flush deepened, and she licked her lips; now it wasn't excitement that filled her, it was frustration, and an emotion she was vaguely surprised to recognize as jealousy. It took a lot of self-control not to snap at him. "Of course not," she said, immensely proud of how neutral her voice was. "If you insisted on *that*, there would be a lot fewer babies born in these Kingdoms."

"I expect they'll have one eventually, though," Randolf continued artlessly. "Wedding, that is, not a baby, though they'll probably have one of those, too. More than one, if they keep on like that all the time."

The jealousy grew, and she finally took herself in hand and mentally sat on it. After all, what right had she to be jealous? "Well," she replied, trying to sound as light and care-free as possible, "if they do that, it will certainly keep Arachnia out of any more mischief."

She couldn't bring herself to say anything more, but fortunately Randolf, who was by nature oblivious to human emotions, began nattering on about something else, and she was able to get herself back under control again. She was even able to laugh at some of his outrageous jokes before she excused herself for the night and went off to her rooms to prepare for bed.

But she did not read as she usually did; instead, she pulled the curtains wide and sat in the window-seat of her bedroom, staring out at the rising moon. Somewhere under that moon, Arachnia and her Poet were locked in a passionate embrace. Elena knew very well what that kind of embrace led to; by the time she'd become "Ella Cinders," no one in the household had cared what she saw. Servants had little or no privacy, and when coupling went on, it happened wherever they could find a corner where they wouldn't be disturbed. The cook and old Jacques had rutted shamelessly in the kitchen, the maids had done it with the footmen in the laundry. No one paid any attention to Ella; it was up skirts and down drawers, and away they went—on a heap of linen, against a wall, a pile of hay in the stable—

Oh, she knew what went on—what was *going* on, somewhere out there, under that bright moon. And that was what she was jealous of.

Because that wasn't just lust; that was *love*. Only love could soften and strengthen two people the way those two had been. Only love could have turned rut into passion. And it had been passion between them. She had *no* doubt of that. Just the memory of it made her heart beat faster, her knees feel weak, and that flush and tingling spread all over her body.

She couldn't say it wasn't fair—first of all, what was fair? Arachnia had endured a horrible childhood, much worse than Elena's, if Madame was to be believed. Maybe she'd done a deal of harm, but not as much as she *could* have, and anyway, she was making up for it now—so who was to say she hadn't earned her happy ending at last? Not The Tradition, and not Elena, and anyway, it was a Godmother's job to make the happy endings, not take them away from someone. Plenty of people got happy endings that some might say they didn't deserve.

Oh, but—

But what? asked a ruthless, inner voice. *Are you going to try to claim that what you have now is not a happy ending? Look at you! Fed, housed, clothed beautifully, with work in front of you that means something—*

Yes, but—

And that isn't enough for you? the voice continued, as her throat thickened and her eyes stung, and the moon blurred a little from unshed tears of loneliness. *Oh, well, aren't we a selfish little bitch! We want it all, do we? And just what have we done to earn it, hmm?*

Nothing, but—

Exactly right. Not even to earn as much as we've gotten! The inner voice was not going to go away. And it wasn't going to be less truthful, either. *Think about the Rosalindas, before you start feeling too sorry for yourself. Think about the other ugly turns The Tradition can take. Then think about how lucky you are that Madame Bella came along, and stop being like the spoiled child who cries herself to sleep because she can't have the moon.*

Now the voice went quiet, and left her alone. She swallowed down the lump in her throat; she wiped her eyes with the back of her hand. That inner voice was right. She knew it was right. And just because she thought she was a little lonely, that didn't stop if from being right.

She needed to take herself in hand, and count her blessings. And she would. She would.

Tomorrow....

But tonight—tonight she would think about how much she wished it *was* her that was in a true lover's arms, and weep for the moon.

Just a little....

By the time the winter snows were calf-deep on the ground, the time that Elena spent as an Apprentice was no longer so much a matter of lessons as it was of practice. Elena knew the theory, virtually everything that Madame Bella could teach; she was not comfortable in it yet, but she knew what to do. And now, unless it so happened that she would ever find herself required for some Great Work, she was as strong in magic as she would ever be. She still had the majority of her own power, and the power she had gotten from Rosalie—twice now, because things were *not* getting better, they were getting worse. The Tradition definitely wanted Rosalie, or her child or both. And it was not giving up.

So Madame Bella began taking her out to actually do the

Godmothering herself, while Madame supervised; most of
it was minor, such as taking the power from Rosalie; once
she played "the old woman at the crossroads," giving the
correct directions to the one young man who was polite to
her, and sending the other four who were not down a long
wilderness road that would leave them in the middle of
nowhere. Another time, she made a point of getting a *particular* pot of flowers into the hands of a young woman, and
once she ensured that a handsome kitten was adopted by
a mill-owner with three sons. She knew what both of those
were about, of course, but it would be years before either
story came to fruition. What was more, neither the Black
Magician nor the Ogre would be remotely aware of what
was coming before it was too late. *They* were too busy fending off knights at the moment to even think about what a
Godmother might be preparing for them.

And last of all, Madame taught her Magical Combat.

With the assistance of the Fair Folk, Elena learned all of
the ways that duels could take place between Magicians—
whether it was the Duel Direct where one threw powerful
magical attacks at the foe, the Transformation Duel where
each magician kept changing his form until one or the other
was able to devour or otherwise incapacitate the opposition,
or the Duel by Avatar where each magician transformed
into a magical monster and physical *and* magical combat
took place between them. And she got as much practice in
dueling as was possible under the circumstances, which was
not a great deal; dueling took such huge stores of energy that
no one really *practiced* it. Instead, they did what she did; they

studied the great combats of the past, and the Fair Folk were the past masters at summoning such things into blazing life.

"I have never actually gotten into combat myself," Madame told her warningly. "Quite frankly, I leave that sort of thing to Sorcerers—it's what they're supposed to do. Just remember, if you are ever in a position where combat can't be avoided, call for help. The best thing you can do is stay out of the way; if you can't, never forget that evil will cheat."

The rest of it was fairly innocuous; selling potions at a market stall, giving advice, sending one young lady on an errand that would intersect her course with a particular shepherd boy who was eminently well-suited to her. Godmothering was as much about small things as large, and about the lives of ordinary people as well as those that The Tradition was trying to steer. And sometimes The Tradition could be as implacable a foe as any twenty powerful Magicians.

"Take you, for instance," said Bella one day. "Suppose, just suppose, mind, you happened to encounter a Prince outside of your role. Because you were supposed to marry a Prince, you *would* be attracted to him, and if he happened to kiss you, you *would* feel the urge to melt into his arms and you might very well fall in love with him. But," she added darkly, "you are a Godmother, not a deserving orphan anymore. You are outside of your role, where he is concerned, and The Tradition could very likely try to put him into another role altogether. The Rake, for instance, the Cad, the Seducer, who will have his way with you, steal your heart, and abandon you. Do you recall my discussion of just how I selected Arachnia's young man? That is why I was so exceedingly careful. If I had not been, *he* could easily have fallen into one of those roles and made things worse, in the end."

Elena felt very uneasy. "And—what if that happened?" she asked.

Bella shrugged. "It is a bitter thing to have your heart broken. That is how Godmothers *themselves* sometimes go to the bad. Just remember, dear, that if you decide to step out of your role, you had better do it in such a way that you thoroughly break with The Tradition, not just try to get around it."

She didn't need to be reminded of that, for The Tradition was in ponderous motion within a few miles of the cottage.

The situation with Rosalie was clearly not going to improve. Despite all of Madame's attempts to prevent it, the young wife when less than a month from confinement was so overcome by a craving for fresh rampion that she could stomach little else, she sent word to Madame immediately. There was little doubt in either Bella or Elena's minds that if she did not get the vegetable soon, she would sicken and perhaps die.

Snow lay a foot thick in every garden. Only magic could produce fresh rampion at this point, and Rosalie knew it. Fortunately, she was stubborn as well as intelligent, and determined that as she had escaped the fate that The Tradition had set for her, so would her child. So she hid her craving from her husband until she could convey her plight to Madame Bella.

Madame called Elena into her study, after hours closeted with Randolf.

"Rosalie *must* have rampion. Randolf has found an Evil Sorceress sniffing around the village. We have little time." She looked searchingly at Elena. "I know what I would do, but what would you do in this situation?"

"First—The Tradition is going to force a magician into that village to grow the rampion to be stolen," she said, slowly. "Is there any reason why that magician cannot be me?"

There was only one possible house in the village that would suit; only one had a great stone wall all the way around it. The Tradition would demand that Rosalie's husband climb a wall or pass some other barrier to steal the rampion.

The fact that it was already occupied was a detail that needed to be taken care of. The Dark One could use trickery, or might simply dispose of the woman and take her place; not being bound by laws or decency made things a bit easier for their kind. It was a trifle more difficult for the Godmother and her Apprentice.

However, a Godmother has many resources at her disposal. Elena never learned what it was that Madame promised to the widow in order to get her to agree to vacate for a month or two, but it was evidently enough to have her packed and gone on the instant. It was only an hour or two after Madame paid the woman a visit, that Elena could move into that isolated, walled house at the end of the village, a house shrouded by tall cypress and pine, usually occupied only by the widow and her two servants. Madame whisked the widow off quietly, in a closed carriage; no one in the village would ever even guess that she had gone. Elena took her place, in disguise, as soon as the carriage was out of sight.

The disguise was made easier by Elena adopting the widow's mourning; to most folk, all black dresses look alike, and the widow held herself so aloof from the rest of the village that so long as her face looked right, it was doubtful that anyone would note a difference in height or weight.

The house was terribly silent compared to Madame Bella's. Elena hadn't really noticed it before, but there was always the sound of *someone* moving about the place; one of the House-Elves at some task or other, Madame bustling about the place, or even Randolf singing to himself in Madame's parlor, or speaking with her about something. The two servants here, however, had very little to do, and had been trained to do it all silently. The house was mostly cold; the only fires were in the kitchen and in the widow's bedroom. The contrast with Madame's cheerful home could not have been more dramatic.

And when Elena went up to the widow's room, she got a bit of another shock; she saw a stranger in the mirror, an older woman, statuesque, aloof, and nothing like *her*.

Madame had arranged this part. It was an illusion, but a very, very good one. Elena reached for the mirror, and the stranger reached back.

Feeling a little shaken by the encounter, Elena went straight to bed. But she slept lightly, and not well. Unless she was watching the house all the time—not likely—the Sorceress would not know that a substitution had been made. Shortly she would make her first attempts to take the widow's place herself. During the night, in fact, Elena woke up twice, hearing *something* sniffing about under the windows, and trying the doors.

She woke the third time as something rattled at a window. It could have been the wind, which had picked up, but she remained wide-eyed and awake until dawn.

As soon as there was light, she went ahead and got up to dress. No sooner had she finished, but there was a knock at the door.

One of the two servants answered it, and summoned Elena in her guise as the mistress of the house.

She had half expected the Evil Sorceress to appear herself, but instead it was a supercilious-looking manservant. He gazed at her down his long nose; *she* was wearing the guise of that wealthy widow, perfectly ordinary in every way, and he evidently didn't recognize her for what she was. He wore a livery so rich with gold braid that if one actually had to buy it, the clothing would probably fetch twice as much as the gown that Elena was wearing.

So, the Sorceress was taking the indirect option. That was interesting. It suggested that she might not be the sort to resort to outright murder. Or at least, not yet.

"My mistress wishes to purchase this house," he began.

"It's not for sale," she said, rudely, and slammed the door in his face. It was not in *her* best interest to give him—or rather, his mistress—a good look at her. A magician's disguise is seldom proof against the probing of another magician; at the least, the other would be able to tell that there was a disguise in place, if not the true identity beneath it.

The knocking began again; she ignored it and directed her servants to do the same, and eventually, from an upper window, saw him trudge away.

The Sorceress was clever, more so than the usual, because the next person she sent was the village constable. A spell on him that Elena could read from her window like one of her favorite books meant to make him think that Elena was to be evicted.

She opened her door to him, and before he got more than the word "You—" out, she struck him with the counterspell. She stood there in the doorway, while he stood stupidly in the snow, trying to remember why he had come there in the first place.

"Well, Constable?" she asked. "Have you come about that prowler the neighbors have been talking about?"

"Ah—" He actually shook himself, then brightened. "Ah, yes, mum. The prowler! Your neighbors said there was something or someone around their walls last night, and it fair gave them a turn. Did you have any sight of him yourself?"

"Not a bit of it," she lied, because of course, there *had* been a prowler around her walls, but if it had been another servant of the Evil One, her protections had probably kept it off. But the neighbors had evidently seen it as well, and been frightened out of their wits.

That was a stroke of luck, though it wasn't anything that she needed to count on. There was always someone in every village who saw prowlers at night, every night, and would berate the constable about them in the morning. "I have stout walls and good locks, and if there *was* a prowler and not something out of the bottom of a bottle, he'd know better than to try my door."

"Right enough, mum," the constable said agreeably, and turned to go about his business. As he left her gate, she saw that he was going to talk to the neighbors. Another stroke of luck; the Sorceress would not be able to get at him until he was alone again, and that might not happen for the rest of the day.

Three times was the usual number for frontal assaults, and sure enough, just after sundown, the Evil Sorceress arrived herself.

She came in full array, parading down the road from the forest in a black carriage drawn by black horses with fiery eyes; "horses" that Elena sensed were not horses at all. Where she walked up the path to the front door, the snow melted. When she struck the door with her fist, it sounded like the pounding at the gates of a tomb. It even shook Elena, and she was ready for it; she had the feeling that the neighbors were all hiding under their beds, shivering.

But now that the moment was at hand, somehow she didn't feel quite so frightened anymore.

In fact, the imperious pounding on the door just woke Elena's native stubbornness, and her anger, too, along with the weapon that Bella had given her. She gathered her courage, made sure she had the weapon in her hand, went to the front door, and flung it open.

The Sorceress's hand was raised for a second volley of knocks. Caught by surprise, Elena did not give her a chance to recover. She jabbed the needle-sharp spindle of a spinning wheel right into the upraised hand.

There was a flash of light and the smell of lightning.

The Spell of Sleep hit the Sorceress like the fist of doom, and she crumpled. It was a good spell; solid and well-turned. It should be; it had been diverted from being used on yet another Princess several years ago. Taking down one Evil Sorceress with the spell crafted by another had a certain satisfying irony about it. And anyway, Madame liked to conserve effort whenever possible. The magic had been expended for this weapon of the enemy; it only made sense to make use of it if they could.

This spell had been meant to hold a Princess for a hundred years. It would only hold an Evil Sorceress for about a month, but that was all that Elena needed.

Now, at last, Robin appeared, from where he had been waiting in the cypresses in case Elena's attack failed. He helped her drag the unconscious Sorceress into the house. Together they installed her in a spare room, arranging her on the bed—then Elena sealed the room with triple bindings to make sure the woman *stayed* there.

As she closed the door, she felt, and saw, the weight of magic around the house shift, and took a deep and steadying breath. The Sorceress was now *in* the house. The real owner was gone, and someone in her image was now mistress of the place. The first part of the tale was complete.

Elena looked out at the walled garden at the back of the building, and was not at all surprised to see the snow melting away from the raised vegetable beds, as if it was springtime, even though it lacked but three days to Christmas. That was The Tradition at work; if the Sorceress herself was not capable of enchanting the garden so that the fateful rampion could grow, The Tradition would take care of that little detail for her.

In a way, the sight was more terrifying than the Sorceress and her dreadful horses at the door. Here The Tradition revealed the power that it could exert in the Five Hundred Kingdoms; here was magic moving and working without any human medium at all. At that moment, Elena felt The Tradition looming over her like a giant wave about to crash down on her, like a silent avalanche about to overwhelm her.

Unless she could direct it. She could not *control* it, but if she was careful, perhaps she could make it work for her.

Elena went to bed, and in the morning, when she checked the garden again, the little plants were already sprouting from beds in which the earth was warm to the touch. Her lips tightened with anger, but she took care not to show it. What she *did* do was to check again to see that the Sorceress was fast asleep.

By Christmas, the rampion was half grown. By New Year's it was full grown, lush, and luscious. And on New Year's Day, Rosalie's husband came over the wall in the early morning, to steal the verdantly green plants for his wife. The roots were at their most perfect, crisp and sweet, about the size of prize carrots, but with a white flesh. Peasant food, which made it all the more ironic, for this peasant food would nourish a peasant child who would, one day, marry a prince.

But only after royal blood had soaked the earth beneath her tower.

Once he came, pulling up a handful of roots before fleeing. Twice, a bit more boldly this time, when no one appeared to stop him. And the third time, in the dusk, Elena was waiting for him, as the Sorceress would have been.

He bent to rip up a plant, hastily, but without a lot of fear. He *should* have been afraid; it should have occurred to him that nothing natural could have produced these plants in the heart of winter. Nothing like this had ever happened in the widow's garden before. He should have realized that there was something very, very wrong.

He was thinking only of his wife, his beloved, the mother of his child-to-be. The widow who lived in this house might be angry at him for stealing her property, but the worst that would happen would be that she would summon the village constable, and the constable was a man with a family himself. There might be a punishment, the stocks perhaps, but everyone in the village knew about pregnant women and their cravings, and the punishment wouldn't be harsh—

—surely—

The Tradition demanded a dramatic entrance, and Elena obliged.

"So!" she cried in a cold voice, stepping out of the darkness in a flash of greenish light. *"Thief!"*

While she wore the widow's face, she also wore the sweeping black gown and winglike cape that the Sorceress had worn, the cape streaming out behind her in a self-created wind. Rosalie's husband dropped to his knees, his face transfixed with terror, the plants falling from his hands.

He might not have been very clever, but he was brave.

He might have blamed Rosalie, but the explanation he babbled out held no touch of accusation for his wife. In fact, he begged only for mercy because Rosalie was with child and would need him; he said nothing of her craving for the magical rampion.

There was no doubt in Elena's mind at that moment why Rosalie loved this man, who would willingly sacrifice himself to save her. But The Tradition had a certain momentum of its own, and it demanded the child. She felt it impelling her on.

Well, she already knew what she would do about this— The Tradition demanded that this child become a part of one of its tales. Very well. She would give it a tale.

A different tale. *Not* Ladderlocks.

"You will take me to your wife," she decreed, sternly. "You have stolen my property; there must be restitution, and there must be punishment. *I* know that your wife's hunger for my plants brought you here. She must pay, as well as you."

He, no less than she, was impelled by the weight of The Tradition. He could not have disobeyed her if he had been possessed of a stronger will and more wits than he actually owned. As if he was sleepwalking, he rose. His face a mask of despair, he led her to his little home, the lovely garden now shrouded in snow, the lights of their home streaming out into the darkness from the open door. Rosalie, now heavily pregnant, stood in the doorway; she was expecting this, and praying that the woman who followed her too-loving husband was Elena, not a stranger.

Still The Tradition demanded this child, and in that, it was too strong even for a Godmother like Bella to withstand. So, the child would be Elena's to do with as she pleased. In that much, The Tradition would be obeyed.

The man stopped, and Elena pushed past him, imperious, and unstoppable. "Come," she said coldly, and head hanging, he obeyed.

One month later, Elena stood again in Rosalie's cottage, this time to look down into the face of a tiny baby. Elena had seen her share of newborns over the years, and most infants looked like wizened, red-faced old men with sour dispositions. This child was enchanting, with a perfect little pink rosebud of a face, and wide blue eyes that stared blankly up at the Apprentice.

This only made her feel terribly guilty about what she was going to do next.

"I'm sorry," she murmured, then took a hard, dried pea, jamming it with her thumb into one of the baby's tender little buttocks, whispering a spell that she *knew* was going to bring pain, until the infant's face crumpled and the mouth opened in a wail of discomfort.

Elena instantly left off torturing the poor little mite, and after making certain that the offending pea was going to leave a satisfactorily livid bruise, handed the baby back to her mother.

And she felt the power shift again. The pea in her hand became oddly heavy, and when she dropped it into the little silver casket she had brought, it nestled into the velvet like a jewel. The Tradition felt what she had done, and had begun to alter its impetus. And even as Elena stood there, she could see the glowing drifts of power leaving Rosalie and beginning a slow, circling spiral towards the baby.

"That's all?" Rosalie whispered, bouncing the baby and hushing her with kisses and petting.

"That's all," Elena replied, then added, as she had to. "For now. You'll lose her when she turns sixteen, of course—" It was, almost as cruel a fate, in a way, but—

Rosalie sighed, and bent her head over the baby. She probably thought that Elena couldn't see that she had wiped a tear away, surreptitiously. "It could be so much worse. And we would lose her to a husband anyway, eventually...."

But it was clear that Rosalie was only waiting for Elena to leave to break down weeping. Who could blame her? Hearing that you will lose your child after only sixteen short years is never easy.

But it could have been so much worse. She could have had Clarissa snatched out of her arms to be locked away from her forever.

Elena left, quickly. She could not bear to be here a moment longer; there was relief in this little cottage, but there was pain as well. When little Clarissa turned sixteen, something would happen to her that would mean that her parents could never see her again, except at a distance, and that was a hard thing for a mother to learn.

Besides, she had another journey to make, and she had borrowed the help of Sergei, the Little Humpback Horse; she wouldn't keep him standing about waiting any longer than she had to.

He stood in the traces of the gaily painted cart, shaking his head sadly. *He* knew what she had been forced to do in order to avert the greater tragedy of the birth of a Ladderlocks child.

"This is a sad thing," he said, and Elena's dragon's-blood gift of the Speech of Animals allowed her to understand him, as she had not been able to the last time she had seen him. "To have your child for only sixteen years—"

"Or to know that she is the cause of many deaths?" Elena replied, climbing into the cart. "Do you know how many young men died to save the *last* Ladderlocks?"

"It is hard to weigh sorrow against sorrow, and I fear you have made the only possible choice," the Horse agreed. "But I cannot like it. Her grief pulls at my heart. Come. Let us be gone from this place." He looked back over his shoulder at the cottage, and his skin shivered all over. "It is better not to linger."

He took off at a trot; once beyond sight of the village, he rose into the air, taking the cart, and Elena, with him. Now she was prepared for the ascent—

Well, as prepared as anyone *could* be. She clutched the wood of the seat as her heart jumped right into her throat. She clenched her eyes tight shut, but then decided that she had to face this some time, and opened them again.

The ground was not very far away. The Horse was just skimming the tops of the trees this time, in fact, he was using the trees to hide their progress from below.

"You ought to put the disguise on," he called over his shoulder. "No one will be surprised to see a Godmother flying in a magical sleigh."

She blinked; Bella was right, the Horse was exceedingly clever. She summoned power from within her and pulling her wand from the pocket of her gown, *pulled* the power into a shape. It drifted just above them, a glowing cloud that only she and the Horse could see. With a shudder of effort, she pulled it down to cover both of them; it settled over the Horse, the cart, and her, and obscured them for just a moment.

Then as he ran on across the treetops, *he* became a snow-white stallion and the cart transmuted into a silver sleigh overflowing with furs.

"Ha!" said the Horse. "Now that's more like it!"

He didn't rise much more than a foot or so higher, though, which made Elena feel very much better. This, she could cope with. She'd climbed all manner of things as a child, before Madame Klovis arrived to blight her life—trees, clock towers, up onto the roof of the house. This wasn't much higher than that. This, she could cope with.

The Tradition demanded a tale; it demanded a tale that had at least a modicum of tragedy about it, and it demanded a tale in which the ending made a Princess of a peasant. There was only one Path that Elena had been able to think of that matched those demands. She was on her way now to meet Madame Bella to establish the second half of the tale's beginnings.

She was, in fact, on the way to a place she had not really expected to ever see again—the Royal Palace of Otraria, where King Colin and Queen Sophia were meeting with the Godmother who had brought them together. Bella was the only possible person to explain all this to them; they trusted her as they did not yet trust her Apprentice, and no wonder. If it had not been for Bella, the Princess (now the Queen) would still be pining away in her room, unable even to smile. And Colin would still be a goose-boy.

Elena was already dressed for the occasion, and not merely as Bella's Apprentice this time, but in the full formal garb of a Godmother when visiting royalty. From the tiara of rosebuds carved from pink crystal in her powdered wig, to the same crystal rosebuds set into the silver buckles of her high-heeled, pink satin slippers, she was garbed as Madame's equal and counterpart, in a pink that favored her coloring, rather than the lilac that favored Madame's. Wrapped in an ermine mantel, her hands in a matching muff, she had probably been an odd sight, sitting on the bench-seat of that little painted cart. Rosalie had been too overcome with emotion to really pay any attention to what the Apprentice was wearing, or perhaps she would have been more than a bit overawed.

They landed well outside the city, and the Horse paused on the road for just a moment. He looked over his shoulder again while she caught her breath and added a little more power to the spell, making the changes *real*, solid, tangible. She very much wanted tangible; she wanted those furs tucked in around her. In this state, she drove to the Palace, and had the rare privilege of seeing people she knew, both well and only slightly, gaping at her with a total lack of recognition.

No one saw Ella Cinders in the fancifully arrayed Godmother—but it was clear from the startled gazes and the sudden deference that the people she passed knew exactly what she was. In a way, she enjoyed it—and in a way, it was rather sad. For the first time, she felt the widening gulf between her, and the people she had grown up among. She had always been lonely, but now she felt *alone*.

The sleigh glided past the Klovis house, which was still unoccupied, and Elena had the melancholy satisfaction of seeing that someone—perhaps the creditors—had actually begun the process of dismantling it. The slate roof was half gone, and the stone wall down to no more than knee high. She suspected that the elegant paneling had been stripped away by now, and any of the built-in furnishings taken out first of all.

When Madame Klovis reappeared, she would have a great deal more to worry about than her missing step-daughter....

What did they think those people who were taking the house apart, bit by bit? Did they ever wonder what had become of the missing Elena? Or had she dropped out of their minds, relegated to some unimportant corner of their memories? "Oh, Elena Klovis—Ella Cinders, you mean? Dunno. Went to the Mop Fair after Madame did the runner, never saw her again. Suppose she must've hired out after all."

The Horse brought the sleigh neatly to the steps of the Palace; a footman hurried to help her alight, and she descended from the sleigh in a swirl of pink silk and white fur. She climbed the steps, the silver-heeled slippers she wore clicking with every pace. Two footmen sprang to hold the brass-bound door open for her. As soon as she was inside, her mantel was taken by another servant stationed just inside the door, and she was conducted immediately by a fourth footman to a small, gold-and-white audience chamber where, as she had expected, Madame was waiting with the King and Queen.

What she had *not* expected was that the Queen would

immediately throw herself at Elena's feet and seize her hand, covering it with grateful kisses and tears.

"Queen Sophia, please!" Elena cried, trying to raise the weeping woman to her feet. "What in heaven's name—"

"Our Godmother decided to do a divination on what would have happened if we'd played unwitting host to the Ladderlocks child in Otraria," said King Colin, white-faced. "It seems that our son would have been the first to die at the hands of the Sorceress who held her captive."

For a moment, Elena really did not understand what had just been told to her. Then, when the meaning struck home, she looked to Madame Bella, who nodded slightly.

"Blessed saints," she whispered, feeling as if she had been hit with a deluge of cold water. "I had no idea—it only occurred to me that the Prince was the right age to be the baby's suitor when she turned sixteen—and that he was near enough to encounter her by chance, perhaps when out hunting—"

Except that the "chance" would not have been "chance" at all. The Tradition would impel the boy—who would be a handsome young man by then—towards the girl as steel was drawn towards a lodestone. The moment she turned sixteen, it would be inevitable. In fact, in either scenario, the Ladderlocks or the Tender Princess, that attraction would have taken place.

But the Ladderlocks would have killed him, it seemed. "When she turned sixteen, even if she was a Ladderlocks—" She faltered.

"But she would not have been rescued until she was eighteen," Madame Bella said quietly. "And before then, the Sor-

ceress would have battened on the potential power of—
well, far too many young men who died trying to bring the
girl away." For The Tradition did that; throwing Questers at
the Quest, even if they died of it, until one of them achieved
it. The power it invested in them would go to the nearest
magician who was ruthless enough to take it. *That* was why
the Dark Ones went along with The Tradition; they could
batten on the power inherent in those who failed, for as long
as they could keep the task so difficult that there would be
plenty of failures.

"And our dear son would have been the first." The
Queen had risen gracefully to her feet, at last, and dabbed
at her tear-streaked face with a dainty, lace-edged bit of
linen. "If you had not had the wit and the will to turn the
infant's tale from one course to another—"

And at that reminder, Elena hastily brought out the tiny
silver casket, in which resided the perfectly ordinary looking dried pea. She pressed it into the Queen's hands—

And there it was; that strange feeling of something looming, then as suddenly settling, turning away. As if a mountain had silently rotated to face a new direction, or an
avalanche "decided" that it would fall some other day.

The path was altered.

"There you are," Elena said, seeing from Bella's expression that she, too, had felt the change. "Keep it safe. And
when, in sixteen years, your son brings home a beauteous
young woman, and your courtiers demand proof that she
is worthy to become their next Queen, place this beneath a
pile of twenty mattresses and announce that this will be the
test to prove that she is of royal blood—for only a Princess

born would be tender enough to feel a pea beneath so much padding."

"We will," Colin pledged, taking possession of the casket. "And until then, it will reside in the Treasury."

Elena felt a little dizzy now with the effort she had expended in resetting the course of the tale, and let Madame do all of the talking after that. Not that there was much of it; even Kings and Queens did not engage in idle chat with one Godmother, much less two. It had occurred to Elena, and more than once, that people were happy to see a Godmother when there was trouble brewing, but as soon as the trouble had been sorted, they were just as happy to see the Godmother go. She wondered if that was the case with all magicians.

Perhaps it is even the case with heroes....

Nevertheless, though King Colin and Queen Sophia were far too polite to make it obvious that Bella and Elena made them uncomfortable, the uncomfortable pauses began to stretch into uncomfortable silences, and at that point, Madame very gracefully stood up and took her leave.

Very shortly after that, Elena and Bella were bundled up together in the sleigh, and the sleigh itself was soaring over the treetops, on the way home.

"Oh, heavens," Elena said, then inexplicably felt herself bursting into tears.

Bella gathered her against her shoulder. "There, now," she soothed. "It's all over. You've given Rosalie a daughter to raise, you've saved Colin's son from death, you've eliminated a Ladderlocks, and—well, I've done something a bit naughty. While you were dealing with Rosalie, I had Arach-

nia discharge some of her misgotten power by further enchanting *our* Sorceress, and locking her up asleep inside a
ring of fire in a cave. It will take a hero to get past the fire
and wake her, and there is quite a warning carved into the
rock bed she is lying on. Maybe if she sleeps for a hundred
years or so, she'll wake up in a better frame of mind."

"And if she doesn't?" asked Elena, through her tears.

Bella shrugged; Elena felt her shoulder move. "She won't
be our problem anymore, she'll be the hero's."

Her ironic tone of voice startled a shaky laugh out of
Elena, who pulled a handkerchief of her own out of a
pocket, and wiped her face with it. "This is horrible,
though—we're taking one woman's daughter away once
she's sixteen, which I think is too young to marry—we're
turning a poor bewildered peasant girl who will barely have
seen a knife, fork, and spoon at place settings together, and
imprisoning her in that golden cage of Manners. And The
Tradition is going to *make* her wed a man she won't ever
have seen before!"

"Rosalie will have her daughter for as long as most
women do," Bella pointed out reasonably, as the Horse increased his pace and the height they were flying at. "The
girl would probably have married as young as fifteen otherwise; most peasant girls wed early. Colin knows very well
what it is like to be a peasant in a King's Court, and he will
see to it that no one is unkind to her while he has teachers
show her how to behave. And last of all, even if she remained with Rosalie, she *still* could have wound up in an
arranged marriage with someone she didn't know!"

Elena blotted her eyes, and had to admit the justice of Madame Bella's words. Most of them, anyway.

"But marrying a man she doesn't know?"

"The Tradition will ensure that she falls in love with him directly when she sees him," Bella replied, patting her hand soothingly, as the Horse tossed his head and whickered agreement. "Colin and Sophia are raising a well-grounded boy; I believe that Clarissa will remain as much in love with her Prince as Colin and Sophia have with each other. Eleven years between their ages is no worse than most royal marriages, and a great deal better than many."

"Maybe, but—" Elena began.

"So what have we possibly done that is wrong?" Madame asked.

"I don't know—but we did the best we could." On that point, at least, Elena was sure. She looked out over the head of the Horse, and saw that they were approaching the cottage. She had never been so glad to see a place in her life. She could talk this over with Randolf; he would understand. She could have a good meal, and Rose and Lily could talk of small things, and she could forget the cruel fates that The Tradition forced on people.

The sleigh touched down with a bump on the snow, and drew up to the front door. Madame patted her hand. "And there you are. That is all we can do, we magicians. The best we can. I think you're ready now."

She was halfway out of the sleigh before she realized what Madame had said. *Ready? Ready? Good heavens, surely not—*

But both her feet were already on the ground; before she

could clamber back in, the Horse tossed his head and the sleigh moved off.

"Madame!" she cried, desperately, panic overwhelming her. "Madame Bella! Please! Come back! You can't! I'm not—"

"You are as ready as I was," Madame called over her shoulder, and the sleigh rose into the sky, over the treetops, and vanished among the clouds, leaving her standing on what was now *her* doorstep, now the Godmother of some Seven Kingdoms.

And she had never felt more alone, or been more terrified in her life.

10

Deep in the middle of decanting a tincture, Elena heard the sound of something *crunching* in the garden, just outside the window of the stillroom. "Crunching" was not the sort of sound you wanted to hear coming from the kitchen garden. She looked up, already prepared to yell at whatever was out there.

She was not sure just *what* it would be—there was supposed to be a barrier that kept things like rabbits and deer out, but sometimes the spells failed. And such spells did nothing to keep out other visitors, some of whom seemed to be of the opinion that the garden had been planted for *their* benefit.

There was a Unicorn in the garden, eating the new peas,

daintily taking each pod and munching them up between his strong white teeth with every evidence of enjoyment. Elena thrust her head out of the window, indignantly.

"You!" she shouted at him. "Shoo! I put out an entire flower bed of lilies for you lot, go eat *those!*"

The Unicorn looked up, and focused his attention on her. Then went cross-eyed with the immediate onset of the stupefied devotion every Unicorn was overcome by when in the presence of a virgin. His big brown eyes misted over, his ears swiveled towards her, and his ivory horn began to glow with magic. Unicorns, like the Fair Folk, were practically made of magic; Elena made a note to ask one of the mares later if the stallions who kept coming around would be willing to allow her to siphon some of it off. If they were going to plague her and eat her garden, the least they could do was to contribute to the cause, so to speak.

It was no use asking the stallions, of course. They went entirely idiotic at the sight of her. The mares went idiotic, too, of course, but only for virgin *boys*. Fortunately, those were in even shorter supply than virgin girls....

"Don't like lilies," he said, absently, around a mouthful of pods he had forgotten to chew the moment he spotted her. Half chewed pods fell out of his mouth as he spoke. He had, of course, also forgotten that he was supposed to look noble. "Like peas."

"Well I don't care!" she snapped in irritation. "You'll eat the lilies, and you'll *learn* to like them."

"Ah," the Unicorn replied, then dreamily turned and looked at the bed of pastel lilies on the edge of the garden.

He turned his bearded head back to look at her. "If I eat the lilies, may I lay my head in your lap?"

"No, you may not—" she began, then at the sight of his ears drooping with dejection, changed her mind. She could spare a minute or two. "Oh, all right."

The Unicorn's head and ears came up, and his tufted tail flagged. He trotted over to the lily bed, and began eating with unbridled—well, of course, unbridled—enthusiasm.

A Unicorn would do just about anything that a virgin asked of him.

Elena finished her potions and dried her hands, before going out into the garden with a feeling of resignation. This was the fourteenth Unicorn loitering about, eating up the garden this spring. The first one had taken her breath away, and it was only after an entire afternoon spent petting him that she realized that he had destroyed the roses. She'd been warier at the second. She was getting tired of them now. Why had there never been Unicorns when Madame Bella was the Godmother here?

Maybe because she didn't qualify as a Unicorn attractor....

As soon as she sat down on the wooden seat that Robin and Lily had fitted around the trunk of the apple tree, the Unicorn knelt at her side and his head dropped into her lap, his round, brown eyes gazing up at her soulfully. With a sigh, she stroked his head and scratched behind his ears, while he moaned in ecstasy.

"Shouldn't you be making those sort of noises at a mate?" she asked, crossly. What *was* it about virgins that made them go so idiotic?

"Not until autumn, Godmother," the Unicorn replied,

shivering all over at her touch. "Oh. Uh, I was sent. I'm supposed to tell you something."

She waited, still scratching. Unicorns were not the brightest of beasts at the best of times—they tended to remind her of highly inbred lapdogs, to tell the truth, all beauty and no brains. There was no point in rushing him while the stray thought fluttered around in his thick skull like a butterfly in a box, and he tried to catch it.

At least once you told one something, he never forgot it. It might take him a while to remember what it was, but he never actually *forgot* it.

"Questers," he said at last. "In Phaelin's Wood. For the Glass Mountain. Three Princes. They came just after Karelina left. There's no one there to guide and test them."

Ah. That explained why he was here; she'd had a message yesterday morning by way of Randolf that the Witch of Phaelin's Wood was off attending to a difficult birth that had a lot of Traditional potential behind it. Twins, if you please, which meant that someone had to be there, not only to make sure that mother and babies survived the birth, but to figure out just what The Tradition was going to try to do with them. Karelina had the same problem with Unicorns that Elena had. She too had a Mirror-Slave, inherited from her Grandmother the previous Witch, and she had sent a message by way of Randolf this morning that she was going to be out of her Wood for a while. Well, this meant that no one would be able to meet the Questers at the crossroads and test them unless Elena took the task herself. "Did Karelina send you?" she asked. Karelina might be away from her mirror, but she was never far from a Unicorn.

The Unicorn gave another faint moan of pleasure, but answered, sensibly enough, "Yes. We came and told her that they had gone in, and she sent me to you. She's put the tanglefoot on their path until you can get to the crossroads."

The "tanglefoot" spell would make sure that all three of the Questers would travel in circles without realizing it, and without meeting each other, until Elena got into place. Small wonder that the woods that Questers entered always seemed to be much bigger than they had thought!

At least in this case, she was going to have no crisis of conscience over the quest. King Stancia of Fleurberg had only one child, a daughter, and he was old. He was understandably concerned that the husband she took be clever, intelligent, and kind, as well as strong, iron-willed, and tough, because he knew that *he* was probably not going to be around for very much longer to protect her from the consequences of a bad choice. He had a great many neighbors, most of whom had several sons—and he also wanted to be sure that whoever wedded his daughter would rule his Kingdom as Stancia would have wanted.

So he had obtained the services of a powerful Sorcerer, and placed her in a tower atop a mountain—

The mountain wasn't really glass, or at least, it wasn't man-made glass, and the tower was hardly a place of imprisonment. The mountain was volcanic; there *were* obsidian boulders and shards everywhere, and it would take a very strong man with immense stamina merely to endure the path to the top. To complicate matters further, there were many tests and trials for anyone who wanted to earn the reward of her hand and throne. As for the tower, it was the Sorcerers' own home, and the Princess was, by all reports, having a delightful time exploring it.

The King and the Sorcerer had been very careful in deciding what trials the Questers would face. Unless a man was very stupid, or exceedingly stubborn, there was no chance that anyone would actually *die* along the way—not unless he kept trying until he perished of exhaustion or did something monumentally foolish. Everyone understood The Tradition in this case, and making it work *for* them. The Sorcerer had a great many truly dreadful tests of courage, intelligence, quick-thinking, and so forth set up once the Questers set foot on his mountain.

But the first of these trials was the simplest, and it weeded out any seeker who was *not* kind, generous, and unselfish. There were at least a dozen magicians who were tasked to provide this particular test, and for once, it was something that Elena had no second thoughts in agreeing to, not now, and not when she had first heard of the Quest.

She gave the Unicorn one last scratch, and pushed his head out of her lap, gently. "All right," she said. "The sooner I get on my way, the sooner I get this over with. And *you* can't lie here in my lap all day, either. Now, shoo."

The Unicorn heaved a final, sorrowful sigh, got to his feet, cast a last, longing look at her, and slipped off into the forest.

Elena stood looking after him for a moment, shaking her head. "Unicorns!" she said, to nobody at all. "I'm not surprised they're easy to hunt. It's a good thing for them that the bait is so hard to find."

Then she went back into the cottage to get her stoutest walking shoes and a staff.

Poor old Dobbin had finally dropped dead of extreme old age last February, and she still hadn't replaced him, so she was going to have to get to where she needed to go by walking.

Well—sort of.

She pulled out her wand—the simple one today, anything else would be drastically out-of-character for the old peasant woman that she was going to appear to be. She released a tiny packet of power, and sent it into the path ahead of her, concentrating on where she was *now*, and where she wanted to be—the crossroads in the middle of Phaelin's Wood, which would be where she would meet and test the Questers. She held up her staff. "Shorten my way, please," she told the path.

The glowing power circled over her head like a swarm of tiny star-bees, then dropped down and *zoomed* down the path, out of sight in a moment. The forest became very still for a moment.

And then she felt the path shiver beneath her feet, and braced herself. She knew what was coming. She hadn't necessarily expected *this*, but this was a forest that the Fair Folk as well as many other magical creatures lived in, and when that happened, even inanimate objects and bits of landscape could take on a life of their own.

The path rose up about a foot beneath her, and suddenly began to move.

She'd done this before, when Bella was still the Godmother. *She* remained perfectly still, but the path was carrying her along on top of a little mound, at a pace that a horse would be hard put to equal. The last time she'd cast the Way-Shortening spell, the path hadn't moved, but every step she'd taken had covered a dozen yards. And the time before that, she'd apparently re-awakened the remnants of an "All Forests Are One" spell, because she just strolled down the path a few yards and found herself where she wanted to be.

It was a chancy thing, living in a magical forest. Things tended to get minds of their own. Not long after Bella turned over the position to Elena, one of the few true Fairy Godmothers had paid a call, and had told Elena that the cottage and the forest had once been the home of another of the original Fairy Godmothers, and had hinted that this uncanny semi-intelligence of the very forest itself was a common thing where the Fair Folk dwelled. Elena had not precisely gotten used to it, but she was no longer surprised by what happened.

She had also taken to saying "Please" and "Thank you" when the forest responded with something to help her. Anything that allowed her to conserve power was a fine thing, and if the forest was going to help her, she was willing to let it help her in its own way.

Bella had never stood for that sort of thing; when she'd cast a spell, she by-Heaven wanted the *same* spell to do the *same* thing, every time, and no free-will nonsense. But that took a lot more power—and perhaps because of coming from a childhood where the next meal was not taken for granted, Elena did not feel at all comfortable with simply using all the power that was available to her. Instead, her style was to use the minimum possible to get the result she wanted, and if the *means* to that result was a bit unnerving now and again, well, that was the chance she was willing to take.

Elena leaned forward a little, into the wind created by her passing, and the path responded by speeding up still more. She hoped that there was no one else actually *on* this path— if she came up on them before they had a chance to get out of the way, they'd be bowled over like tenpins. As it was, there were half a dozen small animals left scattered to the right and left of the path in her wake.

Still, it was a novel form of transportation, and peculiarly enjoyable—like running, but without the effort. She was almost disappointed when she felt the path begin to slow, recognized the landmarks, and knew she was nearly at journey's end.

The path dropped her gently where the road that would ultimately lead out of Otraria crossed the one that led to the Kingdom of Kohlstania. And Kohlstania was, presumably, where the three Princes were coming from.

Elena stepped out into the road and sat down on a stone at the crossroads, taking a little book out of her pocket. Now *this* was a very useful bit of conjury that she had worked out for herself, and she was terribly proud of it. Working with the spell that allowed a Godmother or other powerful magician to copy his or her chronicles to the libraries of other magicians, *this* little book was able to repeat what was on the pages of every other book in her library, if she knew what to ask for.

She opened the blank pages, waved the head of her staff over them, and let a little sparkle of power drift down over them. "The current Royal Family of Kohlstania, please," she ordered.

Something appeared, like blurred writing beneath a smudge; a moment later, the writing resolved itself, and so did the smudge, and she saw an image of the stern visage of a man who appeared to have never laughed in his life. *King Henrick of Kohlstania*, read the caption beneath the picture. *Widower, three sons—*

Yes, those would be the Questers—

—has held the throne for twenty-seven years. Took the crown in— She skipped the rest, and moved on to the next page. Three more smudges resolved into three more drawings. Three young men. Octavian, Alexander, Julian. Well, it was easy enough to see where this tale was going. Octavian and Alexander looked like hard, uncompromising men formed in the image of their stern father. Julian, however, must have taken after the now-gone mother; while no one could possibly say that he looked *soft*, he certainly looked *softer*, and there was a very gentle and humorous look to his eyes that Elena liked quite a bit.

"Laws, attitude and recent history in Kohlstania regarding magic, magicians, and Godmothers, please," she said aloud, and the pages filled with notations. She read through it all swiftly; nothing there to be particularly concerned about, although there had not been any magical intervention in a major way in the Kingdom for three generations. There was, in fact, no one alive there who had any experience of any magician more powerful than a Witch, much less a Godmother, and Witches and Hedge-Wizards were creatures that the country-folk depended on, not city-dwellers, and certainly not the upper crust of nobility.

For the King and his family, magic was probably a thing

of nursery-tales, and this did not seem like a family in which nursery-tales were encouraged.

On the whole, that was not a bad thing at all. It meant that none of the young men would even guess she was testing them. She closed the book and put it back in her pocket.

Now, because Elena liked to conserve power as much as possible, she had a number of clever ways to do things using a minimum of magic that Bella would have accomplished with several spells. And the next item she pulled from her pocket was a false nose.

It was a particularly beaky object, carved and colored by Robin, and held onto her face by means of two pink ribbons that tied in the back. Ludicrous, one might say—until she put it on.

For the nose was ensorcelled with a spell of illusion; whoever put it on would appear as an old crone or an old man. In this way, Elena only ever had to cast *one* disguise spell; thus conserving her power and allowing her to disguise other people as well, if there was need. She was rather proud of herself for coming up with such a thing.

She tied on her false nose over her real one, and although *she* felt no differently, anyone looking at her would have seen a bent and feeble old woman with a great beak of a nose and a dowager's hump. Her hair had gone from golden to white as snowdrops; her face was a mass of wrinkles and her hands were spotted with age.

Although she was *standing* straight, she would appear to have a dowager's hump, and her clothing aged just as she had. The colors faded, the seams took on the look of having been unpicked and resewn as the cloth was turned and turned again, and the hems looked tattered.

Now she was ready.

She looked down at the crossroads at her feet; there were conventions that any Witch would have followed, the more especially when she knew that someone else would have to take up the task in her place. Karelina had, as expected, cast the tanglefoot spell from this very crossroads. There were three threads to the skein, one for each Prince, ending in a knot practically at her feet.

She took her staff and touched it to the knot. Tradition must be served; eldest must be tested first. "Octavian," she said aloud, and a little spark of power jumped from the wand and ran down the thread to release him from the spell and bring him to her.

Prince Alexander of Kohlstania was hot, thirsty, and exasperated. It was quite bad enough that he found himself on this ridiculous "Quest," though he could certainly understand his Royal Father's reasoning, but to have been wandering in this stupid forest for days was outside of enough. Now he was sorry he had ever agreed to this—

But I had to, he reminded himself. All of Kohlstania's immediate neighbors were, if not allies, at least not overtly hostile, but King Henrick had not held his throne for this long by being naive. King Stancia did not particularly *care* about the politics of the man who would win his daughter and his throne, so long as that man would treat daughter and country alike with care and gentleness. How he treated his neighbors did not matter a whit to Stancia, although he certainly would never actually come out and admit that.

Father is right. We can't just sit by and hope that whoever won the girl would follow Stancia's policies. King Henrick could not take the chance that some enemy would win girl and country, and then proceed to sit on Kohlstania's border and cast covetous eyes on what Henrick ruled as well. Stancia's land was prosperous, and could easily afford to field a large army. This would never do.

He had gathered his three sons before him the moment that he got the messenger from Stancia throwing open the contest to any and all comers. "You will go to Fleurberg, and one of you will conquer this so-called 'Glass Mountain' and win and wed the girl," he ordered. "If it is you, Octavian, all to the good; we can unite the Kingdoms into one. If it is you, Alexander, that will be excellent too, since it will give you a Kingdom of your own. If it is you, Julian— which, may I add, I do *not* anticipate—" he had cast a jaundiced eye on his youngest son then "—at least we will be spared having to try to find something for you to do with your life."

Alexander also understood why his father had given his youngest son such a poisonous look. Julian was considered by the King and by his eldest brother to be a fool and a dreamer. Alexander, nearer in age to Julian, was not so sure of *that*, but he doubted whether Julian had the necessary abilities to go through whatever tests Stancia was going to put in front of them. Most likely he would be eliminated at the first. Poor Julian; he seemed content enough with his lot, but Alexander wondered, sometimes, if it was all a facade.

But maybe he simply didn't have any ambition at all, and was perfectly happy with his books and his horses.

Octavian had been the first out of the gates, somewhat to Alexander's chagrin. He would have thought that being heir to one Kingdom was enough, but apparently not. With the prospect of not one, but *two* Kingdoms within his grasp, one of which he would not have to wait for (or at least, not very long, since Stancia was well over sixty), Octavian had ordered up his provisioning and been in the saddle within an hour.

Alexander had taken longer; he hadn't left until later that afternoon, for he had been taking careful consideration of what he should and should not pack, and had decided to forego speed for preparation. *He* had a packhorse tied to the back of the saddle of his destrier. He did not intend to fail one of the tests because he lacked, say, fifty feet of rope, or a storm-lantern that the wind could not blow out.

When he had left, Julian was still not ready, and oddly enough, he seemed to be taking as little as Octavian. Furthermore, he wasn't taking any armor, and in fact, was carrying little more than his sword and a bow by way of weapons.

For a moment, Alexander had considered staying long enough to advise him, but he shrugged the impulse off. Octavian would probably fail this Quest for lack of preparation; well and good, he was the heir, and he already *had* his Kingdom guaranteed. Julian would fail because of foolishness, and too bad for him; well and good, that would get him out of Alexander's way.

He had trotted off on his best warhorse in a very positive frame of mind. This "Quest" should cause him no great difficulty; he was prepared for every possible eventuality. *He* was the one, after all, who had been sent to military school, and had learned everything there was to know about tactics and campaigns. Octavian, though the elder, could not best him on that score, and Octavian's haste and greed would probably be his undoing.

Not that he *blamed* Octavian. Their Royal Father showed no signs of shuffling off the mortal coil any time in the near future, and Octavian was not the sort of fellow to enjoy sitting about, kicking his heels, as the King-In-Waiting. Not that any of them *wanted* the King to die—or at least, Alexander didn't think either of the others did—but it was hard to be trained to rule but not actually get a chance to do so.

As for Alexander, he had long ago resigned himself to playing Commander-In-Chief to the Army of Kohlstania under his brother's rule for the rest of his life. He *wanted* a Kingdom of his own, and although he would rather it had come without the need to marry some brainless bit of fluff probably spoiled into uselessness by her father, he would put up with the girl to get the throne. This opportunity was *not* going to slip through his fingers; Princesses and thrones for the taking were not presented to one on a platter every day, even if one was a Prince himself.

He thought that he would be generous once he had won, and find Julian some pretty young heiress to marry, once he had settled into the position. He *liked* Julian well enough— certainly more than Octavian did, and Julian would be much more comfortable in Alexander's court than in Octavian's.

And far more comfortable than under Father's eye.

He had been full of these plans right up until he got well into these cursed woods and found the first night falling without any sign that he was going to get *out* of them before darkness fell. And without any sign that Octavian was on the road ahead of him, either, though initially that didn't worry him as much as the coming of darkness.

Of course he had made camp—an excellent camp—long before the last of the twilight had faded. And because he had made careful provisioning, he had not gone hungry or cold, either. But he *had* gone to sleep seriously concerned. For where was Octavian?

He had a map, of course, and a compass, so *he* could not be lost, and at any rate, the road simply didn't branch at all until it came to a marked crossroads. Therefore, Octavian must have somehow strayed off the road, unlikely though that seemed. There was, of course, the possibility that he could have been waylaid, but Alexander had interrogated peasants outside the woods very carefully before he went in, and they had all assured him that there were no bandit bands living in Phaelin's Wood. There might, they said, be a robber or two, but there were no *groups* of outlaws. And no single robber could have overcome Octavian, even Octavian only lightly armed.

Besides, there had been no sign of a struggle anywhere. Octavian would *never* have given up without a fight.

He had gone to sleep still worrying over the problem, and not really even thinking about the fact that this Wood, which he should have crossed in a few hours, was still all around him.

However, the longer he traveled the next day, the more he began to think that there was something more going on than met the eye. He had certainly been thinking about that very problem when he camped for the second night.

He had gotten out his map and compass at first light, and gone over them, and then his irritation had only increased. The road on the map ran straight and true right to a crossroads in the middle of the Wood. The road he had been following had twisted and turned like a snake in its death-throes. The road on the Map represented a journey of no more than half a day to cross the Wood entirely. He had been here for two days now, and there was still no sign of the crossroads!

Which left only one answer. And it wasn't that he was lost.

"Magic," he said aloud, savagely. *Someone* was plaguing him with some sort of magical impediment.

He did not *like* magic. It was not logical, it was not ordered, and any sort of riff-raff could use it. It might have been a very useful weapon in war, but the trouble was, the only time that the so-called "good" magicians would consent to do such a thing was when you were fighting against an "evil" magician. You could employ an "evil" magician, of course, but you could never trust him not to turn on you, and anyway, the moment you made use of such a tool, every "good" magician for hundreds of leagues around would come fight for your enemies because you were using an "evil" magician.

And then there were the other things that were associated with magic—beasts and birds and things that were neither, people who did not answer to any laws that *he* recognized and could not be depended upon to act logically. He didn't like any of them. When you fought a man, you should be able to use straightforward tactics on him, and not have to wonder if he was going to set fire to you. When you met a woman, you should be able to tell at a glance what her station in life was, and know what to expect from her, and not have to wonder if she would seduce you or let you think you were seducing her, and then wake up turned into a pig.

No, he did not like magic at all, and if this was King Stancia's idea of a good first test—

It might well be, too. He'd heard a rumor that Stancia had got the aid of a Sorcerer in setting up this Quest. Sorcerers had a habit of showing complete disregard for such niceties as borders. The Sorcerer might think it amusing to set the first "test" in Phaelin's Wood, on the Kohlstania side of the border.

The more he thought about it, the angrier he became. He packed up his camp, seething, and mounted his destrier in a foul mood. Magic! It might as well be cheating!

Wretched magicians. Stupid, senile old men who depended on them. Well, *he* would show them! From now on, he would depend on his compass and not the map, if he had to cut his own road to do so.

He took his compass out of the saddlebag and opened the case with a smirk that swiftly turned to a teeth-clenched frown.

For the compass needle was spinning merrily, with no sign that it intended to stop.

Magic!

* * *

Elena waited, sitting on a rock in the concealment of a dense clump of birch-saplings, just before the crossroads. She had the advantage that the crossroads itself was on the far side of a relatively cleared space in the forest; she was able to get a good long look at the Questers as they emerged from the denser growth. The first Prince, Octavian, approached on a great bay warhorse looking rather the worse for two nights spent in the forest. He was wearing light armor, but he didn't seem to have a great deal of kit about him, and it showed in his appearance. From the look of him—moving stiffly, dark circles under his eyes, twigs in his hair—he'd spent both nights on the ground, under the stars, with his saddle for a pillow. All three boys had reminded her of animals, actually—Julian an amiable hound and Alexander an arrogant and rather sleek fox. This one was the gruff wolf, and the resemblance was only heightened by his state.

She waited on her rock, quietly, to see if he'd notice her. She saw his eyes flicker towards her, then saw, just as clearly, that he dismissed her as unimportant.

Oh, yes, do that. She waited until he was just passing her before speaking up.

"Have ye a crust of bread, milord?" she whined. "They've turned me out as too old to work, and I'm perishing of hunger."

He ignored her. She raised her voice. "Please? Milord? Please, good sir?"

Nothing.

Now, at this point, he *could* have stopped, offered her something, and asked for directions. She would have given them to him. She would *not* have told him the keys to the puzzles that the Sorcerer was going to set him, but at least he would have gotten to the Glass Mountain.

He did neither; he rode on as if she was of no more importance than a beetle.

Fine, she thought, and touched her staff to the path again as he rode out of sight under the trees.

> *"Twist me and turn me, and bring me to grief.*
> *Muddle my pathway and give no relief.*
> *Send me to wander a month and a day,*
> *Give me no guidance and keep me astray.*
> *Then when a month and a day will have sped,*
> *If I am kinder and my pride's been shed,*
> *Then send me on homeward.*
> *But if I'm too high*
> *Then keep me astray till a year has gone by."*

There, that would take care of him. He'd stumble along in Phaelin's Wood—and possibly several others, if Kare-lina decided to invoke the "All Forests Are One" spell against him when she got back—and he'd do so while his provisions ran out, spring thunderstorms deluged him, and every possible minor disaster that could would arise to plague him. After a month and a day of this, if he'd learned his lesson, he'd finally come out of the Wood right where he went in. If he was smart, he would go home again. If he wasn't—well, Karelina would have to decide what to do with him. Hopefully, he would come out a humbler and wiser man than he'd been when he went in a mere month, because otherwise he'd be stumbling around for the next year.

Smiling to herself, she touched her staff to the path again, on the knot representing the tanglefoot spell. "Alexander," she told it, and the spark of power leaped from the wand and raced down the tangled skein of the spell.

It was not more than an hour later that she heard hoof-beats on the road, and saw her quarry approaching. And she had to give him a few points for preparation, anyway. Unlike his brother, he not only was fully armed but he had a packhorse laden with armor and apparently quite a bit of other luggage as well. From the look of things, *he* had not been spending his last two nights huddled next to a pathetic little fire. She hid behind her sapling screen and waited to get a good look at him before he could see her.

Elena parted the branches of the birches and peered through them as the sound of hooves on the path stopped. And there he was, framed by two of the saplings, looking exactly as he had when she'd seen him in the book. He had stopped at the edge of the clearing that held the crossroads, frowning.

Truth to tell, she hadn't paid a lot of attention to his appearance, other than to make sure she wouldn't mistake him for some other Prince-errant, or one of his two brothers. Now, as he paused staring at the crossroads, his frown turning into a scowl as he tried to make up his mind which way to go, she studied him.

And she didn't much care for what she saw. Not that he wasn't handsome enough; he was all of that. His wavy brown hair, thick and shining, fell down past his shoulders, giving him a very romantic appearance, especially combined with the rakish tilt of his cap, and the fact that he was much better groomed than his older brother. Of course, part of that was due to the fact that he hadn't been sleeping in the open, but still....

Vain, she thought to herself, cynically. *I've never yet seen a long-haired man who wasn't a popinjay. And clean-shaven, too. He must spend as much time in his valet's hands as any primping girl.*

As for his face—square chin, chiseled cheekbones, broad brow—well, it was shapely enough, even if his nose was entirely too aquiline to suit her.

He could plow a field with that nose.

But the regular features were spoiled entirely by the unpleasant frown, and the furrowed brow, and the air of unbending rigidity about him that, together with a tunic that managed to suggest a military uniform without actually being one, made her think that this was a man for whom there was, always and for everything, One Right Way from which he would never deviate. Even when it was wrong.

Well, this isn't going to be much fun, she thought with resignation. And with a sigh, steeling herself for unpleasantness, she stepped out onto the path. If The Tradition held true to form, the first Prince had been merely rude and haughty— this one would be haughty and rude *and* arrogant *and* aggressive.

His frown deepened the moment he saw her, if that was possible. What was more, he added suspicion to the emotions of irritation and arrogance on his face.

Suspicion! What could he possibly suspect her of?

"Have ye a crust of bread to spare, good milord?" she quavered, holding empty hands out towards him. "They've—"

"I have nought to spare," he interrupted. "Get from my path, old hag."

Well! Not that she'd expected politeness, but that really was more than a bit much. Still, she kept hold of her temper, reminding herself that she *was* the Tester here, and she could make sure he got sent down an even longer path to wander than his brother. "But, milord," she whined pathetically. "They've turned me off as too old to work, and I'm—"

"Then find work or die," he said, now turning his frown away from her and looking about, as if trying to find something that might be hidden. "Those who cannot work, will not be fed. We'll have no beggars here."

You wretched little— Once again she caught hold of her temper. But something like this could not go unpunished, and wandering around for a month or even a year was not going to teach this arrogant lad what he needed to learn. No, this was something that needed a more imaginative punishment.

Still, she would give him one more chance. But if he failed this time, she was going to take his lessoning into her own hands. "But can you—"

He ignored her, as his brother had. Instead he touched the spur to his horse's flank, and rode straight at her at a canter, so she had to scramble out of his way or be run down.

Now she was angry. What if she *had* been a poor old

woman? She could have been hurt, or even killed! What right had he to run people over as if they were nothing?

Oh, that tore it. As he passed, she whirled, and took her staff in both hands. *"You!"* she cried out in her own voice, pointing it at him.

Startled by the change in her voice, he pulled up his horse and turned in his saddle to stare at her.

She did not bother with a rhyme this time; the force of her anger was more than enough to shape the power. She aimed her staff at him, like an accusation. *"You are as ill-mannered, as stubborn, and as stupid as an ass!"* she shouted, *"So* BE *one!"*

The power exploded out of her, coursed down her arm, and shot from her staff in a stream of red-gold light. If he'd had eyes to see it, he'd have been terrified. It hit him full on, covered him, enveloped him in a single moment, hiding him from sight inside a great globe of light that held him and the horse he was riding on.

He cried out in fear, though, as he felt *it* take him. And in the next moment, the cries changed, deepened, and hoarsened. The globe pulsed; once, twice, and on the third time, there was another flash of light.

There were three beasts on the path now, not two. A great bewildered warhorse, the packhorse tied to its saddle, and—

—and a donkey, standing petrified, all four hooves splayed, still trying to wheeze out a terrified bray.

"Hah," she said, looking at him with satisfaction. "I need a donkey. You'll do."

He was clearly in a great deal of shock, too much so to

move—though likely if he had tried, he'd have fallen to the ground, for he was not used to moving on four feet instead of two. She had plenty of time to rummage through his packs, find the rope she was sure was in there, and fashion a crude nose-pinch halter and choke rope, and get it on him before he even began to react to his much-changed situation.

And by the time he did, she had him right where she wanted him. If he tried to rear, she could choke him at the neck. If he tried to bite, she could pinch off his nose and choke his breathing from that end.

He tried both, not once, but several times, until she finally picked up her staff and pointed it at him again.

He froze.

"You *will* behave," she told him, "Or I'll take your horse instead of you, and turn *you* into a frog."

At that, his ears flattened against his head, but it was clear he didn't doubt either her ability or her willingness to do so. Instead he allowed her to lead him, stumbling, into the cover of some bushes and tether him there, the horses beside him. She wasn't going to take any chances, though; she used more of the rope for hobbles, and tethered all four feet.

She waited until she was back on the road before she took a deep breath, paused, and steadied herself. She was still angry with him, and that was no mood to be in to Test the last of the Princes. She counted to ten twice, took another deep breath, and let the anger run out of her. When she was sure she was steady again, she shook herself all over, and took her staff in hand.

Besides, this would be the easy one.

"Right," she said aloud, to the empty air, and touched the staff to the knot of the tanglefoot spell. *"Julian."*

And for the third time, the spark of light sped away.

11

Alexander suspected that the appearance of the old woman was some sort of trick; how had she gotten out here, anyway? She didn't look as if she could travel six feet, much less limp her way into the middle of the wood! She might be the bait for a trap, or something in disguise, and if he stopped for her, the trap would be sprung. All he could think of was that if he charged her, she'd get out of his way, and whatever magic the Sorcerer had been hexing him with might be broken. Then she'd shouted *"You!"* and he'd been stupid enough to stop and turn to look back at her. Then he knew, the moment that he saw the old hag pointing a stick at him, that he had been right. Someone *had* been working magic against him—but it had been *her*, not some Sorcerer working for King Stancia! But he didn't even have a chance to duck, much less do anything about her, before she shouted out something else.

Something about being as arrogant and rude as an ass—

And in the next moment, he was engulfed in more pain than he had ever felt in his entire life put together. It felt as if his bones were melting and his insides turning to water; he tried to cry out, but his very voice changed, and he felt himself falling off his horse and hitting the ground on all fours, and—

Well, he really didn't know *what* it felt like then, for there were no words to describe how it seemed as if he was made of warm wax, and a pair of giant hands was remolding him. Remolding even his head. His eyes felt as if they were going to pop out of their sockets, his mouth like something had hold of his teeth and lips and was stretching his face, and his ears—well, they burned and hurt past all reason. Then as if that wasn't enough, he began to *itch*.

Finally, as quickly as it had come upon him, the pain left him. But it left him dazed and very confused, because now, although he could see exceedingly well to either side, and somehow actually see *behind* his head, he couldn't see much of anything that was straight ahead of him. And when he tried to stand up—he couldn't.

And when he looked down at his feet, he saw four hooves.

Four hooves?

The old hag! What she'd said! *"You are as stubborn as an ass! So* BE *one!"*

He blinked. He stared. The sight did not change. Four

hooves—and if he craned his head around, he saw a round, barrel-shaped body covered with grey hair, and a tufted tail.

If his legs hadn't been locked at the knees, he'd have fallen to the ground. If his throat hadn't been choked with despair, he'd have howled.

She'd done more than confuse his path. She'd turned him into an animal.

He scarcely noticed that the old hag had come up to him, until it was too late, and she had some sort of fiendish torture device made of his own rope around his neck and nose. Too late, he tried to fight her, and finally, when after the third time she choked off his breathing until he began to black out, he gave up.

He allowed her to drag him into the shelter of some bushes, and watched with even greater despair as she hobbled him so he couldn't move. Then she went back to the crossroads.

So this is what happened to Octavian? he thought, dully. He could not imagine why; what enemy had managed to set a Witch on his family? Had the business with Stancia and the Glass Mountain all been a ruse to lure them into this cursed forest and her clutches? *I wonder what she turned Octavian into....*

Oh, bloody hell! What if she'd turned him into a bug, or a frog! What if he'd *trampled* his own brother? He tried to fight the hobbles, and all he did was nearly fall over; his horses stared at him down their long noses with astonishment, as if they couldn't imagine what he was doing or why he was there. He tried to fight the ropes around his neck, but the Witch had tied them cunningly; if he fought them, they choked him and only when he hung his head in resignation did they relax and let him breathe.

I have to warn Julian— That was his thought, but it came too late, for Julian rode into the clearing on his handsome black palfrey just as he realized the danger, and Alexander couldn't get the breath even to bray a warning.

"Kind sir?" whined the old hag, both hands outstretched. "They've turned me out as too old to work, kind sir, and—"

And Julian, soft, foolish Julian, was out of his saddle in a moment, helping the old witch to her rock, fussing over her as if she was his own grandmother. He ran to get water for her, then rummaged through his saddlebags.

She's going to kill him! Or worse than kill him! He tried and tried, but he couldn't get free, his balance wasn't right and he kept falling to his knees—he kept blacking out from lack of air!

"Here, old mother," Julian said, gently putting half a loaf of bread in her hands and closing her hands around it. "It's all I have—I wish I had more, but if you'll bide just a bit, I'll see what I can hunt for you—"

"Ah, nay, good sir—you're too kind, too kind—" the old woman said, sounding absolutely delighted, and of course, she *would*, she'd just gotten all of Julian's provisions off him, and he was a *terrible* hunter—

Oh, Julian, Julian! he thought in despair, waiting for that stick to come out, for Julian to be turned into something horrid. It was a plot, that was what it was. It was all a plot by Stancia or that Sorcerer or both, to strip Kohlstania of its heirs and send their father into despair. There probably wasn't a Quest—there never had been a Quest—

"Now, then, old mother, just you wait," Julian was saying, with that good-natured grin on his face that drove his father mad. "You'll have a good meal, and I'll put you up on Morgana here, and we'll all go on into Fleurberg together."

Now he froze, eyes bulging with fear, but unable to understand what was going on. She hadn't done anything to him. Why hadn't she turned him into something? Nothing was happening as he'd thought! He stared at them through the underbrush, feeling his upside-down world flipping for a second time.

The old hag was hiding her face in her hands, and for a moment, Alexander hoped again. Was her conscience overcoming her? Was she going to let Julian go?

But then something—odd—happened. She seemed to shimmer all over, as if she was caught in a heat-haze, and then—

Then she changed.

Her clothing was what he saw first; it—*un-aged*. Somehow, all in a moment, it got newer. The fading, the frayed bits, they all went away, and as her clothing changed, she began to stand straighter, that old-lady hump on her back vanished, her hair went from straggling and grey to golden and curling and her face—

Well, she *certainly* wasn't an old hag anymore!

Julian stared, too, gape-mouthed, as the handsome young woman lifted her head and looked him over boldly with a twinkle in her eye. "You are certainly an improvement over your brothers," she said.

She lifted the stick and made a tiny gesture, and the peasant's clothing she was wearing transformed again, this time into something pink and satiny and shining, a gown his own mother would not have been ashamed to wear, and there were diamonds at her throat and wrists and ears, and the stick in her hand was now a long, slender, ivory-white wand.

Alexander stared and stared, blinking in disbelief. So, too, did Julian.

What's going on here?

There was something about the way the woman looked—it tickled the back of his mind, something he remembered from a long time ago. From a distant part of his memory, he heard a voice he'd thought he'd forgotten, a woman's voice, speaking softly. *"Once upon a time, there was a lovely princess who was guarded by her Fairy Godmother...."*

Julian, poor fool, stood there with his mouth dropping open. Not that Alexander was in much better case.

She's got to be an Elven Queen. But why ambush us? Why go through all of this to intercept us?

Finally— "Are you—one of the—" Julian stumbled over the words, not surprisingly, as they didn't come readily to one from Kohlstania "—one of the Fair Folk?"

She laughed; there she did *not* resemble a fine lady of a lofty court at all. It was a hearty laugh, and rang around the clearing; it didn't tinkle like a tiny silver bell, nor did she hide her mouth behind her hand when she laughed.

"No, Julian, but I *am* a Fairy Godmother. And your kindness and courtesy to an old woman shall have its reward. I am here to help you on your Quest."

She's here to help us? Alexander could hardly believe his ears. *Fine help she's been to me! And what did she do with Octavian?*

But then, from somewhere deep inside, perhaps the same place as that memory, came another set of thoughts. *When you thought she was nothing but an old peasant woman, you would have dismissed her as something less than the dirt in your path. And you tried to run her down the moment you thought she might be a threat, without waiting to see what she would do or answering her cry for aid. You seem to have forgotten all those knightly vows you took, and you haven't exactly proved yourself worthy of help. Have you?*

He felt his ears flattening against his head, and he gritted his teeth. *I am a Prince of the blood! Why should I care about some stupid old base born woman? Julian bleats about the peasantry all the time, and this is where his concern leads him! Let her family take care of her, or let her go to the poorhouse where decent people won't be bothered by such as her! Isn't that why we built the things?*

The voice in the back of his head—snickered. Nastily. *Ah. I see. So long as you don't have to look at "such as her," you needn't concern yourself. Is that it?*

Of course it was—but somehow, that felt like exactly the wrong answer. And he didn't know why.

The woman who was calling herself a Fairy Godmother made a tiny gesture with the wand. As Alexander watched her with his ears still flattened against his skull, beside him in the bushes something moved, snakelike.

His attention was distracted, away from the woman, to

the horses. And as he stared, the reins of both horses came unknotted from where they'd been tied.

They moved as if they were alive, or as if there was someone actually undoing the knots.

But that wasn't the least of it, oh no. Before his very eyes, they changed color. The bay became a grey, and the packhorse a dapple; the armor packed onto the latter simply vanished altogether, and the shield with it.

She gestured again, and the two horses tossed their heads to free the reins and ambled out into the clearing as if she had called them.

And then, as calmly as if the horses and their burdens were *her* property to give away, she handed the reins over to Julian. "Here is all you will need for the physical tests you will face," she said, as Alexander nearly choked, his fear for his brother turning to outrage at her high-handed behavior. "But it will take more than strength to win the Princess. It will take cunning."

Julian bent his head to her, as humbly as if she was some sort of Queen, instead of a thief and a trickster. "Tell me," he begged. "What must I do?"

The next half hour was the worst period in all of Alexander's life, as he watched and listened, unable to move, speak, or interfere in any way, while that infernal woman coached his younger brother through *everything* he needed to win through the trials and get King Stancia's daughter and throne. Not that some of it made any real sense—some babble about freeing trapped foxes, rescuing baby hawks, feeding ants—

But that didn't matter. She was *cheating*, helping Julian,

and why? Because he'd stopped to help a worthless old woman! Where was the sense in that?

She'd stolen *his* gear too, and given it to an idiot who didn't have the sense not to leave without the proper equipment! The more he watched and listened, the angrier he got, until he was nearly faint with rage and trembling in every limb.

Of all the Questers that Elena had ever tested, this one was probably the best. He was even better-looking in person, with the animation of a good intellect in his eyes, and a ready smile on his lips. Like his brother, Alexander, he was clean-shaven and long-haired, but somehow (and perhaps it was the faint air of untidiness about him, the *lack* of perfection in his dress) she got the impression that Julian was not given to much thought about how he looked. To tell the truth, his horse was better groomed than he was; his brown doublet was just a bit faded, and someone else probably would have given it to a servant by now. His linen was clean, but it was clear that he hadn't changed his shirt before he left. And his breeches, of soft doeskin, were made for use, not for looks.

Everything he said was intelligent and to the point. Prince Julian was a fine, considerate young man—but more than that, he was much cleverer than his brothers and father gave him credit for. That was borne out in his conversation.

"Have you done something with Octavian and Alexander?" he asked, quietly, when he accepted the reins of the two horses that Prince Alexander had brought with him. By the tone of his voice, it wasn't exactly a question; he knew, he just wanted it confirmed. "I can't imagine them getting past you, you see—"

He didn't quite accuse her, but he clearly remembered the sorts of things that Godmothers did. Which was more than his brothers had.

She raised an eyebrow. "I'll tell you that they're as safe as I could make them," she said, finally, "but that they won't be competing with you for Stancia's daughter, and neither of them will be seeing Kohlstania for a while."

"Ah," he replied, and grimaced, and for a moment, those fine, dark eyes were shadowed. "Alexander has always been kind to me. And I don't wish any harm even on Octavian."

Hmm. "Even" on Octavian? Some bullying there, I suspect. Well, if that's the sort of fellow Octavian is, he won't be seeing home next month.

"I'll keep my eye on Alexander then," she promised, repressing a little smile. Oh, she would be doing that, all right.

She took note of the angle of the sunlight across the clearing; in fact, the clearing was entirely in shadow at the moment and it wouldn't be long until sunset. She needed to get him on his way, and soon. He probably wouldn't make it out of Phaelin's Wood tonight, but at least now he'd have the gear for a night in the forest. "Never mind them, Julian. It's you who will be needing help, all right? Now, before you ever get to the Glass Mountain, you'll probably encounter several tests like mine. Perhaps there will be a trapped fox that you will need to free—perhaps you will have to rescue a young hawk or eagle and return it to its nest—perhaps you will have to save an ant colony from flooding. I can't tell you what it will be, but I can give you this."

She handed him a tiny, red glass vial that contained, in part, some of the dragon's blood that she herself had once drunk. This, however, was not the straight, undiluted stuff. This was a potion, created by her, which would last no longer than it took to finish the trials.

Being able to converse with animals could cause a great deal of trouble. It was not a gift given lightly, and few deserved or needed to be burdened with it for very long.

"When you are a mile or two down the road, stop and drink this," she told him. "When it takes effect, you'll be able to speak with the animals for several days. At some point, you'll get the chance to save the lives of one or more wild creatures, and by doing so, you'll earn the right to their help later in the tasks. Now, when you get to the Glass Mountain, the first task you'll encounter will be to find a way to get past a lion *without* fighting him."

She did not actually give him the answers; that would be for him to work out for himself. That was why it was a trial. And every other Quester who got past the initial test of kindness and courtesy would be getting the same sort of advice, so it wasn't as if they weren't all on the same footing. There was no guarantee that Julian would be the one to win the Princess, though she had a good feeling about him.

No, this was just a way of making sure that the best Questers were not only the ones that actually made it to the testing, but were properly equipped when they arrived. And she had to admit that it tickled her to use the arrogant Alexander's equipment to outfit the quiet and considerate Julian.

After about a half an hour of coaching, he was as ready as he was ever going to be.

"Time to go," she said, and he mounted onto the warhorse. He looked back uncertainly at his palfrey; there was no way that he was going to be able to manage three horses, and he knew it.

"I'll take care of Morgana," she promised, then hesitated, and decided to add one more little bit of advice. It wasn't exactly the sort of thing that went with The Tradition—but it was still good advice. "Prince Julian, in the future, you do not need to be *quite* so generous."

He blinked at her. "What do you mean?" he asked.

"Well! When someone begs you for food, for instance, as I did—it is *quite* generous of you to say, 'I have food and I'll share it with you,' and quite unnecessary to do what you did and give *it* all to me. The former is noble-minded and generous; the latter is daft." She gave him a long and level look. "Not everyone you meet is going to be a Fairy God-mother."

"Oh," he said, and "Ah," and colored up. "I—do things without thinking, sometimes."

"Well, if you want to win King Stancia's daughter, you'd better practice thinking *first* and acting second. Now, good luck and godspeed," she told him, and she sent him off down the path, into whatever The Tradition had in store for him. He rode off into the shadows under the trees as the air in the clearing cooled noticeably, and the sky in the west turned to red and gold.

At least, if he failed this Quest, the worst that would happen to him was to be sent home. Too many of these things ended up with Questers dead.

She had difficulty with her conscience over those, never

mind that the reward in the end was a good one, the point was that there was only *one* reward and that failure was fatal. She always warned the ones she sent on, too, and some of them even turned back. Not enough, though.

Did Bella ever have trouble sleeping at night after testing Questers? Does anyone else? she wondered. It wasn't the sort of thing you brought up at the little Godmother gatherings that happened at christenings and weddings.

She let the illusion of her court gown fall once the lad was gone; no point in looking overdressed out here, and she didn't feel the need to impress Alexander. Well, with Julian safely out of the way, there were only two things to be dealt with. Julian's palfrey, which he had left in her hands—and Julian's brother.

The horse first; she was easiest.

For a moment, Elena toyed with the idea of keeping her. She was a beautiful creature, with a fine, arched neck, flowing mane and tail, and a broad forehead. But while Elena did not own a horse at the moment and presumably Alexander would learn his lessons and be gone so that they would not even have *him* to do the chores, this was not the sort of beast that was of any real use to her. She needed a carthorse, not a palfrey.

She sighed with regret though; she couldn't ride, but she couldn't help thinking about how nice it would be to be able to. She toyed, just a moment, with the image of herself in an elegant riding habit, the sort she had seen the Sorceress Lilliana wearing, riding along the green-shadowed paths of the forest. Ah, she could see it, the palfrey's mane and tail shivering and rippling with every step, she could feel it, a freedom like flying through the air when the Little Humpback Horse pulled the cart—

Silly. When would I have the time to learn to ride properly? Besides, there's a Traditional use for Julian's horse, and I need to cement the path to it. Nothing like doing the job right, and getting the whole family in one go. She turned her attention towards the pretty black mare and put herself in the right frame of mind to talk to it.

"I want you to go home," she told the palfrey, which flicked its ears forward to listen to her, two liquid-brown eyes gazing into hers.

"Why?" the mare asked.

"Because home is where the food is," Elena replied, knowing what every horse is most concerned with, at bottom.

The palfrey licked her lips. "The oats," she said, longingly. "*My* stall. *My* manger."

"That's right. You need to go home," Elena seconded. Then she used just a touch of magic to reinforce her command. "Go *straight* home, as fast as you can, and do *not* allow anyone to touch you until you are in your stall."

The mare tossed her head as the magic *geas* settled over her; Elena made her stay while she cut the reins away from her halter so that she wouldn't get hung up on them anywhere—and so that anyone who tried to catch her would not have anything to hold onto. Then she stood back, and the mare was off like an arrow, cantering back down the path she had just come on.

She would arrive back at the castle with cut reins, without Julian, and in a lather. All of these things combined should manage to raise a great cloud of alarm and guilt in even the King of Kohlstania, who would discover that there was no more word of them after they had entered the Wood. With good luck and The Tradition on her side, King Henrick would learn that there are things more important than one's ambition—things like one's children. When Octavian returned, he would be welcomed back with tears of relief and the warmth that he probably had not felt since he was a child. And *that* would reinforce the lessons of humility he had learned. *"Behold, my son who was lost to me is returned!"* she thought, and smiled. It would even be good for King Henrick—who would spend his last days as a *beloved* King as well as a strong one.

But that was for the future, and now that she had put it all in motion, it was out of her hands.

So much for the horse. Now for the ass.

Overhead, the sky was growing dark, and in the far east there the first few stars were coming out, pale diamond-dust against the velvet blue. Not only was it time to get home, but she and the ass both needed to be out of these woods quickly. *She* would be safe enough, but it was going to get cold, and she didn't want to try to negotiate the path in the dark. As for Alexander—asses didn't see well in the dark. Even if she could get him moving, which was debatable, he'd be stumbling over every little stone and root. She sauntered back to where she had left Alexander tied up, and was not particularly surprised to find she was being glared at out of a pair of eyes nearly red with rage.

His ears were back, his teeth were bared, and his neck was stretched out towards her. Now, unlike a real ass,

Alexander probably *wouldn't* bite her; it simply wouldn't occur to him to do so. But he was angry enough that he *might*, and besides, he was certainly likely to try to step on her or kick her. "A good thing that I hobbled you, I think," she said, regarding him thoughtfully. "However, this does present a problem; how to get you home with me."

"Let me go!" brayed the ass, angrily. "Witch! Slut! Traitor! Let me *go!*"

"Oh, no," she said, amused in spite of herself. "First of all, you brought this on yourself, so don't blame me, blame your own behavior. For your information, I'm not a Witch, I'm a Godmother, and I am charged with seeing to it that virtue is rewarded and—now how shall I put this?—" She regarded him with a raised eyebrow. "Hmm—nasty little boys who behave like cruel, rude brats get their comeuppance."

The ass nearly burst with anger at being called a "nasty little boy."

"Now, just to complete your edification on this business of Stancia's daughter," she continued, really beginning to enjoy herself, "your brother Octavian is currently wandering in the woods, very nearly as ill-provisioned as your brother Julian *was*. He will continue to do so until he learns to treat all people with the same politeness that he would give to his equals, and to give them the consideration he would expect for himself." She tilted her head to the side and matched him glare for glare. She also tried not to laugh; the donkey looked absolutely ridiculous, trying to twist his face into an expression of affronted outrage. "Does that sound familiar? It should. I suspect he will be quite ragged—

and very well acquainted with the kind of hunger, cold, and misery the poorest of the poor live with—by the time he mends his manners. And I suppose that you're wondering why I let him go his way still human? *He* only ignored the poor, starving old woman. *You* attempted to run her down."

The ass's eyes flashed warningly. She feigned surprise. "What, you don't think there was anything particularly wrong with your behavior? I suppose you're under the impression that your birth gives you the right to trample whoever you please under your horse's hooves."

He looked for one moment as if he was about to say something; she didn't care to hear it. "Well, your punishment is in *my* hands, my lad, and as it happens, I'm going to see to it that while you are not as well-acquainted with hunger and misery as your brother, you *will* learn all about the hard labor that turns your peasants old before their time. I told you; I need a donkey, and you will do. The main problem now is, how to get you home, since I doubt that you're going to cooperate of your own free will."

She crossed her arms over her chest, and tapped her cheek with the tip of her wand while she thought out loud. "I *could* put a spell of coercion on you, but you might hurt yourself trying to fight it." That was a distinct possibility, for as angry as he was, although she doubted he could break it, he might well wrench muscles or even break a bone trying to keep from obeying it. Such things had happened in the past, because the sort of coercion spell that good magicians used only worked on the subject's body, and imperfectly at that. Now, the coercions used by practitioners of the Dark Arts were more insidious. *They* worked inside the subject's head. And sometimes, even when the spell had been lifted, the subject was never quite right again.

"I *could* blindfold you and ask the path to take us home," she continued. But if she did that the odds were good that he would fall off. He'd try to escape or try to hurt her, and he'd fall off, possibly hurting himself, certainly ending the magic right there. Then it would be all to do all over again, and most of it in the dark. Probably a bad choice.

Considering her options, she decided on a third. "On the whole, I believe I will see what magic and The Tradition have around us that might suit best."

In the time since Bella had turned over the position to her, Elena had learned something very interesting about The Tradition—which was that when it had no set path that it was trying to follow, it could be very helpful indeed. Apparently The Tradition always had to do *something* whenever magic was used, and if she merely used a very little magic to get its attention, she often got a very large benefit in return. Now this was more to Elena's liking, again, conserving magical power.

If she was not specific in *how* she wanted something done, it also tended to happen much more efficiently and faster than if she had been. The Tradition would bring whatever help she requested that was nearest and best suited to the task, and in the process of doing so, laid down a trace to follow at some other time, in some other place. She was, in effect, using The Tradition itself to build new paths. The more paths The Tradition had to choose from, the easier it would be to keep it to one she and other good magicians preferred.

So she released another thread of power, and sent it *seeking*, saying only, "I need some help in getting the pair of us to my home quickly, please," to the twilight air.

She saw the little wisp of glowing light waver uncertainly, like a thin stream of smoke from a pipe, for a moment. Then, suddenly, it compacted itself into a tight ball, and shot off into the east at tremendous speed.

So! That suggested that there would be an answer to her request very soon—

There was; so soon that she barely had time to finish that thought before she heard something large, *very* large, crashing and crunching its way through the forest towards them. It wasn't just twigs that were snapping out there, it was large branches.

And she had no idea what could be *that* big.

But she didn't go anywhere beyond the walls of her cottage without at least one talisman that would react to the presence of *anything* evil—really wicked, not merely "bad" as Octavian and Alexander had been—and whatever was coming was not making her talismans the least uneasy. So she waited with anticipation, but no trepidation, to see what her magic had called to her side.

Now, Phaelin's Wood was a very old forest, and the trees were enormous, much taller than the tallest building that Elena had ever seen, and since becoming an Apprentice she had seen quite a bit. So she wasn't at all surprised that she couldn't actually see what was coming. What *did* surprise her was that when it stepped into the clearing, it—he—certainly stood *as* tall as, say, the average Town Hall.

He was a giant, the first one that Elena had ever set eyes on.

I didn't know there were any giants in this Kingdom!

A very civilized giant he was, and clearly visible in the twilight, nicely clothed in a patchwork leather jerkin which had probably taken the hides of six or eight cattle to make, a canvas shirt which had probably been sewn from ships' sails, a good pair of woolen breeches likely made from blankets, and in place of boots—which obviously would have been very difficult to have made for one so large—heavy felt shoes with wooden soles. He was bearded, but his beard was neatly trimmed, and though his hair was a little wild, it did look as if he made an effort to keep it tended.

He looked around the clearing for a moment, and she helped him out by stepping out where he could see her. His gaze fell on her, and his face lit up with a smile.

"Ah, our Godmother! I wondered why I'd felt a summoning!" he said in a voice like a flood of warm, dark velvet. She smiled with delight in return; you couldn't *not* like someone who sounded like that. "How can I serve you, Godmother?"

"An exchange of services is in order, I think," she replied. "I've changed a fool into an ass, and I don't think he's going to cooperate in coming home with me, so I need a bit of help in bringing him along."

The giant laced his fingers together and pushed his hands outwards, cracking the joints, with a laugh. "Well, I'm your man for that! And if it's an exchange you're offering—well, I could use a new ram."

For some reason completely unfathomable to Elena—or any of the chroniclers of The Tradition that she had ever read—sheepherding was a Traditional occupation for giants, along with woodcutting. And as it happened, although this was not normally the case, Elena *had* a ram penned up in the old donkey paddock, given her by one of the women she'd made haying charms for. It was completely useless to her, and she'd been searching for something she could barter it for.

This was not unlikely coincidence; this was how, given free rein and the nudge of a little magical power, The Tradition worked for a Godmother who knew how to manipulate it. She needed a way to get Alexander home, he needed a ram, she had a ram, and a touch of magic and The Tradition put them together. It could have been a farmer passing through with an animal cart; it could have been one of the Fair Folk who could whisk them home in a breath. Anything would serve so long as she had something that the other wanted. This time, it was a giant who was nearest and fit the bill.

"Done!" she said, and to the giant's delight, spit in her hand to seal the bargain in the country way.

"They told me the Godmother who'd Apprenticed for our Bella was a right lass," he said, with that broad grin spreading across his face again. "And so you are, Godmother Elena. I'm Titch. Howler Titchfen, in full, but mostly they call me Titch."

"And I'm pleased to meet you, Titch," she replied, almost giggling at the notion that anyone with so mellow a voice as this giant's would be called "Howler." "How do you propose to help me?"

"Let's see your wee donkey," he replied, and she led him in the gathering gloom to where Alexander was tied up.

The ass was petrified with fear. All four legs were rigid, and his eyes practically bulged out of his head. His ears were flat down against his back, and he shook so hard it was almost comical.

Evidently Alexander had never seen a giant before, either.

"I don't think this one's likely to give me much trouble, Godmother," Titch said, with a chuckle like thunder in the distance. "I reckon the easiest is to carry the two of you—him 'neath my arm, and you on my shoulder."

And so it was; Titch knelt down and offered her his hand to step up onto; from there she got into a comfortable sitting position on his shoulder and took a good hold of his hair. He seized the trembling ass with both hands and tucked Alexander under his arm, and away they went, back down the path to her cottage. Each one of Titch's strides covered a good thirty feet, so Elena reckoned that was probably how tall he was, since a man can usually stride the length of his own height when he's in a hurry. It was a very good thing that she no longer had any difficulties with heights, though.

The giant's hair was like strands of yarn, so it was easy to hold onto, and his broad shoulder made a surprisingly comfortable seat. He kept up a lively conversation with her as they walked, modulating his voice so as not to deafen her. She suspected that he must spend a reasonable amount of time around humans to be that sensitive about their needs, and a moment later, he confirmed that.

"And the wife says to me, 'Titch,' she says, 'Your old mam's getting creaky in her bones, and I'm not so young anymore. Can you find me a couple of human lasses and lads to help with the cleaning? They can get where I can't.' And

Godmother Bella, she set us up with some lively folk that don't mind living off in the beyond. Said they was tenant farmers turned out by the lord for havin' sauce. 'Sauce away,' says I, 'I like a man who'll tell me what he thinks to me face!' and we get on as right as rain."

She hoped that Alexander was listening to this. It was the sort of thing he needed to hear. For here was a giant, a monster, giving help to humans who'd been dismissed, not because they hadn't done their work and done it well, but for speaking their minds. And furthermore, this same giant *approved* of men speaking their minds.

Then again, at this point, he had probably passed out from fear.

Before they were home, Elena learned all about Titch, his half-deaf old mother, his wife of thirty years, the four humans who helped them tend house and the herds and the sheep themselves.

Now, sheep don't live in forests, they live in grasslands, and Elena finally asked Titch what had brought him down into Phaelin's Wood.

"Oh," he replied, "That's no secret. Got a bargain with the Elves; when there's a storm I clear deadfall and leave it in four special places. Humans around about know where I leave it, and they go there for their firewood and stay out of the deep woods. So no trees get cut, and there's no one trampin' around where they shouldn't be. And I get deer when I get tired of mutton. When I felt that tuggin', I thought 'twas maybe one of the Elves that wanted something."

By this time, the lights of the cottage were gleaming

warmly through the trees, and Elena felt her stomach whisper a complaint that it had been too long since breakfast. And that made her offer—though not without trepidation, since she wasn't sure they had enough food to feed a giant—"Look, we're here! Would you care to stay for supper?"

Titch laughed. "Ah, no, thankee, Godmother. I'll be taking my ram and be on my way. The wee wife'll be in a taking if I spoil her meal by coming home late!"

And it appeared that Titch was no stranger to the cottage, for once he'd set Elena down at her door and the House-Elves came out to see who was there, there was a round of friendly greetings and banter before Alexander was put down in the stable with strong charms about him to keep him from running away. Then Titch collected his ram, tucked it under his arm, and was off, striding away under the stars.

"So," Lily said, hands on hips, looking at the ass, who was still shaking. The lantern in the stable shone down on him, and she had to admit that he made a very good ass; strong, well-muscled. "What's the tale behind this one?"

Elena told her, and Lily raised her eyebrows. "Well," she said judiciously, "I hope you know what you're getting into."

I don't, actually, she thought, but she wasn't going to admit that. "It's within The Tradition," she pointed out. "Oh, I know, it's a little grey to haul him home with me and make him work for a while, but I could hardly have left him out in the forest. He'd probably have gotten eaten by something. And it's not as if I've put some impossible conditions for him to meet on his state."

"Hmm," Lily replied, as they walked back towards the house. "That wasn't what I was thinking. I'm more thinking what's going to happen when you give him his days as a man. You'll have to do that, you know."

She nodded; she'd given thought to that herself. Only the most powerful of Sorcerers and Sorceresses—good *or* evil—could do a transformation on someone without the risk that the person transformed would lose himself in the creature. For anyone else, there was the need to allow the person time as himself, in human form, on a regular basis. "I'll have him hedged around, believe me," she replied as they stepped into the warm, fragrant kitchen. "He won't be able to even think about violence, or about running off—"

"That wasn't what I meant—ah, never mind," Lily replied, somewhat to Elena's puzzlement. "We'll see what happens the first time he gets his day as a man."

"And in the meanwhile, we have an ass again," Robin said with *great* satisfaction. "Poor Dobbin was so old I was afraid to work him as much as we needed. I have plans for a great gathering of firewood tomorrow."

And Elena hid her smile behind a spoonful of soup. Tonight, the Prince of the Blood would be eating dry hay and drinking water. His only companions would be three cows. And in the morning, he would find himself roused at dawn and working harder than he ever had in his life until sunset.

She could hardly wait.

Alexander woke slowly to the sound of roosters crowing. He'd always come awake slowly, for as long as he could remember, no matter how much racket anyone made. In his days at the military academy he might have gotten into trouble over that, if he hadn't been the Prince.

As it was, some—adjustments—were made to the usual procedures for cadets. Not to allow him to lie abed longer, good God, no—King Henrick would never have countenanced that. No, another arrangement was made. While the officers did *not* allow him to lie abed at reveille until he was actually awake, they *did* allow his batman to come in and begin the waking process for him alone, specially, a half hour early. He had a batman, of course, though the other cadets did not. And he had his own room, though the other cadets shared a dormitory. He was a Prince of the Blood, after all. While he was expected to abide by discipline and study as hard as the rest, he could scarcely be expected to shine his own boots or make his own bed. It was thanks to the batman that by the time the bugle sounded, he was awake and ready to fall out with the rest of the class.

As thoughts began to form with glacial slowness, he gradually realized that something wasn't right. He didn't feel right, and there was something different about his surroundings. He was lying all wrong, and he wasn't in a bed.

A new thought oozed to the surface; of course, he wasn't in his bed at home, he was on his way to win Stancia's daughter. He couldn't be in an inn, though, or he would be in a bed.

No, of course he wasn't in an inn. He'd been wandering around for days in the wilderness. He should have been in the forest, but there weren't any roosters in the forest. So something was still wrong.

He managed to move a little, and a foreign aroma—not unpleasant, but foreign—came to his nose, along with the crackle of something underneath him. From the scent, he seemed to be lying in straw.

He managed to move again, although he could not get his eyes open. His foot hit a wooden wall. He was lying against another. He got one eye open, got a hazy impression through sleep-fog and predawn light, of a narrow space hemmed in by crude wooden walls.

He was in a stable, in a stall. He was lying in a very odd

position; he should have felt cramped, but he wasn't. He looked down at himself.

He had four legs. Four stubby, hairy legs, ending in hooves.

He had in his life, on a very few memorable occasions, come awake in a single moment. This was not the first time such a thing had happened, but it was certainly the worst.

He *remembered* everything, all in a rush. That horrible woman. The curse. Julian. The giant.

The memory sent a cold shock through him, jolting him into movement fueled by anger. All four hooves scrambling, he heaved himself up, braying at the top of his lungs, full of rage and despair.

And knocked himself senseless on the manger he'd somehow wedged himself underneath in the night.

The second time he awoke that morning, it was with a head that pounded as if five men were playing bass drums inside it, and a pain behind his eyes that stabbed all the way through his brain with every beat of his heart. And this time, he couldn't remember where he was or what he was doing there; he gazed around at what was clearly a stall in a stable without any idea of how he had gotten there. Before he could get his thoughts clear, he realized that there was someone standing over him.

"All right with you, lad," said the voice above him. "Time for you to go to work."

Work? But—

Then it hit him all over again. For a second time the memories came back to him in a rush, but this time he was feeling too sick and his head hurt too much to sustain the rage.

He lifted his head from the straw and looked blearily at his captor.

It took him a moment to realize that it wasn't a human, although it was a male.

The—man?—couldn't have been taller than three feet, but he was as weather-beaten and wizened as an old man. He had overlarge ears that came to hairy points, and wore clothing that Alexander associated with common laborers or peasants; homespun shirt, leather breeks, canvas tunic. His clothing looked new and clean, though, and the creature had a bridle in his hands.

A bridle? He wouldn't! The man wouldn't dare!

Alexander opened his mouth. He was *going* to say, "I am a Prince of Kohlstania, and I demand to be restored!" except that what he started to say came out in a bray, and anyway, as soon as he opened his mouth, the creature jammed a bit into it. And the next thing he knew, his head had been trussed up in the bridle, and the creature had the reins firmly in his hand.

"*Up* with you!" the creature said, and he must have been immensely strong, because somehow he hauled Alexander to his feet by main force. The Prince swayed there a moment, torn between rage and fear. He'd always thought of himself as a brave man, but this time it was the fear that won, and he tried to bolt, only to find himself brought up short by the reins that were now tied to the manger. He reared and fought the bridle, kicking not at the man, but wildly, at random, trying desperately to break free.

"Hold *still* ye daft bugger!" said the little man, who then brought his fist down on Alexander's nose.

Hitting the manger with the top of his head had been bad. This was infinitely worse. Alexander went nearly cross-eyed with the pain. His knees buckled, and he almost fell. Darkness speckled with little dancing sparks covered his vision, and when he could see again, there was a harness on his back as well as the bridle on his head.

The little man came around to the front of him and seized both sides of the bridle, pulling Alexander's head level with his. "Now you *listen* to me, my fine young Prince," said the man, staring into Alexander's eyes with an expression that was perfectly readable. Alexander had seen that expression on his father's face many a time; it meant, *cross me and you'll pay for it.* "We know who you are, and we know how you come to be *what* you are, and we don't give a toss. You're not in Kohlstania now. You're in Godmother Elena's house, and what *she* says is law. You stepped over the line, my buck, and you'll take what's coming to ye like a man, or ye'll be treated like the brat she says ye are. You understand me?"

He was seething with every passionate emotion in the book, and they all tangled up with one another and got in each other's way. *Run!* said fear, and *fight!* said anger, and *lie down and die* said despair. He was trapped, trapped in the web of a Witch and even if he could *get* free, where could he go? He didn't know how to get home again, he didn't know where he was, and even if he did, how could he *tell* anyone what he was?

"There's no use you trying to run," the little man went on remorselessly. "Any peasant that sees you running loose is going to grab you to work his land and bear his burdens. Half of them can't read nor write, so it's no use thinking you can scratch out what you are in the dirt. And anyway, the ones that *are* literate around here are all beholden to God-mother Elena and before you can say 'knife' they'll bring you right back here. So. Until you mend your ways, *I'm* your master. You do what I say, and do it honestly, and we'll get along all right. You try to cross me up or give less than your best, and you'll find out that I'm no bad hand at fitting the punishment to the crime myself."

He *believed* the little man. He believed every word. They had that ring of truth about them that he used to hear in his instructors' voices at the military academy. Despair won out over every other emotion, and his knees went weak. *Oh, God, help me!* he prayed. *Deliver me from the hands of my enemies!* He wanted to weep, and he was denied even that, for he was trapped in the body of an ass and animals could not cry. And God did not seem to be answering him today.

"I see we understand one another," the little man said, with immense satisfaction. Then he looked up, and when Alexander in turn raised *his* head to see what the man was looking at, he found himself gazing into the knowing eyes of that terrible woman....

"No beating him, Hob," said the woman.

The man frowned. "But, Godmother—"

"I'm not saying not to give him a sharp stripe or two if you have to get his attention, but no *beating*. If you beat him, all he'll learn is the old lesson he already knows, that the strong have the right to enslave the weak. If he's *ever* going to warrant getting his old shape back, he has to learn better than that." The way she was talking about him as if he wasn't there or couldn't understand her made him mad all over again. But the little man was still holding his bridle, and the memory of that blow to his nose was a powerful incentive to him to stand quietly.

"Now, my lad," said the little man, "it's time for you to earn your keep and get to work."

Well, maybe he wasn't going to fight where he couldn't win, but he would be *damned* if he was going to be this woman's slave!

He set all four hooves and refused to move, staring at her and her minion defiantly.

"Ah. So that's how it's going to be," said the woman, when all of the man's hauling could not make him move an inch. "Good enough, then. Hob, tie him up and make sure there isn't a scrap of hay or a grain of corn about. But do put fresh water within reach; I want to teach him a lesson, not kill him or drive him mad." She put both her hands on her hips and matched his defiant glare. "If you won't work, you don't eat."

He snorted angrily at her.

"Very well, have it your own way," she replied. The little man tied his reins short, and left a bucket of water hung within reach. Then he, too, left, and Alexander was alone in the stable.

It didn't take long for him to get bored; there wasn't much to look at. The high walls of the stall cut off his view of anything outside, so he was left with the rough wooden walls, the old bucket on a peg, the manger, and the straw-strewn dirt floor to stare at. The view palled pretty quickly.

He closed his eyes, and listened. Roosters crowed occasionally or *a* rooster did; he didn't know enough about chickens to tell if there was more than one. Hens clucked, and beyond that, he could hear several sorts of birdsong and jackdaws calling. And someone humming, someone female. He couldn't imagine a Witch humming under her breath, so it must be yet another servant.

His stomach growled. It had been a long time since yesterday's lunch. He buried his nose in the water bucket, and then snorted and choked as the water went up his nose.

It took several tries before he figured out how to drink as a donkey.

The water eased his hunger temporarily, but what began to creep in on him was another sense, so much sharper that it might have been an entirely new one. He could *smell* everything!

The straw under his feet, for instance, strong and strangely appetizing. The damp earth under the straw. Green growing things, a smell which began to tease him mercilessly with need. Baking bread, which drove him *mad* with wanting it. The scent of roasting meat which, oddly, was faintly nauseating. A whiff of honey, which made his mouth water.

He'd never actually missed a meal in his life before this. He was behind by two, now.

Could you eat straw, if you were a donkey? He strained at the rope and reins holding his head to the manger, but they were tight, and so were the knots. The straw was just out of reach.

Damn them!

Could he bite through the bonds holding him?

He gave it a try, but the leather was tough and wouldn't

yield to his teeth. And the additional lead-rope was thick; even if he could get through the reins, he didn't think he could chew through the rope.

He almost gave up, but the thought of the Witch's smirk galvanized him. He started in on the rope. At least it was something to chew.

Elena heard Randolf laugh, and looked up from her writing. "What's so funny?" she asked.

"He's chewing on the ever-renewing rope," Randolf replied, with unconcealed glee. "Oh, I know it's not *that* funny, but I can't wait for the moment when he figures out that however many strands he breaks, they always get replaced."

Sometimes Randolf shows his origins a little too clearly to be comfortable, she thought. *And the personality traits he picked up from his previous owners.* It was like the wicked Sorceress to whom he had belonged to take delight in the pain of others.

She kept her tone light, however; there was no point in rebuking Randolf, as he wouldn't understand why he was being chided. "I think it will be more interesting to see how many meals he misses before he gives in," she replied.

"You ought to let me give him a good hiding," Hob said from the door. She turned her head to see him standing there with his arms full of clean linens. She wondered how long he had been there.

"I'm not going to kill him with kindness; he's already had much too much spoiling in his life, and I've no desire to reinforce that. But I told you before, and I will repeat it, there will be no beatings," she said adamantly. "It will just make him feel martyred and justified. Think, Hob—if you beat him, he'll be *certain* that he is in the right. Can't you see that? No, we have to do this the hard way. Nothing to make him feel that we are worse than he is. *Everything* to make him see that our way is the better way."

"Hmph," Robin said from behind Hob, *his* arms full of clean clothing. "Spare the rod and spoil the child is what *my* old father used to say."

Elena pursed her lips and frowned. "But he's not a child. Not by our count of years, anyway. No, the lessons he learns have to come from *his* pain, things that he essentially brings on himself, not from anything we actively do to him."

She returned to writing her part in the tale of Stancia's daughter thus far. She already knew, thanks to another volume that was writing itself down in the library, that Prince Julian had passed the second of his tasks, freeing a fox whose tail had been caught in a log. It was not just *any* fox, of course, but he was not to know that, and the *Fairy* Godmother who was responsible for that task did not elaborate on just what sort of "fox" it had been. Prince Octavian was nowhere to be found at the moment, but she wasn't worried. There wasn't much in Phaelin's Wood that could harm a fully armed man the size of Octavian, though by now he was surely getting tired, unkempt, and rather hungry.

Now, if he ran across a segment of road where an "All Forests Are One" spell had been put in place and was still active, there was no telling what he might run into. And, of course, there was always the chance that an evil magician would get wind of his wanderings and intercept him. But that was out of Elena's hands now; Karelina was back in her place, and what happened to Octavian was largely up to her.

And when she began to feel a little pity for him she just thought of his stone-cold expression as he looked right past her and moved on. No, he deserved what he got, and like Alexander, the end of his punishment was in his own hands.

She finished her chronicle and fanned at the ink to dry it. "I think it'll be tomorrow before he gives up," she said, consideringly. "And at the end of six days, I'll have to give him a day as a man, you know."

"Hmm. Dangerous, that," Hob said. "And Madame, we're not much help if he decides to attack you."

"I know; I've planned for that," she replied. "At least, I hope I have."

If missing breakfast had been a torment, missing lunch was an agony. All Alexander could think about was food. The hot summer breeze from the garden brought him the scent of the vegetables out there, and to his surprise, he could *identify* them by their scent, if he didn't think too hard about it. Not that it helped; if anything, it made it worse. And the scent of baking bread—oh, if there was a heaven for horses, Alexander now knew, intimately, that it was full of loaves of fresh-baked bread. The aroma of fresh-cut grass made his mouth water. The scents of other things were not at all tempting, but the *memories* of the foods he had enjoyed as a man were maddening. And no matter how hard he tried not to think of them, more memories of sumptuous breakfasts, *al fresco* luncheons, and amazing feasts piled into his mind to the point where he could *taste* his favorites.

It didn't help at all that there was nothing to see or do in this stall, with his head tied up to the manger. He was able to hear things perfectly well, but it wasn't enough to occupy his mind, and what he could scent for the most part only made him hungrier.

By nightfall he had learned two more things. The first, that not even three buckets of water are enough to keep hunger at bay for long, and the second, that all that water has to go somewhere. That was when his final humiliation occurred, that of having to stand in his own—well. He could only hold it for so long, after all.

If he'd thought it smelled when he was a man, it was a lot stronger to a donkey's nose.

The strange little man came and carried the soiled straw away, but still—he'd had to stand over it for hours. He vowed that if he was ever himself again, he would assign a stableboy the task of doing nothing else but carrying away mess as soon as it was made.

It was humiliating. Dreadfully humiliating.

Darkness fell without anyone coming to look in on him but that little man, who elected not to speak to him. When it was pitch-dark in the stable, he managed to fall asleep again, actually standing up as horses did, even with his stomach growling at him.

He woke in the middle of the night, out of restless dreams interrupted by hunger and emotions he couldn't exactly put a name to. It was very dark in the stable, too dark to see anything. His ears twitched, and it was an *extremely* strange sensation to feel them twitching, to feel the air moving over the surface of them, to be *aware* of how big they were. He'd never been aware of his ears before, only of the sounds they brought him.

There were owls hooting out there. His ears twitched again, and he realized he could pinpoint where they were, or close to it. They were moving, flying from tree to tree, he guessed, calling to each other. Were they mates?

Why couldn't she have turned him into an owl?

He heard crickets outside the stable, frogs somewhere in the distance; the night was a rich tapestry of sound the like of which he had never experienced before. Was this what life was like for an animal?

Why couldn't she have turned him into a frog? A frog would be better than a donkey.

He heard something else, then. Something coming in out of the forest. Two things; hooved beasts, he thought, walking so lightly they hardly made a sound. Deer?

Being a deer wouldn't be bad.

He felt his nostrils spreading as he tried to scent what it was that was out there. And what he got was a bizarre odor that his donkey-instincts couldn't identify....

It was sweet, with musky overtones. Not horse, certainly not deer or goat—too sweet for any of those. If a flower could have been an animal, or an animal a flower, it would have smelled like that.

"The Godmother said to eat the lilies," whispered a voice out there in the darkness. "Not the peas."

A second voice sighed. "But I like peas," it objected. Then he heard a snort. "Enemy!" it said, more loudly. "I smell—"

"Godmother's," said the first voice dismissively. "A Quester who failed."

"But it is *not* a virgin!" the second objected, disapproval heavy in its voice.

"It is also not a *man*," said the first. "And the Brownies are not virgins, either. Let the Godmother deal with it."

"All right, you two!" snapped a third voice that was altogether and detestably familiar to Alexander. His tormentor, the little man with the bad temper. "We figured some of you would be here tonight. Come along; the Godmother wants a word with you."

"But we didn't touch the peas!" objected the first voice indignantly.

"Yet," said the voice of the Witch's little servant, darkly. "Now, come along."

"Will we get to lay our heads in her lap?" asked the second voice, so full of hope and yearning that it made Alexander blink. Then blink again. *Why* would someone want to put his head in that Witch's lap?

"We'll see," the little servant replied. "Just come along."

The sound of hooves and feet moving off was the last he heard of that conversation.

He finally fell asleep again, falling back into troubled dreams that were interrupted at the first hint of light when the chickens began fussing over something. If anything, he was more hungry—and more stubborn—than ever.

This day was a repeat of the first. At this point, he would so gladly have eaten even the dry straw at his feet that he found himself tearing at the lead-rope on his halter in a frenzy of activity that ceased only when his jaws tired.

That was when he took a good look at the place he'd been gnawing on, and cursed the Witch fervently and thoroughly.

There was no sign, none whatsoever, that he had been chewing on it for most of two days. It was magic of some sort, of course.

More of that cursed magic! A surfeit of magic! When had *he* ever had anything to do with magic? Oh, he knew it existed, but at a distance. The peasants called on Witches and other magicians to help them, because they were—well—stupid peasants. It was not the habit of the sophisticated folk of the towns to do so; or if they did, they did not do so openly. Certainly not one of the people of King Henrick's Court ever used magicians, for his father prided himself on surrounding himself and his sons with people who were rational and logical, and had no need of magic. Magic was for those who did not have the intelligence to come up with other solutions. Magic was for the weak, for it relied on weak little things like potions and talismans. The strong used their own will and force of arm to bring about what *they* desired. It appalled him in a way, how quickly he had come to accept so quickly that magic really was strong enough, after all, to bring *him* to his knees.

And it had. It had brought him to his knees. Because when the little man arrived just before darkness fell, with the last bucket of water for him, he heard himself saying—or rather, braying— *"Stop."*

The little man looked down his long nose at him. "Oh?" he replied. "You have something to say to me?"

"I'll work," he said, in despair, so hungry now that he was positively nauseous. "I'll work tomorrow."

"I see." The little man put his bucket down, and regarded him skeptically. "So I feed you now, and in the morning, you decide that you *won't* work, after all. I didn't fall off the turnip cart yesterday, young man."

Alexander shook his head impatiently, unable to comprehend just what *that* was supposed to mean. "I pledge it. My word of honor. Feed me, and I'll work."

The little man *hmphed* and glared at him.

"Word of honor. My word as a Prince of the Blood and a knight," he repeated, his temper starting to rise. Just who did this dwarf think he was, to question *his* word?

"Just now you're an Ass of the Blood, and more like the thing the knight would use to carry his squire's bags," the little man observed, crossly. "And you certainly weren't acting like a knight when you tried to run the Godmother down. But the Godmother said you might make that sort of pledge, and that I was to accept it if you did. All right, then. Pledge accepted."

He left the bucket of water, went off somewhere, and returned with a pottle of hay and a great wooden scoop of something. Alexander felt his nostrils widening again as he greedily drank in the scents, and identified them as not only the best clover-hay, but a scoop of grain as well. The oats went in the manger, the hay in a hay-bag the little man tied to the side of the stall, and then it was a matter of a moment and the little man had the bridle off as well.

Alexander had no thought for him; his nose was deep in the grain and he was on his first mouthful when the man hit him—lightly, this time—between the ears.

"Mind!" the man said sharply. "You're a man, *think* like one, ye gurt fool! Eat too fast and ye'll founder!"

Curse it! He's right. So though his empty stomach was crying out for him to shove the food as quickly down his throat as he could, he did nothing of the sort. He chewed each mouthful slowly and carefully, counting to twenty before he took the next—and he wasn't taking big mouthfuls, either, just dainty little bites. He didn't shove all the grain in first, either; he alternated. One bite of grain, one mouthful of hay torn from the net, one sip of water.

He would never have believed that anything could taste as good. It surprised him, actually; he'd expected the hay to taste like—well, *hay*. It didn't; it was a little like dry cake, a little like new peas, and there was just the faintest hint of nectar; in fact, it tasted like new-mown hay smelled, utterly delicious. As for the grain, it was earthy, a little bit truffle-flavored, and a lot like bread-crust from the best bread he'd ever eaten. Well, no wonder horses seemed to enjoy these foods so much! It made him wonder what grass tasted like.

When the little man was certain that he wasn't going to eat fast enough to make himself sick, he took himself off with a grunt and a word of warning.

"I'm not going to leave you tied up tonight," the man said, "but remember what I said about running away. Try and run off, and you'll soon find yourself in more trouble than you think. If you're lucky, someone will eventually figure out you belong to Madame Elena. If you aren't, the work you'll be doing will make what I have planned for you seem like mild exercise. And if by some chance you actually manage to get into the deep forest—"

Something about the relish with which the little man said that made Alexander look up at him. He was grinning. It was not a sign of mirth.

"—let me just say that the packs of wolves in the forest would find donkey-flesh quite the tastiest thing to come their way in a long time. Fancy yourself being able to take on a wolf pack in your current shape?"

Since Alexander had no illusions about being able to take on a wolf pack in *human* shape, he shook his head.

"And that's just the wolves. There's other things in there you'd rather not learn about." The little man slapped him on the rump. Alexander elected not to protest the insult to his dignity. "So be a good little Prince and stay where I've left you."

Only then did the little man walk out, leaving Alexander alone again. Only now he had a full stomach, and the ability to pick a clean spot to lie down in, and when he did so, he slept the dreamless sleep of the utterly spent.

It was Alexander's fourth day of working for the little man, whom he learned he was supposed to refer to as "Master Hob," and he ached in every limb.

He had thought, when he underwent his training as a knight, that he had worked hard. He had certainly exercised until he was ready to drop, and he had certainly gone from dawn to dusk—but it was not this bad. He had thought that he had exerted himself when he had been in the military academy. And he had indeed done hours of drilling in all weathers, but that had been *nothing* compared to this.

They had gone out every single day at dawn and he had spent every morning hauling deadfall out of the forest. This meant that he was hitched to a tree, and had to pull and strain until he pulled it loose from the undergrowth, *then* had to drag it all the way back to the cottage, where the little man unhitched it at the woodpile. Then they went back after another tree.

Then, after a break for a meal, he spent every afternoon but one hauling stones to build a wall—the one he did not spend in hauling stones, he spent hitched to a cart on a trip to and from some village nearby. Relatively nearby, that is; he had never before appreciated the difference between being the one doing the riding or driving, and being the one doing the pulling.

Then, after a final meal, he spent each evening until twilight with panniers over his back, in the company of someone he was supposed to call "Mistress Lily," tramping about in the forest again, this time so that Mistress Lily could pick wild herbs and berries and bits of things he couldn't identify.

He had to admit that the little man worked just as hard as he did—*he* was the one hacking the brush away from the fallen trees, hitching them to the harness, and guiding them, and he walked the entire way. *He* was the one piling the stones into the garden cart, dumping them at the wall, and building the dry-stone wall himself. And it hadn't been Master Hob who had driven the cart to the village, it had been a second little woman whose name he did not know, for Master Hob had been busy with some other task.

If this sort of thing was *easy* work, he did not want to contemplate what the peasants outside of the grounds of the cottage would do with him if they caught him trying to escape.

But his memory was giving him some hints, with bits of

recollection of things he hadn't paid a lot of attention to at the time. Donkeys with bundles strapped to their backs to the point where it was hard to see anything but four staggering legs and a nose. Donkeys hitched to carts that a warhorse would have been hard put to move. Donkeys so thin you could have played a tune on their ribs, their patchy hides showing raw, rubbed places and sores where flies had been feasting on them. He'd seen these poor beasts, often enough, in the streets of Eisenberg, the capital of Kohlstania, and in Polterkranz, the city where the military academy had been. He'd seen them, and his eyes had skimmed right over them. He certainly hadn't *done* anything about them.

He had plenty of time to think about them now; hauling things didn't take a lot of mental concentration. *Why did you look right past us?* said those sad, reproachful eyes in his memory. *Why did you ignore us? Why didn't you help us?*

But they were just donkeys, brute beasts, he tried to rationalize. *They weren't men, they hadn't been men! They couldn't suffer as I am suffering!*

Oh, no? replied that other, hateful voice in the back of his mind. *Really?* And it would force him to remember those thin bodies, those sores, those hopeless, glazed eyes.

Those thoughts, well, plagued him like the flies he'd been cursed with until another little man, this one called "Master Robin," had come out with a bottle of something that Master Hob had rubbed into his hair and hide. It smelled sharply of herbs, but whatever it was, it kept the flies away.

Nothing kept the thoughts away.

Nor was that all; it was only when he hurt the most that he thought about those donkeys. When he was resting, other thoughts swarmed him. What was his father thinking? Julian's palfrey must have gotten home by now. Riderless, with cut reins. What was the King thinking? What was he doing? Had he sent out riders to look for Julian— to ask after Octavian and Alexander? If he had, he would have found only that their trail stopped at the forest, and he could scour the forest all he liked, but he'd find no trace of any of the three of them.

Would he send to King Stancia? If he did, he'd find out that Julian, at least, was there. What was going on for Julian? Were the trials of the Glass Mountain over? Had he won the girl and the throne, or had he already started his defeated way homeward? And what would he tell their father, in either case?

The questions buzzed in his head like the flies, and tormented him. They were his last thoughts before he went to sleep at night, and his first thoughts when he awoke in the morning. There were other questions too, but they were not as urgent—

Still, when his mind wearied of going around and around in the same fruitless track, they did float to the surface. Just who—and what—*was* this "Fairy Godmother" person? What did she want with him? It wasn't ransom, or anything else he could understand. It wasn't some sick desire to see him suffer, because she was never around, or at least, never around *him*. What did she want? What did she think she would gain from keeping him in the shape of a donkey? If she was *this* powerful a magician, what in heaven's name was she doing in this cottage out in the middle of nowhere? Why wasn't she ruling a Kingdom herself? It made no sense!

It all made his head ache—and none of it stopped the anger inside him from building, either. He worked it out during the day by throwing himself into the tasks he'd been given, but it burned in him all the time.

Such was the state of his mind and heart when, on the morning of the seventh day of his captivity, he woke—slowly, as ever, in the thin grey light of predawn—to find that he was himself again.

And the mysterious "Godmother" was standing over him, magic wand in her hand.

He lay there, staring up at her stupidly for a moment. His vision was a bit foggy, and more than a bit distorted; he had trouble focusing until he realized that his eyes were now on the *front* of his head, not the sides. He shook his head, trying to make his mind wake up. Then, of all the ridiculous things to be worried about, his first reaction was of horror—that he had come back as a man and was now lying there naked in front of her, at her feet, like some sort of—of—

Naked slave boy? the voice in the back of his mind suggested slyly.

But in the next moment, relief washed over him, for no, he was exactly as he had been when he was transformed into an ass in the first place. He was still wearing the same clothing, in fact, though it was a bit worse for wear.

He blinked again, his eyes still having trouble focusing. And the feeling of having only two legs again was extremely disorienting.

"Wake up, *your highness*," she said, prodding him in the ribs with a toe, her tone of voice making the honorific sound very sarcastic. "I can't leave you a donkey forever, much as I would like to. If I do, you'll become more ass and less man with every passing day. Not that you weren't an ass already," she added matter-of-factly, "but it was a rather different sort of ass."

He really wasn't *thinking* as she was speaking; he was really still waking up, right up until the moment she finished talking to him. Then, with a jolt, his mind started working.

And he didn't exactly *think*. Instead he reacted in the way he had fantasized he would in the first hours of his captivity.

He leaped to his feet.

He meant to lunge at her, at this vile Witch who had ruined his life. He had done it so many times in his mind, he would throw her to the ground and truss her up, then demand that she restore him his possessions and send him home—

But his balance was all wrong. His legs didn't work right. But after tripping and falling, he scrambled to his feet again, anyway.

He made a grab for her—

—and there was a sort of *bang,* and a flash of light—

—and he found himself flat on his back in the straw with a monumental headache.

"As I was saying," the woman said, calmly, but with an edge to her voice, and her blue eyes flashing with suppressed anger. "I can't leave you in the donkey-skin for more than a few days without your mind becoming more donkeylike." She looked down at him and shook her head. "Not that it would be a huge difference, apparently. So once a week or so, you'll get to be a man for a day and—"

He leaped to his feet for a third time, despite pain in his head that threatened to send him to his knees. This time he didn't make the mistake of trying to attack her; instead, he just shoved blindly past her and ran.

He blundered into the wall of the stable, but the clean, chill air braced him, and he staggered a few more paces, then broke into a real run, his steps growing more sure with every moment.

In the thin grey predawn light, he got his bearings by the cottage. *He* could get away; the Witch hadn't a prayer of catching him. After all, he *knew* the forest around here, now. He even knew how to get to the village. And while the villagers might not treat an enchanted donkey with any consideration, they couldn't ignore the demands of a Prince of Kohlstania!

He sprinted down the path to the cottage, then leaped the low stone wall around the garden and pelted for the road. In a moment, he'd be in the forest, under the trees, and *she* didn't have a horse to chase him on, nor did she have a hound to track him with. He—

—found himself pelting down the path to the stable.

He whirled, and reversed himself, running this time for the forest itself rather than the road. There must be some sort of spell on the road; *fine,* he'd get into the forest and get onto the road again later, he'd get to the village that way. That would be even better! She couldn't possibly find him in the forest and—

—he found himself running down the path to the stable.

"So, how many tries you going to make before you figure it out, boy?" asked a voice to his right. He stopped, and looked. The little woman called Lily stepped out from between two blackberry canes, her head, crowned by a flat straw hat, bobbing with suppressed laughter. "You reckon we're all as big a set of fools as you are? It's you the enchantment's on, not the path, nor the forest. You can't leave here unless the Godmother lets you."

He heard footsteps coming towards him, and saw the Witch emerging from the stable and walking towards him in a leisurely fashion, a smug smile on her face. And rage completely overcame him.

He seized a pointed stake supporting a plant and yanked it out of the ground; he hadn't intended to kill her before, but this was clearly war, and none of the laws of chivalry applied! And if he couldn't *touch* her, he was a prize-winner at the spear and javelin—

He pulled his arm back to impale her at the same time he caught a kind of silvery flash out of the corner of his eye.

And suddenly, he found himself looking at something very sharp, the tip of which was less than an inch from his eye.

It was the shining silver tip of a Unicorn's horn.

He clutched at his improvised spear, wondering if he could manage to duck under the threatening horn to kill it before it killed him—

There was a second flash, and a second Unicorn in his path. This one was braced to charge, and the tip of its horn was pointed somewhat lower than the first's. Very much lower.

He gulped, and his hands clenched hard on the stake.

"I wouldn't do that if I were you," said the first Unicorn, its voice hard and angry.

"That's right. *You* aren't a virgin," the second said, in a tone of accusation. Then it snickered. "But try it, go ahead, and you'll wish you *were*."

His mind raced for a moment. What did being a virgin have to do with—

Oh.

Of course. Unicorns were not only held spellbound by virgins, but they were the *protectors* of virgins.

He remembered the things in the night-shrouded garden, the conversation he'd overheard. So—the Witch was a virgin?

Not a big surprise, he thought sullenly, *if this is how she treats real men.*

He dropped the stake, and the Unicorn imperiling his eyeball backed away a pace or two, without dropping its threatening posture. The Witch came up even with the second Unicorn, and placed a hand on its shoulder.

Oh, yes. The bitch is a virgin, all right.

It would have been funny, under other circumstances, to see how the Unicorn tried simultaneously to melt under the Witch's touch and maintain its threatening posture towards

Alexander. She would have been attractive, under other circumstances. He wouldn't have minded tumbling her if he found her serving as pot-girl in an inn. But at the moment—

"Now, if I may continue," the woman said, one hand absently petting the Unicorn's neck, "you will be permitted to wear your shape as a man from sunrise to sunset, when you will become an ass again." He thought for a moment that she was going to make another one of those nasty comments, but she evidently restrained herself.

"But just because you're wearin' your man-shape, my lad, don't think that means you don't work," said that detestable Master Hob from behind him. "The same rules hold true whether you're a man or a beast; if you don't work, you don't eat."

The Unicorns both seemed to wake up a bit, and became all threat again. And perhaps that was because Master Hob stepped past Alexander and shoved an axe into his empty hands.

He hefted it experimentally. It was a woodman's axe, of course, and not a war-axe, but—

"Don't even think about it," Master Hob warned, and poked him hard in the ribs with the stake he'd dropped. "She's been easy on ye until now. And there's more Unicorns where these twain come from."

"Don't I even get some breakfast, first?" he said, plaintively. His voice sounded unpleasantly whiny, even to him.

The Witch raised one eyebrow. Master Hob nodded at the east. "Sun isn't up yet," he countered. "You go over to the woodpile, and you chop some wood. Your breakfast'll be ready when it's ready."

* * *

"You ought to let us poke him, Godmother," said one of the Unicorns, as the Prince slouched angrily away in the direction of the woodpile. "You ought to drop the spell and let us chase him away with holes in his hide. You don't need him here."

"Of course I don't *need* him here," she replied, looking after him thoughtfully. "But he needs to *be* here. He has lessons to learn."

"Then let him learn them in the forest," said the second, in an uncanny echo of what Master Hob had said to her just this morning before she transformed him.

"That one's all trouble, Madame Elena," he'd said, shaking his head. *"Let me go down to the village and buy us a new donkey. Drive him out into the forest like his brother."*

She tapped her cheek with her wand, looking after him—astonishing how like a sulky adolescent he looked from the back!—and finally shook her own head and walked briskly back up the path to the cottage.

She was of two minds about letting him inside to eat. On the one hand, she wanted to keep an eye on him to assess him; on the other, the rest of the household was divided over keeping him on, and that sort of tension would only be increased if he shared the breakfast table with the rest of them.

Lily thought he was hilarious, and so did Rose. Robin was of two minds about him. Hob thought he was trouble waiting to happen.

Randolf's reaction was predictable; to Randolf, Prince Alexander and his family were a fresh new source of entertainment.

Julian's horse had returned to its stable with the desired effect. King Henrick had frantically sent searchers on the path of the Princes, only to learn that once they entered Phaelin's Wood, they vanished. He was frantic; he had sent messengers on to King Stancia to determine if any of the Princes had arrived, but the messengers were being delayed by Stancia's Sorcerer. Prince Julian had only *just* completed the last of the tasks—which was to play chess with the Sorcerer with impossible stakes.

Now, the Sorcerer's intention there had been something that was the talk of all of the white magicians that had heard about it. Everyone agreed that the way he set up the final task was a brilliant bit of trickery. If Julian lost, two things would happen. The Princess would be "spared"—the Sorcerer cleverly did not specify *what* she would be spared. The second thing was "you will meet your fate." But of course at this point, Julian was putting the worst possible interpretations on everything. He assumed that it meant that the Princess would live and he, Julian, would die.

On the other hand, if Julian won, the outcome would be just as bad, from the point of view of someone who was worried about the Princess. "You will live. The Princess will be no more—" Of course, what he didn't know was that the Princess would be no more, because her father intended to make her Queen and co-ruler, with her new husband.

And Julian, of course, being the gallant young fellow that he was (and probably hoping that somehow he could wiggle out of the "fate" that awaited him), threw the game. So by losing, he won, which was the whole point of the trial, not the outcome of the game itself.

At this point, of course The Tradition was in full flood, and the moment they set eyes on each other they were passionately in love. The Sorcerer was making certain that the wedding went off unhindered in order to have King Henrick's messengers arrive at the wedding-feast itself. Beautiful timing. This put any idea of Julian returning home out of the question; he was Prince Regnant now, and had his own Kingdom to rule, King Stancia having established Julian and his daughter as co-Rulers, and intending to abdicate in a year or so. So the messengers would return home with the news that the most despised of the three had triumphed, but with only the vaguest hints of what had happened to the other two Princes.

Meanwhile, Karelina in Phaelin's Wood had passed Octavian on to Arachnia. And that was proving to be a stroke of genius. Arachnia and her consort *looked* the part of Evil Sorcerers, and at this point, they really enjoyed playing the part so long as they could do so without ever harming anyone. So Octavian was now wandering about in Arachnia's forest, a place perpetually shrouded in gloom, dripping with rain, thick with will-o-the-wisps and foxfire, abounding in giant frogs, enormous insects, and colossal spiders. Some of the weirder tribes of the Fair Folk liked to live in such surroundings, and they were all of the mischief-making sort. The place was tailor-made to give Octavian the sort of lesson he deserved, and eventually Arachnia herself would take over the final portion of it, as he was reduced to begging at the door of her kitchen for shelter and work. And when he proved himself worthy, he would be sent home, beautifully clothed and armed, on a finer horse than anything King Henrick had in the stables. Randolf had done some delving into the past for her, and it seemed that Octavian was less of a bully than Elena had thought; the "bullying" was Octavian's clumsy attempt to get Julian to come up to the standard that their father thought was acceptable. It wasn't done out of sadism or spite; in fact, Octavian was dimly worried for his youngest brother, afraid—

Well, what he was afraid of was the sort of thing that one didn't *talk* about in Kohlstania. But one single conversation that Randolf dug up explained it all. Octavian had been talking to *his* best friend, the Master-At-Arms of the castle. "Afraid he's turning into a—" Octavian's voice had dropped to a whisper "—a *nancy-boy*." Both men had shuddered, as at a fate so much worse than death it didn't bear thinking about. Octavian had straightened his shoulders. "Gotta cure him of *that,* by God," he'd said gruffly. "Can't have *that* in the family. Disgrace! Besides, Papa'd kill him." And Octavian had then gone about, making his clumsy, simpleminded best effort to turn Julian into a Real Man for his Own Good.

Alexander had missed all of this, of course, having been packed off to the military academy to get him away from Julian's possible "taint."

All of which explained a great deal about the youngest and oldest scions of the Kohlstanian Royal Family. Julian was the rebel, in his own quiet way, and had come out of it all the better man—certainly the more humane man. Octavian desperately needed some of that moral superiority shaken out of him.

But Alexander—Alexander was a different kettle of fish altogether.

He was afflicted with Octavian's sense of moral superiority; he was also afflicted with a case of *class* superiority. But there was one more little problem with Prince Alexander. It was what the military academy had made out of him.

She sighed. She did not understand it, and could only observe the results, which were dire. There was no apparent connection in his mind between himself and the vast majority of mankind. The only people that mattered were the ones of "his" class and a little below. Everyone else was chattel.

She suspected this was because the military academy to which he had been sent turned out officers that treated their men like little counters on a game-board. Fodder for the front lines, and not human at all. And it was a place reserved *only* for the sons of the elite of Kohlstania, which only reinforced the cadets' sense of superiority.

Whatever the reason, it would take more than wandering about as Octavian was doing to drive it home to him that he was, when all else was stripped away, no better than any other man, and quite a bit worse than a lot of them.

"I believe he'd better eat in the garden," she decided aloud, and went on to help Robin in the kitchen.

At least he had learned his first lesson as a donkey; according to Rose, who brought him his breakfast, there was quite a pile of chopped and split wood already stacked up for seasoning. Elena had *almost* brought him his breakfast herself.

Except that she had realized, even as she was reaching for plates, that there was something other than her own thoughts nudging her down that particular path.

And when she realized that, she stopped, closed her eyes, and felt the unmistakable presence of The Tradition.

When Rose brought the dirty plates back, she took a moment to check again. And there was no doubt. The Tradition was trying to fit them into a tale.

At that moment, she thought she could hear Madame Bella, and her warning about what having a Prince hanging about a Godmother could mean.

She tightened her lips, and realized that it was far more important for her to keep the upper hand with him than she had realized. There *was* no place in The Tradition for a Godmother to be courted honorably by a Prince—therefore, The Tradition would be hunting for some other option that might fit. The most logical one was to fit him in as The Prisoner, which, in effect, he was. And there was a precedent for *good* magicians holding royalty prisoner in order to facilitate their going through a set of trials. That was the path *she* wanted this thing to take.

The trouble was, in that case, the magician was usually old and male.

The Tradition was having some difficulty with her being neither.

So the next logical role for Alexander was that of the Seducer, and ultimately, the Betrayer.

And as for her—she remembered all too well what Bella had told her. She was *supposed* to have been the bride of a Prince, and hence, every unmarried Prince that crossed *her* path was going to be irresistibly attractive to her. She was going to have to fight that, every moment that he was not a donkey.

Hob was right. The man was trouble.

The problem was, she had taken the situation on; she was honor-bound now to see it through.

"I'm an idiot," she muttered under her breath, and went off to see the Unicorns. The stallions had agreed to let her have as much magic as she wanted—which was considerably *less* than she was going to take.

There was at least one bright spot in all of this. If The Tradition was going to start trying to manipulate her again, there was going to be magic accumulating around *her,* magic she could siphon off of herself for the first time since she had become a Godmother. There was a sort of ironic justice in it; she was going to have the magic she needed to fight the will of The Tradition from the magic The Tradition was using to try to force her to its will. And using that magic to fight The Tradition was only going to make The Tradition bring more magic to bear on her, which she could in her turn use to fight it....

It was enough to make a sane person dizzy.

At least she was getting firewood for the winter out of all of this!

Confined to the cottage and grounds as he was, Alexander got his fill of looking at the Witch early in the day. As the sun rose and the heat increased, Hob took him off cutting wood and moved him to carrying water for the Brownie, Lily, to water the garden. At several points in the proceedings, that woman sauntered past with a Unicorn following her like a faithful dog, and finally he muttered something under his breath.

The Brownie had sharper ears than he had reckoned on. "She's not a Witch," Lily said, matter-of-factly, as she carefully watered the base of each of the squash plants.

"What?" he asked.

"She's not a Witch," Lily repeated. "She's a Fairy Godmother. Except that she's mortal, not one of the Fair Folk."

He muttered something under his breath. The Brownie evidently took this to mean that he was interested, and proceeded to lecture him at length about Witches, Godmothers and Sorceresses, and how they were different from each other. He got some relief from the lecture when he had to go fetch more water, but not much, since she took it up again where she had left off the moment he returned.

And she asked him *questions* about what she'd told him, just as if she was one of his tutors! If he didn't answer to her satisfaction, she went on about it until his head was full of it, and he took to paying attention just so she wouldn't natter endlessly about it so much. So by the time he got to take a break for something to eat at around noon, he knew a thousand times more about magicians than he'd ever learned in his entire life.

At least he knew enough not to call that woman a "Witch" again. Though he was damned if he'd call her "Godmother." He thought about "Mistress," with the sarcastic inflection that would turn it into an insult, but decided, on the whole, he'd better stick to what the Brownies called her. "Madame Elena."

Arrogant bitch.

After lunch, Master Hob came and dragged him off to some other work, helping to lay the drystone wall that he had hauled stone for as a donkey. At least Hob didn't lecture.

Finally, though, when he saw that woman wander by three times in the course of what could not even have been an hour, he growled under his breath, "Oh, *Godmother*, is it? Base-born peasant more like! Belongs in the kitchen, she does; too stupid to recognize her betters, cleaning pots would be good enough for her. Doesn't she ever do any work?"

Hob stopped what he was doing. Stopped dead. And in a cold voice that put goose bumps on Alexander's arms, said, "Don't ever say that in my hearing again."

No threat. No punishment. Just that. And somehow, that simple sentence felt more imperiling than a cold knife-blade laid along his neck.

He coughed. Hob ignored him. Not, as in merely *ignored* him, but as in, "paid no attention to him because his intelligence was less than that of the village idiot." To say he resented that was an understatement, but he was also not going to push things.

Because thanks to Lily's lecture, he knew what, exactly, the four little people were. Though they might play at being servants, they were Fair Folk, and if the tales of his childhood were anything to go by, they *could* be powerful. He already knew that Hob was physically stronger than any two adult human men and all you had to do was look at the amount of wall he'd built today, by himself, to know that there was something quite formidable about the Brownie; Hob had magic himself, for sure, because every stone he laid (and he laid them twice as fast as a human mason) was placed perfectly and never moved or shifted. Alexander wasn't particularly anxious to see Hob perform some sort of magic on *him*.

He must have offended Hob more deeply than he guessed, for about dinnertime, Hob simply got up and stalked off, leaving him there beside the stone wall, wondering what to do. It was Lily who came for him a moment later.

"Come along, young fool," she said, beckoning to him. "You've gotten Hob in a temper, you have, and that takes some doing."

Alexander got up and followed her obediently, as she led the way to the kitchen yard. She pointed at the pump.

"Wash yourself up," she told him curtly. "And yes, I know what you said around Hob. Maybe your kind don't think that much of an insult, but I'm going to tell you why our kind does."

And while he stripped himself to the waist, while he washed himself in cold water and harsh soap until *she* was satisfied, and while he donned the clean, coarse clothing of a base-born laborer that she handed to him, she told him.

He got the main idea early on; how it was the Godmothers and the Wizards who worked tirelessly to keep things running smoothly. But as she elaborated on her theme, detailing all that Madame Elena had, herself, accomplished in the last several weeks, he found himself grudgingly impressed against his will. It wasn't so much the steering of lives into the most pleasant—or at least, the least harmful—path. It was something else; the way that the Godmothers also served as intermediaries between the world of the *fully* magical and the "real" world that he had (until now, at least) lived in.

Madame Elena had been doing a respectable amount of what he would call "herding"—protecting the Fair Folk from human encroachment, and the humans from Fair Folk meddling. "Used to be, before there was a lot of God-mothers and Wizards, half the time a farmer wouldn't know when he went out to his barn of a morning whether he'd find his horses lathered up from being stolen for a Wild Hunt in the night, or whether his cows had been milked dry. And as for you so-called highborn lot, well! Used to be unless you had nursery-maids awake all night, and horseshoes over the cradle, you'd end up with a changeling in place of your firstborn! There'd be Fair Folk coming around at feast-time, and woe betide if you failed in courtesy! There's many a noble house was in ruins within a year, or still has some dreadful curse hanging over it, because the door got slammed in some Fae Queen or Elven Knight's face! And then there was what you Mortals used to do to our kind!"

Now, as it happened, this was one aspect of which Alexander himself had direct experience, and no reason to doubt.

When he had first been sent to the military academy, his best friend had been another young Prince, the only other royal scion in the place at the time, Robert of Bedroford. The instructors, and indeed, some of the other pupils, had kept their distance from the likable young lad, for no reason that Alexander had been able to see. His own valet had tried to discourage the friendship, but when he had been unable to dissuade Alexander by indirect means, had finally shrugged and said, enigmatically, "Well, perhaps it won't come, being as he isn't home."

What "it" was, no one would tell him, and Robert had seemed blissfully unaware of the existence of "it."

Then came the morning of Robert's seventeenth birthday.

The two of them had planned to spend it together, once drills and lessons were done, but Robert was missing from his bed at reveille.

Frantic searching and questioning of the servants finally uncovered a single kitchen-girl who'd seen him, just after midnight, going down to the stables, white-faced, and moving like a man in a nightmare. He'd emerged a short while later, astride a huge black, red-eyed stallion, and galloped off into the night.

Now, as Alexander himself knew, there were no stallions of any color, and no black horses, red-eyed or otherwise, in the academy stables. In point of fact, because the academy uniform was a handsome dark blue, all of the academy horses were a carefully dappled-grey, so that all of them matched. And all of them were geldings.

A search party was organized—but it had seemed to Alexander that it was a singularly *dis*organized party, with no sense of urgency to it. And in fact, nothing was found.

A week later, a letter had come from Bedroford, which Alexander, as Robert's friend, had been permitted to read. Prince Robert's body had been deposited "as anticipated" on the threshold of the Palace by a huge, black, red-eyed stallion at dawn on the morning of his birthday. It was the phrase "as anticipated" that had come as a shock.

Even more of a shock had been the explanation, carefully and clinically given to him. The Royal House of Bedroford, it seemed, was under a curse, incurred when the firstborn son and heir had insulted an Elven Queen and stolen her favorite stallion five hundred years before. Since that time, the firstborn son of every generation was doomed to try to ride the Elven Stallion between midnight and dawn of his seventeenth birthday. Very few of them survived the experience, as the Stallion could, and usually did, perform antics such as galloping along the bottoms of rivers and charging along the tops of mountains where the air was too thin to breathe. And, of course, it could (and did) gallop through the Faerie Realms as well, which contained things that were not meant for mortal eyes. Of all of the firstborn Princes of Bedroford, only three had survived the ride, and of those three, only one had emerged sane.

All this Alexander had learned only after Robert's death. His family had hoped that the curse might be subverted if he was not raised at home, that when the Stallion came for him, it would look for him at Bedroford and, not finding him, give up.

Clearly, nothing of the kind had happened.

"Have you ever heard of the curse on Bedroford?" he asked, hesitantly.

She put her hands on her hips and raised an eyebrow. "Oh, yes. And have *you* ever heard *our* side of it?" She didn't give him a chance to answer. "Young fool makes a drunken bet, marches into the High Hall as drunk as a tinker, sits down at the Queen's Table, and treats her like his doxy. Then, if you please, he steals the Black Horse. Bad enough. *Except,* the Black Horse is her brother, and the bridle he bound the Horse with was made with Cold Iron. He was a year in healing, can't show his face, now, without a mask. He bears the scars and the pain of them to this day; mark one of us with Cold Iron and we suffer from it forever. And thanks to that, he'll never be made King, for our Kings must be without flaw."

Alexander thought about Robert, thought about all of the Princes before Robert who had died. Then thought about living forever—in pain, denied the right to your own throne. It might drive you mad.

"It's thanks to the Godmothers and the Wizards that sort of thing doesn't happen nearly as often anymore. And you lot don't see any of this," Lily finished crossly, handing him a thick wooden comb to get the tangles out of his hair with. "Because that's the way it's supposed to be. Them as don't *want* to be bothered with magic, doesn't have to see it. Which lets us as *is* magic go about our business without having to turn the likes of you into toads out of temper. And that doesn't even begin to cover what all the White Mages do, keeping the Dark Court Fae away from you, and the Black Mages in check. So don't you *dare* even hint that Madame Elena doesn't work."

She reclaimed the soap and her comb, snatched up his filthy clothing, and stalked off. She returned with his dinner and shoved it at him, then stalked off again.

Apparently, no one was going to invite him to the table....

He glanced around and finally elected to sit on another section of drystone wall to eat. He could hear the murmur of voices in the kitchen, and occasional laughter. He wondered if they were laughing at him.

Sunrise to sunset— He didn't have much longer as himself; he'd better enjoy it.

As the sun began to set, Elena reluctantly finished the last of her pastry and went out to look for the Prince. A bit to her surprise—because it wouldn't have been out of keeping with his attitude for him to try to make a few more attempts at escape—she found him waiting in the garden, back in his princely (now clean) clothing again. There was a stubborn set to his chin and a rebellious glare in his eyes, but she ignored both and crooked her little finger at him.

"Down to the stable, my lad," she said, leading the way. Another surprise; he followed.

He had looked quite different in the sort of loose shirt and breeches that common folks wore, with his hair all tousled and rough-combed. He wouldn't have been out of place in the village, though she had to admit, he was quite a bit handsomer than most of the village lads.

Hmm. Break hearts and promises and never give a damn, either, she reminded herself.

As the last light of sunset faded from the sky, she watched her spell take hold again, watched the despair on his face before it turned into that of a donkey. And decided, out of fairness to him, to at least tell him what had happened to his brothers.

She perched on an upturned bucket. "Your brother Julian has won King Stancia's daughter," she began.

"Oh, yes," the donkey grumbled. "With your help. Cheating."

"No, it wasn't," she retorted. "My test was as valid as

any of the others, and for your information, twenty young men, both royal and common, passed that same test at the hands of other White Mages. Julian was the twenty-first Quester to make it that far. But he was the only one to get the help of all three wilderness spirits before he got there."

"Wilderness spirits? Was that what you were gabbling about with him?" the donkey asked reluctantly, as if the words were being pulled from him.

"The first was a fox-spirit, whose tail was caught in a tree. That one was fairly obvious. The second was a lark, whose nest was being threatened by a snake; that one, only about half of the Questers spotted. The final one was something you truly had to *look* for." She smiled to herself, but the donkey noticed; his ears flattened a little, sulkily. "A Queen ant on her maiden flight was caught in a spiderweb; he heard her crying and freed her."

"What good is an ant?" the donkey asked crossly.

"Now, the first task on the mountain was to get into the maze that surrounds it, by going past the lion at the obvious entrance," she continued, ignoring him. "That was where the fox came in; she could slip through a rabbit tunnel dug under the wall and trip the latch to a locked door on the other side. The second task was to thread the maze, and that was where the lark came in; she could hover above and call out the right turnings. But the third task was to separate a bushel of wheat from a bushel of oats and place the oats in one measure of a scale and the wheat in the other. Only if the scale balanced correctly, proving you'd separated them all, would the door to the Sorcerer's Tower open. It was the ants that separated the grain for Julian; the Queen he had saved called on them and got them to help him."

"Those are *stupid* tasks!" the donkey burst out. "What about fighting a terrible monster, or climbing a cliff? Things that would prove a Quester is a good warrior!"

"What about them?" she replied. "The Mountain itself is enough to prove whether or not you are strong and can endure. As for fighting—" She shrugged. "Any fool can fight. The wise man is one who knows when not to, and when to rely on the cleverness of others."

There was a long moment of quiet; shadows had begun to fill the stable, and she wondered if Alexander had fallen asleep.

"So what was the final task?" the donkey asked suddenly, out of the darkness.

She told him.

"Huh," he grunted. "So where's the cleverness in that?"

"He had to lose without making it look as if he was losing on purpose. Otherwise, the Sorcerer would have known he was stupid, not gallant and willing to sacrifice himself," she replied.

"Huh." Another silence. "Does my father know?"

"Yes," she told him, and left it at that. "Now, I have things to do. Good night."

"Huh," said the donkey as she rose. She waited a moment longer, but there was not even a curt "good night" coming from the shadowy corner of the stall where he stood.

Still no more manners than a donkey, she thought in disgust, and left him alone in the dark.

Alexander bided his time during the next six days, working—well, like a donkey—waiting for the seventh day when he would be himself again. All right, so he couldn't escape because of that woman's spell. Very well, he would break the spell by breaking her wand. He had tried to remember as many nursery-tales about magic as he could, and every one of them said that when you broke a magician's wand, you broke all the spells that had been cast with it.

And if that didn't work, he had some other ideas.

Sure enough, at dawn on the seventh day, he woke up to find himself in his own shape again, and in his old clothes, with the woman standing over him as before. This time, though, he feigned sleep until his disorientation and dizziness passed, waiting for her to poke him with a toe again.

"Wake up, *your highness*," she said again, with that smirk in her voice that turned it into an insult. "This is no holiday—"

That was when he jumped up out of the straw, seized her wand before she or Master Hob could react, and broke it over his knee.

At the least, he expected a flash of light and a peal of thunder as all of her spells fell apart.

What he got was a peal of laughter.

In fact, that woman was so convulsed with laughter that she had to hold onto the wall of his stall to keep standing up; she bent nearly double, with one hand on her stomach, tears leaking out of the corners of her eyes as she laughed. It was Master Hob who supplied the explanation, around peals of laughter of his own.

"Ye gurt fool!" he howled. "What sort of ignoramuses are they growing in your country? Ye think a magician's power is in a puny thing like her *wand?*"

His face must have fallen a mile, for one look at it set Master Hob off a second time, and that woman, too. And when she picked up the pieces and fitted them back together again as if the wand had never been broken at all, that just put the icing on the cake for him.

All his energy ran out of him in a single moment, like water out of a broken jug. Utterly crestfallen, he slouched his way up to the woodpile without being ordered, eager to get away from their pitiless laughter. Thank heavens, they did *not* follow him, and he picked up the axe waiting for him in a foul, angry state of mind.

He worked off his anger on the wood. All right. So his

first ploy had failed. He still had a second string to his bow, and he'd bide his time and watch for an opportunity to try it today. It had to be today; he *didn't* want to spend another week as a beast.

He wanted to go home.

He had to be careful, though; the one thing he didn't want around when he tried his second plan was a Unicorn.

It wouldn't be hard to carry off, really. The wench was pretty enough; curled, golden hair that she wore without powder (surely a sign that she was base born), sparkling blue eyes, a luscious red mouth that practically begged for kisses, skin like cream. And the peasant-costume she wore most often displayed the best and most interesting of her attributes to the fullest; a pair of ripe breasts that made his groin tighten even when he was around her as a donkey. If he'd seen her working in the castle, he'd have tried for her, assuming Octavian hadn't gotten there first. Of course, his father wouldn't have liked it—he didn't like the idea of *anyone* trifling with the staff—but he wouldn't have been more than annoyed about it. *I'd have gotten a lecture, but no worse than that.*

A woman like that, still a virgin—she'd probably been mewed up here with some old stick teaching her magic, never seeing a proper man alone. A waste, that was, a damned waste. She'd be easy, so long as he could corner her somewhere without a Unicorn or one of those Brownies about to interfere. He was angry now, and it made him want to humiliate her, bring her to heel, show her who was the rightful master here. Master! That's what she needed, all right, a master! And women needed that, needed to be shown their place. Whether or not they realized it, they wanted it, too. Especially a base-born peasant. Wooing was too subtle for them. A woman like that wanted to be conquered, wanted to be overwhelmed. That's all these peasants knew, really, they were like rutting animals, no subtlety to their lovemaking. Once she had an idea of what a real man could do, she'd quit this nonsense about "teaching him lessons" and come to heel like a proper wench.

Not before lunch, though. He had to work off his anger, and besides, he wanted the memory of his humiliation to have faded before he tried.

It was after luncheon that his opportunity came. The last of the drystone wall was laid, the woman Lily was off somewhere doing something else and didn't need his hand at watering the garden just then, and he was alone in the kitchen yard. That was when she came by, basket full of some herbage or other, without a Unicorn in tow, and not a Brownie in sight.

He stepped into her path; her thoughts were clearly elsewhere, and she practically ran into him. She stopped; looked up at him with a frown as if just now really seeing him. For a moment he thought she was going to say something, then she shrugged. He moved to block her way completely as she tried to step around him, and her frown deepened, those eyes beginning to take on the hue of storm-clouds.

"Shouldn't you be doing something?" she asked, irritably.

"Yes," he replied, and seized her, crushing his mouth down on hers, ruthlessly, left hand around her waist, right hand thrust into the top of her bodice. For one glorious moment he felt her warm breast under his hand, the nipple hardening against his palm, tasted the faint, sweet taste of her mouth as he thrust his tongue past unresisting lips.

There was a flash of light, and a sound like a churchbell booming right in his ear.

Then nothing.

And he woke up, flat on his back, in the straw in his stall, his head aching as if from a dozen blows. And when he tried to move, he realized that every headache he'd ever had, *including* the other ones her magic had left him with, was nothing compared with this one.

"What's the matter?" cried Robin in alarm, as Elena stormed into the kitchen and threw the basket of herbs at the table. It skidded across the tabletop and landed on the floor.

"That—that—that *man*!" she shouted, scrubbing at her mouth with the back of her hand to get the taste of him out of it. "He tried to—to seduce me!"

"I warned you," Rose said, dourly, coming into the kitchen and rescuing the basket and its contents. "I told you he was going to be trouble. I'll just take these to the stillroom, shall I?"

"Well, he's trouble with an aching head now," she replied savagely. "And if he tries that again, I'll—I'll *geld* him!"

"I doubt that'll be necessary," Hob put in his bit, coming in through the door from the yard himself. "But I think I'll just go threaten him with it. After he wakes up from your spell that is. I saw you knock him down just now, and I just dragged him off and put him in the stall, by the way."

"He'll be unconscious for an hour at least." That much gave her some satisfaction; he was going to lose some of his precious time as a man, and serve him right. "I'm going up-stairs; leave me alone until dinner, please."

The House-Elves exchanged significant looks, but she pretended not to see them. At the moment, she wanted to be alone to get herself under control again, and not because she was angry.

Or to be completely accurate, not *just* because she was angry, and not *just* because she was angry at him.

She ran up the stairs and through the sitting room to fling herself into a chair at the window. Fortunately, the curtains over Randolf's mirror were closed. Not that he couldn't have seen what happened for himself, of course, but at least she wouldn't have to talk to him about it.

Once again she rubbed her mouth with the back of her hand in a very unladylike fashion; her lips felt bruised.

Well, he'd be feeling a bit *bruised* himself when he woke up. She didn't actually know how hard her magic had hit him when she'd finally gotten over her shock; she was so angry that she had lashed out without thinking. He was lucky she hadn't used a killing-stroke instead of the dis-abling one.

Brute. Beast. How *dare* he try to overpower her like that? Did he think she was some idiot milkmaid in a bawdy song, ready to spread her legs for the first good-looking man who came her way?

Actually, that was probably *exactly* what he'd thought.

And The Tradition had done its best to make his thought a reality. Evidently, bawdy songs created as many paths as the Traditional tales did. She would have to remember that from now on.

She'd felt it, when he kissed her; felt it hit her nearly as hard as her spell had hit him. Felt the weight of it crashing down on both of them, making her knees go weak, parting her lips for him, making her secret places feel tight and hot with a rush of longing as she—

She realized what was happening and slashed at the thought with venom.

Damn it! It was doing it again!

Furious now, she got up and splashed cold water on her hot face. *No,* she thought at it, summoning up images of ice and snow, of frozen rivers and chill grey skies. *No, damn you! You will not do that to me!*

Half of her wanted to send him away, now, this instant. Sending him away, perhaps to a Wizard, would be so much safer! She would never have to see him again, and surely there was *someone* she could trust with his education!

Half of her refused to even consider the idea of giving up.

It wasn't only that she hated to concede that she had failed—which she hadn't, not yet! It wasn't only that now that she was looking into his past with Randolf, she had an idea that if she could just get past the arrogance and the assumption of superiority, there was something there that could be worked with. Well, look at Octavian! She would have been willing to bet that it was going to take until winter set in before he humbled himself to appear at Arachnia's castle to offer himself as a kitchen-boy! But there he was, scrubbing pots, submitting himself to the insults of her cook—

"I think it was the Mirrormede," Arachnia had said in her letter, brought by bat just last night. *"He managed to find his way to the Mirrormede—you know, that naiad pool I have that shows people what they most need to see. About half the time it shows people the present, about a quarter of the time it shows them what other people think of them, and about a quarter of the time it shows them their future as it will be if they go on as they are. I don't know what he saw in it, but whatever it was, it's shaken him to the core."*

Whatever it was—and Elena had to wonder if it wasn't a glimpse of the future—the image of him that Randolf showed her was a far cry from the arrogant Prince that had passed her by without a word. He was working as Arachnia's lowest stablehand. He took the abuse that her coachman heaped on him without a word of complaint.

And he had begun to take notice of the timid little tweenie who served as the cook's scullery-maid. If he was moved to protect her rather than abuse her himself, that would signal the moment when the ruse would be dropped and Arachnia would send him home.

So; it was clear that Julian was already a decent fellow. It appeared that Octavian was good enough stock to have an unexpectedly swift redemption. So there was plenty of hope for Alexander.

Plenty of hope for such a handsome fellow, with such fine, broad shoulders and hard, strong body, with a face like a young god and hands that knew how to caress a—

STOP THAT!

Furious all over again, she stood up out of her chair and

gazed up at the ceiling. Without really thinking about it, she gathered her power around her, like storm clouds filled with the lightning of her anger. And she confronted The Tradition in her mind as if she was a Sorceress facing off against a Great Enemy of her own. "Now you can just listen to me right now," she told The Tradition—and Anything or Anyone else that might overhear. "I will *not* go play the green-sick goose-girl to suit your tales and your plans! You *cannot* seduce me with a pretty face. I am Godmother Elena, by all that's holy, and I was Elena Klovis before that, me, myself, and no puppet to be danced about on a path you choose! I did not lie down for my stepmother to be Ella Cinders, and I will not lie down for a Prince with a handsome face! I refuse to be any man's doxy, to be flung aside and forgotten! I will be *me*, on my own terms, by my own rules, with my own plans and my own decisions!"

Everything went very still, then. Very, very still. Once again, Elena had the feeling of great power looming over her—but this time, it was waiting. Waiting for something. Some direction, perhaps?

Whatever it was—it was certainly listening to her now.

Not even a breath of breeze stirred in the room. She realized that she could not hear anything outside the room—not the cackling of the chickens in the garden, not the House-Elves working inside or outside, not the birds in the sky nor the wind in the birches. The skin on the back of her neck prickled. Her back was to the window, but she wondered—if she dared to turn around and look, would she see the world going on as usual out there? Or would she see nothing at all?

Something very odd, perhaps even unprecedented, was happening here. Godmother Bella had never, ever told her about anything like this—

She needed to say something. She *knew* that, as certain as the blood flowed in her veins. She felt it in her bones. Something wanted—shaping.

Words are power in a magician's mouth. Choose them carefully.

And yet—she always got her best results when she wasn't too specific, when she let the power choose its own shape.

She took a deep breath. One by one, the words fell, carefully, from her lips. "A playfellow I'll be, but no man's toy. A partner, helper, but no one's servant nor slave. I will be captain of my fate, and commander of my destiny, though the path I may share and the course I chart be followed by others. What I have, I'll share, but I'll not give it over. What I am, I am, and I'll not change it. What I will be, I will be, by my own will and no other. Now. Take *that* and make something of it!"

There was something like a great intaking of breath. Something like a sigh.

Then the world gave a shake, like a dog, and dropped back to normal.

She wondered what she had bound—or what she had unleashed.

Alexander was getting used to waking up to find people standing over him, wearing unpleasant expressions. What he was *not* used to was finding people standing over him holding a crude metal instrument in one hand that he happened to recognize.

Master Hob must have seen his eyes track immediately to that hand and what it held, because he smiled, grimly. "I assume ye know what this is, ye cream-faced loon?" he asked. "Happens I'm practiced in the use of it. Never seen any reason to keep jack or stallion around here, when a gelding's so much steadier."

A great shudder of horror convulsed Alexander as he stared at the hideous thing.

"And it'd be wise for ye to remember, my lad," Master Hob continued, softly, but with great menace, "what happens to the ass happens to *you*."

It felt as if a cold hand closed around his throat, and he nodded, slowly.

"Good. Now we understand each other." Master Hob turned, but only to stow the dreadful object in the pocket of a leather apron hanging on a hook next to his stall. "*She* might be put out if she found I'd been altering ye, but it'd be too late by that time. She'd rather just keep you in the ass's skin for longer; I take a more direct approach to the problem."

He shuddered again. He had no doubt that the little man would follow through on the threat if it suited him.

"Now then, up with ye," Master Hob continued. "And I doubt not ye've an aching head, and too bad. Mistress Lily needs help with her watering again."

So, aching head or no aching head, he got up and followed the little man back up to the cottage garden. It had been a long day; it was getting longer by the moment.

* * *

It took two days before his fear wore itself out and his anger came back to the surface.

He wanted to kill her. She had ruined his life; and that assumed he was ever going to have a life again, at least, a "life" as he had known it.

No, he didn't want to *kill* her, he wanted to humiliate her. He wanted to see her crawl, wanted to see her humbled, wanted to see her made lower than the lowest whore in the cheapest tavern in the scummiest city in the Five Hundred Kingdoms.

And he didn't dare touch her.

He might be many things, but "stupid" wasn't one of them. The Unicorns never left her side anymore, two of them at a time. If he touched her, they'd kill him. If they didn't kill him, her magic would knock him arse over end again. He didn't care to repeat *that* experience.

The days were bad enough, slaving away in harness, sunup to sundown, angry thoughts buzzing around in his head like bees in a disturbed hive. The nights were worse.

He dreamed, at night. He dreamed of Julian, and nearly went mad with envy, seeing him ruling his new Kingdom, with his exquisite young bride at his side. It nearly made him sick, and yet he couldn't hate Julian—that woman had made it quite clear that Julian had won his prize fairly, and if he was honest with himself (and in dreams, he had to be) he had to admit that given the nature of the trials, *he* would have lost. But bloody Hell! How it grated on him! It was only made worse when in those dreams, Julian proved himself to be a fairly good ruler. Not perfect; it was clear enough from one or two of the decisions that Alexander saw that Julian had a lot to learn. But he was respected and admired by his underlings, and loved by his bride and his people.

He dreamed of Octavian, too, dreamed of *him* humbled as badly as Alexander was, slaving away in a stable in some grim, dark keep, eating whatever he could beg from the kitchen, cleaning filthy stalls. It shocked him, to see Octavian brought so low. It shocked him even more when he realized that (in his dreams, at least) Octavian believed that he *deserved* this terrible punishment.

And he dreamed of his father—seeing King Henrick as he had *never* seen him before; not a broken man, but a severely battered and lonely man, pale, silent, and grieving. Two of his sons gone, the only one left being not at all the favored one. And in his way, Henrick feared to approach the only son that he knew he had left, fearing what that son would say to him, the father who had held him in scorn. No, the third son was not lost, but certainly out of reach, so far as Henrick was concerned. It cut Alexander to the heart to see his father in such a state, and in his dreams, he tried to reach out to the King, to *tell* him what had happened to all of his sons. But he was like a phantom; he could hear and see all, but no one could hear or see him.

He would awaken from these dreams in the middle of the night, sweating. If he had been a man, he could have wept, but he was a donkey, and beasts couldn't cry. The best he could manage was a fit of dry, wheezing sobs that shook his bones and made him ache all over, and finally tired him out until he could sleep again.

He hated everything at that point, including himself.

But most of all, he hated *her*.

He watched her as she went about her business, as she came and went from the cottage, sometimes garbed as richly as any queen, sometimes in the dress of the merely wealthy, but mostly in her peasant guise. He never knew where she was going, or what she was going to do when she got there, but at least twice she went out in a strange, colorful cart pulled by the oddest looking excuse for a horse he had ever seen. Even when she was gone, the work did not stop; her House-Elf minions acted exactly as they did when she was there to supervise them, and so, perforce, did he.

Finally, the seventh day arrived again, and he was back to being himself. For whatever good it did him. He couldn't think of any new plans to get himself free, and the moment he was a man again, the Unicorns doubled their guard on her.

What was more, he discovered by making the attempt that the cottage wouldn't allow him inside it. Literally. There was a barrier at the doors and windows that he not only could not cross, but could not see past. So trying to sneak in and catch her unawares (and de-unicorned) was not going to do him any good, either.

He wanted, with a physical ache, to go *home*.

He was reduced to throwing insults at her, but although Master Hob bristled and the Unicorns glowered, all *she* did was laugh. "In a contest of wit, your highness, I fear you are but half-armed," she said, mockingly. "And you can call me whatever you like, if it makes you feel any better. Being called a whore does not make me one, any more than calling Master Hob a giant makes him thirty feet tall."

And she sailed off on some errand or other, leaving him seething and speechless.

It was almost a relief when night fell and he became a donkey again.

Another week began in anger, but something odd was happening to him as the days passed. There was nothing wrong with his physical energy, but—but he felt drained anyway. The moment he was left alone without anything to do, he found himself sinking into a dull lethargy. It took nearly three days before he realized what was wrong, and when he did, the realization of what was happening took him by surprise.

It was getting harder and harder to sustain his anger. It was as if he was blunting it against the rock of that woman's indifference; she clearly did not care if he was angry, or in despair, or indeed, in *any* emotional state. She did not even care if he hated her.

For the first time in his life he was *below* someone's notice. It did not matter to anyone here what he thought, of her or anything else. What his opinions were was of no more consequence to her than the price of corn in some far distant land. How could *anyone* sustain any emotion in the face of that?

He was never going home.

He was certain of that, now.

And no one would really miss him, either. To whom had he really endeared himself? Not to Octavian. Julian—well, perhaps, but Julian knew what had become of him, and if

Julian had really cared, wouldn't he have sent someone to come looking for him?

His father? But his father didn't really know him; he was a cipher, the "spare," useful if something happened to Octavian. He recalled the day he had graduated and come home, home to a room that looked like every other guest chamber in the Palace, to a father whose presents on any occasion had always been the same thing; books on military history with money tucked inside. His instructors at the Academy knew him better than his own father did. He had not had a good friend since Robert had died. In a month, he'd been given up on. In a year, people might remember him with the words, "poor Alexander." In ten, you would not find one person in a hundred in Kohlstania who would remember he had even existed.

His bulwark of anger collapsed like a fortress of snow in the spring at that point.

Without it, he had nothing to sustain him. And he sank into a kind of insensate despair, saying nothing to Hob, doing what he was told, eating what was placed in his manger, more and more lost in a grey fog of apathy. He just could not muster the mental energy even to decide to go out in the meadow and eat grass instead of the hay that was in front of him.

When he woke as a man for the fourth time, he was still sunk in that state of despair, and even Hob noticed it when he came to fetch him for the morning's work.

The little man looked at him sharply. For his part, Alexander just looked back at him, dully, without getting out of a sitting position.

"What ails you?" the Brownie asked. "Sickening over something?"

He shook his head. *And why should you care?* he thought. *Except that you would be able to go buy a beast that's less trouble if I were to die.* It occurred to him that perhaps he ought to ask that woman to leave him as a donkey from now on. Surely getting lost in the beast would be better than this.

Hob gave him another look. "Even the lowest scut gets a half-day a month," he said gruffly. "No working for you today."

That penetrated his fug, and he raised his head a little. "What?"

"Take it, ye green-goose, afore I change my mind," the Brownie growled, and promptly turned on his heel and stomped off, leaving Alexander alone in the stable again.

No work? Then what was he supposed to do with himself?

He sat there for a long moment in the gloom—but the straw prickled him, and there were little rustlings of mice and insects that didn't bother him as a beast, but made his skin crawl as a man. With a sigh, he got to his feet and wandered outside.

He looked around, for the first time, really *looked* around, at the cottage and its grounds lying quietly in the predawn. There was a light mist lying along the ground, just at knee-height, giving the place an air of mystery. To his right lay the stone cottage, grey-walled and thickly thatched. The only signs of life were the birds twittering in the thatch around the windows. He knew from experience that it would not be until the sun actually rose that anyone would be stirring there.

In front of him was the bare, hard dirt of the stableyard, though "yard" was a bit of a misnomer, as there was not a great deal of space there, just enough to turn a small cart around. To his left were the kitchen-gardens and beyond that, the drystone wall he had been working on.

So far, there didn't seem to be anywhere to go.

Behind the cottage were some little sheds, the ricks of curing firewood, and the chopping block, where he would have been if Hob hadn't ordered him to take a rest. That was no help.

In front of the cottage was a flower and herb garden, but he was hardly the sort to putter in a garden, even if it had been his.

But all around the cottage grounds, separating it from the forest, was a meadow left to grow as it would, where he was allowed to graze when he was a donkey.

He already knew that his "boundary" was the edge of the wood; that was where he was turned back any time he tried to pass on his own. But the meadow was wide and irregularly shaped. He hadn't seen most of it yet, and there were probably places where he could be alone for as long as Hob didn't actually come looking for him.

For lack of anything better, he wandered out through the kitchen-gardens, over the stile, and into the bottom meadow. He thought there was a pond out there.

Sure enough, he found, when he'd waded through mist and grass for a bit, that there was a pond fed by a lively little stream, rimmed with willow and birch. Someone—Hob, perhaps—had tied a little boat up to the bank. It was far too small to take someone of Alexander's size and weight, or he might have gone for a row, just because the boat was there. But if he sat down on the bank, he couldn't see the cottage from here; maybe he was no good at pretending that he wasn't held in this bizarre captivity, but at least, he wouldn't have it thrust in his nose.

Blackbirds sang a few experimental notes in the reeds, and off in the woods, he heard a cuckoo. It was peaceful here, and somehow soothing to the aches in his soul. He sank down on the bank and watched the sun come up, the clear, thin light streaking across the hazy blue of the sky, as the birds began their morning carol.

He let his mind empty of everything. He had never done that before. But then, he'd never been at a place in his life where he could. In Kohlstania, he'd been Prince Alexander, one day to be Commander in Chief of the Army, currently standing duty under the present Commander, and second in line for the throne. In the Academy, he'd been Cadet Alexander, Squad Leader and Prefect, responsible for the behavior of all of the Cadets subordinate to himself. He'd always had things to remember, duties to perform.

Here he was no one and nothing. His rank mattered not at all, his titles were meaningless, his value only so much as paid for the food he ate. And for today at least, he had no responsibilities at all.

There was a curious freedom in that. Perhaps that was all that freedom really was, in the end, the knowledge that you had nothing and were nothing, and thus, had nothing to lose or gain. "Free as a bird" was synonymous with "tied to nothing" after all.

So he sat and watched the new day unfold as he had

never quite watched a dawn before. And for an hour, at least, he stopped being "Prince," stopped even being "Alexander," and just *was*.

The sun swiftly burned off the mist, the sun dried the dew off the grass, and he lay back on the soft grass and stared up at the sky. He thought about going up to the cottage for breakfast, but since he hadn't been working like a dog, he wasn't particularly hungry. *I'll just lie here a little,* he decided. *After everyone else has gotten food, I'll slip up there and get what's left. If I get hungry. If...*

And somehow, he slipped into a drowse without ever noticing that he had done so.

He dreamed—or thought he dreamed—and in his dream, he opened his eyes at a little sound, and looked into a pair of extraordinary eyes. They were an intense violet color, and belonged to a creature that was about the size of Hob, but nothing like him. This was a girl, a very young child, wraith-thin but bright with health, clothed, so far as he could tell, in nothing but water-weeds. There were water-lilies in her streaming wet hair, and she gazed down at him with all the solemnity of a judge.

"Why are you so unhappy, son of Adam?" she asked, in a voice that reminded him of the sound of a brook flowing over stones.

"Because—I want to be free," he replied without thinking. "I want to go home, before people forget I ever existed."

"Ah," the child said, looking wise. "Are you sure that is what you want?"

"Of course I'm sure!" he replied. "I'd do anything to figure out how to get out of here!"

"Oh, that is a dangerous thing to pledge, *anything*, son of Adam," said the child. "You are lucky I am a small Fae, and have so little power. I could do you a mischief with that pledge, if I were minded." She gurgled a laugh. "But it is a lovely day, and I am a lazy Fae, as well as small. And—" She tilted her head to the side, considering. "It is in my mind that you are the thing, maybe, that our King called for, on a day not unlike this one, on a spring morning, when a girl old in pain but young in power came to be weighed and judged and gifted. So I will give you what you ask, the thing that will help you, though it may not seem that way at first to you." She stood up, and held out her hands, which seemed to fill with light.

And then she spilled the light over him. It floated down on him in incandescent motes that filled him with warmth as they touched him.

"Mortal, here's the key to free you," she half-sung, and half-chanted. "See yourself as others see you!"

Then she suddenly lifted up on one toe, spun in place, and vanished with a tinkling laugh and a glow that blinded him.

There was nothing standing above him, and no sign there ever had been anything but dream.

He blinked, and raised a hand to rub his eyes. "Maybe I am sickening for something," he muttered to himself. What kind of a daft dream had *that* been?

His stomach growled, and he sat up; and maybe some of the leaden lethargy had lifted. He was hungry, anyway.

Breakfast first. Then—see what would happen, on a day when nothing was happening as he had come to expect.

He got to his feet and brushed himself off, and really *saw* the clothing he was wearing.

Each day that he had spent as himself, he had awakened in it, and despite all the heavy labor he did while working in it, the clothing looked exactly as it had the moment he had been transformed into a donkey. The first day, after he had washed, Lily had taken it from him and given him coarse, common laborer's clothing; he'd taken back his own and put it on damp when she'd washed it. After that first day, he had refused to surrender it. But now, as he brushed grass and bits of leaf and twig from the tight military-style breeches and tunic, he paused in dismay.

Not because it was filthy, because it wasn't—it was no dirtier than it had been when he'd been so unceremoniously transfigured. But—he realized at that moment how utterly ridiculous it was.

It was completely unsuitable for doing the sort of work he'd been put to; too tight, too ornamented, too ostentatious, too impractical, too hot. There was a reason why that woman swanned about in her peasant garb; *this was a farm, and she was working just as hard as the rest of them.* He'd *seen* her; milking the cows, tending the garden, and presumably, doing things in the cottage as well. You couldn't do any of those jobs trussed up in a Court Gown, teetering on high-heeled slippers.

And apparently the rule of "if you don't work, you don't eat" applied to her as well.

He wasn't proving anything by clinging to this ridiculous suit of clothing except that he was stubborn. And, possibly, stupid as well.

Yes; well, look what she turned you into, after all, commented that voice in the back of his mind. *Making the outside match the inside?*

He would have had a hard time denying it at that moment, so he didn't even bother to try.

Instead, he made his way slowly up to the cottage, with another request besides food on his mind.

To his intense relief, there was no sign of the Unicorns or that woman, but the Brownie Lily was already at work in her garden. She straightened as he came up the path and gave him a measuring look.

"Robin says he thinks your sickening for something," she said abruptly. "Well?"

"Not that I know of, Mistress Lily," he said. "But I would like something to eat—and—" he hesitated, then blundered on "—if you still have the shirt and breeches you gave me to work in, I would like to get rid of these. For now, anyway."

Her expression didn't change, except that her eyes narrowed a little. In speculation? Perhaps.

He wondered what she saw when she looked at him, then got a kind of flash of what it might be. *Sullen, rude, restless, stubborn. Foolish, insisting on working in his stupid quasi-uniform, as if anyone around here, where magic flowed and your dress could change in a wink, would be impressed! Pig-headed, too. And very, very young.* Of course, he'd seem young to one of the Fair Folk; however not? He had no idea how old Lily was, but she'd mentioned serving several of this Godmother's predecessors, so he must seem like an infant to her.

He flushed. And added, belatedly. "If you please?"

"If I—ah, right. Come along with you, then," she said, and got to her feet.

She led him to the kitchen door, left him there, and came
out with the clothing and a basket. "Here," she said, thrust-
ing both at him. "You can't go far, but—well, breaking your
fast by the pond is—and a book—ah, here!"

Startled, he took the clothing and basket, remembered at
the last minute to thank her, and decided to leave while she
was still treating him nicely. What had gotten into these people? First Master Hob, thinking he was ill and giving him no
work for the day, and now Mistress Lily!

Feeling unwontedly modest, he got out of sight around
a shed and changed into the commoner's clothing. And
knew in an instant that he had been a fool to refuse it before this. It wasn't coarse; on the contrary, the loose shirt
was of linen as fine as anything he owned. For the first time
he felt *comfortable*, not hot and sweaty, with a collar and
waistband that were both too tight.

That left the boots—

He looked at them, looked at his bare feet, and wriggled
his toes in the grass, experimentally. Riding boots, especially
cavalry boots, were not made for walking. He hadn't gone
barefoot since he was a child....

He left the boots on top of the clothing on the kitchen
step, and took the basket back down to the pond.

There was a book on top of the napkin that covered the
food. He picked it up, curiously.

The Five Hundred Kingdoms: A History of Godmothers,
said the faintly luminous letters on the cover. He hesitated
a moment, then chose a piece of fruit and began to read
while he ate.

* * *

"Hmm," Elena said, when Lily had finished explaining why the pile of clothing was beside the kitchen door and the Prince was nowhere in sight. "You don't suppose——"

"He did say 'if you please,'" Lily pointed out. "And 'Thank you.' It's possible he's finally turned the corner."

"And it's possible that pigs will fly, but I'm not running out to buy any manure-proof umbrellas just yet," Rose replied dourly, before Elena could say anything.

"His brother is just about to earn his freedom," Elena felt moved to counter. "And I'd have given that lower odds than this."

"Hmph. I'd have said it would take magic to get *that* one to see what faults brought him here," said Rose, and gathered up the quasi-military uniform to clean and put in storage. From now on, Elena's spell would transform Alexander's current gear, rather than his original clothing.

"Maybe. Maybe not," Lily said to Rose's retreating back.

"I don't know that it would matter," Elena replied, picking up a bread roll dripping with melted butter, and biting into it thoughtfully. "Once the blinders are off, it's rather hard to go back to seeing things the way you used to."

Lily's glance was startled. "You don't suppose——" Then she stopped.

"I don't *suppose* anything," Elena told her. "But I do know this much. Some of the other Fae have been *very* interested in him. There have been a great many of them flitting about on the edges of the forest, far more than usual, and I don't think it's entirely because of the presence of all the Unicorns here. Some of them have even come to me directly to ask about him."

"Welladay." Lily's eyes widened a little, as Elena helped herself to another roll. "The Wild Fae don't talk much to us; we've not much in common with them. Like a fish trying to talk to a bird, I suppose, or a rock to a star. I hadn't noticed them about, but then, I wouldn't. But interfering—"

"Just tell me this—what would one of them do if—just speculating, mind you—he happened to wish aloud to know how to get himself out of here?" Elena raised an eyebrow at Lily, who clapped her hand to her mouth.

"By Huon's horn! *That* would appeal to the mischiefs!" Lily exclaimed. "Because—the only way for him to get out of here *without* even bending your magic is—"

"To change his ways," they said together, and Elena smiled.

"And it has to be sincere and permanent, just like what his brother's going through," she added. "So—maybe. The Wild Fae don't, won't bind if they can help it. But they'll change, oh, yes, or else, they'll midwife change along. We'll see. I'm not entirely agreeing with Rose, either, but it doesn't take much to backslide."

"And The Tradition?" Lily asked cautiously. Elena shook her head. The truth was, that since that odd day in her room, when she had confronted the faceless force that was The Tradition with her own will, although she had *still* felt its power circling around her to the extent that she felt like one of the Great Sorceresses, with enough magic at her command to move the world, she had *not* felt that terrible pressure of it on her, forcing her to walk a path she was not at all willing to take.

"This doesn't feel like The Tradition," she said only. "This is—new."

Lily blinked. Then said, "Well—good."

"It will be, if he can hold to this course," Elena replied. *"If."*

"'If ifs and ands were pots and pans, there'd be no work for tinkers,'" quoted Lily briskly. "And my garden is not getting weeded by me sitting here."

"Nor those harvest-potions getting brewed by themselves," Elena agreed, finishing the last of her breakfast. "Still—" She took a long thought. "Let's make a point of rewarding virtue, shall we?"

She and Lily exchanged a smile that might have been called "conspiratorial."

"Good idea," said Lily. "A very good idea. 'Catching more flies with honey,' eh?"

"There's truth in old saws," Elena agreed.

And maybe in a Wild Fae's help as well.

Whatever had happened to the Prince—whether it was a bit of helpful interference from one of the Fair Folk, getting sense beat into him, as Hob opined, a bout of brain-fever the way Robin suggested, Rose's suggestion that he'd managed to wear out his stupidity, or just simply that he realized that there was a *reason* why he'd wound up as a donkey—that day marked the turning-point.

He still got angry, insulted people, and showed his temper. But it was in short bursts, usually after a long and exhausting task, and he had even begun apologizing for it afterwards. And as the season moved into harvest-time, Elena made good on her determination to "reward virtue" by making a profound change. She allowed him to spend every *fourth* day as himself. Then every third. Then every other day, and told Hob to find a real donkey—"or really, whatever you think we need"—to purchase when the Horse Fair came to the village.

Hob left in the morning with a purse full of silver, and returned that evening, well before sunset, just as Alexander came up to the cottage for his supper.

The sound of hooves on the road made him look up, and brought Elena to the door. The look on his face when he saw Hob arrive riding one donkey and leading two mules was worth every silver penny that Hob had spent.

Nevertheless, he hastened to help the Brownie to unharness and put the three new animals in the stable—and put one of them into the very stall that *he* had been occupying since he had been brought to the cottage.

He was still enough of a Prince not to go to the subordinate for answers, though; when the work was done, as she had expected, he came straight out and looked about to see if she was anywhere in sight. Since she had been waiting for him to do just that, he didn't have far to look.

And he walked straight over to her, his demeanor a mixture of emotions and attitude that was so comical in its way that she had to fight to keep a straight face. For all that he was being scrupulously polite to her, he still deeply resented what she was doing to him. For all that he recognized what an idiot he had been, he resented that she was punishing him for it. And he was sullenly, burningly angry that he was still, in effect, her prisoner. She was, in a way, the Enemy—and now he had to come to the Enemy to find out what was in store for him now.

She watched him try to find a way to ask what her intentions were without asking the question directly. He didn't want to hope too much—yet hope was hard to keep down. Finally, he settled, and asked, harshly (probably more harshly than he intended), "Am I sharing my stable with animals, now?"

"In a manner of speaking," she replied, "since I expect you'll be using the room in the loft, now." She watched varied emotions chasing themselves across his face—no real surprise that there was some bitter disappointment there, since this might have meant, and he surely hoped it had meant, that his term of correction was over. "Unless, of course," she added, so he understood *why* she was not letting him go quite yet, "you backslide."

"I—" She watched the temper rise; watched him struggle to control it. And expected the outburst of anger and insults.

It never came.

"Very well, Madame," he got out, through gritted teeth, then turned on his heel and stalked back into the stable.

"Well, I like that!" Rose said indignantly from the door.

"Actually, I *do* like that," Elena said thoughtfully, turning to go back inside herself. "He could have done, or said, much worse. I believe we're getting somewhere, my thorny Rose."

"I'm still not buying manure-proof umbrellas," was all Rose said—but as she also turned to go back into the house, Elena caught a glimpse of a grudging smile.

Lily was already in the kitchen, setting out plates on the table. "Take him out some fresh linens and things, would you, Lily?" she asked. She wasn't going to do so herself, not because she thought herself above the task, but because she wasn't going to give The Tradition a second chance at going down the bawdy-ballad path. Oh, no. That was *still* the easiest road, and if she was going to keep it from happening, she had to keep her wits about her at all times.

"Already have, Godmother," Lily said with a sidelong look and a smile. "When you told Hob to go off to the Horse Fair, we knew what was toward. Saw to it this morning, while he was down clearing the nettles out."

She had to laugh at that, and she did. "You know what I'm going to do before I do, don't you?" she asked the Brownie.

"Have to, don't we?" Lily countered, with a tilt of her head. "Been serving Godmothers a mort of years now; you'll be our ninth, I reckon. Be a sad thing if we hadn't learned a bit by now."

"Nine!" That surprised her; she hadn't known that the quartet had been doing this sort of thing for so very long. "Are you weary of it yet? Have you ever wanted to—to—stop serving anyone but yourself?" There it was, the question she hadn't dared ask when she first became Godmother—did they want to be free? She didn't know what she would do without them but—

Lily laughed at her, and her fears dissolved. "Bless you, no! What's a Brownie without a home? We're the Fae of *housen*, Godmother, not the Wild Fae of the woods! Oh, I'll admit that now and again we wish we had a whole family to serve, instead of just the one Godmother, but you've managed to keep us on our toes enough to keep us busy. That's why Hob brought back the extra beasts; he reckons we'll need them."

"Ah." She was a bit nonplussed at that. "For what?"

"Oh," Lily replied, waving her hand vaguely. "Things."

Robin came in at that moment, with an empty basket that held a napkin; evidently Lily had also sent down the Prince's dinner, figuring he would not want to come to the door for it tonight. Lily took it from the other Brownie, then continued after he left. "Hadn't you noticed that some of the Witches and Hedge-Wizards of other Kingdoms have been asking you for help? We reckon you're going to get made Godmother of a couple more realms before the year is out. That means you'll be getting more people coming to *you*, and that means guests, and guests means a bigger house and more work. We *think* the house is getting ready to bud off a couple new rooms. There's a funny feeling upstairs, off the old Apprentice rooms you used to be in, and downstairs, too. The Library'll probably bud—expand—first, and then all those books Madame Bella put in the parlor and the dining room will move themselves into the new space so we'll have proper places to receive guests."

Lily said all of this so matter-of-factly that Elena's head reeled. The house—had she said *budding* rooms, as if it was some sort of plant? And the books were going to move themselves?

It was, in a way, one thing to work magic herself. It was quite enough thing to hear that it was going to be working without her intervention....

And was she really going to be given the keeping of other Kingdoms? But which ones?

In the course of an hour, once again, her life was taking

on a brand-new direction, and one she had never anticipated.

If only she had a way to contact Madame Bella! Right
now she badly wanted advice—she wanted to talk to an
older, more experienced Godmother! She needed to learn
more than Madame Bella had initially taught her, and she
had the feeling she needed to learn it quickly.

But wait—there was advice, advice in plenty, already
written down and waiting for her. She had only to find it.

"Ah—I see," she said, carefully, and laughed a little. "I
suppose you must be used to it by now."

"Oh, aye," Lily said, cheerfully, but shrewdly, and she was
watching Elena's face quite narrowly. Elena remembered
something that Bella had told her.

*"The House-Elves might seem common as clay and with-
out any kind of magic sometimes; don't allow yourself ever to
believe that. They're Fair Folk, as truly Fae as any you've seen,
through and through; they serve us because it amuses them to,
and this house and everything around it is their creation. If they
wished to, they could snap their fingers, and it would be gone
in an instant, and them with it."*

"I'll be in the library, I think," she said. Then, a little nervously, "It isn't going to do anything while I'm there, is it?"

"Bless you, no!" Lily replied. "Whatever it does, it'll be
while you're asleep. It knows that budding unsettles the
Sons of Adam and Daughters of Eve, and it's sensitive about
that sort of thing."

Oh my, she thought. *She talks about the house as if it's alive.*
Then came a more comforting thought. *But so is a tree alive,*

and I've no qualms about walking inside one of them to take tea with a dryad.

And like her house, the dryads' trees were all bigger on the inside than the outside. Perhaps that was what the cottage was; a kind of dryadic tree.

"Well, I'll be in the Library," she repeated, more confidently now. "All evening, probably."

"Very good, Godmother," Lily said, looking pleased out of all proportion to what Elena had just told her. "I'll let the others know."

Now what did I say that's made her smile so? Elena wondered, as she waved the lamps to light in the Library, and prepared a simple Seeking Spell to help her find the exact books she needed. *Or—was it what I didn't say?*

But she couldn't spare any more time in wondering one way or the other. She had to find out just how it was that Godmothers were assigned more responsibilities—and what it meant to the Godmother in question when it happened.

The Seeking Spell led her to book after book, until she had a pile of them, twenty deep, on the table she used as a desk. She looked at them and sighed. It was going to be a very long night.

Alexander was racked with so many conflicting emotions that he knew better than to be around anyone else, so he strode rigidly off back to the stable. That woman's casual pronouncement had left him both elated and crushed. When he'd realized that Hob had brought back other work animals he had hoped—and simultaneously told himself *not* to hope—that his term of punishment was at an end. To learn that it wasn't made him want to howl.

But on the other hand—

On the other hand, tonight I go to sleep as myself, and wake up as myself. In a bed! Or at least, in whatever passes for a bed in that loft....

And he realized then that he didn't even know what was up there; *he* had never been there, and—

—*and I guess I was just taking it for granted that Master Hob slept up there. But come to think of it, I never heard any footsteps up there in all the time I've been here, so it must be empty.*

He'd gone back to the stable, of course, out of habit. It was nearly dark, and he "should" have been in "his" stall, waiting bitterly for the magic to turn him back into a beast.

Tonight, it wouldn't, and that felt—unsettling.

To shake off the feeling, he sought the ladder that led to the loft and climbed it. Might as well find out what his new domain looked like.

He pushed open the hatch at the top of the ladder, and warm, welcoming light spilled down around him. Blinking, he finished his climb, poking his head up into an odd, but quite comfortable room.

The attics at the Academy had been like this; right under the roof, so that you could only walk upright down through the center. This was a thatched building, but someone had gone to the trouble of putting in tongue-and-groove boarding lining the ceiling so that at least he wouldn't have wildlife dropping into his bed and belongings out of the thatch. There was one very tiny window at each end of the single long room, curtained, with the shutters opened wide to the night air. There was a table under each window and a brass lamp on each table. That made sense; you wouldn't want candles with open flames around so much hay and straw. The lamps looked very heavy; you'd have to work hard to tip one over.

In the center of the room was an odd box that *looked* like a brick stove, except there was no chimney. He couldn't imagine what it was, so he dismissed it for the moment from his mind.

His bed was on the right; somewhat to his surprise, it was a *real* bed. Somehow he'd expected a pallet on the floor or something similar. But no, this was a real wood-framed bed, with a dark wooden blanket-chest at the foot of it, neatly made up, faded blue linen coverlet and pillows and all, and if he wasn't mistaken, beneath the sheets and coverlet was a featherbed mattress.

To his left, the lamp shared the table with a floral-figured pottery pitcher and basin. And fitted in under the slope of the roof, down both sides, were shelves. There was clothing on those shelves, and a pair of sturdy boots he didn't recognize, along with the carefully folded and familiar pieces of his princely garb and his riding-boots.

And there were books....

Now that, he had not expected at all.

He hadn't laid his hands on single book except for that strange little history that Lily had given him since he'd arrived here. That, he had read from cover to cover, and had thought about it quite a bit. But here were more books, many more, and though he was not the bookworm that Julian was, he was still fond of reading, and he had missed it.

So the first thing he did, the first things he inspected, were the books.

Now, this *was* a stable, and these *were* (presumably) the quarters of a stablehand. He expected books about horses and mules and donkeys.

These were histories and practical books on magic.

And it didn't take very long to discover that, like the book that Lily had gotten into his hands, they were written from, and for, the very peculiar viewpoint of the Godmothers and Wizards.

The Godmother's Book of Days, read one, and that was the one he settled in with, reading propped up in his new (and oh, so comfortable) bed, after blowing out the lamp at the farther end of the room.

Elena glanced out the window of the Library after darkness fell, and frowned for a moment to see a square of light where she hadn't ever noticed a light before. Then after a moment, she realized what it must be, and smiled ruefully.

The room over the stable, of course. So the Prince was in his new quarters.

Probably nothing like what he's used to, she thought, then had to laugh at herself. Of course! Lately he was used to bedding down in straw at the clean end of his loose-box! A bed of any kind should seem like a luxury to him now.

It was certainly better than his brother Octavian's lot. Octavian got an empty stall and slept on what he could find. He hadn't sunk so low as to use dirty straw, but he wasn't allowed the new, clean stuff the horses got. No, the best he could manage was fusty stuff from last year, that had gotten a bit moldy, the thin heap of it covered over with rags. He slept under several moth-eaten blankets, arranged so that the holes at least didn't intersect.

Octavian would have regarded the clean little loft room with raw envy, and his reaction to the featherbed would have been disbelief.

She wondered what Alexander was thinking. She *hoped* he was grateful. She wanted him to be grateful; he hadn't been grateful for much of anything in his previous life, instead, he had accepted the good things that had come to him as his due. The more feelings of things like gratitude he could muster, the better off he would be.

Reluctantly she turned her eyes away from the window and back to her books.

Apparently there was some mechanism whereby Godmothers just *got* authority over Kingdoms as their experience, cleverness, and strength warranted. There was no formal announcement of the fact, it just *happened*. But there were unmistakable signs that one had gotten the Kingdom; the Witches and Hedge-Wizards would begin reporting information to one, and at some point, the Godmother would have the opportunity dropped in her lap to make some Grand Gesture at the Royal Court. A gesture like—

—*like returning a lost Prince, a former failed Quester who has learned his lessons, to his parents*—

There it was, unmistakable. And here was Arachnia's latest letter, brought by bat, lying open on the table next to her.

"—*and I can't risk ruining my reputation as the Dark Lady by bringing Octavian back myself, Elena. That's the job of a Godmother. So you might want to think about how you want to do this, because I expect he'll be ready within the month, and unless he backslides, I really don't want to risk his health out there in that drafty stable in the winter. My stableman does fine, but he's a troll. No, really, a troll; a good enough fellow, but as stupid as a block of wood and as hard to hurt as a stone. The conditions he likes might kill a man.*"

Elena chewed on the end of an ivory pen. Arachnia was right; she was *much* too useful as a stalking-horse, the faux Evil Queen who was actually in charge of a failed Quester's ordeals. She was far enough away from Kohlstania that someone would have to invoke "All Forests Are One" to bring Octavian back. And ideally, in order to wake up Kohlstania to the fact that magic was very *much* alive and a force in the Kingdoms, as well as to cement King Henrick's change of heart as well as Octavian's changed ways, the return of the "lost" Prince would have to be conducted with a great deal of fanfare.

Which meant—

Which means, I fear, that Kohlstania is now mine. She wasn't certain whether to be pleased or worried. Kohlstania was certainly an *orderly* place. Perhaps a little too orderly. When things were too orderly, The Tradition had the unsettling habit of stirring matters up by creating an opening for a Dark One to move in.

Well, all right; at least I'm forewarned. I'll have to have Karelina put me in touch with the Witches and Hedge-Wizards. I might be able to nip trouble early.

She made a note of that on the tablet she was filling, right underneath, *Octavian? Make him my helmeted Knight-Escort until I reveal him to his father?*

She glanced out the window again; the lamp was still burning over the stable. It looked as if Alexander was celebrating his first night as a man again by staying up a bit. She thought she recalled Lily asking for some of the duplicate copies of books in the Library. Had she put them up there? Well, where else would they go?

If so, she hoped he was something of a reader. The more he learned about magic and The Tradition, the sooner he would really come to understand the path that he had made for himself that had brought him here.

A bat flew in the open window and fluttered around for a few moments before catching itself on a beam and hanging upside down, staring warily at Alexander.

He had been startled when it flapped past his ear, but he wasn't the sort to think that bats were somehow evil, or to want to chase it out. The Palace gamekeeper had once had a bat with a broken wing that he'd rescued and nursed back to health before turning it loose, and he'd shown it to the two youngest Princes, explaining how bats ate all manner of insects and were very useful to have about. Alexander had found the tiny thing fascinating, with its delicate wings, soft fur, and miniature features. It was nothing at all like a flying mouse.

So Alexander watched the bat watching him without moving from his bed, and finally the bat had relaxed, dropped off the ceiling, and fluttered around the room for a bit, catching the moths that had been attracted by the lamplight.

The arrival of the bat had been a useful interruption, because at this point, Alexander's head was beginning to feel very full.

When the bat flew out again, having swept the room clean of moths, rather than returning to his reading he put the book aside, and turned over on his stomach to blow out the lamp. And when he had done so, he saw a square of light down below, and in it, the unmistakable silhouette of Elena.

He supposed that he ought to be thinking of her as "Madame" Elena, but somehow the title really didn't fit her. It was like trying to put a collar on a wild doe; you could embellish it with gems and gold filigree all you wanted, but the doe was still a wild thing and would never be a pet. "Godmother" suited her, but only when she was becoiffed and powdered and tripping about on her silver-heeled slippers in court garb. In her ordinary clothing, she seemed, to him at least, nothing more imposing than simply "Elena."

Of course, if he dared address her that way, Hob would probably lay him out on the ground.

He wondered what she was doing; it looked as if she was writing, or reading, or perhaps both. Well, so much for thinking she was an illiterate peasant.

He wasn't doing very well on his analysis of the situation that he had found himself in. Truth to tell, he'd fouled it up almost beyond recognition with his assumptions. For someone who was supposed to be trained in assessing conditions correctly and making the right decisions based on those assessments, he was doing a damned poor job of it. And to think he was *supposed* to become Octavian's Commander-in-Chief! If this was how he would have fared in a war, maybe the Academy hadn't trained him all that well after all.

From what he had read in the *Godmother's Book of Days,* he was what was known as a Quester. Or, to be more accurate, a *Failed* Quester. It was his brother Julian who was the real Quester; Julian had succeeded. He had passed the trials and won the Princess. Alexander and Octavian had failed the very first test put in front of them—the test of courtesy.

He had been knighted, and so had Octavian, but he knew now that they had been knights in name only. He *knew* it now, or rather, acknowledged it, at least to himself.

He wasn't quite ready to confess it to anyone else.

But there was something else that he was finally putting together in his mind that was beginning to make him feel a smoldering anger that was *nothing* like the anger he had so unthinkingly loaded onto Godmother Elena. The first book he had read had left him a little baffled, referring to something called The Tradition, but in a way that had not left him with any sort of clear definition of what was meant.

In the first chapter of the *Book of Days,* everything that The Tradition was had been boldly and clearly spelled out. It was that which was making him so angry.

But not at Godmother Elena. Not anymore.

It was quite clear to him now that Elena was doing quite a bit more than the average Godmother to use The Tradition against itself. She should *never* have brought him here, for instance. Godmothers just did not intervene personally with Failed Questers. There was no place in The Tradition for a Godmother to take the training of a Failed Quester on herself. She properly should have done to him what she'd done to Octavian; turned him loose to wander without being able to get home until he either died or learned his lessons—lessons that would make him a much better King than he would ever have been without this humiliation. And if he died, well, that was too bad—either the second Failed Quester, himself, would survive *his* lessoning, or Julian would inherit both Kingdoms.

And if Elena had not intervened, it was the latter that was the most likely. The *Book of Days* had unflinchingly given the odds of a Failed Quester surviving long enough to redeem himself, and the odds weren't at all good.

Elena had gone out of her way to get both himself and Octavian into situations where, even if they were brought down lower than the humblest commoner, they were not in any danger of dying. Except, perhaps, by being monumentally stupid.

Alexander turned over on his back and stared up into the darkness above his bed. Now that he knew about The Tradition, he had an explanation for something he had felt all of his life—a ponderous, implacable sort of weight hanging over him from the moment he'd been born. He'd often ascribed that feeling to God, the weight of the Almighty's regard upon a young Prince.

Now he knew better. It hadn't been God. It had been this faceless, formless, impersonal *Force* that went about shoving people down the way it wanted them to go, just because it fit a sort of well-worn path. It didn't *care* what they wanted. It didn't give a toss about pain or pleasure. It only wanted things to happen in a predictable way.

Oh, how he *hated* it!

He wondered if Robert had been aware of such a thing, for surely Robert was a victim of The Tradition in all its cruelty. On the whole, he hoped not. To live your life feeling yourself impelled towards your early death—as if your fate was a cliff that you were rushing towards, with no way to stop—

That would have been unthinkably horrible, turning what had been a tragedy into something infinitely worse.

He sighed, and the sound filled the little loft room. He became aware that outside the window, crickets sang and frogs croaked, much quieter to his human ears than to the donkey's. For the first time in too long, he was in a bed, feeling two arms, two legs, all the parts of him what they should be and *where* they should be, resting on a feather mattress as good as any in the Palace of Kohlstania and better than the ones at the Academy. He was himself again.

I won't backslide, he vowed fiercely to himself. *I swear it. No matter how provoked I am, no matter what that damned Tradition wants and tried to make me do, I won't backslide! I will be courteous, I will be considerate, I will remember my knightly vows and I will live up to them instead of merely giving lip service to them.* There was nothing, absolutely nothing he would not do to avoid feeling his body warp and change into the beast.

Which meant he would have to be careful, very careful. If The Tradition could not force him into one role (*dead* failed Quester) it would probably try and force him into another. He would have to read and study to find out what that role might be, and whether or not it was one that would get him out of here. He might hate The Tradition, but there was no point in pretending it did not exist, nor that it was not very, very powerful. Clearly it took knowledge *and* magic to beat it. He only had a chance at half of that equation.

He closed his eyes, and for the moment, felt rather disinclined to open them again.

Strange, he thought, as he felt sleep creeping up on him. Strange how things worked out. He might have discovered that he was little more than a fancy pawn on some giant chessboard—but at least now he had a better target for his hate and anger than a pretty woman....

Shortly after midnight, Elena blinked, looked down at her notes, and realized that her handwriting was just short of illegible. It was time to call a halt to all of this and go to bed, before she dropped off to sleep right here at the table. She really wasn't minded to wake up at dawn with a crick in her neck and an inkblot on her cheek.

She tidied her papers, put up the quill, corked the ink, and with a wave of her hand, extinguished the lamps. A glance out the window showed her that Alexander had already given up for the night. He was probably smarter than she was.

She made her way up to her room; behind his curtain, Randolf was very quiet. He might not even "be" there at the moment; it was likeliest that he was off watching something or someone else. She waved the lamps in this room to darkness, and went on into her bedroom.

With a few touches, it was very much as Madame Bella had left it. By the time she had moved into it, Elena had decided that she liked it that way and saw no reason to change anything that was there. It felt—old. Very old. She had to wonder, in fact, if the furnishings in this room dated all the way back to the first human Godmother to live here.

For the furniture was, in fact, rather more antique than anything in the Klovis household had been, and far more than anything in any other room in the house except, perhaps, the kitchen. The walls were of wood, but there were tapestries hung on all of them. The bed was huge, a whole family could have slept there comfortably; it stood on a little dais of its own, and it was curtained twice. The inner curtains were of thin gauze, the outer of heavy velvet. In the summer she closed only the inner ones, to keep insects out, so that she could leave the windows open without resorting to a spell. The rest of the furnishings, wardrobe, a sort of couch, backless chairs, chests, and her dressing table, were just as massive, and had an air of comfort about them that was rather surprising given how heavily they were built. The walls were dark oak paneling, the floor darker yet, the colors of the curtains and cushions all dark burgundy and garnet. The tapestries all around the walls were of magical creatures; the one above the fireplace showed Unicorns *sans* maidens. Sometimes she wondered if a Godmother had woven it herself, and why. It certainly managed to portray them accurately—beautiful, but with a certain vacuity in their eyes.

She left her clothing draped neatly over the blanket-chest at the foot of the bed for Rose to deal with in the morning and slipped into the clean nightgown that was waiting for her, left lying on the pillows. It smelled pleasantly of violets and lavender. She waved the lights out and climbed up into the bed, feeling fairly satisfied. Of course, there was no way of knowing what Alexander would actually do or think following his first night of freedom from his curse, but she had high hopes for him, given that he had managed to remain in control of his temper. And she could hardly blame him for being angry that she hadn't just freed him outright. He still hadn't, in his heart, acknowledged that he had failed some crucial tests of character.

On the other hand, if he was reading her spare histories, they might point his mind in the right direction.

It would be a bit awkward to have him around in his natural form, though. When he'd been an ass, she hadn't thought twice about acting as she always had in his presence. The more she had allowed him to be himself, the more *conscious* she had been of the presence of an admittedly good-looking young man about the place. And now, if he was going to be himself all of the time—

But he'll be gone soon, she told herself. *By winter. I'm sure of it. Besides, he's made it quite clear that he considers me very much his inferior in birth, if our births were to be compared. So although he may begin to treat me with courtesy at last—* she yawned, and closed her eyes—*of course the courtesy—* her thoughts began to ooze away from her—*will be the kind...a Prince...gives....*

She did not often dream, or at least, she did not often dream in ways that could be linked back to the real world. That was deliberate; the dreams of a Godmother had the potential to take on a life of their own, and one of the things that Bella had taught her was how to dream in pleasant nonsense. So when her dream began, and she found herself walking along a shore of purple sand by an amethyst sea beneath a silver sky with three azure moons in it, she felt quite relaxed and comfortable. So comfortable, that she did not in the least mind when she realized that Alexander was walking beside her.

They did not speak, but after a while, quite easily and naturally, her hand stretched out a little of its own accord, and encountered his reaching for hers. Their fingers entwined, and they walked on, climbing up the purple dunes, through sand as soft as powdered velvet. There they sat down together, on the top of the tallest dune, listening to the sea and watching as the moons set, one after another, like blue pearls on an invisible chain being pulled below the horizon. She leaned her head to the side, and quite naturally found that she was leaning it against his shoulder, and just as naturally his arm came around her and pulled her closer.

Then her heart started to pound, and her skin came alive, so that she was acutely aware of the brush of his fingers against it, the touch of the warm breeze on her face. She felt her stomach tighten, and when he bent his head down to hers and she lifted hers to meet his and their lips met, she felt as if lightning had jumped between them, or maybe the spark of life itself, though she could not have told if it went from her into him or the other way around.

He turned more towards her, and his free hand came to

cup her breast; her nipples hardened and the soft teasing of his fingers sent jolts of pleasure through her that made the secret parts between her legs tighten and burn with anticipation. She moaned a little, and her lips parted insensibly beneath his kiss, and his tongue slipped between them, teasing and tickling her lips and teeth and playing with her tongue, until she—

—*Damn it!*

She came awake all at once, and in a fury. The benighted Tradition couldn't manipulate her when she was awake, so now it was trying to do so in her sleep!

"No." That was all she said into the darkness, but she put every bit of her will behind it.

Nothing answered her. There was neither an increase in pressure upon her, nor a decrease—nor was there any change in the amount of the magic she could sense swirling in potential around her.

Could it possibly be that what she had just dreamed had come, not out of what The Tradition wanted, but out of what *she* wanted? Or what her body wanted, anyway.

She lay there afire with *wanting* and not knowing, well, not really, not *truly,* what it was she wanted. Madame Klovis's servants hadn't bothered to hide themselves when they dallied, but her curiosity had never been enough to overcome her embarrassment and past a certain point, she'd always covered her eyes.

But she *ached* with frustration and need. And it took a very, very long time to get back to sleep again. And when she did, it was to toss the rest of the night as part of her tried to get back to that purple sand dune, and part of her utterly refused to go there, which left *all* of her so bleary-eyed when she woke at dawn that Rose took one look at her and ordered her to sleep in late for a change.

When Alexander woke the next morning, it was with strange dream-fragments echoing in the back of his mind; blue moons and purple sand, and a very sweet and lissome lady in his arms. For the very first time since he had left Kohlstania, he woke feeling good, warm and very pleased with himself. It had been a *wonderful* dream, apparently. He just wished that he could remember more of it.

But just because he wasn't waking as a donkey didn't mean that the work was going to stop. Hob had made sure he knew that weeks ago. Back when he'd been thinking he'd only be spending every other day as a donkey rather than most of a week, Hob had told him in bald terms that man or ass, if he didn't do his share, the same rule held: no work, no food. Alexander didn't think that things would have changed just because the Godmother had decided that he was going to be spending his time as himself from now on. This was the season of harvest, and there was work even for the untutored hands of a Prince.

"Alexander!" bellowed Hob from somewhere beneath him. "Get your lazy royal ass down here!"

Royal ass— Maybe it was the good mood that he had awakened in, but the phrase that would have made him livid with anger yesterday struck him this morning as inexpressibly funny. He rolled out of bed and stuck his head through the hole in the floor. Hob was looking up at him.

"Lazy I am, but today, at least, I am no ass," he replied. "Give me but a moment."

There were *three* new beasts to tend now, and one of the few good things about being a donkey had meant that he didn't have to tend himself. His first chore on his first morning waking as a man were quite enough to drive the last fragment of erotic dream out of his mind; nothing was *less* erotic than mucking out a stall.

Still it didn't spoil his good mood at all. The beasts were mild-tempered and easy to work around and he was done reasonably quickly. He joined Hob at the pump in the kitchen-yard just as the sun came up, the two of them doing a thorough-wash-up in the cold water. "We won't be able to do that much longer," Hob said, shaking his head, and sending droplets flying everywhere. "Be too bloody cold before long. I don't fancy icicles off my nose."

"I don't fancy them hanging off elsewhere on my anatomy," replied Alexander, who had been a bit more thorough in his washing-up. But then, Hob hadn't been mucking out the stable, either.

Hob grinned at him.

"Come *on,* lad," he said, and led the way up the kitchen stairs.

Alexander stopped where he was. "Ah—"

"Come on, lad," Hob repeated. Dubiously, and certain that he would be stopped dead at the door as he always had been before, Alexander followed him.

Followed him right into the warm and fragrant kitchen, where he stood in the doorway, blinking stupidly in the light, just as Rose entered from the door opposite.

"Godmother won't be coming down until later," she informed Master Robin, who was the source of the wonderful smells of sausage and egg, of baking bread and frying ham. "She looks as if she hasn't had nearly enough sleep."

"She was awake rather late last night," Alexander offered. Both Rose, and Lily, who was already seated at the table, gave him odd looks. "She was reading, I suppose," he added. "I could see her from my window."

"I trust your room meets with your approval?" Rose asked tartly, managing to sound only the slightest bit sarcastic.

"Rosie—" Hob injected, with a note of warning in his voice. "Lad, sit down, have some breakfast."

Alexander did sit where Hob indicated, but he also answered Rose. "Mistress Rose, it is exceedingly comfortable, thank you," he replied as courteously as if she really had asked him the question seriously. "And I thank you for asking."

Rose blinked at him for a moment, then sat down without another word.

She ignored him during the meal, speaking only to the other Brownies, but Hob, Robin, and even Lily addressed him from time to time, making him a part of the conversation whether Rose liked it or not.

"So, you'll be going out with Lily and a cart today, past the water-meadow," Hob told him, after some discussion of what needed to be "got in." "Time we beat them deer t'the orchard fruit, I'm thinking."

"A fine plan, Hob," Robin said, nodding with enthusiasm, as he cleared up the plates from the table. "I've always said there was almost no point in having the orchard, we get so little out of it each fall. And nuts! With Alexander and the new beasts to help, we can rob the squirrels of the harvest of the nut orchard as well, later this fall!" He grinned. "I mind me that there's none of you would object to apple cake and spiced nuts."

So Alexander found himself harnessing up one of the mules to a small, two-wheeled cart, loading it with empty sacks and a couple of baskets and a ladder, and leading it out to meet the Brownie woman Lily. It was she who beckoned him down a path he was *sure* hadn't been there before today, past the meadow with the pond in it, and into what he had thought was just forest.

But it wasn't a forest; it was an incredibly ancient apple orchard.

The trees were huge and gnarled with age; the apples were small and a very bright red, but when he pulled one off a low-hanging branch and bit into it experimentally, expecting it to be sour or woody, he found it utterly delectable, tart and sweet at the same time, and bursting with juice.

"Finish that and let's get on with it," Lily chided, but with a smile. "I've a mind to fill the cart before the morning's over, at the least."

In fact, about the time that breakfast was beginning to wear off, Robin appeared with a second cart, mule, and their luncheon of bread, onion, and chunks of cheese. He brought water, too, but they hardly needed it with the juicy apples all about.

"We'll have cider this year, I think," Lily said with satisfaction as Robin led the mule and laden cart away. "And preserves, and plenty of apples in store, too. First year we'll have had cider of our own pressing in a while."

"Um—" He paused, not sure how to word the question he had delicately. Then he decided to just blunder on with it. "Why? I mean, why are we doing this by hand?"

"Why not use magic, you mean?" Lily didn't look in the least offended by his question. "Well, it's like this. *We* Brownie-folk don't have all that much magic to use for that sort of thing. We're small Fae, as such things go. The Great Fae, they've no need of mortal foods, for they create such things out of their own power if they choose—we little Fae, who haven't the magic, either feast at *their* tables or live as mortals do by the work of our hands."

"But surely the Godmother—"

"Ah." She laid a finger alongside of her nose and nodded. "Well, here's the thing. Aye, Godmother Elena *could* use magic for suchlike things if she chose, but she don't choose. And that's because she's a saving wench. She don't see the need to do with magic what can be done with hands, ye see. There's only so much magic that she *has,* without gathering more, and she reckons she can't always count on gathering more. Am I making sense?"

"You mean—" He groped to understand Lily's words. "You mean, magic is like rain, and sometimes there's a drought, and you can't always tell when a drought is going to come so you—you save it in a cistern?"

"Very like!" Lily applauded. "Now not all Godmothers think like ours. There's plenty who do a lot more with their magic. But Madame Elena always thinks, 'what if something really terrible happened, and I *didn't* have the magic to fix it,' every time she goes to do something. So there you are."

"I—see." And actually, he *did* see, though it seemed a rather novel and perhaps parsimonious approach to him. After all, what was the point of having magic if you didn't use it?

But then again, what if she did go about squandering magic, then didn't have it to turn *him* from donkey back into man again? He'd supposed that he'd have felt very differently about her approach if he'd been the one feeling the "drought."

"Now, one of our Godmothers, one we served a long time ago, was like that," Lily continued thoughtfully. "Using her magic to do this and that, cleaning her rooms and appearing and vanishing where she chose and suchlike. And something bad *did* happen. The Kingdom of Lorendil was invaded, and a Black Sorcerer took the throne and held it for three generations. And our Godmother didn't have the power to stop him because she'd used so much of it on things we could have done, traded for, or done without."

At the name "Lorendil," Alexander found himself feeling cold. Even in Kohlstania they had heard of the Black Beast of Lorendil, a Sorcerer whose atrocities were the stuff of nightmare. "*Could* she have?" he asked. "I mean—she was a Godmother, but *he* was a Sorcerer...."

"We'll never know, will we?" Lily countered. "But Lorendil was her responsibility, and it went down on her watch, and it took a Prophecy, a Child of Prophecy, and a Sorcerer to set it all right again."

He pondered that for a moment. There was just so much he didn't know about magic—

"Well, in that case," he said, finally, licking the juice of his last apple off his fingers and wiping them clean on the napkin his luncheon had come wrapped in, "let's get back to these apples."

They filled that cart as well, and a third, before Lily decreed an end to the harvest for that day and they headed back to the cottage. And that was when something odd occurred to him.

The kitchen that he had sat in this morning was huge. It should have filled the entire ground floor of the cottage.

Except that it hadn't, for Rose had come in from what was clearly another room, and Elena had been sitting at a table that had *not* been in a kitchen.

"Lily," he said hesitantly, as they neared the building. "That cottage—"

"Is bigger on the inside than the outside, I know," she said nonchalantly. "No worries. You'll get used to it after a bit, and not even think about it."

"Ah," he replied. And tried not to, because the very idea made his head begin to hurt. How could a building be bigger on the inside than the outside? It sounded mad, and yet he knew that his own eyes had given him contrary evidence.

Hob came to take charge of the cart and its contents, and Alexander and Lily proceeded on to the kitchen yard, and if Alexander had thought that the aromas issuing from that chamber had been delicious this morning, they made his mouth water this evening.

But Lily drew him away from the kitchen door to one of the outbuildings. "Men's bathhouse," she laughed, pushing him at the door. "Go make use of it. And when the weather is too cold to bathe at the pump, you can come here, but you'll have to fire the stove yourself."

It was his first bath since he had left home.

He would have lingered, except that he was far too hungry. Even so, to revel in hot water was something of a revelation. *Now* he felt wholly human again. Hob had washed him down regularly as a donkey, and what had happened to the donkey had, of course, happened to the human. In fact, washing him as a donkey seemed to clean his clothing as well. But that was no substitute for a real hot bath.

Nor for real clean clothing, with the scent of the hot sun that had dried it still in the folds. He walked alone into the kitchen with some of the same euphoria that had buoyed him this morning.

There he found that the others were already sitting down to their dinner, the Godmother sitting at the kitchen table among them. And that surprised him a little. Ladies did not eat in the kitchen among their servants. But then, again, this was no ordinary lady, nor were these creatures strictly "servants."

Quietly he took his own seat, and held his peace while they talked of the day. The Godmother kept sending odd glances in his direction, and though he kept his mouth shut, he wondered what was going through her mind. Did she regret her decision to allow him to remain himself? But why?

Whatever the cause of her behavior, she said nothing to him. And eventually, he gave up trying to figure out what was in her mind, and just listened.

And ate, of course. The food was marvelous, and the results of today's work appeared at the end of the meal in the form of a huge apple pie.

Robin's food had always been good—it was just a great deal better eaten like a civilized man, on a table, in company with others. However strange that company might be.

Strange company, indeed. While casual talk of what must be done over the next several days went on all around him, he felt curiously detached from it all; it occurred to him that had anyone described this situation, these surroundings to him a year ago, he would have considered them to be mad. Sitting in a room in a building that was larger on the inside than the outside, in company with a magician and four Fae. And if he made one misstep, he might be spending the *night* as a donkey again.

"There's a new room in the cellar," Robin was saying, in answer to some question of Lily's that he had not been paying attention to. "Complete with barrels for the cider."

"Ah, well, that's one problem sorted," Lily said with satisfaction.

Elena was looking from one to the other of them with a look that was something between a smile and a grimace. "Would any of you mind telling me just how the house does this? Gets bigger when we need space, I mean?"

"We don't know," Rose replied, as it finally dawned on Alexander just what they had been talking about. "It's some magic that the first Godmother to live here did. Actually I don't think that the house is actually getting bigger. I think that it is merely giving us access to parts of it we didn't have before. We've never actually seen it growing, you know, even though Robin talks about it budding."

"Did you not say," Alexander said, thinking quite hard about some of his recent reading, "that the first Godmother to live here was one of the Great Fae?"

They all turned to stare at him as if they had not realized that he was there.

"Yes," Lily said. "So?"

"I always thought—" he shrugged "—children's tales in Kohlstania speak of the Elven Queens living in great palaces. Well, what if this is—and always has been—a great palace?"

"Ah!" Robin said, his wizened face lighting up. "Yes! One of the Great Halls of Faerie! So that the house we see is— is just the entrance hall to it, so to speak!"

"It's as good an explanation as any other, I suppose," Elena said, after a moment of thought. But she looked relieved. "It makes sense. But why didn't any of you know this?"

"Because we weren't here, except Hob, and he was in the stable," said Lily, matter-of-factly. "We did not take service until here until the first of the mortal Godmothers was in residence. Then, the place was as you have seen, with fewer storage rooms and workrooms. And a much smaller Library."

Alexander shook his head. This was only contributing to his sensation of living in a dream. But the food in his belly was warm and solid, and the scent of sweet apples was still in his nostrils—

"We're all mad, you know," Elena said aloud, looking straight at him.

"I had begun to suspect this," he said in all seriousness.

She broke into a smile, a completely unexpected smile. She had never really smiled a great deal around him, and never *at* him before—or at least, she had never done so without a great deal of ironic mockery to her expression. This smile accepted the joke as being on both of them, and invited him to share in it. It hit him with an almost physical impact. He managed to return it, but not without a struggle to get his heart and breathing going again.

She's beautiful. How had he never noticed that before?

"Well, if that is the explanation—and thank you, Prince Alexander, for thinking of it—I will confess that I am much relieved," Elena said to all of them. "It had occurred to me that if this house was capable of growing, it might also be capable of *shrinking*. What would happen, for instance, if some enemy were to somehow drain away some of its magic? Would it shrink? With us in it?" She shuddered. "But one of the Palaces of the Great Fae, slowly opening rooms as we need them—now _that,_ I feel much more comfortable with. And on that note, I shall go back to my studies."

That seemed to be a sort of dismissal for all of them. Elena got up and left, Robin collected the dishes, Rose left through the same door that the Godmother had used, Lily moving to help Robin. Hob stood up, and gave him a sharp look.

"We've had our dinner," he said, with a meaningful glance towards the stable.

Alexander understood him. "Time to feed the beasts," he replied, and got to his feet, himself.

Hob actually fed them; it was Alexander who gave them all water and made sure they were comfortable. Then Hob left, and Alexander climbed the ladder to his loft room, taking the lantern with him. When he got there, he stripped down to his breeks, and slipped into bed, taking a book with him.

Many pages later, he felt his eyelids drooping, and put the book aside, turning to blow out the lantern. As he did so, he glanced out the window, and saw the silhouette of Elena, also bent over a book, in the window that faced the stable.

It was another long night, but at the end of it, Elena felt as if she had a better idea, not only of what would be expected of _her_ on taking the responsibility for a new Kingdom, but what she could expect from Kohlstania. And she had a bat-delivered note from Arachnia, to the effect that Octavian had passed, not only _her_ trials, but a few little tests that her consort had contrived. She made a few notes, based on other Restoration spectacles in the various chronicles, and her imagination began to get to work. She fell asleep with her head full of ideas.

But the next morning, she had to work hard to wrench her concentration back to her plans for restoring Octavian to his proper place, for she had had a second one of those dreams about his brother.

Wretched man! she thought, irritated beyond all reason by the fact that he had so sensuously invaded her dreams. She put off going down to breakfast until after she saw Lily taking him back down to the apple orchard again.

The sooner I get all of them off my hands, the better, she decided, feeling very glad that Lily had taken responsibility for Alexander for the day. She told Rose that she would be gone overnight, and with a sense of relief, drove the donkey-cart out into the forest and evoked the "All Forests Are One" spell to take her to Arachnia's dark and forbidding palace.

There, she gave Octavian one last test—resuming her guise as the old woman, she came to the back entrance to beg for food. Not only did Octavian give her half of his share, but he prevented the stable-troll from running her off and he was about to give up his sleeping place to her as well, when she dropped her disguise and revealed herself to him.

That went well. Arachnia appeared right on cue, dropping *her* guise as the Evil Sorceress, and the two of them played out the first act of Octavian's Redemption precisely as The Tradition preferred. In fact, The Tradition unleashed a veritable flood of magic upon the scene—presumably to ensure that Acts Two and Three would take place as well. Arachnia's servants took Octavian off to be bathed and re-clothed, feasted, and finally put to bed until the morrow, when they would take him back to his father.

When the hurly-burly was over, Elena and Arachnia retired to the peace and quiet in Arachnia's Library. It was
nothing like her own, cozy little chamber; this was a Library,
stretching up three full stories, with two balconies ringing
it. Dark banners hung down from the rafters above them—
banners that featured, not the arms of defeated enemies nor
of ancestors, but beautifully rendered images of creatures
normally associated with night—several species of owls,
bats, wolves, and cats, as well as a dragon or two, the rare
Ebon Unicorn, and the Nightmare. There was a fireplace in
one wall of a size sufficient to make any ox placed on a spit
therein look like a suckling piglet.

"Dare I ask how you got all of this—?" Elena said, looking about her.

Arachnia laughed. She was, all in all, very much prettier
than she had been when Elena had first seen her, and for all
that she and her Poet-Prince preferred being seminocturnal,
much rosier. Being in love and beloved evidently suited her
well indeed. "I killed the owner," she said.

Elena felt her eyes widen. "You're joking?"

"Oh, no," Arachnia assured her. "I was her servant. She
had a Sleeper here—she wasn't playing by The Tradition, and
after she enchanted the poor thing, she carried the girl off to
here, *her* palace. She wanted to ensure herself of a steady diet
of Failed Questers without having to work at it too hard."

"Ah." Elena nodded. She remembered Bella telling her
that like those whom The Tradition was trying to set down
a path *not* of their choosing, there was a great deal of magical power invested in the life of a Quester. When one Failed,
all that magical power was available to the evil magician—

—and it was also possible to transmute life-force into magical power as well. So it was in the interest of an evil magician to attract and slay as many Questers as possible.

"She had half a dozen human servants that she had kidnapped or lured here, and easily three times that in magical servants or enslaved magical creatures. She was really dreadful to all of us, but I was the only one who dared to think about killing her." Arachnia shook her head over the cowardice of her former fellow servants. "I watched for my chance, and one day when she was gloating over murdering yet another Quester and feasting on the magic that his death had released, I pushed her out a window."

Arachnia's eyes glinted at the memory; Elena had to wonder just how bad "dreadful" had been in order to bring *that* look to her face.

"The Sleeper awoke and ran off with the stableboy," Arachnia continued. "In fact, everyone ran off except me and the talking statue—" She indicated a statue in the corner of the library of a very graceful, half-nude woman. The statue gave Elena a stiff little bow; Elena bowed back. "—and, of course, a few ghosts. I decided to stay, partly because I hadn't anywhere else to go, and the statue began to talk to me. She was the one who discovered that I could see magic; she pointed out that this meant that I could *be* a magician, and I decided that *I* would be the Sorceress here. I knew that the ghosts would keep everyone away until I had learned enough to be formidable." She shrugged. "Not a very exciting story, but the statue tells me that I was supposed to have been a Witch-killer except that the Spider-queen's hunters found me wandering around in the forest before I could find the evil Witch's hut. Which is probably why I could see magic in the first place."

"And why you shoved the Spider-queen out a window, I suppose," Elena said thoughtfully, as she watched the swirls and eddies of magic play about the banners overhead. It was so thick up there you could practically read by it; The Tradition really, truly wanted Octavian reunited with his father and reinstated as the Heir, and it was putting all sorts of effort to bear on the situation. Perhaps because not one, but *two* magicians with a habit of opposing it were sitting here with Octavian's fate in their hands. "Don't Witch-killing children usually shove the Witches into their own ovens, or down wells? I suppose *shoving* just was the natural thing for you to do. How old were you?"

"Seven," Arachnia said serenely. "The statue taught me how to read. There were plenty of provisions stored under preservation spells, more than enough to feed me while I learned magic. What I didn't learn from the books here, some of the ghosts taught me, but of course it was all a bit slanted."

Slanted? Considering that this has apparently been a stronghold of Evil Sorceresses for the last three hundred years? I'm surprised that she didn't go completely to the bad!

But of course, Elena didn't say that aloud.

"The ghosts are mostly very sweet," she continued thoughtfully. "They were all victims of my former mistress and her predecessors, so they were disposed to like me and wish me well. And the statue was stolen by *her* mistress, so she wasn't particularly upset about seeing me get rid of the Spider-queen, either. Now, what are we going to do with Octavian? Have you any ideas?"

"You do realize that whoever brings Octavian back is going to become Kohlstania's Godmother, don't you?" she asked instead of answering directly. It was only fair to give Arachnia the chance at having the place—it *would* mean another source of magic for her—

"Hellfire and damnation!" Arachnia swore with a start. "No! Elena, if *you* don't take him back, I swear, I will revert and curse you!"

Elena choked on a laugh. Well, *that* was certainly vehement enough! "I thought I ought to at least give you the option—"

"I do *not* want to be a Godmother! The wretched man is *yours*, and his Kingdom with him! Now, have you any ideas?" Two pink spots flared on Arachnia's cheeks as she calmed herself.

"I don't suppose you have any sort of transportation that flies?" said Elena.

Of all of the means of transportation Elena had used as a Godmother, this was by far the most unique. She'd had to do some quick cosmetic work on it, though, or it would have frightened three-quarters of the citizenry of Kohlstania into fits, and had the remaining quarter running for the spears and bows.

It appeared that there was a reason for the dragon-banners in the library. The traditional means of transport for the occupant of this castle was—formidable. An elaborate black war-chariot, apparently forged of blackened silver, drawn by two black dragonets—which were the much smaller, unintelligent subspecies of *Draconis Sapiens*. A third dragonet generally served as the mount for the chariot-driver's outrider. This was why the stableman was a troll. When the beasts were feeling fractious, nothing short of a troll could control them. These were not the beasts that Octavian usually had charge of, although he was familiar with them and they with him.

Elena didn't change much about the rig other than to make it far less menacing—she made the chariot and dragonets white, an opalescent rose and gold instead of black and silver, and she made a few cosmetic changes to the beasts' heads, giving them more a look of scaly horses than of man-eating carnivores. Octavian got armor to match, of course, and she herself had donned her most impressive costume as the Rose Fairy—complete with powdered wig and six-foot staff topped with a pink diamond in the shape of a star.

Octavian was in full armor—enameled in white and rose, with gilding. Luckily for him, it was magic in nature, which made it a great deal lighter than "real" armor. He had gotten very carefully detailed instructions from Elena, but she was taking no chances; there was such a superabundance of magic available that Elena took the precaution of putting a tiny *geas* on him to *obey* those instructions. This time, at least, she was going to give The Tradition what it wanted; a full spectacle which would probably turn into a tale that traveled through the Kingdoms for generations. Maybe that would make it leave her alone for a bit.

And no more dreams! she told it fiercely. Not that she had any evidence that the dreams of Alexander—of which she had had another last night—were coming out of The Tradition. But she had no evidence to the contrary, either, and in absence of evidence...

So the whole outre procession went flying off into the morning sky, heading for Kohlstania and the Royal Palace; she driving the splendid chariot, Octavian riding beside her on his winged mount, the whole of it buoyed on swirling clouds of magic that would have enveloped them in a thick, pea-soup fog except that only she could see it. It was practically thick enough to cut; she had stored as much of it away in wand and staff, whatever talismans she had on her person and could put together last night, and in her own reserves, and *still* it was like this. And *that* was after she insisted that Arachnia divide the power with her! The Tradition was making certain that the Kingdom of Kohlstania got its Godmother with a vengeance!

Or perhaps it was trying to bribe her into being more cooperative and conciliatory.

Well, it wasn't going to work. On the other hand, there was no harm in taking the bounty that was given.

Naturally—since she insisted on flying at a little above tree-height, to ensure being seen—they attracted a great deal of attention, and even with her cosmetic changes, they excited a good deal of fear. For every face upturned to watch them pass, there was someone running for concealment down below. So by the time they landed in the courtyard of the Royal Palace, all of the Royal Guard had turned out, armed to the teeth, and she suspected that most of the Army was on its way from the Royal Barracks on the outskirts of the city.

The dragons pulled the vehicle around to stand as near

to the door as the Guards would allow. She remained in her chariot; Octavian, however, dismounted from his dragon, and took his place between her and the Guard; with his visor down, he looked very formidable indeed. She surveyed them all haughtily as the dragons tossed their heads.

"Is *this* any way to greet me?" she demanded "One woman, with a single escort-knight? Where is your King?"

She suppressed a smile at her own words, though— *Oh yes, one "mere" woman, clearly some sort of extremely powerful magician, three dragons, and a fellow whose face no one can see! You're right to be nervous, my lads!*

"He is here, lady," said a weary, wary voice, and the Guard reluctantly parted to let King Henrick through. "What is it you would have of me?"

The King was armed as well, though he'd only had time to buckle on a breastplate over his velvet doublet, and replace his crown with an open-face helm. Still, he was brave, she had to give him that. He wasn't hiding in his throne room, depending on his Guards to protect him; he had his sword in his hand, and he looked as if he was prepared to use it.

"You have three sons, King Henrick," she said, sternly. "Where are they? Answer me true, for I am a magician of no little power, and I will know falsehood if I hear it. And the cost of falsehood may be more than you can ever dream."

Of course, the cost of falsehood would be that she would *not* allow Octavian to reveal himself. Not that she expected to hear anything but truth out of Henrick; if everything Randolf had shown her was true, he had spent a very long time learning a great deal about himself since his sons had vanished, and he did not much care for what he had learned.

He reeled as if she had struck him a blow, and yet, from the expression on his face, it was a blow he had, in part, expected. It did not break him—but in that moment, she saw him look at her and admit his own defeat and his own failures.

"I know only what has befallen my son Julian, lady," he replied, bitterly. "In my folly, in my greed, I sent them out, all three of them, to answer my neighbor's Quest and win his daughter, thinking to add his Kingdom to my own. And it is true that of the three, I sent Julian out expecting that he would fail and rid me of the one son I did not understand and could not care for. My cold-heartedness was well-repaid; it is Julian who has won the maid and the throne for himself, and not for me, and my other sons are lost. And in a sense, all three are lost to me, for I fear that Julian knew my heart only too well, and will never forgive me. So here I am—surrounded by wealth that I care nothing for, facing my own declining years with neither friend nor son at my side." He straightened, then, and looked her in the eyes. "So work your will on me, Witch. I am already living in the worst I can dream, and I brought it all upon myself!"

She caught Octavian's eye, and nodded slightly. He needed no further encouragement.

"Father!" he cried, pulling off his helm, and flinging himself to King Henrick's feet. "Father, I am here! I am home again!"

There was a moment of stunned silence. Then the King fell upon his son, weeping, and embracing him, as the Royal

Guard erupted into a cheer. And after that—well, that was when things got very interesting indeed.

It was long after dark that Elena finally headed back home to her cottage, and she was just about ready to drop with exhaustion. First, there had been the whole Reconciliation scene to play out, then *some* (by no means all) of the explanation of what had happened to Octavian and why, then (this time, in private) Elena had delivered herself of a bit of a lecture to King and Prince. Not *much* of a lecture, but she had made it very clear that their first act must be to reconcile with Julian by delivering the one thing that the King had not been able to bring himself to send—

—an apology, a long one, for a long list of wrongs and neglect going back into his childhood.

It was the newly-humbled Octavian who'd had no difficulty with this rather obvious necessity, and in the euphoria of having his favorite son back, Henrick had agreed.

As for the rest—well, that would mostly be in Octavian's hands, but his Redemption had been very real, and she didn't think he was going to backslide. There would be some gradual improvement in the lot of the common people of Kohlstania, and it would begin with being accorded the common courtesies that had heretofore been honored more in the breech than the observance. She had left, flying off into the sunset, with the third dragon harnessed with the other two, and had returned the whole rig to Arachnia by the time darkness fell. And by the time she had left, there was one very interesting change already visible in Kohlstania. Out in the marketplace, there were stalls and shops hung with the signs of various sorts of magicians. *Those* hadn't been there when she flew over that morning. So, magic and magicians were already been accorded a great deal more respect by the "sophisticated" city folk.

Well, it only took looking up and seeing a dragon flying overhead to make a believer out of you, she supposed.

That was yet another change that had been badly needed here; from what Elena had learned from Alexander and her own readings, Kohlstania had been rapidly on its way to banishing magic altogether. And that would have had a very serious effect on the very soul of the country, for a country whose people ceased to believe in magic soon lost much of their ability to imagine and dream, and before long, they ceased to believe—or hope—for anything. This was one of the fundamental truths of the Five Hundred Kingdoms. Even the lowest of swineherds could believe that he, or his son, or his son's son could one day be a Prince—because all it took was magic, and being the right person in the right place. And the highest of Kings could know that at any moment, an act of dishonor or cruelty could send him tumbling out of his throne—because all it took was magic, and doing the wrong thing to the wrong person. In this way, The Tradition could be a blessing, and the magic by which it operated certainly was. "The carrot and the stick," Madame Bella had once said dryly, when explaining it all to Elena. "The carrot for the lowly, the stick for the mighty. It is quite astonishing how effective these things are when applied in that particular order."

Elena left the dragons and their chariot with Arachnia's troll, and enjoyed a fortifying and amusing dinner with the Dark Lady and her Lord.

At least, it had been amusing right up until the moment that they said their farewells and she drove off into the forest—alone. At that point, she was overcome by a spasm of envy so powerful it felt akin to pain.

She clutched at the reins, and slapped them over the donkey's back to make him hurry his pace. Wise little fellow that he was, he ignored her; he was going no faster than a walk, for he could not see the road well in the darkness. She had evoked the "All Forests Are One" spell, of course, and he might even be *in* her home forest even now, but it had never taken less than an hour to traverse the distance between *where she was* and *where she was going,* and she very much doubted that was going to change tonight, just because she was feeling miserable and wanted to be home.

She stared into the darkness, and felt tears dripping down her cheeks.

Arachnia hadn't meant to hurt her, of course. In fact, she had no idea that her words had left Elena feeling as if she had been stabbed. She'd only meant to explain why she had no intention of being the Godmother to Kohlstania, or any other Kingdom. And she had meant it as a compliment.

"I could never be as strong as you, Elena," she had said, earnestly. *"You Godmothers, living all alone as you do, I don't know how you can bear it. You completely amaze me. Now that I've found it, I could never stand to be alone the way you are, to live my life without love."*

If she could see Elena now, she would be horrified, for she could have no way of knowing how bitter those words had been, and how they had made Elena's heart ache with pain.

Not just because of what they meant *now*, but what they meant for the future.

Because, of course, Godmothers did live alone. Who had ever heard of a Godmother's Consort, or a Fairy Godfather? It was one thing to manipulate The Tradition; it was quite another to forge a new one that would create such a monumental change as that.

In the back of her mind, she had been planning on having Alexander with her all winter—had been looking forward to his company during the days when snow would confine them all within doors. She had not been thinking at all, or at least, she had not been thinking like a Godmother. If anything, she had been thinking like an ordinary woman.

Which, of course, she was not.

That was what Arachnia's words had made her realize. That she would have to put more effort into Alexander's redemption, so that he could be back in Kohlstania himself by the time the snows came.

That she was going to be spending another long winter alone.

As she would, for the rest of her life.

17

"**I** don't know why you're letting him watch this," Rose complained aloud for the fourth or fifth time, as Alexander stared intently into the depths of the magic mirror and the scene that was playing out there. It would have been fascinating enough to watch just about *anything* there, and know that he was seeing a reflection of something that was going on elsewhere, far away. But to be able to see his own father and brother—well, he simply could not tear himself away. It was a pity that he could not hear as well as see, but Randolf was giving a fairly good precis of what was going on.

Rose, however, was speaking, not to Alexander, who probably would not have answered, but to Lily.

"Because, oh impossibly obdurate one, *I told her to bring him here,*" replied the mirror-spirit Randolf, in a bored tone.

"And to repeat myself one more time, I told her to bring him here this morning, because I *am* something of a predictive Mirror-Slave, and it seemed imperative to me, and important to the lad's Redemption, that the Prince see and understand what was happening to his father and brother today. The Godmother has given me fairly broad scope for me to use my own judgment in such matters, and this is how I choose to use it." The spirit of the mirror paused. "You *do* want the boy redeemed, don't you?"

Out of the corner of his eye, Alexander saw Rose glare at the mirror, but she said nothing.

Instead of going out to work in the orchard today, directly after breakfast Lily had insisted on bringing him into the house, right up to this rather feminine chamber, where she had placed him on a hassock in front of a mirror that was not silvered, but black.

He thought he had gotten used to magic and the idea of it, but when a face appeared in the mirror that was clearly not a reflection of anyone in the room—and then, when it spoke to him!—he had nearly jumped up and gone looking for a weapon.

His self-control had the upper hand, however, and quite honestly it was impossible to listen to Randolf without being amused and forgetting that he was basically a disembodied head. And before too long, he was talking with Randolf almost as if the spirit was an ordinary person rather than something that only lived in a mirror.

Then Randolf began showing him what had taken the Godmother away from home—and that it had to do entirely with his brother Octavian.

Now, the Godmother had been keeping him fairly, if sketchily, up-to-date on the rest of his family, but it was one thing to hear about it, and quite another to see it. Octavian just astonished him; his brother had never been a weakling, but the amount of muscle that he had put on was matched only by the changed look of his face. There was thoughtfulness there, and intelligence; Octavian had once seemed a bit imitative, reflecting what others thought rather than thinking for himself.

Alexander scarcely left the mirror for anything; Lily brought him a ploughman's lunch and he ate it without even tasting it. It was not only that he was half-starved for the sight of familiar faces, and anxious to know the welfare of his father and brother. It was that, if *Octavian* had managed to win his freedom, how had it been done? And could he manage, as well?

At least, that was how he had begun his vigil. But as he watched his father and brother together, and heard from Randolf what they were all saying, he had realized something quite profound.

They did not need him.

Oh, they wanted to know that he was all right, and when Elena had assured them, in rather vague terms, that he was, they clearly dismissed him and his current situation with some relief. But it had been Octavian who had been brought up at their father's side; it had been Octavian who was the Crown Prince. The problem that had occurred with Julian had, in a lesser fashion, been going on between Alexander and his father. He'd been raised by nurses and tutors, educated by the Academy, and although he idolized his father, he realized that before his return on graduation, he had probably spent less than a month in his father's presence, all told. Realistically he was the Spare. And with Octavian hale and hearty and as like to their father as if they'd been hatched from the same egg, there was no place at the Kohlstanian court for Alexander except as a perpetual Prince-in-Waiting. Even that promised position as Octavian's Commander-in-Chief would probably have been in name only. The Commanders of Kohlstania's army were practiced and competent, and he was unblooded. Exceptionally well-trained, but unblooded.

So, by the time that Randolf showed them Elena, in her little donkey-cart, on her way home again, the question had been significantly altered in Alexander's mind. It was no longer *How can I get home*, but *Do I want to go home?*

What would he do, when he got home again? Oh, he could take command of the Army, he supposed, but to what purpose? To watch them drill, and take them out on parades, and make some effort at keeping them sharp? The current commanders would be better at that than he was. He didn't know a great deal about anything other than military matters, and to put it bluntly, he doubted that seasoned Commanders would give more than lip service to his leadership. He had no practice, and no real experience, and they had no reason to trust his judgment. So what would he do when he got back? He had a taste of real work and real *life* now, and while he wouldn't miss the blisters and the sweat and the dead-stupid physical labor, the artificial surroundings of the Court did not seem particularly attractive anymore. Watching the intrigues going on, playing politics, sitting in on the Council sessions and pretending he was actually contributing to the discussions seemed an utter waste of time. And a day "filled" with games, hunting, flirting, wenching, and the like wasn't particularly attractive, either.

Well, perhaps the wenching. But a man could only rise to the occasion so many times in a day. You couldn't actually fill a day with wenching.

As a grumbling Rose made certain that he was *out* of the house and heading back to the stables, he was no longer sure that he belonged in Kohlstania anymore.

He'd had more of those dreams, of purple sands and a lovely lady. He was not altogether certain of her identity, but by now, he had a shrewd guess.

Oh, yes indeed, he could guess. The strange light had given an odd color to her hair, but under proper sun, he reckoned it would be golden. And while he'd never seen Elena in quite so *little* clothing, well, that could just be chalked up to the fact that his imagination was very good at creating a picture from a small amount of information.

Not that he was under any illusions that the dreams meant anything, except that *he* had stopped thinking of Madame Elena as an enemy and someone to blame all of his troubles upon. No, he was not *about* to make any overtures in that direction. He had no particular wish to go back to being a donkey most of the time. Not that she wasn't a tasty little thing, and not that she wasn't exactly to his particular taste, but—no. And not that she still couldn't make his groin ache if he thought about her in that way, but— definitely no. Even if she didn't turn him back into a donkey, it wasn't worth finding himself flat on his back with *that* sort of headache for a second time.

It was enough that as he had become less of an ass, in both senses, she had become friendlier. If she didn't yet treat him as an equal—well, maybe he didn't yet deserve to be treated like an equal. A Godmother was both above birth-rank and apart from it—

So, if you want respect from a Godmother, you have to earn it, I suppose.

He climbed the ladder to his loft-room slowly, and as he poked his head through the hole in the floor, he realized that tonight he was disinclined to read anything. He didn't even light his lamp; he merely blew out the one he had brought with him and stripped down in the darkness. Instead of reading, he climbed into his bed, and lay there with his hands clasped behind his head, thinking.

No, I don't think I want to go home. Not unless something horrible happens to Octavian; Father would need me then. But as long as they know that I'm all right, I suppose it wouldn't matter to them where I am. So where should I go, and what could I do?

Julian might be able to use him; he'd always gotten along reasonably well with Julian. Truth to tell, though his brother was probably handling the civilians in his new land well enough, where the military was concerned, Julian wouldn't have a clue. According to Alexander's instructors, it was usually better all the way around for a ruler's Commander-in-Chief to be someone he trusted and knew, personally.

He could probably talk Julian into giving him the position. The real question was how Julian's new people would feel about it. And there were other things to consider; what the shape of Julian's army was, if he even *had* an army. If he didn't—well, in that case there was no doubt; there *was* a place for him at Julian's side. Building an army up from nothing, or back up from decay—yes, he knew how to do that, in theory at least.

But of course, if Julian happened to have a perfectly good army, and a Commander-in-Chief that suited him, then even if Alexander talked him into the job, there would be a colossal amount of resentment. No, he wouldn't walk into that particular tiger-pit...not without a lot of forethought and planning, anyway.

It might be worth it. Especially if he'd actually be able to accomplish something.

He tried to think of all of the possible ramifications and repercussions, and found himself drifting off to sleep. And as he relaxed and his concentration faded away, one final, very odd thought floated up through the formless, shapeless stuff of his dreams.

I wish—it's a pity the Godmothers don't need an army....

It was probably a good thing, after all, that it *had* taken Elena the better part of two hours to get home again. By the time she drove up to her door, she had managed to cry herself out, find a stream, wash her face, and get herself looking no worse than tired.

Hob was waiting for her, ready to take the donkey and cart, but surprisingly, Rose was right at the door. And she hadn't even gotten across the threshold before Rose made it very clear *why* she'd been waiting—or rather, lying in wait—in order to get a very particular complaint lodged before anyone else could say anything. She started at the front entry and continued her complaint all the way up the stairs and on into the suite.

"—in your rooms, if you please, the whole day. Not a jot of work done, and that Randolf acting like the lord of the manor—"

"I did *not* act like the lord of the manor," came Randolf's voice, muffled by the velvet drapes that had been drawn across the face of the mirror. "I merely told Lily that in *my* opinion, and based on *my* presentiment, the young man needed to be here to see what you were doing with his brother."

Elena went to the mirror and pulled back the drapes. Randolf was ensconced squarely in the center of the mirror, looking seriously miffed. "I do not often have premonitory feelings, Godmother," he said stiffly, "but when I do, I am not accustomed to having them questioned." He looked down his long nose at Rose, who sniffed scornfully. "*Really,* Godmother. Particularly from a creature with no experience at predictive magic, and no—"

"Thank you, Randolf," Elena said, interrupting him by holding up her hand. "I do understand your feelings, but it is Rose's duty to act in a manner that protects my interests." Rose looked smug for a moment, but Elena continued. "However, you are entirely correct; your previous owners *did* use you to foretell the future in a very limited way as we both know, and although you lost some of that ability when Bella gave you more freedom, when you do feel a prescient impulse, it is wise for us to act upon it. If this happens again in my absence, I would wish you to speak with the others first, and let them know your reasons before you act, just so that everyone knows what is happening and why."

Now *both* of them gave a derisive sniff, which—since it probably meant that neither of them felt the victor in the disagreement—was the best she was going to manage.

Silly geese. Randolf took the attitude that since he was *entirely* a magical entity, and had served only Queens and Kings among Dark Sorcerers, he was somehow higher up in the Faerie ranks than a mere House-Elf. He was, in his nonexistent bones, a snob. While Rose, who had served Godmothers for hundreds of years here, believed in her heart of hearts that any decision *she* made in a Godmother's absence should take precedence; in her own way, she was just as much of a snob as Randolf, which meant that they were doomed to clash. Robin and Hob either humored her or ignored her when she was in this mood, but Lily enjoyed slyly tweaking her skirts, and it was clear to Elena that this time Randolf and Lily had conspired together to take Rose down a peg.

Well, here was the one valuable piece of advice that Madame Klovis had ever given regarding the staff— *When the servants begin quarreling, stay out of it.* The rest of the advice, *All you will do is inflate their already bloated opinions of themselves,* was utter nonsense, but the first part was right enough.

"I would have told the Prince everything anyway," Elena continued, ignoring the sniffs, "but I don't think anything but good can come of his actually *seeing* it all unfold. It will probably give him extra motivation to prove that he has re-formed and is ready to go back to his family himself."

That last cost her a pang; she ignored it. Rose looked a lit-tle more mollified, but Randolf frowned. "But, Godmother, that's—" he began, but once again Elena cut him off. "Rose, I am wearied to death. Could the rest of this wait until morning?"

Rose flushed, mortified at being caught at permitting her own grudge to interfere with the well-being of the God-mother in residence; as Elena well knew, it was the only thing that would shake her off her current crusade. "I beg your pardon, Madame Elena!" she said. "Of course it can wait. Your bed has been turned down and warmed, and there's a tidbit waiting on your bedside table."

"Thank you, Rose," Elena said, but she was already gone, whisking herself away as only an embarrassed House-Elf could.

Now she turned back to Randolf. "So what was it about your presentiment that was so important you were going to set Rose off *again?*" she asked with more than a touch of im-patience.

"Madame," Randolf said, with immense dignity. "God-mother. It *was* important, because if I am correct, what is going to happen is unprecedented. My sense is absolute that Prince Alexander is perfectly ready to pass any trials of his nature that you or anyone else may set him—and also, that when he does so, he will *never leave here.* Make of that what you will; it ut-terly baffles me. I certainly cannot imagine a Prince of the Blood being content with laboring as a common farmhand."

Elena controlled her expression, somehow, and managed

to thank Randolf gravely before dropping the curtains over his mirror. But inside, the emotions that she thought she had brought into check roiled up again.

If she had not been so tired, Randolf's words probably would have kept her up late into the night. But after a glance out the window to see that there was no light in Alexander's loft-room, she found herself so exhausted that she nearly fell asleep with the glass of honeyed milk in her hand. She caught herself just as it started to slip from her grip; she drank it down quickly and got into bed, and was literally asleep before she even turned on her side to her usual sleeping position.

The little, shallow waves of the amethyst ocean were as warm against the skin of her feet and calves as the milk she had just drunk. She noticed that the filmy little halfhearted excuse for a skirt she was wearing barely came to her knees; well, at least it wasn't going to get wet while she waded. The silky-soft sand was even softer under the water. Experimentally she reached down to touch the slowly undulating waves, then brought her fingers to her lips.

The water was sweet, not salty. Interesting; she wondered what that meant, since dreams had their own logic.

"Elena! Are you going to paddle out there all night?"

She looked up; Alexander was standing just above the waterline, watching her with a huge grin on his face. Unlike her, *he* was attired in real clothing, rather than the few bits of veils that *she* was wearing.

What on earth was her dream trying to tell her?

She waded obliquely towards him, enjoying the feel of

the water on her feet. When she was near enough, he held out his hand to her, and she took it.

"You called me by my name," she said, curious to hear what the dream-Alexander would say to that. "You've never done that before."

"Well, I finally figured out who you were," he replied. "And it doesn't matter what I say to you *here*, anyway," he continued, impudently. "You aren't a Godmother here; you can't punish me in a dream. I can say what I like and I won't end up as a donkey, or on my back with a splitting head. I can do *this*—" he took her in his arms "—and *this*—"

He wound both his hands in her hair, bent his head and kissed her; his lips were already open, and hers were parted, but in surprise rather than initial arousal, because she had just realized, not only what he had just said, but what it *meant*.

This wasn't her dream.

Or to be more accurate, it wasn't *just* her dream; it was *their* dream. They were sharing it.

His tongue teased hers, and his hand slipped inside the flimsy bodice of her gown to caress her naked nipple, which hardened immediately. She thrust all other thoughts aside for later. This *was* a dream, and she was going to enjoy it—

He slipped the straps of her gown off her shoulders, and her breasts slid free of the silky fabric. The warm breeze played over her shoulders. Each of his hands cupped a breast now, and his thumbs made little circles on the exquisitely sensitive skin. Little lances of pure pleasure and incredible sensation followed every movement of his fingers, and her groin tightened as she opened her mouth to his probing.

He took his mouth from hers and began to lick and nibble at her neck; she discovered that (ah, the wonders of the dream-state!) his shirt had vanished altogether, and she moved her hands over his chest, the muscles moving marvelously under her palms as he breathed, until her fingers found *his* nipples, and it was her turn to make *him* gasp.

But he took his revenge immediately; before she knew what he was about, his head had moved lower, and he fastened his mouth on her breast.

And his tongue and teeth were so much cleverer than his fingers had been that it was all she could do to stand upright.

Dream-logic again, for the very next moment they were lying in the soft sand, both of them utterly naked. He moved the attentions of his mouth to her left breast, and she moaned aloud, her hands in his hair, wanting to keep him there forever, but also wanting more. He chuckled; his free hand went to work on her right breast, and she felt her back arching without her even thinking about moving, and then his hand began to move lower—lower—her legs parted involuntarily as his fingers just stirred the first soft hairs of her sex and—

A rooster crowed. Right in her ear.

Swearing, she woke up.

The wretched bird crowed again. It wasn't *right* in her ear, but it was certainly just under her window.

She was breathing as hard as if she had been running; her secret parts were still tight and hot with need, and if at that moment she could have gotten her hands on an axe, there would have been poultry for dinner.

Instead she closed her eyes and forced herself to think rationally, difficult though that was under the circumstances. It wasn't the damned bird's fault. It must not have gotten into the coop with the rest before Lily closed them all in for the night. It was lucky it had escaped the ferrets, foxes, and owls. It *was* dawn. It was only behaving like a rooster.

There was some cold comfort in knowing that Alexander had been jolted just as rudely out of the same dream.

Think about this, she reminded herself. *Rationally. You were sharing the same dream. That doesn't happen to just anyone.*

Unless she was *greatly* mistaken, that meant that Alexander had a touch of magic himself. Probably not a lot, or he would have been able to put up some resistance to her spells even with no training at all. But even a little magic was certainly enough to qualify as a Hedge-Wizard.

That put something of a different complexion on things. Even a little magic would allow him into the brotherhood of magicians. Which meant—

Which meant he could stay. He wouldn't be a common—or uncommon—outsider anymore. He could be *allowed* free access to everything here.

I have to find out if the Elves will give him the power to see magic. If they will—

If they did, then there was no question. If he chose to remain here as part of the household, the mere fact that the Elves gave him a magical ability of that nature would mean that not only could he stay if he wanted to, but that they *intended* for him to stay. Even Rose would have to give in to the will of the Great Ones of Faerie.

Only those born to be among the Sorcerers could see magic naturally, as Arachnia did, and there were plenty of

Witches and Hedge-Wizards who, never having the chance to gain that power, went on and blithely worked with magic without being able to see it. You didn't *need* to see it to be effective, it simply made things much easier for the God-mothers and Wizards if they were able to see the magic following the will of The Tradition and could gauge how strong it was at a glance. That was why they were *always* given the gift after they were accepted by the Fae.

And when she remembered that, a plan fell into place in her mind, whole and entire. And despite the level of her frustration, she very nearly laughed aloud. If it worked—if it worked, well—there would be some changes. If it didn't, she'd be no worse off than she was now.

And with that, she was able to fall back to sleep. This time, *without* dreams.

"I take it you can hunt," Lily said to Alexander over breakfast. "Never heard of a noble who couldn't. But are you any good at it?"

He blinked at her in surprise, still feeling a bit muzzy-headed from the dream that had been so rudely interrupted by that wretched rooster. If he'd had ready access to an axe, there'd have been poultry for Robin's stew pot this morning....

Rose was assiduously ignoring him, but everyone else seemed interested in his answer, so he took the time to think about it before he said anything. "Well, I'd have to ask what you wanted me to hunt for, and with," he said, wondering what had prompted the question. "I'm good with any kind of bow. Pheasant, quail, waterfowl—I'm quite good at hunting those. Rabbit and hare are best taken with snares; you're more likely to lose or break arrows going after them with a bow, and I have to be honest with you, I never learned how to set a snare." He was *not* going to say that the snare was considered to be fit only for peasants to use. "If it's deer you're wanting, I would feel more comfortable with a cross-bow; without a hound to help me track a wounded one, I want to be able to take the beast down at once, not let it run off to die slowly." At that, he saw Hob smile approvingly, and went on, feeling encouraged. "I won't hunt boar alone; that's for fools and braggarts—although, if there's a boar giving one of your villages trouble, you can count on me for the hunt. And I won't hunt anything I can't eat, and I count swan, stork, crane, and heron in that category. Does that an-swer your question?"

"Perfectly," said Lily, with great satisfaction. "We have beef and chicken, and goose, too, but Robin wants deer in storage, and some wild fowl—"

"The house has a larder that preserves anything put into it and keeps it at the state it was when it went in," Robin said gravely, turning away from his cooking for a moment. "You've heard us speaking about the house growing? And you recall from yesterday that Madame Elena is now the Godmother for Kohlstania as well as her other Kingdoms? As a Godmother's responsibilities grow, so do her obliga-tions, and we believe that we may be required shortly to be able to play host to visitors. I wish to have something more on hand than the ingredients for simple country-fare."

"And we don't hunt," Lily concluded. "If you do, and

you're good at it, then Godmother thinks you're ready to have the bounds taken down so you can go hunting."

A few months ago, that pronouncement would have set his plans for running into motion. What more could he have possibly asked? He was being made free of the forest and fields, with a weapon in his hands! No matter *how* far away Kohlstania was, he was certain he would be able to find his way there.

Of course, that was before he learned—thanks to what had happened to Octavian—that the Godmother was perfectly capable of putting a curse on someone that would make him wander in circles until she cared to collect him.

He might still have considered making the attempt to escape, but—no. When he left this place, he wanted it to be because he was deemed ready to go. Like Octavian.

"I'd prefer fowl, to begin with," Robin was saying, interrupting his thoughts. "Since I don't believe we'll be seeing more than one or two important visitors at a time, at least at first. Frankly wild boar is no tastier than domestic swine, and we have plenty of farmers prepared to sell or trade us for pork."

"I'd like to be deeper into fall before I hunt deer," he replied, "and since we're hunting for the pot, I would prefer to draw them to a bait-spot where I've set up a blind, anyway. It might not be as sporting, but it will give me a better chance to select a target, and the best chance for a clean, quick kill. I'll leave the does and the King-stag, given my choice, and cull out some of the younger bucks."

"That sounds like a fine plan." Robin nodded agreeably. "Hob?"

"Finished your plate?" Hob asked, and at Alexander's nod, said, "Come with me, then. We'll get something that suits you, and I'll point you in a good direction for some fowling."

It was to another of the outbuildings that Hob led him, one that was no bigger than a gardening shed on the outside, and in fact, the last time Alexander had looked at it, it *had* been a gardening shed, empty but for a few pots. But when Hob opened the door—

"Ah, I thought that might've happened," Hob said with satisfaction.

Alexander *knew* he should not have been surprised, and yet he foolishly was. Outside was a shed he could have circled in ten paces. Inside was a royal hunting-lodge, with polished wooden floors covered with bright carpets, polished wooden walls adorned with hunting-trophies from all manner of animals (including a span of antlers that must of once belonged to a creature the size of a small elephant), and furnished with massively constructed chairs and benches. And there must have been a second, perhaps even a third floor, since there was a staircase beside the door. There were no windows on the outside. Ten enormous glass windows on the inside let in the light from a landscape of stunning beauty, a wide meadow studded with flowers on one side, and a forest with tall, graceful trees of no species *he* recognized on the other. It was mountainous, too, the purple, snow-capped mountains rising above the trees at the far edge of the meadow, and of course, there were *no* mountains within sight of the Godmother's cottage....

"Good place for putting visitors," said Hob matter-of-factly. "'Course, the Great Fae can come a-visiting by coming through here, an' they choose." And as Alexander stumbled across the threshold, Hob strode the length of the lodge to the racks of hunting-bows on the wall at the far end—which also had a door in it. "Come along, lad!" he called over his shoulder, reaching for a longbow. "You'll want to check the pull on these for yourself."

Alexander hurried across the room, which did not show a single sign of wear, dust, or occupancy, and took the bow that Hob had selected; it was a thing of beauty, the work of a master craftsman, who had not wasted time, skill or the strength of the wood on foolish carving or inlay-work. It was a thing of perfectly polished simplicity, the close grain of the wood speaking for itself, the surface like satin. Only the ends were sweetly capped with silver-chased fittings. Alexander nocked the string and tried the pull.

"Too light," he said with disappointment, for it was an otherwise exquisite piece, and had roused an unexpected avarice in him.

"Aye, well, you've muscled up a bit since you came here," Hob replied, with a smug smile. "Doubt you could still fit in that candy-soldier tunic you showed up wearing." And before Alexander could react to that statement, Hob handed him another.

This one, just as fine as the first, differing only in the chasing on the silver tip-caps, was still a bit light. But the third choice felt perfect, and Hob took down a quiver full of fowling arrows and a second of target-arrows, and led him back outside again.

"Have you—seen that place before?" Alexander asked, as they set up a target at the bottom of the garden.

"Oh, aye, back when the Godmother here—that'd be Madame Beaubaton—was the first mortal after the Fae Godmother, the Emerald Fairy," replied Hob, eying the distance between Alexander and the target. "Back up a bit, lad. I think you'll find with that pull you have more distance to work with. Aye, by rights, she should've been a Sorceress, should Madame, but she was more minded to the *herding* of things, so to speak. Happens that way, sometimes. Them as should be Sorcerers decides they want to be more active. Said she didn't care to sit on a mountain and wait for a Great Quest to set things aright when she could nip trouble in the bud." He sighed, reminiscently. "That there was the hunting-lodge of the Emerald Fairy, and that's Fae lands you see outside the windows, and since Madame was so powerful and all, the lodge stayed put until we didn't need it again. Last of the outbuildings to shut up, and first to open. Fae can come and go from there, and now, probably will. Oh, aye, we had visitors in them days. Great Sorcerers, mortal Kings, and Fae—needed the room then. Me and the rest, we was under servants then, serving under Ald Kelm, he's *Sir* Kelm now, if you please, him as runs the Elven Queen's household as her Seneschal now. Never dull, but a mort'o work, I tell you. We scarce need magic now, but then—crikey! Couldn't get through a day without casting till you was dizzy with it, and that was just to keep the stables clean! So many invisible servants the air fair buzzed with 'em!"

"Do you miss it?" Alexander asked, taking careful aim.

"Truth to tell—no. Ah, good! See, I told you that you've

got more range with this one." As Alexander took aim
again—his first shot having hit the target, but high—Hob
continued. "No, I'm a simple fellow, and I like a simpler life.
We *all* do, or we wouldn't be here. *But*—now, well done
there!—that's not to say I wouldn't like things a *little* live-
lier. A visitor, now and again, that's a good thing. Seeing
some of the Great Fae. Madame Elena's like Madame Bella
before her; she's got some good notions, not minded to just
react to what The Tradition does, more inclined to do a bit
more *pushing* and a bit less following, if you take my meaning. I'd like to see some of the Great Ones putting some consideration into her notions. But a Court here again? Like
Madame Beaubaton and the Emerald Fairy before her? No,
no. Now *there* you go! You've got the range of her now!"

Alexander's last arrow hit dead in the center, and he felt
comfortable with the bow now. "Well," he replied. "I agree
with you. Now, where do you suggest I go?"

Much to Rose's exasperation, Elena was taking Alexander's place out in the old orchard—though little did Rose
guess that Elena was doing so in order to talk with Lily pri-
vately. All that Rose knew was that Elena and Hob had decided to see what Alexander would do with the freedom to
hunt alone and unescorted. She didn't know that this was
part of a much larger plan, nor that Lily had gone to see if
she could have an audience with the Elven King before the
sun rose this morning.

"So, Madame, like you thought, when I mentioned the
lad, they took me right to His Majesty. And like you said, I
made no suggestions." Lily upended her basket of apples

into the back of the cart, and Elena followed it with hers a moment after. "I just said that you were looking for a *real* trial for the Prince, knowing that he'd recognize all the usual sorts of things, and that you were sending him out hunting today. And His Majesty did give me a look, then told me to tell you that he'd see to it personally." She gave Elena a look of her own; pleased, but wary. Well, she was right to be wary.

Elena shivered a little. "It is chancy, leaving this sort of thing to *them*," she said soberly. "The Great Fae don't always think like us...." She included the House-Elf in that; Brownies were as close to mortal in their ways of thinking as any Fae could get.

"True enough," Lily agreed. "Whatever trial they give him is going to be dangerous. But letting him wander about in the forest like a donkey would have been dangerous. Sending him off on *any* redemption trial would have been dangerous. Questing *is* dangerous—and with all that reading he's been doing, he *will* recognize just about any trial that you could put him to. That the Great Fae don't think like mortals will just mean that he's not likely to recognize a trial for what it is until after he's passed it."

Or it's too late, Elena thought, but kept that thought to herself.

So they worked on, side by side, with a tacit agreement to say no more about it. If Alexander passed his trial, and *if* he was the something that the King had been looking for, and *if* he was so unusual that Randolf was right, and he was suited to remain here, only the King and Queen could make that judgment and mark him in a way that even Rose would respect. Elena knew now, as she had not known when she first came as an Apprentice, that the first Godmother, the Emerald Fairy, was the sister of Huon, the King of the Sylvan Elves of this part of the Fae Lands. He had a particular association with the Godmothers of this place; though his Queen made most of the decisions concerning the mortals who lived here, *he* had the right of direct intervention whenever he cared to exercise it. But she still worried. Had she been within her rights to call on the Elven King and Queen for this? Had she been within her rights to subject Alexander to that sort of danger? The Fae operated by laws and rules that few mortals really understood. But how else was she to test him? And if Randolf was right about him—how else was she to get the authority to allow him to stay?

Well, it was out of her hands now. And whatever happened, she would have to live with the result—or the blame.

Now this is the way to hunt, Alexander thought, with great satisfaction, as he stood on the edge of a sun-drenched meadow, waist-deep in waving grass, a light breeze stirring his hair.

Hob had outfitted him with moleskin breeches, stout boots, a doeskin jerkin, and a most remarkable game bag. "Made it myself, back in the day," he'd said with great pride—and besides being of fine workmanship, there was another reason for the pride. It was magical; it would hold virtually as much as you cared to put into it, without ever getting an ounce heavier.

Alexander had already stuffed two pheasants and a half dozen quail into it. It was much better than trying to carry around a conventional game bag, or tying the game to your belt. It was better even than having to trail around with a crew of servants to carry what you shot, since a pack of servants always managed to scare off so much game that it hardly seemed worth having them along.

He missed having beaters or a dog, though; having to go it alone, flushing his own game, was chancy. When confronted with a single man, quail and pheasants were as likely to run away under the cover of the grass as they were to flush into the air.

On the other hand, given those circumstances, he wasn't doing badly, and it was wonderful being out here, without anyone looking over his shoulder. It was a perfect day, too; sun bright in a blue sky, air crisp, not enough breeze to give him any serious windage problems.

In fact, he could almost believe that he was a free man, free to do whatever he—

A shriek cut across the peace of the meadow, startling a covey of quail into the air practically at his feet.

They whirred away, tiny wings a blur, presenting him with five clear shots. But he had no time for game now, not when a second scream rent the air, and he knew it for the cry of a woman in terror.

The quail were barely in the air, and he was already half across the meadow, running in the direction from which the scream had come.

A third scream put more speed into his heels, and he burst through a coppice of birch trees to find himself at what was clearly a woodcutter's cottage, with an axe still in the stump and a pile of wood chopped that was as tall as the cottage, and a second and third beside it. A chestnut pal-

frey in fancy tack was tied to a sapling nearby. He took little more note than that of his surroundings, though—not
with the bleeding body of what must have been the woodcutter himself lying facedown on the ground, and a young
woman struggling in the grasp of a richly dressed man not
thirty feet away.

Without even thinking about it, he had an arrow nocked
and flying, and a second one drawn. The first flew right past
the man's ear, close enough to brush him with the fletching,
and *thunked* into the tree behind him—just as Alexander had
intended.

The man froze, the struggling girl still in his grasp.

She could not have been much older than fourteen or fifteen, and only just woman-ripe. And once, maybe Alexander would have laughed to see this, and gone on his way,
for the girl and the man on the ground were only peasants,
after all. And had he not come down the path that Madame
Elena had laid for his feet, some future, harder Alexander
might even have demanded *his* share of the girl—

But that past Alexander was gone, and the future one
erased. And this bastard, be he never so noble, was not of
a like kind with the Alexander who stood there with his second arrow aimed for the eye.

The stranger slowly met Alexander's gaze. He was clad
in blue velvet and silk, and around his neck was a thick chain
of golden links. Otherwise he was nondescript, with short
hair cut to fit beneath a helm, and an ordinary enough,
moustached face. "Well met, fellow," the man said, coolly.
"Come to take a share of the spoils? I saw her first, but
you're welcome to her when—"

"Let her go," said Alexander, feeling an icy fury rising up in him at the sight of the poor child's terror.

"I don't think you *quite* understand the situation here," the man replied, without turning a hair. "These are my lands. I own these peasants. They are mine to—"

"Let her go!" Alexander interrupted with a roar. "Lands you may well own, but people, never! Now unless you want my arrow in your eye—"

The man barked a laugh. "And what if my men have you in *their* sight? What then?"

"I can drop you before they can reach me," Alexander countered, instantly. He knew it for truth; he also knew that it was unlikely the man would have positioned his men in hiding, if he'd even come with men at all. "If *they* had bows, I'd be dead already. Assuming they even exist. Now *let her go*. You have until the count of three, or you die like the base-born cur you are. One."

Slowly the man's grip loosened on the terrified girl.

"Two."

The girl wrenched herself free and threw herself down beside the man on the ground. Alexander did not lower his bow.

"Girl," he barked. *"Girl!"*

Weeping, she looked up from the victim.

"Does that man live?" he asked harshly.

She nodded, tears streaming down her face.

"Good. Then he'll last long enough for us to find him help—*and* deal with this dog here. Give him what tending you can, then get you rope from the house."

The face of the nobleman went blank. "Just what, precisely, do you intend, fellow?" he asked, carefully, and the girl ran back to the house.

"Justice," Alexander replied succinctly. "I see by the belt you wear that you are a knight—or you pretend to that rank. By the laws of chivalry, I could kill you where you stand for the insult you gave that maiden."

The man's face went black with rage, and he shook as he made his reply. "You *dare*!" he howled. "You *dare* take me to task for what I do with *my* cattle on *my*—"

"Shut your mouth!" Alexander roared again. "Yes, I take you to task, for people are *not* cattle, to do with as you will, and the vows you swore as a knight bind you to honor *all* women, be they never so base! And speaking of bind—*bind him,* girl. Bind his hands behind him, and bind his arms to his body. Then take up that poor man and put him on that horse I see over there." He jerked his head in the direction of the richly caparisoned palfrey that clearly belonged to the knight. "You will lead the horse, and *I* will prod this dog before us, and we will go to a lady who will see justice done for you, and to this—"

And the man—and the maid—abruptly burst into peals of delighted laughter, like the wild pealing of joyful bells ringing out for a great victory, and the triumphant trumpeting of bugles on the battlefield.

And before Alexander could even begin to react to that, the body on the ground—vanished. And the cottage vanished. And the peasant maid and the richly clad knight also vanished.

But in their places stood two beings the like of which Alexander had never before seen.

That they were Fae, Elves, he had no doubt—but they were to the Brownies and that odd little creature he might or might not have met down at the pond what a brilliantly faceted diamond was to a quartz crystal. Or perhaps, what lightning and thunder were to the little spark that came from rubbing silk against amber. There were no words to describe them adequately, and now he knew why, when the books in Elena's Library had tried to tell what the Great Fae were like, they simply said, "Their like is not in the world."

There were things that marked them the delicately pointed ears, the long and narrow faces, the slender, graceful bodies, the ground-sweeping manes of silken hair that graced both sexes, the strange, intricately wrought garb that they wore that was both jewelry and clothing in all the colors of green that ever there were. But none of that *was* what they were. If enchantment had a form, it was theirs.

"Well done, Prince Alexander," said the she—who was a Queen among her people, surely. "And well and truly said and meant, for meaning is as important as action. You have passed our test."

"More than passed, pearl of my heart," the male—also, most surely, royal. "We looked only to see he intended a rescue. Instead he dared to think of *justice,* and against one he might well have sought common cause with, once." As Alexander slowly lowered his bow, the string going slack in his fingers, they both approached him, with deliberate grace and gliding steps. "Yes," the King continued, fixing Alexander with a penetrating gaze. "Yes. I believe he is what I hoped for."

"Then a gift I grant to you, Prince among mortals," said

the Queen, "for it is, I think, a gift that you will use wisely and well." And she reached out with one long, slender finger and touched him lightly in the middle of his forehead, and a second time on his lips; he licked them involuntarily, and tasted something like honey.

It was as if some dam inside him burst, and suddenly he was flooded with sensation. *Mostly* vision, as swirls and clouds of glowing light sprang up around him and all about him, but mostly circling the two Elves. But there were other things, sensations he couldn't quite put a name to, but which left him dazzled, nonetheless.

Then the King did the same—

But this time nothing happened, or at least, nothing obvious.

"Now go you back to dwelling of the mortal Godmother called Elena," said the King, with a pleased chuckle.

"And tell her—?" Alexander managed.

"Oh, she will know what to make of you," the Queen said, amid more peals of that silvery laughter, that he joined in with, without quite knowing why he did so. "Trust me, she will know!"

18

"**M**adame Elena," said Rose, in a rather strained voice. She peered into the doorway of Elena's study, to which Elena had been "banished" when Lily felt that she had done more than her share of apple-picking. "The Prince has returned. I think you had better see him."

Elena looked up; Rose looked as if she had seen something she still *could* not believe, yet *dared* not disbelieve. She looked shocked, rather than smug, but shocked as in having her own view of the world turned upside down, rather than if something truly dreadful had happened to the Prince that even *she* was appalled by.

So. He's returned in triumph, I suspect! Elena took a deep breath, and let it out in a sigh of relief, all of her tension going with it. It was over, and it had gone well. Alexander had passed the trial—and apparently managed to do a great deal better than merely pass it.

Behind his curtain, she heard Randolf chuckle with immense satisfaction. Rose did not even glance his way.

"Very well, I'll come down," Elena said, setting aside the chronicle she was reading. Rose turned and was gone by the time she reached the door onto the staircase.

She went down the stairs and passed through the parlor and the library, and noted that most of the books had left the parlor, though whether the House-Elves had moved them or they had moved themselves, she could not say. What mattered was that the new library room must have opened up in the night. *I shall have to look into that in a bit,* she thought, hastening her steps at the sound of voices in the kitchen.

There she found all of the House-Elves, Rose included, and Alexander. They were standing; he was sitting at the table, dressed in hunting-gear, cradling a cup of ale, and looking bewildered.

There was no doubt why Rose had reacted to the sight of him in the way that she had. The amount of magic about him was matched only by the magic that had swirled around Octavian when it was time for him to return to Kohlstania. But that could have been explained away—what could *not* be explained away was the forms that had been laid over him, and that was what had given Rose her shock.

The same forms had been laid upon Elena, though she had not known it, when she was accepted as an Apprentice. The Elf-Queen's mark was on the Prince, in the form of a crimson bird with flaming wings, the sign of the Protector, laid over his head and shoulders, visible to those with the eyes to see magic, and—yes, the Elf-King's as well, a circlet of emerald fire around his brow that raised a narrow, mild-eyed head at her approach and showed itself to be, not a circlet at all, but the emerald serpent, the symbol of Wisdom. Both would fade in time, probably by morning—but the mark upon the spirit was there for all time.

There it was. The Elven Royalty had accepted him. If he chose to remain here, he could not be turned away. Small wonder that Rose had been shaken.

Alexander looked up at the sound of her footstep, and it was very clear from his expression that he was utterly bewildered. She knew how he felt; to see magic itself, raw and primal, for the first time, and not to know what it was—he must think himself going mad.

"It's all right," she said, immediately, and sat down beside him, patting his hand. "You're not moonstruck. The Elves marked you, and when they did, they opened your eyes to see magic. You must have some magical ability of your own, or they wouldn't have been able to do that. It means that not only did you pass the trial they set you, but they've accepted you as a kind of—of Knight of Magic. Like I am, actually. You have to be able to *see* magic to use it with finesse. If you can see it, you can do more with a very little ability than someone with more ability, but unable to see."

"It's—very disorienting," he said carefully.

"Just *want* it to go away," she told him. "These things answer to the trained will, and I *know* you have that; all that military training you had must have given you discipline. At first, it might help to close your eyes before you concentrate on making it go away. Then, when you *want* to see magic again, want it to come back. It's probably the easiest of all of the magic powers to control."

He closed his eyes and opened them again, and relief spread over his features. "It's gone!"

"I told you it would be." She patted his hand again. "I don't think you heard me the first time—you've passed your final trial, Prince Alexander, just like your brother. Would you like to go home?"

That last cost her to ask, but the offer had to be made. And if he said yes, she would have to honor his request.

But he opened his mouth, then closed it again, without saying anything. Then opened it again. "I'm a magician?" he asked, instead of answering her.

They all nodded, even Rose. "Now that you can see magic, even though you don't know how to use it yet, aye," said Hob. "And seeing it, you'll train up right quick."

He looked thoughtful. "How powerful am I?" he asked, this time looking to Elena.

She shook her head. "I don't know for certain," she cautioned, "but I would guess, not very. No more than a country Witch or a Hedge-Wizard. If you were more powerful than that, you'd have come into your powers earlier, and you'd at least have felt them—*every* day, *all* the time, as if there was something you should be doing, something amazing that was going to happen to you, though you didn't know what it was."

He rubbed at a scratch on his cheek, absently. "What about now and again feeling like there was someone looming over me, watching me?"

"Hedge-Wizard," all the Brownies chorused at once, with Rose looking relieved. "That's just the sense that the power is *there*, lad," said Hob. "As it was, of course; it looms over everyone born royal, from time to time. Now—huh. I've a thought—"

He glanced at Elena, who nodded encouragement.

"Well," he said slowly. "It's been a long, long time since I've seen such a man, but it's also a long time since anyone wizard-born was also warrior-trained—it comes to me that you don't need a lot of magic to be a Champion."

"A what?" asked Elena, but she was drowned out by a chorus of what sounded like fervent curses from the other three House-Elves.

"Now why didn't I see *that* coming?" Lily said aloud, throwing her hands up in the air. "Of course!"

"It would be nice if someone would explain this to both of us mere mortals," the Prince said, but so plaintively that it would have been impossible for anyone to take offense.

"You've heard of the Green Knight? The Knight of the Black Rose? Sir Gavin the Hawk?" At each of those names, Alexander nodded vigorously. "Well, they was all Champions. The Great Fae have 'em among them, of course— warriors with a bit of magic—but sometimes they see a mortal they think worthy, and make *him* one, too. 'Specially if they think he's the kind to go charging in without regard for his own safety seeking justice, protecting the innocent, defending the virtuous, all that knightly sort of thing."

For some reason that Elena could not fathom, Alexander blushed, but nodded.

"Thing is, you see—now, you know not everything that comes out of Faerie thinks kindly of mortals, eh? And some of those things just laugh at ordinary swords and arrows and what-all." Hob waited to see if Alexander was following him, and as the Prince nodded, he went on. "Now, of course, you know that there's magic swords and so on that can take such an enemy down, but a Champion don't *need* a magic sword, or arrow, or spear, because whatever weapon he has is magic when he chooses. You see? You may not be able to channel *much* magic into your weapon, but any magic is enough to make it bite, and bite as hard as you can hit."

Elena felt her eyes widen, and Alexander's mouth formed a silent "oh."

"Ye see?" said Hob with satisfaction. "You mind Gavin the Hawk? That's how he got through the Scorpion King's black armor."

"How do I learn to do this?" Alexander asked, eagerly.

"We-ell, I'd say to go look in the Chronicles to be sure, but I think you'll find you don't need to learn it," Lily put in. "I think once you can see magic, it's more a matter of will and instinct than learned. And practice. Lots of practice, with someone who can see magic to supervise."

Now Alexander turned to Elena. "You said I can go—" he said, hesitantly. "But may I stay instead? Just until I understand all this," he added quickly, flushing. "But there's probably not anyone in all of Kohlstania who could help me, and, and—" he averted his eyes "—well, Father's got Octavian back. They don't exactly need me. And I would be truly, deeply grateful if you could help me. I don't know why

I was given this thing, but I can't see having it and going off to kick my heels at home and not use it."

Elena looked at him gravely. "Prince Alexander, you *do* realize what it means if you take this on yourself? Being a Champion is not—not—"

"I know it means my life won't be my own," he replied, and now he looked up to meet her eyes again. "But it never was, was it? It's just trading one set of responsibilities for another." Then an altogetherly unexpected bitter tone crept into his voice. "At least I'll *have* real responsibilities, and a real job that no one else can do."

She was taken aback by that for a moment; in fact, everyone in the kitchen seemed to be. And strangely enough, it was Rose who answered him.

"That's no less than the truth, Prince Alexander," she replied, and for once there was no half-hidden scorn or irony in her voice. "Become a Champion, truly, and there'll be no second-son make-work for you."

"Then that's what I want," he said firmly, and looked back at Elena. "May I stay?"

But she looked at the other four. "It's not only up to me," she said. "You only play at being servants here, when all's said and done. You have as much say in this as I do. I have never, ever heard of a Champion in the household of a Godmother before."

"Be damned useful," Hob said, stroking his chin thoughtfully.

"Can't think of anyone else to send him to," observed Robin. "And I can show him what to do, I think. It can't be much different than using a wand."

"I'll get his things," said Lily, and "I'll make up the guest-suite," said Rose, both at the same time.

"Well, then, it's unanimous," Elena said, trying not to show her elation. "But I will insist on one thing. You *must* inform your father that you are well. Whatever else you tell him is up to you. I can arrange to have the letter to him by nightfall."

He grinned. "I'll use the things in the study, shall I? Or will you require me to write it in blood?"

She aimed a blow at his ear, which he ducked. "In the study with you, *your highness*," she said, and still grinning, he obeyed.

Oh, me, she thought, looking after him, half in pleasure, half in dismay. *What have I bound—and what have I unleashed?*

The letter went off, carried by one of the wise old white ravens that hung about the place, which were fed from the leftovers carefully saved from meals. As Arachnia used bats as her messengers, so Elena, as had Madame Bella before her, used the clever white ravens. And she watched in Randolf's mirror as King Henrick, and Prince Octavian, read the letter, sighed a great sigh of relief, and then went on with their lives.

So there it was; Alexander had been right. All that had awaited him in Kohlstania was make-work, cooling his heels, and no real responsibility.

And she—she had a Champion-in-Training in her household, and she did not know whether to be glad of it. Champions could be called out to any need, at any time, to right any injustice, fight any good fight—

And so can Godmothers.

Champions' lives were not their own.

No more are Godmothers'.

But he was busy here, and, she thought, happy. Robin was making good on his promise to teach Alexander the channeling of magic power, which was coming harder for him than it had for her—yet another proof, had she needed one, that he had not been born with the ability of a full Wizard.

That was a relief to her, for if he *had* been a Wizard he would, eventually, been given responsibility for Kingdoms of his own, and he would have had to set up his own household in the midst of them. Now that she knew what to look for, she had gone back through all of the Library books and the Godmother chronicles, and had found Champions after all. She had paid little attention to the mentions of them before this, partly because she had been under the mistaken impression that they were just a different sort of knight, and that their ability to slay the terrible creatures of the Black Fae and those enslaved by Dark Sorcerers was merely that somewhere along the line they had gotten hold of those rare magical weapons. It had never occurred to her that they *were* magical weapons in and of themselves.

Silly of her, now that she came to think of it.

Still, in all of it, she never came across a reference to a Champion attached to the household of a Godmother. To Sorcerers and Sorceresses, yes. To Kings, certainly. Most of them seemed to wander about, singly, or with a group of adventurers, looking for trouble to eliminate. She was put in mind—which would, at this point, *not* be the thing to tell Alexander, even though it was awfully funny—of the bands of traveling rat-catchers, with their rat-charmers, rat-trappers, and ferreters, who went from town to town getting rid of pests of all sorts.

It seemed that no matter what, she would have him with her, undisturbed, through the winter at least, for as the season turned, it became quite clear that magic did not answer readily to Alexander's hand. The last of the harvest was gathered in, as the leaves turned and fell from the trees and the cruel November winds began to blow, and only by that time was he getting the knack of directing power into material objects and having it *remain* there. He did turn his hand to the household work without being asked—but Elena had the distinct feeling that there was a lot more being harvested from the orchards and gardens than could be accounted for by only overt work of the six members of the household. She had a shrewd guess that the Brownies were now using more of *their* magical powers than they used to. But of course, by The Tradition, that sort of thing had to happen in secret, where and when no mortals could see, so she just averted her eyes from the huge stores of apples, vegetables, and nuts in the cellars and went on about her business.

There was still an abundance of magical power looming over the household; not *pushing,* as she was accustomed to feeling The Tradition, but just—hovering. If a mountain could "hover" that is, for that is what it felt like to her. The Tradition was clearly nonplussed by what was going on here, but as she was operating completely outside of any Traditional path, it didn't quite know what to do with her and Alexander. For the moment, she was not going to argue; it kept her personal stores of magic topped up, and provided extra for all the things that the House-Elves were doing.

Meanwhile it appeared that Hob and Robin were calling in favors from Fae outside the household. Piece by piece, armor was appearing, wonderful stuff as light as cork, but stronger than steel, and fitted to Alexander exactly. He had a bow already from the hunting-lodge; Hob found him a sword and an axe and shield, and Robin made him a lance.

He was a proper part of the household now, and even the house responded by opening up an entirely new suite of rooms, uncompromisingly masculine and suited to a warrior, complete with an armor-stand and a big, empty, barn-like room in which he could practice. The windows looked out into some other part of Faerie than the hunting-lodge did; his rooms appeared to have been built in the edge of a sheer cliff overlooking the sea. It gave Rose vertigo; she had to leave the cleaning there to Robin or Lily.

It was not an amethyst-colored sea under a sky with two moons, though. Elena expected him to comment on that—but he did not. In fact, even though the delicious, frustrating dreams continued, he said nothing.

He treated her with respect, with honor, with courtesy; in fact, he was acting in the most Knightly fashion possible. It was utterly maddening. Not that she didn't *want* respect, honor and courtesy; but—

But she also *would* not let The Tradition turn this into a bedroom farce. Or worse. She would not let it undo all the work she had done to help him become someone that the *Great Fae*—the Great Fae!—had been willing to make into a Champion.

She would not allow all of that to be wasted, no matter what it cost her. On that, she was determined.

Even if all she got out of this was respect, honor, and courtesy....

Alexander stood quietly, looking out of the window of the library at the road to the cottage, which was disappearing under a thick snowfall as dusk fell. The House-Elves had gone to bed—or at least, they had gone to wherever *their* private quarters were, leaving the house quiet.

Elena had sent them off early tonight, insisting that they could and should take a kind of half-holiday. "We can manage dinner for ourselves," she'd said.

He hadn't objected, though she had looked at him oddly, as if she had expected him to. This fit in altogether perfectly with some half-formed ideas of his own, and even if he had to eat stale bread and rancid cheese tonight, he wasn't going to discourage anything that left the house empty for once.

Because having the Brownies around was, frankly, awkward. You never knew when they were going to just pop in a doorway. And he was very tired of awakening in the morning with his groin aching from one of those delightful and frustrating dreams.

He had decided that he was going to court Elena. *Court,* not seduce, because his intentions were ultimately honorable. That is, if Godmothers were permitted to wed. Mind, if the bedding preceded the wedding by quite some time, he wouldn't object; it wasn't that he objected in the least to a wedding, but—well, he had the feeling that the wedding of a Godmother would turn into an Occasion that would be the talk of a dozen Kingdoms and possibly the center of news for a dozen more. He knew what weddings were like in a *single* Kingdom—bloody hell, you had to plan the wretched things for months or even *years* in advance, and the celebrations generally stretched on for a month or more, which tended to make things a great deal less than comfortable for the newly wedded couple. And the wedding of a Godmother? He rather fervently prayed that he was wrong. Because there were old, old stories that described wedding celebrations between very great heroes and important Princesses that carried on for a year and a day, and—

—no. No. He could *not* manage to perform—for "performance" would be what it was—for an audience of thousands, every day, all day, for a year and a day. And he didn't think that such a thing would really appeal to Elena, either.

If The Tradition even allowed it. A formal wedding might bring down all sorts of horrible calamities on their heads.

But becoming lovers? Well, there was nothing in The Tradition against it, so far as he could see. Witches and Hedge Wizards could, and did, take spouses and lovers. Sorcerers and Sorceresses took lovers all the time. "Consorts," they were called. And even the masculine counterpart to the Godmother, the full Wizards, were mentioned to have companions from time to time. No mention for Godmothers, but there was also nothing against the idea, either. And maybe that was because the Godmothers were all assumed, traditionally, to be Fae—or because they were simply very, very discreet.

But he knew that he was going to have to tread very, very carefully. His old ways were not going to work with Elena; she was not to be "conquered," not to be "seduced," and certainly not to be taken by force. And the truth was that he didn't *want* to do any of those things.

The truth was, he didn't want to change the slowly unfolding friendship that was building between them, especially now that he had some of *her* respect. He just wanted to add to it.

Well, he was going to try, tonight.

And with luck, he wouldn't find himself flat on his back in the stable, with a head like a ringing bell.

As darkness fell, Elena began rummaging among the things in the pantry, and Alexander, probably hearing the clatter, came wandering in with a wistfully hopeful look on his face. "I don't know anything about cooking that doesn't involve spitting a bird over a fire," he admitted. "It's not the sort of thing that Princes are taught."

"Well, it *is* the sort of thing that I had to learn," she replied dryly. "Or did I not ever tell you my sordid little life-history?"

"Actually," he said, looking interested. "No. Of course, I know now that all Godmothers and a lot of Wizards are out of failed Tradition paths, so I assumed you were, too. Which one?"

She told him as she rummaged up the ingredients for

omelettes and began cracking eggs into a bowl. He listened with every evidence of interest, and when she thrust a knife and some mushrooms at him, managed to chop them without losing either the interest or the fingers. "So you would have married a Prince?" he said, when he'd finished. "How—odd. I can't see you in that role, somehow. Oh, maybe it would have been all right for you when you were sixteen or even eighteen, but not now. Crown Princesses don't really do very much other than the occasional Good Work, and I can't imagine you being content with being merely ornamental, wandering about the Palace gardens and posing amongst the peacocks, sitting for hours at your embroidery frame. It seems too passive."

Well—my goodness! "Why, thank you for that," she said, carefully tending the pan over the stove. "I believe that is one of the nicest things you have ever said to me. I must admit, I can't imagine *you* kicking about idly in your father's Court anymore."

"No, neither can I." He watched with interest as she slid the first omelette onto a plate. "I swear, that must be some sort of magic of its own—turning things into *food,* I mean."

"Hmm. Robin would agree with you." She turned out her own omelette, and joined him at the table. "Have you ever thought about how brave the first person to eat an egg must have been? Think about the way they look raw. I mean— *eeeyew!*"

They ate in silence, which she took as a good sign that she hadn't produced a dinner that positively revolted him. But after the food was gone, and the dishes left in the sink, an awkward-silence sprung up between them. It lasted long enough to become uncomfortable, until finally she stood up abruptly.

But so did he, at the exact same moment.

Somehow, either her feet got tangled up in the legs of the chair she had been sitting in, or she lost her balance a little; for whatever reason, she started to fall, and was just catching herself, when she found instead that he had caught her.

For a moment, in which she found herself strangely short of breath, they stood in a frozen tableau, faces mere inches apart, staring into each other's eyes.

She expected him, at that moment, to seize her as he had tried before; expected a hand to paw at her breast, and all the rest of it. Expected, in fact, anything except what actually happened.

"Elena," he said haltingly, "have you been dreaming of purple oceans?"

She nodded, speechless.

He sighed. "Oh, good. Then may I kiss you?"

"Only if you do it the way you do it *there*," she replied without thinking.

And he did.

And it was better than in the dream.

They separated only when it became obvious, at least to her, that if they didn't, they were likely to end up naked on the kitchen floor, which was very hard and very cold.

He was breathing very heavily, as if he had been running. "I—I wasn't intending—not like—I'm not—" he said, "Really. I swear. And I wouldn't—I don't—"

She stared deeply into his eyes for a long moment, then said, "I think we should take this discussion to your rooms."

He blinked. "Why?"

"They're downstairs. They're closer. Randolf." Not that Randolf couldn't watch them anyway, in all likelihood, but at least he wouldn't be in the next room.

"Ah." He cleared his throat. "Elena, may I invite you to my rooms?"

"You may," she replied, suppressing the urge to giggle. "And I accept your invitation."

It struck her that *nothing* he was doing or saying would have fit in with any Traditional path—not a bawdy song, not a tale of seduction and abandonment. Was he deliberately trying to break with The Tradition, or was this purely by accident?

Whichever it was, he gravely led the way to his suite, bowed her in with just as much gravity, and then looked as if he was at a loss for what to do next.

She made up his mind for him, by sitting down on the hearth-rug (which was the skin of a bear bigger than anything *she* had ever seen; it must have been the size of a draft-horse when it was alive). The fire didn't need poking up, but he did it anyway, then sat down beside her.

She was trying to think of something to say when he spoke. "Tell me about your dreams, will you?" he asked. "Do you have them every night? Are they always the same?"

"I've been having them most nights, and they're never *exactly* the same," she said, staring into the fire, leaning back on her elbows. "They always start when I find myself in a— a very odd place. I'm on the shore of some large body of water, and it's night, but very bright, bright enough to see colors."

"Because there are two moons in the sky," he said instantly. "And the sand is purple. So is the water."

"It's sweet, too, not salty," she put in.

"Is it? I never tasted it," he replied, a little surprised. "When my dreams start, I'm usually right at the water's edge."

"So am I, but sometimes I'm wading in the water up to my ankles." She raised an eyebrow at him. "And I don't seem to be wearing very much to speak of."

"Ah—" he flushed, and couldn't look at her for a moment. "When I was very young, I had a book of tales, and that's the sort of thing the Fairies in it wore. Of course—" he continued thoughtfully "—they also looked like ten-year-old children. Which you don't."

"Especially not in *that*," she said dryly, and he flushed again. "Apparently we're having the same dream."

"Does that mean something?" he asked, and ran his fingers through his hair, nervously. "Is it significant?"

"I wish I could tell you." She turned her gaze back to the fire. "What I can tell you is that I—like you, in the dreams and out of them. Very much. I didn't, before, but you're a rather different fellow now than you were when I turned you into an ass. I wouldn't do that now."

That made him laugh, which pleased her. "And if you were to meet me now, what sort of animal would you turn me into?"

"I wouldn't," she replied, and turned back to look at him again. "Because you would treat the poor old woman well."

"Like Julian." He nodded. "Yes, I would like to think that I would, even without knowing all I know about trials and Questers now. But I would *not* go offering you every crumb of food I had!"

She had to laugh at that. "There is such a thing as being too generous," she agreed. "And frankly, I like *you* rather better than your brother. He's blissfully happy with his milk-and-honey princess who is only too delighted to be orna-mental."

"And I prefer the sort of lady who—who can drive a fly-ing chariot pulled by dragons!" he said.

"Are you sure?" she asked archly. And she would have said something else, except that his lips were in the way.

It was different from the kisses in the dreams, and even from the wildly passionate kiss in the kitchen. It was a slow, deliberate kiss, not exactly *gentle,* but not torrid, either. He cupped one hand along her cheek, the fingers just touching her hair, and his lips moved against hers. She closed her eyes and moved closer to him, until they were no more than a few inches apart. Her heart began to beat a little faster, and she felt a warm glow on her cheeks.

He parted his lips a little, and insinuated just the tip of his tongue between them. She opened her mouth beneath his, then gently nibbled his lower lip. He moved his hand behind her neck, playing with her hair, then drawing her closer until there was no space at all between them. She let herself sink into the bearskin so that she could put both her arms around him.

She was acutely aware of every nerve, every bit of skin, and when his hand began to slip from her neck down to her shoulder, she felt his fingers leaving trails of exquisite sensation where they passed, places that ached to feel the touch of his fingers again. He traced the line of her collarbone, pausing in the little hollow of her throat for a moment, then drew his fingers down, into the cleft between her breasts while her breath quickened and she felt a flush spreading from the point where they rested.

His hand slipped inside her chemise, and she was wildly glad that today she was in her simplest garb, with no corsetting to get in the way—then his fingers touched the nipple of her breast and she thought she was going to explode with pleasure. Her hands tightened in the fabric of his shirt, and she gasped at the sensation, which was so much more intense than it had been in her dreams that there was no comparison. His fingers toyed gently with it, and each tiny movement seemed to send a shock straight to her secret parts; her womb tightened, and yet, the feeling made her legs move apart as if of their own will.

He took his hand away, and she groaned with frustration and opened her eyes—only to see and feel that he had removed it just to unlace her bodice. Evidently he'd had plenty of practice, because he did it faster than *she* could....

He slid the chemise down off her shoulders, freeing her breasts, then, as in the dream, he licked and nibbled his way down from her neck until his mouth touched the place where his fingers had lately been playing, and she uttered an involuntary cry of pleasure. Every tiny movement sent a shudder through her, and a tidal wave of urgent desire, until she thought she could not bear it any longer.

And then—he stopped. Her eyes flew open, and she glared at him.

He had the most peculiar expression on his face that she had ever seen, a mixture of tenderness, something she was sure was pure lust, and a touch of surprise.

"Elena," he said, "I—bear with me a moment. I've just had the most extraordinary flash of memory—"

She licked her lips, and nodded, though she wished that he would stop talking and go back to doing what he had been.

"It's the custom among my people for young men of my rank to be—ah—initiated—by ladies of experience." He blushed. "There's a slightly crude saying in Kohlstania; 'two virgins in a bed is one virgin too many.'"

Fine, so *he* wasn't a virgin—as if she hadn't figured *that* out a long time ago.

"And I've just recalled a certain set of instructions that lady gave me regarding this situation. So I'm going to do something you might find rather peculiar, but it's for a reason."

She had no time to ask what on earth he meant, for he went right back to where he'd left off, and it wasn't until he'd stolen up her skirt and suddenly his head was—good heavens! What was he doing between her legs—

She might have tried to push him away, except that she couldn't—because all she could do was melt away as his clever tongue probed all those parts of her that had been longing, aching, for something, and she hadn't known what it was—she had never felt *anything* like the excitement, the pleasure, and she moaned, wanting more—

And then the world exploded. Her entire body spasmed, and she cried out, something between a gasp and a scream.

When it was over, she lay there panting and spent, and opened her eyes again to see him grinning like a boy who has just stolen an entire cake.

"What—exactly—did that lady tell you?" she managed to get out.

He resumed the place beside her that he had temporarily abandoned.

"She said, 'Someday, you will find yourself with another lady, an untried lady, whether your new bride or your new lover, and she will be a lady you wish to make as pleased with her first experience as you were with yours. Now, that is not possible in the conventional sense, but I will teach you the unconventional, so that she will know, truly and completely, that there is very great pleasure waiting for her, once the pain that is sadly inevitable for an untried lady is over.'"

"Oh." She thought about that for a very long moment. Plenty of kitchen-tales about "first times" flashed through her mind. The maids had seemed to take as much glee over telling them as they did over tales of childbirth that went on for days. So *now* she knew what she could expect once the whole painful business of "deflowering" was done with.

Furthermore, she had no doubt he'd do *this* again until they were good enough at the other to make it equally pleasurable for both of them.

"Is there any way I could thank her?" she asked at last.

He chuckled. "Perhaps someday. Oh, and she also said, 'the only woman who will thank you for spoiling her gown is the one you are buying a better gown for.' So—since I'm not in a position to buy you a better gown—" He tugged at her skirt, and raised his eyebrow suggestively.

"Ha. Turnabout is fair, and you've got less skin showing than I do!" she said, a spirit of mischief rising in her as she grabbed for his sleeve and pulled.

It became a rough-and-tumble game for a little while, as clothing got pulled off piecemeal, a stocking there, a shirt here—a game that got more heated when she tried some of what she recalled from her dreams and some of what she'd watched covertly when kitchen-maids trysted with stableboys, and parlor-maids with footmen.

It actually ended in his bed, where he picked her up and tossed her, surprising her with his strength. And by the time they both fell asleep in a tangle of limbs and blankets, she was almost embarrassingly grateful to that unknown lady with her uncommonly good advice.

"**B**lessed Saints!" coughed Alexander, reaching for the second cup Elena handed him. "I'm not sure *that* is worth being able to understand animals!"

"It's a Traditional power of Champions," Rose pointed out, as he drank down the entire hot cup of tea to wash away the taste of dragon's blood. It had taken Elena the better part of a month to find a dragon to trade a bit of blood for one of the jewel-studded trinkets out of the hunting-lodge. A dragon could always find food—but Elven-made treasure for its hoard was worth shedding a little blood over, apparently.

"Bosh! I'm sure you're only getting revenge on me for eating that pie you were saving," Alexander coughed, holding out his mug for a refill. "But if you *will* leave a pie in the middle of the kitchen table and *then* announce that dinner has been put back an hour because the goose was bigger than you thought, what's a man to do?"

Robin only smiled, and handed over a plate full of sausages and eggs to further take away the taste.

"There is only one thing that I am truly sorry for," Alexander said, after polishing off his first helping. "I've deprived you of Unicorns."

Elena burst into peals of laughter, Lily giggled, Hob and Robin chortled, and even Rose unbent enough to chuckle a little.

"Don't be," Elena told him, as he glanced from one to another of them, looking utterly bewildered. "It's a little like being deprived of fawning, brainless lapdogs or a surfeit of Turkish Delight. One is sweet, two are amusing, but after you've been inundated by them a while, you start to think uncharitably of deep ponds and burlap bags."

"And no matter how many beds of lilies and roses you put out for them, they *will* eat my new peas," Lily added, in such an aggrieved tone of voice that they all laughed again.

Elena was definitely of two minds about her new situation. On the one hand, she had never been so contented. Not that she and Alexander were of one accord on all matters; that would have been ridiculous, and besides, she would have immediately suspected that The Tradition was about to unleash something awful on the two of them. They were lovers, they were *still* friends, life was full of wonderful things. Rose was still clearly harboring some reservations, but the other three were as delighted with the new state of things as Elena herself was. Even Randolf approved. Alexander had, overnight, gotten the trick of projecting magical power into his weapons, and now needed only to perfect that skill and hone his fighting abilities to be ready for whatever challenge was put in his path as a Champion.

But on the other hand—

—she kept waiting for the Consequences of her action to occur. No Godmother, so far as she had been able to tell, in all of the Chronicles, had ever broken The Tradition as thoroughly as she had when it came to this. Oh, there *had* been Champions in the households of Godmothers before this, but they had all been true *Fairy* Godmothers, of the Great Fae, and so had their Champions been. The Chronicles were very sketchy concerning those Godmothers, which was hardly surprising, since the Fae did not particularly care to be written about. Nowhere had she found any reference to a Godmother with a lover...much less a princely lover.

It did seem terribly unfair, though. *Wizards* got to take lovers, so why not Godmothers?

"Madame Bella got along perfectly well without Unicorns," Robin said, gesturing emphatically with his fork. "There are plenty of other sources of magic, and Elena is very careful about how she uses the power she has."

"She's that saving, indeed she is," said Rose, bestowing an unusually benevolent gaze on Elena. "She never wasted any bit of magic on indulgences or on show. Usually by this time, a young Godmother's been caught a bit short and had to improvise, but our Madame Elena never has."

"Touch wood," Elena said, automatically.

"Well, if you're sure you don't mind—" Alexander said

after a moment of silence. "But I'd thought you were really fond of them."

"I'm fond of toffee pudding, but that doesn't mean I want to eat it for every meal," she pointed out logically.

"Yes, but if you couldn't ever have it again—" he persisted.

"Oh, it isn't that she'll *never* have Unicorns about," Rose told him. "They'll come if she calls on them magically, or if the Great Fae sends them. She just won't be able to touch them."

He opened his mouth to say something, but no one would ever learn what it was, because at that moment, they all heard the unmistakable sound of something galloping towards the cottage, up the hard-frozen road. And there were missteps in the sound that told them all that whatever was coming was exhausted and on its last legs.

But most of all, there was the unmistakable, yet intangible, sensation of a great "weight" falling on them, as the looming wave of magic and Tradition collapsed upon them.

It completely staggered Elena.

Hob reacted first, running to the kitchen door, wrenching it open, and hurling himself out into the frozen yard. Alexander was right behind him. As Elena burst from the door behind them, the rider tumbled off into Alexander's arms. Hob had seized the horse's bridle and was doing—something. Something magical; Elena saw the blue-green motes of magic power that has been separated from the mass of undifferentiated magic and given a purpose swirling around the beast. They were no thicker than dust in a sunbeam, but whatever Hob was doing gave the horse enough strength to stumble towards the stable. The magic motes sank into the beast rapidly, as Hob's spell took effect.

She clasped her arms around herself, shivering, as she hurried to Alexander's side. The cold hammered at her, but she ignored it as best she could, for the man Alexander was supporting was trying to gasp out something.

"....Prince Julian captive," he croaked hoarsely. "The Princess locked in the East Tower. Trolls everywhere...." and his eyes rolled up in his head as he collapsed. Without a word, Alexander hefted the man over his shoulders and hauled him bodily into the kitchen, where Rose and Lily took the stranger from him. He turned on his heel without a word, his face grim and pale, and would have run straight out again had Elena not caught him by the shoulders and forced him to stop.

"What happened?" she asked, urgently. "What happened to your brother?"

He stared at her wildly. "Julian—blessed Saints, Elena, Julian! Some wicked magician has taken Fleurberg! King Stancia is dead, Princess Kylia is imprisoned, and my brother—my brother—*Julian!*"

She shook his shoulders. "Alexander! Calm down! Make sense! What happened? You have to tell me so I can help you!"

It took a few minutes, and they had to go back into the cottage where Rose and Lily had revived the messenger, but eventually they learned the truth.

A stranger had come striding into King Stancia's Great Hall when the entire court was at dinner. He had not come alone; he had been accompanied by an escort of heavily, baroquely armored men and monsters (the messenger called them "trolls," but they didn't correspond to any description of a troll that Elena knew). He had *not* gotten past the guards on the walls, nor the walls themselves; he had simply appeared in the grounds, his creatures had swarmed the few guards that they encountered within the Palace to clear his path to the Great Hall.

He had announced—nothing. No challenge, no gloating, not a word. He had simply unleashed his escort and his magics. The messenger had been one of the few able to flee the room; he hadn't seen much, but what *he* had seen was terrible.

He was no knight, only a young squire, and fortunately, he was wise enough to know what he could not do. He had hidden himself and waited.

Within the hour, most of Stancia's court had been slaughtered, Stancia was dead, Julian had been thrown into the dungeons, and Kylia imprisoned in her own tower.

The only reason that Julian himself was not dead was that he had come in late to dinner, had joined with Stancia's guards in trying to repel the invader, and had been thrown, unconscious and injured, into the dungeon with the rest of the survivors. The messenger had crept out of hiding to one of the dungeon windows, where Julian had told him what had happened himself. He probably had not been recognized for who he was, but that could not last for long.

"Get help!" Julian had urged. "Go to the Glass Mountain, and if you cannot find the Sorcerer, go to my brother!"

The messenger had stolen a horse and fled to the Sorcerer who had created the Glass Mountain, only to discover that he, too, was dead. The messenger had returned to discover that the city had been sealed off, and Stancia's army was milling about, outside the walls, leaderless. The messenger had gotten another horse, having ridden the first to foundering.

"Go to my brother——" Julian had probably meant his brother Octavian—or had he? Alexander was the one that had always been kindest to him; Alexander was the one who had been trained at the Academy in warfare. Here was the thing about The Tradition; it often found ways of making something happen that were completely without logic.

So if Julian had been *thinking* about Alexander when he had said, "Go to my brother," then The Tradition putting that together with the fact that Alexander was now a Champion, very likely arranged the rest.

How had he gotten here? How had he found his way to *this* remote place? The messenger could not remember. Elena had a guess, though she could not be sure. The Sorcerer might have left a spell, like the "All Forests Are One" spell, that survived his own demise. He might have set something of the sort in the hope that he could escape, only to die before he could reach safety. Certainly the Sorcerer knew that Prince Julian's brother was *here,* and this would be the first place to seek help for King Stancia....

Perhaps that had been the last spell he had cast with his dying breath—to bring whatever messenger sent for help by Stancia directly *here*.

Or perhaps, given a very well-worn Traditional path of sending to a Champion for aid, The Tradition itself had bent distance and magic and made it all happen. Such a thing was not unknown.

That didn't matter now, and it was neither the time nor the place to discuss such things. The messenger was of no more use, for he was unconscious now and Rose was not sanguine about his being in any shape to respond any time soon. And time was most definitely of the essence. If ever the Evil Mage could be dislodged, it had to be *now*. Now, before he discovered that he already had Prince Julian in his grasp, before he replenished all of the magical energy he had used in taking the Palace, and before he cemented his hold on the Kingdom of Fleurberg.

"You can't just—" Elena began.

But Alexander interrupted her. "I know," he replied, his voice hard, and his expression rigid. "I studied military strategy. I cannot merely go haring off wildly; Champion or no Champion, if I charge straight at that Evil Mage, I have no chance at all."

Elena sighed with relief, even while she throttled down a weight of guilt that felt as heavy as the weight of magic that had washed over them all. "We need a three-pronged plan," she said, instantly. "First, I'll send a message to Arachnia and every other Godmother, Wizard, and Sorcerer I know—yes, and my friend the giant, and that dragon I traded for his blood, and even the Unicorn herd. Second, I will send a message to *your* father; if ever there was an act that would redeem him in Julian's eyes, it would be by sending an army to his rescue. And lastly—*now,* while two people actually have a chance to accomplish something, *we* will go."

"Go?" he asked, baffled. "It would take days to get there."

"Less than that. First, I need to contact Arachnia—and someone else. More than anything else, we need something that can *fly*."

No more than two hours later, that something arrived.

Elena had contacted every magician that she could, sending out every one of the white ravens with messages that would not arrive until, at the best, nightfall. She had sent frantic messages via her own chronicles as well, but had no guarantee that anyone would *read* the things any time soon. More than ever, she cursed the fact that there was no good, *fast* way of sending messages from magician to magician. The best one could manage was the better part of a day, and often it was far longer than that.

But by noon, she had the transportation she needed.

It came galloping down out of the sky, and drew attention to itself by drumming excitedly on the rooftop before coming to land in the courtyard.

At the sound of hooves on the roof, Alexander had started up, eyes flashing wildly, but Elena had known exactly what it was and ran out again into the stable-yard, where her help was waiting for her. "Sergei!" she cried with joy, and flung her arms around the neck of the Little Humpbacked Horse.

"This is dreadful, Godmother," the horse said, somberly, in her ear. "The Sorcerer who has taken Fleurberg is one out of *my* countries. I do not know what he is doing here, invading *your* Traditions."

Elena did not say what she was thinking, but she had been fighting terrible and despair guilt from the moment that she had heard of this disaster, and Sergei's words only seemed to confirm her worst fears. That this was happening because of *her*. She had broken The Tradition by taking a lover, and now a Black Mage from another set of Traditional paths had taken advantage of the weakness.

She did not say it, not because she did not want to acknowledge her own guilt, but because doing so would serve no purpose, would weaken Alexander's spirit and resolve, and would only waste time, time that was already precious.

"What can we expect, Sergei?" she asked, pulling away from him and stifling the wish to simply hug his neck and wail.

"I think it is a Katschei," said Sergei in reply, while Alexander stared at them both bemusedly. "Which will mean that his heart is *not* in his body, so you can only kill him by finding his heart. He is in a new land, so he probably has not yet done anything other than encase it in a diamond and place it somewhere he considers safe, which is usually somewhere near him. *I* would guess that it is in the throne room, under the throne. If one of you can penetrate the throne room and find the heart and return it to where it belongs, you can kill him. If you can break the diamond and smash the heart, you can kill him. Of course," he added thoughtfully, "you'll have to get past his army of creatures first."

"I'll—" Alexander began, then stopped at the look on Elena's face. "Tell me," he demanded instead.

"Whoever defeats the Katschei and rescues the Princess can't be you," she said, slowly, "because The Tradition is very strong in Fleurberg, and Princess Kylia is going to *fall in love* with the man who rescues her."

Alexander looked at her for a moment, then licked his lips. "Then what use am I?" But before she could answer, his face lit up. "Wait! If I gather the remains of the army and attack the city and the Palace, the Evil Mage will be distracted!"

"And I can go in and try and find his heart," said Elena. "But I will need more than a distraction, and someone needs to occupy the Mage in a way that will keep all of his attention elsewhere." She took a deep breath, and wondered if she could keep her face from showing her pain. "Champion—"

He straightened, and his entire demeanor changed. He seemed taller, and *larger* somehow.

"Champion," she said, knowing that this was the right thing, the only right thing for *him* as well as for Fleurberg, but feeling her heart whimpering in pain all the same. "Champion, you must challenge this Evil Mage yourself."

"Ah." He took it as she had expected him to; willingly, even eagerly. "And you, meanwhile, will rescue Kylia, free Julian, and find the heart."

"Probably not quite in that order, but I think that I have a plan to do that," she agreed. "Sergei can take both of us—"

"Sergei can take *you,* Godmother," the little horse interrupted. "Mother and I suspected you were going to do something like this, and I brought one of my brothers."

He tossed his head up and whinnied shrilly. He was answered by a deeper whinny from up above; there was a clatter of hooves on the roof again, and a second horse leaped down onto the yard, landing as lightly as a swan on the water.

It was a coal-black stallion, as handsome as the hump-back horse was homely. His mane and tail swept the ground, rippling like waterfalls of silk, and his coat gleamed like the finest satin, and he was both incredibly graceful and massively muscled. His beautifully formed head turned towards Alexander, and the Prince stepped forward, entranced. "Don't expect the kind of intelligence and cleverness that *I* have out of *him,* but he's loyal as a hound, brave as a lion, strong as a bull, and he can fly, just as I can. Mother says that every Champion needs a proper mount," said Sergei, eyes glinting with satisfaction. "So from this moment on, Nightsong is yours."

From somewhere, Hob came up with what must have been armor meant for a young Elven princeling for Elena. It fit well enough, although her breasts were squashed beneath the breastplate. Still, it was no worse than what the flattening corsets favored in Arachnia's Kingdom of Bretagne did to a woman's breasts, and Elena was not going to complain if it kept her alive—and further, that it made her look like a young man, and kept her from being recognized as a Godmother. They knew from the messenger's story where the window into the dungeon was that he had spoken to Julian through. The Princess's tower had a balcony that Sergei could land on. So there was just one more thing that needed to be arranged.

It would take a lot of magic. She hoped that there was

enough still *here* that it would not seriously deplete her own resources.

Hob's magical game bag could actually hold just about anything put into it. The Katschei's creatures were probably things that could only be harmed by magical weapons; Sergei was not sure on that point, but he agreed that it was likely. So the House-Elves and Alexander stripped every room in the cottage and lodge of anything that was remotely weaponlike, right down to the knives and cleavers in the kitchen; Elena enchanted every one of them with just a touch of magic, enough that they could actually hit a magical creature. Then they were stuffed into the game bag.

When she was done, she had exhausted all of the ambient power that had dropped down around them when The Tradition closed its jaws on them, and every bit of power that the Brownies could spare. She hoped that what she had left was going to be enough, but she knew that she was going to have to be very, very clever with every bit of power left to her.

By sunset, they were as ready as they were ever going to be. Alexander was dancing with impatience, wanting to be off; Elena felt as if her heart was so heavy that Sergei would never be able to fly under the weight of it.

But they had no choice, neither of them. With a last, longing look at the cottage, Elena clambered into Sergei's saddle—ungracefully, for she *still* had never learned to ride—as Alexander vaulted lightly into his seat on Nightsong's back and accepted his lance from Hob. He looked every inch the Champion, as bold and brave as a legend, and eager to be off. She closed the visor on her helm; his was already down, and she was glad of it, for it would have been much worse if she had been able to see his face with that weight of guilt on her. It was bad enough, knowing that, with the weight of Tradition along with his own eagerness, Alexander's mind, heart, and soul that of a Champion, and if he thought of anything else, it was fleetingly.

"Ready?" he asked, his voice echoing hollowly out of the depths of the helm.

She nodded. Sergei gathered himself beneath her; she clung to the pommel of the saddle with both hands, and the two sons of the East Wind rose on their hind feet and leaped into the blood-red sky.

It was near midnight when they landed amid the dispirited mob that was what was left of Stancia's army. Alexander had made a proper show of it, too, for had anyone been alert or brave enough, it all might have ended then and there. But calling down from above, "Loyal sons of Fleurberg, we have come to aid you!" and having Elena illuminate him as he landed, meant he had no chance of being mistaken for some warrior of the Katchei's.

Now he stood on a rock, ringed by torches, as the tired old soldiers surrounded him, looking at him with expressions in which fear warred with hope. So far Alexander had said nothing to them, other than to send out word to gather together, and Elena had kept her mouth shut. This was not a Godmother's business; it was the business of a Champion. Here it was Alexander who was the master of the moment.

Finally, when no more men were coming in from the darkness, Alexander drew himself to his full height. "Hear me, men of King Julian!" The voice that rang through the night sounded like Alexander's ordinary speaking voice, but—stronger, deeper, and certainly a great deal louder.

Below him, the men started and gasped as Alexander's words told them what they had feared—that Stancia was dead. Alexander would not have named Julian King, otherwise.

"Hear me, men of King Julian," Alexander repeated. "Your old King is no more. A foul usurper has attempted to seize the throne. King Stancia fought nobly and died as a warrior, his sword in his hand—"

Now that was a complete fabrication, as Elena well knew, but it was the sort of thing that a soldier wanted to hear. No soldier wants to be told that his King was cut down before he could rise from his dinner, that he was slain as he tried to push away from the table by magic against which he had no defense. They wanted to hear that their beloved monarch was a fighter to the end, someone they could emulate, and whose memory they could honor.

"—but Julian lives, and your duty is now to him! Hear me, warriors! I am Alexander, brother of your King, and have come to help you. You must hold until our allies arrive—you must fight to enter the Palace and destroy the evil usurper—"

"How?" bleated one grizzled old man, demandingly, interrupting Alexander's stirring speech. "How, when spears and arrows just bounce off 'em, and swords and spears won't bite?"

But Alexander simply gave the man a pitying look. "With the weapons my squire will give you," Alexander countered, not missing a beat. "Weapons enchanted by the hand of the Fairy Godmother Elena, to strike to the heart of these monsters and give you strength beyond your own!"

That's a bit much! she thought, though she was secretly pleased at being accorded such great power by Alexander. *But—well, it isn't going to hurt, I suppose, to have them think that they're being given magical strength even if they aren't. If they think they are, who knows? It might actually happen.* Taking that for her cue, Elena opened the game bag and began passing out whatever came to hand. There was a moment of reluctance, but then she was engulfed by men who were desperate to have something, anything that would serve them against these creatures that some were already calling "demons" rather than "trolls." They were neither, but that didn't matter, either.

There were still weapons in the bag when the last of Stancia's men, the survivors of what had been a rather pathetic little army in the first place, had each claimed a weapon. Alexander began his rallying speech at that point, and Elena stared up at the castle.

It was not a big castle, and fortunately, it was not surrounded by a moat. But the walls were stout and there were an awful lot of torches and forms moving up there.

"—a frontal assault, to occupy him and keep him from spreading out to conquer the city and the Kingdom," Alexander was saying, when she turned her attention back to him. "Do not spend yourselves needlessly; it is a holding action that we need. Help *is* coming from Kohlstania! My father would never permit his son to languish a prisoner! More help is coming, in the form of magical allies, brought to our aid by the Godmothers themselves!"

Your father would never permit an evil magician to set up shop in the neighboring Kingdom, you mean! she thought, with some irony. This was, in fact, King Henrick's worst nightmare come to pass, the very thing he had hoped to prevent by sending all three of his sons to the Glass Mountain. *And I only hope that the other Godmothers do respond....*

"And what are you doing, while we're doing this?" asked that same troublemaker, dubiously.

Alexander drew himself up, and—yes, there was no doubt of it. His armor began glowing as he took on the full aspect of a Champion. "I," he said, with great dignity, "will be fighting the Evil Mage in challenge combat. Alone."

"All right," Alexander said urgently to her, as the little army organized itself around its few surviving officers, and prepared to make that frontal assault on the gate. "Time for you to go. Find Julian, get him out, and send him around to the front as soon as you hear the fighting start. Then go to the aid of the Princess when you hear the trumpet sound for my challenge."

She nodded, a great lump arising in her throat, rendering her speechless. He was going through with this, and unless she could find the Evil Magician's heart—he could be killed.

"And Elena—" he paused, and his voice lost that quality of "Champion" so that it sounded like nothing more than "Alexander" "—I want to know. I have to know."

"What?" she asked, thickly, expecting some dreadful

question about her own guilt in this mess. But she would answer him truthfully if he asked. She owed him nothing less than the truth.

"Will you consent to marry me?"

She felt as if something had slapped her across the helm so that her head was ringing. She heard her own voice say, joyfully, *"Yes!"* before her head had formulated an answer.

"Good. That's all I needed to know." He grinned at her, and closed his helm down over his face. Before she could say anything else, he had lifted her into Sergei's saddle, and the little horse was off like a shot.

She sawed at Sergei's reins, trying to bring him back around, but the little horse was having none of it. "Godmother, we have a *job* to do," Sergei said, acidly, the bit clamped between his teeth. "Are you going to put all of it to naught?"

She let go the reins, but her heart wanted to be back there, with him, demanding to know just what he had intended with that question—

Except, of course, he was not actually going to be there; by now he was at the forefront of the army, on Nightsong, making himself visible as the attack began, before he and Nightsong flew over the gate and into the forecourt to challenge the Sorcerer. The Evil One would *have* to answer; The Tradition would force him into it. Never had Elena ever heard of a Challenge going unanswered.

Sergei's night vision was better than hers was; he spotted the dungeon window in the shadows and plunged down towards it like an owl on a mouse. Stancia had been a good king, as had all of his ancestors; *his* dungeons might be stout, but they were not lightless nor airless. They had heavily barred windows in their walls that were just about at ground level on the outside—oh, twenty feet above the floor on the inside, of course, but still, windows. It would take magic and cunning to use them for an escape, but magic and cunning Elena had, she hoped, in abundance.

At just that moment, the attack on the front gate began.

There was a roar, and the sound of weapons and a battering-ram hitting the front gate. Virtually every torch on the walls skittered in that direction, and there was more than enough noise to cover anything that Elena was about to do.

Elena slid from Sergei's back, and ran from dungeon window to window, whispering urgently, until she found the one letting into the great room where Stancia's guards, remaining nobles, and Julian were imprisoned. They were, thank heavens, sensible; they did not shout at her whisper, and in fact, she was able to talk to Julian himself.

"Who are you?" he called up.

"The old woman in the forest," she whispered back. "I gave you the gift to speak with animals; I advised you not to be so generous in the matter of your food, sir, if you'll recall!"

"Only that woman knew this," he replied, sounding out of breath. "I believe you, lady! Have you come to succor us?"

"I have. Are you hurt?"

"A bad slash to my shield-arm, but I am alive, and afire to get out," came the whisper up out of the darkness. That was all she needed to know.

Time for a little more magic.

"Give me but a moment, Majesty, and you will be leading your men again!"

She hitched Sergei to the bars of the grate, took out her wand, and ran a trickle of magic along the perimeter, chanting under her breath, giving the magic form and purpose. *"Time erodes all that is made. Weakens iron and crumbles stone. Undermines all that is laid. Time is lord and time alone."* This spell should have the effect of accelerating the hand of time there, and weakening both the bolts and the cement. "Pull!" she whispered to the little horse, who threw himself against the ropes.

Nothing. She ran another trickle around, repeating her incantation. Sergei pulled again, and this time the entire grate came free with a groan—

It would have landed with a clatter, but she caught it before it fell, and lowered it to the ground. She stole a quick glance up at the walls, but so no sign of movement. No one had seen them yet. Perhaps, with luck, there was no one there to watch.

She put her wand away, took the coil of knotted rope from Sergei's saddle, and tied it to the grate that had just been pulled free. She tossed it down through the empty window-frame.

"Climb up!" she cried, and the rope tightened at once. With the little horse bracing against the weight of the men clambering up the rope, the first two, least-injured, came popping out of the window. These two first pulled up anyone who was too injured to climb unaided—Julian was the first—or added their weight and strength to Sergei's. When all of them were out, she cut Sergei free and distributed her remaining magical weapons.

She didn't have to tell them what to do, for the noise of the fighting drew them as soon as they got weapons in their hands. She caught at Julian before he could lead them into the fray.

"Your brother Alexander has rallied the army—" she began.

Julian groaned. "Those poor old men? I—"

"Never mind that; they're just a distraction, but they will still fight better with their King beside them," she interrupted. "More help is on the way, from Kohlstania and other places. If a giant appears, don't attack him, he's on your side, and there may be other beasts coming who will tell you they come from me. They may get here before dawn, in fact. Princess Kylia—"

Now Julian looked about wildly. "Kylia? She didn't escape? I—"

"Majesty!" She gave him a hard shake. "Leave that to me, I'll send her to you, I swear! But I can't get to her if *you* don't keep up the distraction of the attack, and—" She shook her head, wondering how to tell him of everything planned without confusing it more, when he suddenly calmed, and gathered himself together.

"Never mind," he said. "Alex is in command; *he* went to the Academy. Whatever he planned will be the best that can be done."

She slapped him on the back; he staggered a little, for she had forgotten her armor. "Can you fight?"

"Maybe not, but I make a damned good figurehead," he replied, with a grim smile. "Good luck, lady. Send my wife safe to me."

"Good luck, Majesty." She scrambled onto Sergei's back, as the King led his men towards the thick of the fighting. In a moment, the darkness had swallowed them; a moment later, she and Sergei were in the air.

She was supposed to wait until Alexander made his single-combat challenge, but she felt as if she was better off not waiting. For one thing, the longer the attack went on, the more likely it was that extra guards would be sent to watch the Princess. For another—

For another, she wanted to get her hands on that evil magician's heart. Alexander's life would depend on it.

There were no safeguards—*none*—on the Princess's tower. There probably had been something winged up there to keep watch, but all the noise and the fighting must have been irresistible to them. That was one of the odd things about most magical creatures; like Nightsong, like the unicorns, the vast majority of them were not all that bright. It almost seemed as if a creature born of magic could have magical abilities *and* be beautiful, *or* strong, *or* intelligent—but only two of the four. Sergei and his brother were excellent examples of that. That was the reason why the wise magician did not entrust the safekeeping of anything he was concerned about to a magical creature, unless it was an extraordinary one.

Elena and Sergei landed on the balcony without incident; had Sergei been the size of his brother Nightsong, they couldn't have done it, but the balcony was just large enough for something pony-sized. She slid off, and pushed open the balcony door.

Clang!

She staggered back, reeling, from the blow to her head. Which fortunately, had been mostly absorbed by her helm but still—her ears were ringing and for a moment she had seen stars! "Hey!" she shouted indignantly, fending off the angry, poker-wielding young woman who advanced on her. "What do you think you're at, wench? Julian sent me! I'm here to rescue you!"

"What?" the poker dropped from the young woman's hands and clattered to the stone floor as she stared at Elena in shock. "You—"

Once again, Elena felt the weight of The Tradition collapsing around her and even as she seized on the opportunity to replenish her magical stores, she was pulling off her helm. The Tradition had its own path for those who rescued ladies in Durance Vile. And Princess—now Queen—Kylia had spread her arms wide to embrace her "rescuer," automatically, impelled by The Tradition. And in a moment, Kylia was going to find herself a different sort of prisoner, manipulated and pushed into falling in love—or at least, into something that felt just like love. And she might, possibly, recall that once she had felt exactly the same thing for her husband, but at that point, it would already be too late.

"Yes," Elena said, shaking her hair loose, firing the words out as quickly as she could to warp The Tradition back to the path *she* wanted. "I'm Godmother Elena. Your husband, Julian, sent me—he's leading a frontal assault on the gate as a distraction in order to set you free to join him."

Kylia stopped dead in her tracks, as stunned for the moment as Elena would have been if that poker had connected with her skull instead of her helm.

"Oh," she said, in a small, uncertain voice. "A woman?"

"*Julian* sent me," Elena said firmly. "I am a Fairy God-mother, come at his call for aid. He's *single-handedly* lead-ing an *heroic* assault on the front gate to act as a distraction *so you can escape.*"

This was, of course, a lie. That didn't matter. What mat-tered was to deflect The Tradition from the course it was on with certain key words. It wasn't quite a spell, as such, but it had all the force of a spell. Kylia—and through her, The Tradition—heard "Julian—single-handedly, heroic—so you can escape." The force impelling Kylia into falling in love with her rescuer (which had been the source of no end of tragedy in the past) was deflected by the clear impropri-ety of Kylia falling in love with a woman, and by the appar-ent sacrifice that Julian was making of himself. Given those key words, she was impelled right back into the love of her husband.

This was the problem with Tradition-created "love." It was manufactured. In time it would solidify into the real thing, far more often than not, but in the first year or two of marriage, the bond was fragile, easily broken, and easily reformed onto another object of affection.

The Tradition created tragedy as well as happy endings; The Tradition did not care if a story ended happily or in sor-row, so long as the tale was powerful enough. For every Sleeping Princess, there was a Fair Rosalinda. For every Mark and Yseult, the Tradition was perfectly prepared to create a Trystan....

Not in my Kingdoms.

"Julian," Kylia breathed, "he's out there, you say?"

"He is, and waiting for you." Elena took the opportunity to shove her out the door of the balcony before she had a chance to object. And before she had a chance to react to the presence of a horse on the balcony, Elena had lifted her into Sergei's saddle. Just in case, she tied off the poor child's belt to the saddle. Kylia grabbed the pommel reflexively.

"Off!" she shouted, darting back inside. "Good luck!" Sergei shouted back, and leaped from the balcony with Kylia suddenly coming to her senses and shrieking in fear at finding herself several hundred feet above the ground and plummeting towards it like a stone.

But that was not Elena's problem; that was Sergei's.

With luck, if any of the winged things were attracted back to their guard-post by Kylia's shrieks, Sergei would already be on the ground. By that time, Kylia would be silent (or even fainted, poor thing), and they would find the balcony door open and the balcony vacant and assume that, rather than become the bride of their master, she had flung herself from the tower.

And, being no fools, if not very bright—and, as were the minions of most evil creatures, believing firmly in the principle of looking out for themselves first—if they were not magically bound, they would swiftly bugger off before their master found out what had happened, rather than go looking for a body.

She dashed for the door to the room; if winged guardians *did* come back she wanted to be sure that she herself was not here. The door to this level wasn't locked, and she darted into the staircase, closing *and locking* the door behind her, creating one more reason to believe that Kylia had plunged to her death.

It occurred to her, as she began working her way down through the levels of the tower, that Kylia might not be *quite* the milk-and-honey princess that Elena had thought her. She had, after all, armed herself with that poker, yes, and she had been perfectly ready to attack anything coming in the balcony door with it! Well, good; good for her. That boded well for Julian, too....

Get your mind back on what you're doing, she scolded herself. *The most difficult task is yet to come.* And she worked her way down through the empty tower levels until, at last, she found a door that was locked.

She paused, her ear pressed to the keyhole, listening with all of her attention. Was there a guard out there? Was there some other sort of creature? She couldn't hear anything, nor could she sense any sort of magic. All she could hear were the distant echoes of the fighting. Either Alexander had not yet challenged the Sorcerer, or he *had,* but the fighting at the gate was continuing anyway.

That might change at any moment. It was time to take yet another chance, and hope that luck was with them all.

20

Elena knelt beside the door, touched her wand to it, and teased another fragment of magic into the door-lock.

"Open locks, whoever knocks," she whispered to it, and tapped, gently, on the wood of the door beside the lock.

With a *click*, the lock tripped, and she pushed the door open—gently.

She peered around the door, to see that she was in a hallway. There should have been lamps illuminating the whole area, but this hall showed signs of a struggle. Only about half of the lamps were lit; the rest lay on the floor, broken, and the little tables that had once held vases or statues were overturned, their burdens shattered.

Evidently Kylia had not gone to her imprisonment quietly. Once again, Elena found the Princess rising in her estimation. So, she fought, did she? *Well done to her.*

At least the hallway was clear. *If I were the throne room, where would I be?* she wondered. Or did she, in fact, actually want the throne room? Sergei had guessed that this was where the Sorcerer's heart would be, but he had not actually *known.* So who—or what—would?

Well, there was dark magic everywhere, the sort that only evil mages could use without being tainted, for it carried the overburden of death, or of being wrenched away from someone who was afraid and unwilling. That was the bad part; *she* couldn't use it. It hung in the air in clouds, dark and glowing with a sullen red, as if the place was on fire.

The good part was that with so much magic hanging about, a little more wouldn't be noticed. So she eased out a tiny trace, a thread of the stuff, spun it out from her wand, and concentrated on it.

"Clever, cunning, silent, wary;
Come to me and do not tarry.
Anyone who's wise knows that
Nothing will escape a cat's eyes."

The thread of magic formed into a tiny sphere and shot off at floor-level. She closed the door most of the way, sat back on her heels, and waited.

She did not have to wait long, fortunately for her patience. Within a few minutes, a long, slender, black shape oozed through the crack she had left open, and stood looking expectantly up at her.

"Godmother," she said.

Elena was not surprised that the cat identified her immediately. Cats, even the commonest barn and kitchen cats, had an affinity for magic.

"Daughter of Bast," she replied, with a little bow. Cats liked to be reminded that they had once been worshiped. They pretended that they didn't, that they were above flattery, but of course, that only meant that they were all the more susceptible to it. "I am looking for something. It will be strange. It is very precious to the Bad Pack Leader of the Bad Pack that has taken over this castle, and he will have hidden it." She used the word "pack leader," not because cats had a hierarchy anything *like* a pack, but because they very well understood how dogs operated, and tended to think of humans and other two-legged creatures in those terms.

"Strange...." the cat pondered this. *"There is hard shiny no-scent stuff, but it is precious to all of them, and like the hard shiny stuff that was here already. Will it be—"* and here the cat used a word that didn't translate into human terms. This was because it was the complicated, multilayered feline term, incorporating scent, sound, sight, magic-sight, and a sense that only cats seemed to have that somehow involved magic at a level completely alien to humans. It meant "something that is physical but is also extremely magical" with a modifier specifying "bad magic."

"Yes, it will!" Elena whispered, grateful beyond measure that she had somehow managed to attract one of the castle matriarchs, and not a kitchen-cat, a kitten, or a pampered lady's cat.

"Hmm, the size of a six-week kitten? Hard shiny stuff on the outside, but alive inside?" the cat persisted.

Now that could *only* be the heart, as Sergei had described it! *He'll probably encase it in diamond or something, and put the diamond in a box and you'll have to figure out how to get it out....*

"That's it exactly, wisest of the wise!" she exclaimed. "Can you take me to it?"

"Can you walk-through-walls?" the cat asked.

Now, Elena had never been *entirely* certain what that meant. Cats used the term all the time. Sometimes, it seemed to mean only that the cat could ooze through small cracks and holes that seemed too small for it. Sometimes it seemed to mean merely that it could find a way wherever it wanted to go. But *sometimes* it seemed to mean just that, literally— as if there *were* cats who could, indeed, walk through walls.

Mind, knowing cats, she didn't entirely doubt it, though that didn't help her at the moment.

"No," she said with regret. "I am not so clever."

"Clever," in feline, meant a number of things that included being powerful, intelligent, cunning, and very, very magical.

"Can you walk unseen?" the cat persisted. *"We must pass many dogs of the Bad Pack. They are roused by the Good Pack at the gate and the two Pack Leaders fighting, but there are still some along the way who are not distracted."*

Elena felt her throat tighten; so Alexander *was* in combat! She had to move, and move quickly, for he could not battle so powerful a magician for very long....

"I can," she said, electing to spend a great deal of her magic to make herself invisible. She hadn't planned on doing so—it would leave her very little to work with—

But now it was a matter of time, and they had none to waste.

"*Do,*" the cat said, and sat on her haunches, expectantly.

Elena gathered the magic and smoothed it over herself with her wand like a second skin. Then, holding it in place, she concentrated with all of her will, and gave it the direction she wanted it to take—

"*Fool all eyes that look on me; fool each mind that wants to see. Make me clear as purest air; I'm the one who isn't there.*"

She had never done this before, although she had read about it, and it was most unnerving to watch herself, for she just—faded away, growing more and more transparent, until there was nothing where she was, at all. She'd taken pains to form the spell so that it not only worked on the eyes but on the *mind*—so that even if one of the Sorcerer's creatures could ordinarily see things that were invisible, such as spirits, it still would not see her unless it worked a counter-spell, because its *mind* would refuse to acknowledge that she was there.

The cat's mouth opened in a feline grin. "*Well done, God-mother. I see you not. Come.*"

That was proof enough that the spell was properly set, for cats, as everyone knew, were perfectly capable of seeing spirits. The cat oozed around the door again, and Elena pulled off her boots and followed.

The hallway was quite short, and probably represented the point where the tower connected to the castle itself. It led straight into a larger room—much, much larger—that could only have been Stancia's Great Hall where everyone had been at dinner when the Sorcerer came. The bodies had been taken away, but the tables and benches were pretty much still where they'd been when the fight was over. Crockery shards and broken wooden trenchers were scattered everywhere, there were sticky pools of what might have been blood and what might have been drink, mostly dried now. There was no sign of anything edible. Some of the tables and benches were broken or hacked up, the tapestries had been torn off the walls and shredded or were lying in heaps against the walls. There was a foul stench in the air that made both Elena and the cat wrinkle their noses in distaste.

The foul aroma probably came from the creatures still here.

Elena could not put a name to what they were; they were outside *her* expertise, and now she could understand why Stancia's men were calling them "demons." The things that they looked most like were spiders, except that they had a hard armoring skin, and only four legs. All four had nasty cutting pincers on them, though, and they had a manlike torso with two "arms" each as well, with appendages that served as hands. They had oval, hairless heads with masklike faces and large, slanting, glittering eyes. They were all, from the top of the head to the tip of the pincers, a shiny black in color.

There were fifteen of them, and they were simply—immobile. They might have been statues, except that Elena was perfectly certain that they were watching everything that passed around them.

No wonder the cat had asked her if she could be invisible.

They paid no attention to the cat, however. Perhaps they were unconcerned about anything below a certain size. The cat wove her way across the hall, tail in the air, sauntering as if she hadn't a care in the world, and Elena followed in her wake. Elena did note, however, that the path that the cat took was the one that enabled her to keep as far away from each of the things as possible, even though that actually meant that she was weaving her way among them rather than going in a straight line.

Well, that suited Elena. She made herself as small as she could, and was glad that she had thought to take her boots off first. She clutched them to her chest, and walked as silently as stockinged feet would permit. That cat moved slowly as well; perhaps rapid movement would also trigger their interest. That suited Elena just fine as it made it easy to keep right on the cat's heels.

When she was most of the way across the room, with none of those creatures between her and the doorway, something back behind her—fell. There was a tremendous bang and clatter; she froze.

The change in the monsters was instantaneous.

They came alive; they rose up on the tips of their feet, they all turned as swiftly as thought, and then—moved.

They swarmed on some spot near the other door, presumably where the noise came from. They moved like nothing Elena had ever seen before, with a clattering sound, and the ticking of claws on stone. The sight was terrifying, and Elena only gave one horrified glance behind her before turning tail and following the cat into the "safety" of the doorway.

The cat said nothing, but her tail was a bottle-brush and her back humped as she scuttled on.

She led Elena through a succession of three rooms, all of which had been richly appointed, and all of which had been ransacked and not yet cleaned. There were more dried, dark stains here as well, and there was no mistaking that rusty color for anything but blood.

Then came the fourth room.

Elena stopped, and blinked for a moment, eyes dazzled.

It was difficult to say what purpose this room might have served King Stancia; it had no windows, but all the light came from magnificent sconces that had probably held huge, fat candles, but which now supported weirdly glowing balls of green light. But what dazzled her was that around the walls, heaped up as if they stood in a dragon's hoard, was treasure.

There was far, far more of it than there could possibly have been in Stancia's treasury. The heaps were as high as Elena's chest, and there was no order to any of it, except that the heaviest and most massive items were on the bottom. Avalanches of coins, loose jewels, and jewelry, cups, plates, platters, and bowls, boxes and bags, bales of cloth-of-gold and cloth-of-silver, candlesticks, incense-censors, breast-plates, swords, daggers, lamps, bottles—

If it could be made of gold or silver, it was probably in those piles. If it could be studded with precious gems, it was probably in those piles. It reflected the light and dazzled the mind. If it was meant to impress, it certainly did that.

But there was no sense or reason to this display. It was too chaotic to allow anyone to *appreciate* it. A dragon made a hoard like this to sleep on; why would anything human arrange a room like this, a room that could only serve to excite greed and distract anyone who came here from the person who was *supposed* to be the center of attention?

Because in a clear space in the middle of the room was a throne, made of solid gold, ornamented with twisting shapes that looked like nothing Elena recognized, and studded with rubies, each the size of a pigeon's egg. The cat was standing to one side of this monstrosity, waving her tail impatiently.

"There!" she mewed. *"Under there!"*

"Wait!" Elena said, and thought very, very hard. "If I don't appear and the Good Pack takes back the castle, look for a man in a metal skin, called Alexander. He'll be able to understand you. Find him and bring him here."

"All right. I do not like this place. I am leaving."

And she did, whisking herself out the door, leaving Elena standing by herself in the doorway.

No wonder Sergei had said to look for the heart in a "throne room." This was certainly a throne room, although not as Elena understood the term. A "throne room" was meant to concentrate all attention on the ruler. Here, whoever was sitting in that chair was of minimal importance compared to what was in the room.

She shook her head. Maybe Sergei could explain it later. Right now—

She circled around the throne and came at it from the back, somehow not wanting to approach from the front.

Those rubies all felt—however irrational that was—like sleeping eyes. She didn't want them to wake up and notice her.

The back of the throne was plain, unornamented gold. Beneath the throne was a box.

She tried to move it; it was heavier than it looked. She tried again, and discovered that she *could* make it move, though with great difficulty. Carefully she slid it out, making as little sound as possible. She didn't know if those black spidery things could hear anything from this room, but she didn't want to find out that they could, the hard way. The box was horribly, horribly heavy, and if the floor of this room hadn't been of very slippery marble, she would never have been able to manage it. As it was, she could only ease it out a little at a time, biting her lip with the effort.

She'd been afraid that the box would be locked, but it wasn't—because the lock had, at some time in the past, been broken. The hasp that held it shut had broken off. Not a surprise, really; if someone was foolish enough to make a lock and hasp out of soft gold, it should be no great shock to discover it breaks after very little use....

Which made no more sense than this room.

She opened the lid of the box—and there it was, embedded in gold that filled the box, protected by a steel cage.

"It" was a diamond. A diamond the size of her head.

And inside it, seen through the glittering facets, something the size of her fist, something wet and red, pulsed rhythmically.

Her heart sank.

The diamond was embedded in the box. The box was too

heavy to lift. The cage prevented her from smashing the stone, and even if she did, she wouldn't be able to get at the heart immediately—

—and by then, it would be too late. Alexander would have lost the fight. In fact, the only reason she *knew* that he hadn't was that the Sorcerer would have made short work of Julian and *his* "army," and from the faint sounds penetrating the walls of this room, the fighting was still going on.

Seconds ticked by as she tried her dagger on the steel cage, on the gold, and finally broke the tip off trying to shatter the diamond through the cage anyway. Nothing worked, and she became more and more frantic. Dark magics wove a web around it as impervious as the steel cage, preventing *anyone* from getting at it without shattering the diamond. She didn't have enough magic to get the thing out—

—or—did she?

Surely the thing was proof against any spell meant simply to remove it from the diamond.

But the Sorcerer *had* to put it back where it belonged from time to time, and he wouldn't want to bother with dispelling and resetting the magic around it.

Carefully, feeling as if she was wading through sewage, she tried to work her way through the ugly, vicious magic used to protect the heart. Bit by bit, she unraveled the close-woven spells with her mind and identified them—or at least, their purpose. Since she wasn't trying to dispel or break them, the magic left her alone, allowed her to worm her mental probe deeper and deeper into the noisome ball, until finally—

—she touched and identified the last spell.

Which was not a protective spell. Just as she had thought.

She rested for a moment, her stomach heaving, fighting against throwing up. Wading through sewage? This was more like swimming through it, a torrent of sewage and rot and despair, and it engulfed more of her, the deeper into it she went. And she was going to actually have to do more than touch this—stuff.

There was one chance here to save them all. One chance; it would leave her helpless, and if it didn't work, the Sorcerer's minions would find her.

If that happened, if she was lucky, they'd kill her, and if she wasn't lucky, she would spend days, weeks, or months wishing for death with every breath she took.

Even if it did work, the Sorcerer's minions might still find and kill her before Alexander killed the Sorcerer.

All or nothing.

But if she didn't, Alexander, and everyone else, would die.

The Sorcerer could reign unchallenged for generations. He would engulf all of the nearby Kingdoms, *her* Kingdoms, and rain death and terror down on the people she had vowed to help.

And The Tradition would help him.

They had to stop him now, or his conquest would not stop at all for some time to come.

Of all of the spells here, this one was the simplest. It did not need to be able to recognize the person activating it, it did not need to be warded, for it could only do one thing, and that one thing was always, always, to the Sorcerer's advantage, and had no potential to harm him.

He thinks.

It only took a touch of power. She gathered up a tiny mote of it, inserted her wand into the cage of steel, and touched it to the tangled tail of the spell.

"Go home," she whispered to the heart inside the diamond.

It vanished, and there was only one place where it would be "home," only one place for it to go.

She took the last of her power, the very last; she stole the last of the power remaining from her invisibility spell and she saw herself in all of the reflective surfaces, blinking back into place. Then she took all of her own strength, all of her energy, everything she had. She took a deep breath, raised her wand over her head, and cast—

This spell, too, required no finesse. It was simple, and crude. It did one thing; it would engulf the castle and grounds in a single, overwhelming shout that would be heard no matter how loud the fighting.

And as the glittering room blacked out, as she felt herself falling over onto the box, she, too heard it. Three words, in her own voice, if she'd had the voice of a giant and the lungs of a dragon.

"Strike the heart!"

And then she knew nothing more.

"Strike the heart!"

It was Elena's voice, and Alexander was so startled that he missed his stroke.

But so had the Mage.

And Alexander's reactions were those of a fighter. As the

Evil Mage, distracted for that crucial second, glanced to the side, looking for the source of the shout, Alexander dropped his own shield, seized his sword-hilt in both hands, ducked under the Sorcerer's guard and rammed the sword-point home against the Sorcerer's breastplate. As he did so, he willed every particle of magic, every bit of his own strength, into the blow.

As the Mage flailed at him, the sword glowed white-hot. There was a moment of resistance, then it slammed home.

The Mage froze.

With a great clap of thunder, the Evil Mage fell.

He went over like a statue, carrying Alexander's sword with him.

And a silence descended like a hammer, as everything, and everyone, just—stopped.

Alexander fell to his knees, the last of his strength running out of him. He remained there, panting, as a howl shattered the silence, as the sound of great wings rose all around him, as the gate behind him burst open, and as every torch illuminating the courtyard where he and the Mage had fought was blown out, leaving him in darkness.

He could not think; he could only feel. Hammered by the pain of his injuries, fighting for each breath, with sweat running over his face and down his back, he was barely aware that there were people swarming around him until two of them seized his biceps and hauled him to his feet, pounding his back, which he barely felt through his armor. That blessed, blessed, blessedly light and strong armor that had saved his life over and over again in this fight—

"Alex! Alex! Is that really you in there?"

It was his brother Julian's voice. He tried to get enough breath for an answer (the Mage had struck him a blow towards the end of it that had knocked him off his feet and left him with, at the least, a bruised chest) but someone was already fumbling with the straps holding his helmet on. The straps came undone, the helmet came off, and he gasped in great, glorious breaths of cool, clean air, and looked bewildered, into Julian's battered face.

Which he could see only because the other person holding him up, that same grizzled old man who had raised so many doubts during his rallying-speech, was holding a torch in his free hand and peering at his face as if he did not quite believe what had just happened.

"Jules?" he gasped.

"Alex?" said Julian. "My God, man, you've saved us, you and that weird army of yours—"

"Army? What—"

"Let me take him, friend Julian," rumbled a deep voice, like thunder on the mountains.

Then he was scooped up, as a gentle child would scoop up a toy, and he was staring into the face of the sheepherding giant. "Champion," the giant said, slowly and carefully. "Where is the Godmother? When last we heard, she was in the guise of a squire, going in through the Princess's tower. But we cannot find her."

"I don't know," he replied, gathering his wits about him. "I—"

"*Aaaaaaaalexanderrrrr!*"

It was his name, in a long, feline wail, like a cat calling her kittens.

"Aaaaaaaalexanderrrrrr!"

He located where it was coming from; the top window of the tower nearest him.

"Take me to that window! Please!" he shouted to the giant, who obligingly stretched out his arm.

There was a small, black shape in the black of the open window. A cat.

"Aaaaaaaalexanderrrrrr!"

"That's me!" he called to her. "I am Alexander."

"Tell the mountain to hold still!" came the reply.

"Hold still!" he shouted to the giant. "I think a cat—"

A cat flew out of the darkness to land on his chest and slide off the slick surface of the armor into the palm of the giant's hand. She spat and cursed at them both for being fools.

"I'll put you both down, then?" said the giant, hastily, and he carefully lowered Alexander and the cat back down beside Julian. By that time, Alexander had picked up the cat and was cradling her as carefully as his armor would allow. Her claws slipped and scratched on the metal of his armor, and she mewed her irritation until he managed to place her on the stones again at his feet.

"The Godmother said, if she did not appear, to find you!" the cat said when she had all four feet on solid ground again. *"Come! Now!"*

She ran off; he ran after her, pausing only long enough to snatch a black sword out of the hand of the dead man who had been holding it.

The cat kept glancing back at him over her shoulder to make sure that he was following. There were still knots of fighting men and monsters in the rooms that he passed; he and the cat dodged around them. They emerged into an enormous room that held more fighting; a few of Julian's men with enchanted boar-spears, but also three Unicorns, an armored Elf in elaborate armor, and a bleeding, enraged Gryphon, all fighting hideous spider-men that glittered blackly as they moved and shed black blood from their wounds.

The cat rushed past them. He followed.

And stopped dead in the final doorway.

It wasn't the piles of gold and gems that arrested his attention, although that might have, under any other circumstances. It was the terrifying black spider thing bending over Elena's unconscious body.

He had thought that he had no strength left. He had been wrong.

Terrible strength and energy coursed though him, as if he had been struck by a bolt of lightning that had energized him instead of killing him.

The creature was only just starting to turn as he leaped upon it with a scream, sword in both hands, attacking like a mad dancer, a threshing-fiend, a man-machine of death.

His first blow sliced the thing's right arm off. His second took the left, and the third cut the head cleanly from the body, sending it to the top of one of the piles of treasure where it remained, eerily staring out into the room with its sightless, unblinking black eyes.

Its body fell over sideways as all four legs collapsed beneath it.

He did not even look; he threw his sword aside, staggered

to Elena, fell to his knees beside her, and saw with a relief so intense that it made him weep that she was still breathing and outwardly unhurt.

And that was all he knew from that moment until the moment when Julian and some of the strange army of magical creatures found him again, lying beside her, holding her hand in his, the cat standing over both of them, hissing, as if she was guarding her kittens.

Elena tried to keep herself calm as she sat in the hall outside the library of the Keep on Glass Mountain. No matter *what* the convocation of Godmothers, Wizards, and Sorcerers decided, there was one thing they couldn't change; she and Alexander were married. It was the first thing that had happened after the castle had been cleaned up, and it might have happened sooner than that, except that no priest could be induced to come near while the place reeked of evil magic.

They can't separate us, she told herself. *No matter how hard they try. They can't unmake him a Champion, and I don't think they can take my magic away from me if I'm not willing to give it up.*

"How much difficulty do you think we're in?" Alexander asked her, soberly.

"I'm not sure," she replied, yet again, and smiled wanly. "At least we've broken the Traditional paths so completely that there isn't a scrap of Tradition to give them a hint of what to do."

The doors opened, and a servant beckoned them inside. They stood up together, and followed him into the Library.

There were about a dozen people at the long table in the center of the Library, and at least one was a genuine Fairy Godmother. Elena didn't know any of them—which was probably on purpose. And if she didn't have any friends here, at least she didn't have any known enemies, either.

"Champion Alexander and Godmother Elena," said the Fairy Godmother in the center. "Have you any idea what you have done?"

"Um—" said Elena, flushing.

"We had a band of six new Champions that you deprived of a battle," said the Fairy Godmother, ticking the "faults" off on her fingers. "You gave three Unicorns entirely unsuitable ideas of a new vocation, so now we'll have to pair three of those Champions with the Unicorns, and heaven only knows how we'll manage to keep those boys virgins! You *almost* intervened as a Godmother, which is a very, very bad precedent to set."

"But that's why I was dressed as Alexander's squire!" Elena protested.

"We know, dear," said one of the old Wizards. "Not to worry. Very wise of you to think of that. Wiser still that you realized what The Tradition would have done and that you could have made a dreadful mess if Kylia had fallen in love with Alexander. It isn't in the tale now; you're just the Champion's female squire who followed him into battle in disguise—that's two Traditional paths you've combined there, the disguised female serving a boob of a man who hasn't figured out his servant is a she and the brave and cunning girl who follows her lover into battle, so *that's* all right."

"You've opened up the Traditional warrior-woman path

a bit wider now, though, so—" the Fairy Godmother grimaced and shrugged. "What's to come of that, I suppose we'll have to see. But *why* didn't you wait for a few hours to get the replies to your messages? If you had—"

"If she had," Alexander said, his jaw set, "my brother would probably be dead. It wouldn't have taken that— Katschei, was it?—very long to discover he had the Prince in his dungeon."

"Yes, it was a Katschei," said a Sorceress. "A kind of northern-Kingdom half-demon, not entirely human. He shouldn't have been in *your* Kingdoms at all!"

Elena bowed her head, and waited for them to tell her that the Katschei's presence was *her* fault.

But they didn't. "Try this, if you will," said the Fairy Godmother, grimly. "Despite Traditional pressure against anything of *his* sort coming into *our* Kingdoms, he got his foothold by getting an unscrupulous amber-merchant to bring his heart as far south as he could and bury it, a hundred years ago, then he waited for the amber-merchant and anyone else who might remember what had been done to die. Of course, a hundred years is nothing to *his* kind."

Elena's head came up and she gaped at the Fairy Godmother. "You mean—it wasn't my fault?" she squeaked.

"Of course not," the old Wizard replied. "What, were you worried because you'd been breaking Traditions? Good lack, girl, that's what the best of us always do! Bend them, anyway. Shape them the way we want them to go."

"Fretting because you'd gone and married that handsome piece you redeemed?" asked the Sorceress, with a lecherous smile. "Well, generally Godmothers take *lovers*, but if you're going to restrict yourself to just *one* man, that just leaves more choice for the rest of us!"

"Shariss!" scolded the Fairy Godmother, as Elena blushed and Alexander began to grin, "you're telling tales!"

"It's all right, dearie," said a particularly grandmotherly Godmother. "The only thing you did wrong—and I'm not saying it's *wrong* wrong, because as your young man said, his brother might well have been discovered before we could set up a rescue—was to go haring off before you could hear from the rest of us. No, indeed, you *mustn't* do that anymore, and you must *promise* us that you won't."

Elena and Alexander exchanged a look and a nod. "I think," she said, carefully, "that *providing* the next emergency doesn't involve any of Alexander's brothers or father, we can promise that."

The Fairy Godmother looked up, and gave Elena a quick wink. The Wizard chuckled. "She's learning," he said to the air.

"As for Alexander, there is ample precedent for Champions in a Godmother's household as Consort," said the Fairy Godmother. "At least, in the Elven Tradition there is. I see no reason why that can't be extended, although, as Shariss pointed out, I suspect that there are not as many as you might think who will take advantage of it. Champions tend to have wandering ways, you see, and they roam over several Kingdoms in the course of their careers."

Elena's brow wrinkled. "But I'm responsible for several Kingdoms," she pointed out.

"And you're about to get one more," said the Wizard. "There's no one to take Fleurberg. Poor old Hessian never took an Apprentice, and he wasn't strictly a Wizard anyway, he was a Sorcerer who liked to meddle. So Fleurberg's yours, and I expect this young man is going to have his hands full for a while. The Katschei's minions mostly fled. He's going to have to track them down and dispose of them as they pop up. And it's possible that having heard of a way out of an area, other Evil things may try to follow the Katschei's example, so he'll have to look sharp for that." He shrugged. "We'd better get together before we leave and put a Portal to your cottage in the back of an old wardrobe or something. What do you want to do about Glass Mountain?"

"Why don't you bring those six young Champions here and set them up as a sort of Order?" asked Alexander unexpectedly. "That way they have a place to come and go from, you'll have *them* here to clean up the Katschei's monsters, and they'll be able to come directly to Elena if they need magical help."

"Hmm. You didn't do so badly, did you, dear?" Shariss asked Elena, with an upraised eyebrow. "Beauty, brawn, *and* brains!"

Alexander blushed, and Elena flushed.

"Done," said the Fairy Godmother. "An Order of Champions is a fine new Tradition to start. Very useful indeed. I can see that you are going to be a valuable addition to the ranks, Champion Alexander."

She turned to Elena. "As for you—are you *certain* you wish to continue to be a Godmother? You certainly qualify as a Sorceress, if you choose. It seems a waste of your time for you to be puttering about with small problems and making potions and amulets."

She shook her head, vehemently. "No—I *would* much rather take care of things while they are small problems, please. And I really don't mind making potions and amulets for farmers and shepherds. It's only the ones that live in my village that come to me for such things, anyway."

"True enough, there are Witches in plenty in your other Kingdoms. Well, dear, there are those of us who would rather hide away on the mountaintop until terrible situations require resolving, and those of us who prefer to have people about us and nip smaller emergencies in the bud." She smiled. "And, truth to tell, I wouldn't be living among you mortals if I wasn't the latter."

"Nor me," said the old Wizard, cheerfully. "There's room for all sorts, thank heavens! Now, I hate to put you two to work immediately, but you'll have to for a bit. *You,* Alexander—I need you to go help your brothers sort out what to do with that little army that your brother Octavian brought. And help Julian out with his reconciliation letter to your father; from all reports he keeps weeping over it and tearing it up. He's a good boy, but a bit—"

"—*sentimental,*" the Wizard and Alexander said together.

"Anyway, when you get that sorted, *do* something sensible with the Katschei's treasure, too. Just burying it or putting it in the treasury will only invite more trouble. I don't think Julian will need convincing, especially not if you hint at curses."

"You could offer most of it to a dragon," Elena suggested suddenly, recalling her initial impression of a dragon's hoard. "In exchange for monster hunting or something. The dragon could even live up here, as the symbol of the Order."

"Oh, there's a lovely thought!" said the Sorceress, brightening. "And we'd have a source for shed scales and blood!"

"Does that suit you?" the Fairy Godmother asked Alexander. "Good. I'll find the dragon, then."

"And the rest of it can be used to reward Octavian and his force, those magical creatures that came to help us, and repair the damage to the palace and compensate the families of those who were killed," said Alexander.

"And when you finally return home, I believe you'll find that you now have all the resources of the first inhabitant of Emerald Cottage, and the responsibilities that go with it. Which means that you will need to establish a permanent portal—or perhaps, I should say reestablish—with one Witch, Wizard or Sorceress in each of the Kingdoms for which you are responsible." The Fairy Godmother gave Elena a long look. "You will have your Mirror-Slave Randolf contact *my* Mirror-Slave Esteban when you have decided who will play host and where each one will be, and the appropriate Moot will gather to create them—or reopen them, if you decide to use the old ones. This is as much to keep you from acting too impulsively as it is for your convenience. If you know you can get to the source of trouble by stepping across a portal, you'll be less likely to fly off without waiting for answers to your messages."

Elena blushed.

"Now, I believe that this will do." She looked up and down the table, getting nods from all assembled. "Very well. This Grand Council session is closed. Commendations to Godmother Elena and Champion Alexander, who are admonished to go back down into Fleurberg and finish tidying up, keeping in mind that a Godmother *always* cleans up after herself and a Champion never leaves a job half-finished. All agreed?"

"*Agreed,*" came the chorus.

"Opposed? Abstentions? Good." She looked back up at Alexander and Elena. "Well? What are you waiting for? An invitation to join the Grand Council? Be careful or you'll get it!"

Elena made a small sound of alarm in her throat, and to the sound of kindly laughter from around the table, they turned and fled as one. Nightsong was waiting for them at the door, tacked up in a new saddle with a pillion seat. Alexander took the saddle, and greatly relieved *not* to be responsible for being anything other than a passenger, Elena took his hand and pulled herself up onto the pillion behind him.

"Ready?" he asked.

"For anything," she replied, with a soaring heart.

"Be careful what you ask for, Godmother," he warned. "You might get it!"

"And if I do?" she shrugged, gaily. "Then we handle it together."

"So we do," he agreed. "So we do! It can't be any worse than the family reunion we're about to negotiate!"

She laughed, and shook her head. "You're right. Oh, families! All right, Nightsong! To Fleurberg!"

He laughed as well. "To Fleurberg, and my brothers! But this time—we'll take our time about it."

And the great black stallion trotted off—rather than flying—under a cloudless blue sky.

EPILOGUE

Madame Fleur plumped herself down on a chair at the little table in the window of the *Rose and Ivy* with a sigh, and tucked her heavy string shopping-bag beneath the seat. Her sister Blanche did the same.

"Dear saints, what a day!" Blanche said fanning herself with her hand. "I do believe that every living body in town was in the market today."

"I would not disagree," Fleur said. "What a crush! I don't know, dear, perhaps we're getting too old to fight our way through the market. Do you think we ought to hire a boy for it?"

"Or a girl. Actually, I would not be averse to hiring another girl altogether, for more of the household chores." Blanche made a face. "Perhaps we are getting old."

"Well, if we are, then there's no shame in hiring another girl. We've earned it," said Fleur decisively. She looked out of the window. "I must say, it's very convenient, having this inn *right* next door," she added brightly. "So nice, being able to nip over for a bite when we're too tired to cook!"

"Terribly convenient," echoed Blanche, a twinkle in her eye. The potgirl, a bit of hair straggling damply into her eyes, hurried over to take their orders. "Ah, Daphne, there you are. What has Theresa got on the menu today?"

Now, both of them knew very well what Theresa Klovis had on the menu, because it rarely changed, but both of them took a great deal of pleasure in watching Daphne Klovis stand there and recite it all.

Red-faced from her exertions, the formerly-plump daughter of Madame Klovis told over the menu without a flicker of exasperation. She daren't display any bad temper, not now, not when she knew very well that if anyone complained to the debtors who owned what had been the Klovis home, there would be a reckoning.

"Well, I do believe that I will have a Ploughman's Luncheon," said Blanche, as she always did. "With a nice ale to wash it down."

"And cold quiche for me, and a glass of white wine," said Fleur as *she* always did. Daphne hurried off, her back hair straggling down from under her cap. Gone were the silk gowns and ribbons; the Klovis's all wore what any working servant did; a plain smock-dress and canvas skirt, a plain apron to go over it, and a plain mob-cap.

"Well, all this work is doing her good," Blanche observed. "That weight has come off nicely."

When Madame Klovis had returned, without a rich husband, but expecting to find "her" house being cared for by her stepdaughter, she found something else instead. Forewarned by Madame Fleur that she was coming, a committee of those to whom she owed money was waiting.

The committee included a brace of constables, and before you could say "knife," they had hustled off Madame and her daughters, all three of them protesting at the tops of their lungs, while their creditors stripped the coach of everything and divided her belongings among themselves. There was less there than she had taken with her—foreign climes had not been receptive to Madame and the girls, and foreign merchants disinclined to part with anything on credit, and she had been forced to sell a great many things in order to support herself and her daughters in what she considered to be the proper style. There certainly was nothing near enough to settle her enormous debts.

But a solution had been suggested to this problem, by a party who had wished to remain anonymous, and the judge had presented them with this solution as a *fait accompli* the next morning.

"The portion of the home that is hers already having been deeded to the creditors—most generously—by Elena Klovis, the remainder is declared confiscated," the judge had said sternly, as Madame and Delphinium stared at him with angry arrogance, and Daphne wailed. "Being as the debts are still not discharged, your creditors have agreed to refurbish the house as an inn and hire a plain cook until you, Madame, have demonstrated that you have mastered the art of producing edible food. Whereupon you will become the cook and kitchen-maid. Monsieur Rabellet's cousin will serve as innkeeper, and you and your daughters as the inn servants until the debt is fully discharged, at which time, you may either continue to serve as servants for a wage, or go your ways."

Fleur and Blanche had been in the gallery, as had all of the creditors and indeed, nearly anyone who had a dislike for Madame and her daughters. And they really had fallen mightily; even the gowns they had been wearing had been taken from them, and they were now garbed in ugly grey linen prison smocks and caps.

Madame's nostrils had flared, as Daphne wailed still louder. "And if we refuse?" she had asked, icily.

"Then, Madame, you and your daughters will be packed off to the workhouse," the judge replied, just as icily. "And there you will remain until you die, since it is unlikely, at workhouse wages, that your debt will ever be discharged. I advise you to accept."

There really was no choice in the matter. Madame was forced to assent. And so she and her daughters had become exactly what they had forced Elena to be—unpaid servants, sleeping in the attic on whatever was deemed to worn to use in the inn, eating what was left over after all of the customers had been fed. In that, they were treated better than they themselves had treated Elena; they got two new smocks and a skirt a year, (where Elena had gotten rags), a set of sabots and underthings every year, and woolen shawls and stockings for winter. And they never starved.

But Madame and the girls soon found out that if they dared to show any hint of bad temper, Monsieur Rabellet's cousin would summon the debtors and let them know—and the judge would add another month to their "sentence," as a punishment for behaving in a fashion that would drive away customers.

Madame's fair, white hands were now as rough and work-ravaged as Elena's had ever been, with broken nails and reddened skin. Delphinium was developing quite a set of muscles from lugging pots of hot water for the overnight customers' baths. And Daphne actually had a figure that did not require winching down the ties of a corset to produce.

Of the three, Daphne seemed to actually be learning a lesson from the situation, Fleur reflected, as the girl brought them their meal. She had stopped weeping most of the time, and was beginning to show a healthy interest in one of the young farmers who frequented the place on market days. Fleur noted that he was at one of the smaller tables, and that Daphne was stopping there to "make sure he didn't need anything" far more often than she did for any other customer. And her interest seemed to be reciprocated.

"Hmm," she said, catching her sister's attention, and nodding towards the pair.

"Ah, that's the way the wind blows, does it?" said Blanche, with interest. "Well, I must say, her temper and character have improved enormously. She could do worse."

"And so could he," Fleur agreed. She and Blanche were shameless eavesdroppers on the trio, and she was actually beginning to feel some sympathy for Daphne. The girl was trying. And she seemed to have finally gotten it into her dense little skull that not only was taking things from merchants without paying for them *wrong,* but that perhaps what they had done to the now-vanished Elena had been cruel. Fleur had heard her telling their master as much. "And we were that mean to her, and no wonder she ran away to take service from someone as would pay her," she'd said. "Now that I know what she had to do—well, I hope she's better off, is all I can say, and good luck to her."

"No sign of improvement from the others, though," Blanche observed, as Madame's angry voice, berating her daughter for some fault, drifted out from the kitchen.

"That's their choice." Fleur shrugged. "And the way they act, if they don't take a cue from her, they'll be totting up more months onto their service until they'll both be old and grey and scrubbing floors here, while Daphne's off making herself into a proper farmer's wife."

"Ha." Blanche nodded. "It all comes down to what we make of ourselves, eh? The Tradition or no. Who knows? If she really continues to improve her character, maybe a Fairy Godmother will take pity on Daphne and she'll find enough gold under a cabbage in the kitchen-garden to buy her freedom and give her a little dowry."

"Stranger things have happened," said Fleur, making a note of the thought to pass on to the appropriate party. "Like—a Godmother wedding a Champion!" She held up her glass of wine. "To happy endings, however they come about!"

Blanche clinked glasses with her. "To happy endings, indeed!"

A Q&A with Mercedes Lackey...

What does fantasy mean to you?

Fantasy for me has always gone far beyond the magic rings and castles of the classical fairy tale, although heaven knows I love the classical fairy tales! To write or enjoy fantasy requires an open mind and heart, and the ability to believe that things are not always what they seem.

Why do you think women enjoy reading fantasy?

I think it may be because, as Dorothy L. Sayers once pointed out about the mystery genre, fantasy is one of the last bastions of "moral fiction." By this she meant that in mystery—and in fantasy—good triumphs over evil, the wrongdoers get their just deserts, and all ends, if not always strictly happily, at least well. This is the definition of "moral fiction": something that shows the world, perhaps not as it is, but certainly as it could and should be. I think women are, as a whole, a lot less willing to settle for "that's just the way it is" than men are. You tend to find that the men who read fantasy are idealists, in fact.

What makes you write fantasy over any other subject?

I have greater scope in writing fantasy for my imagination than in any other genre. I can write fantasy romances, fantasy mysteries, heroic fantasy, modern-urban fantasy, historical fantasy, dark (or horror) fantasy, alternate-history fantasy, political fantasy even Western fantasy. There is virtually no genre that I could not use for a fantasy novel, and even if I haven't gotten around to it, someone surely has, because I can cite examples of every one of those books, either in my own body of work, or someone else's.

Anything you'd like to say about fantasy or writing, or writing fantasy?

When a reader closes the book with regret, you've done your job. What we all strive for is when a reader goes back to the same book again and again and finds equal pleasure in it each time they read it. That's what every reader is looking for, and every writer is working to accomplish.

And when it comes down to cases, everything written is at least in part a fantasy. Except maybe for the national budget. That's horror.

Mercedes Lackey's DAW books

The Heralds of Valdemar
Arrow of the Queen
Arrow's Flight
Arrow's Fall
Exile's Valor
Exile's Honor
Take a Thief

Vows & Honor
The Oathbound
Oathbreakers
Oathblood

The Last Herald Mage Trilogy
Magic's Pawn
Magic's Promise
Magic's Price

The Mage Winds Trilogy
Winds of Fate
Winds of Change
Winds of Fury
By the Sword

The Mage Wars
Mercedes Lackey & Larry Dixon
The Black Gryphon
The White Gryphon
The Silver Gryphon

Mercedes Lackey's DAW books

The Mage Storms Trilogy
Storm Warning
Storm Rising
Storm Breaking

The Owl Mage Trilogy
Mercedes Lackey & Larry Dixon
Owlflight
Owlsight
Owlknight
Brightly Burning

Non-Valdemar Books From DAW

The Dragon-Jousters
Joust
Rediscovery (1993)
by Marion Zimmer Bradley & Mercedes Lackey

Edwardian Fairy Tales
The Elemental Masters
The Gates of Sleep
The Serpent's Shadow
The Black Swan

Mercedes Lackey's Baen titles

Bard's Tale
Castle of Deception
by Mercedes Lackey & Josepha Sherman
Fortress of Frost and Fire
by Ru Emerson & Mercedes Lackey
Prison of Souls
by Mercedes Lackey & Mark Shepherd

Bardic Voices
Lark and the Wren
The Robin & the Kestrel
The Eagle and the Nightingales
Four and Twenty Blackbirds

Bardic Choices
A Cast of Corbies
by Mercedes Lackey & Josepha Sherman
The Ship Who Searched
by Mercedes Lackey & Anne McCaffrey

Bedlam Bards
Bedlam's Bard (omnibus)
by Ellen Guon & Mercedes Lackey
Knight of Ghosts and Shadows
by Ellen Guon & Mercedes Lackey
Summoned to Tourney
by Ellen Guon & Mercedes Lackey

Spirits White as Lightning
by Mercedes Lackey & Rosemary Edgehill
Beyond World's End
by Mercedes Lackey & Rosemary Edgehill
Mad Maudlin
by Mercedes Lackey & Rosemary Edgehill

Mercedes Lackey's Baen titles

The Serrated Edge
* Born To Run
by Larry Dixon & Mercedes Lackey
* Chrome Circle
by Larry Dixon & Mercedes Lackey
† Wheels of Fire
by Mercedes Lackey & Mark Shepherd
† When the Bough Breaks
by Mercedes Lackey & Holly Lisle

*collected as THE CHROME BORNE †collected as THE OTHERWORLD

Fire Rose
Reap the Whirlwind
by C. J. Cherryh & Mercedes Lackey

Doubled Edge, Elizabethan Magic
This Scepter'd Isle
by Mercedes Lackey & Roberta Gellis

Heirs of Alexandria: Alternate History
The Shadow of the Lion
by Mercedes Lackey, Eric Flint & Dave Freer
This Rough Magic
by Mercedes Lackey, Eric Flint & Dave Freer

Wing Commander: Science Fiction
Freedom Flight
by Ellen Guon & Mercedes Lackey
If I Pay Thee Not In Gold
by Mercedes Lackey & Piers Anthony

Mercedes Lackey's Tor titles

Halfblood Chronicles
by Mercedes Lackey & Andre Norton

The Elvenbane
Elvenblood
Elvenborn

The Shadow Mountain Trilogy
by Mercedes Lackey & James Mallory

The Outstretched Shadow
Firebird

Diana Tregarde/Jenny Talldeer
Burning Water
Children of the Night
Jinx High
Sacred Ground

Mercedes Lackey's Avonova title

Tiger Burning Bright
by Marion Zimmer Bradley, Andre Norton & Mercedes Lackey

Mercedes Lackey's Silhouette Books title
Counting Crows in *Charmed Destinies*

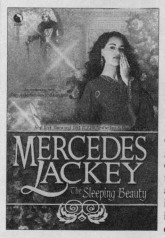

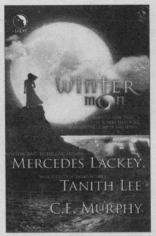